Lizzie

When I Was Yours

FOREVER

New York Boston

Copyright © 2019 by Lizzie Page
Reading group guide copyright © 2020 by Lizzie Page and
Hachette Book Group, Inc.

Cover design by Debbie Clement
Cover photographs © Trevillion; Shutterstock
Cover copyright © 2020 by Hachette Book Group, Inc.

Forever
Hachette Book Group
1290 Avenue of the Americas, New York, NY 10104
read-forever.com
twitter.com/readforeverpub

Originally published in 2019 by Bookouture in the United Kingdom
First US edition: December 2020

Forever is an imprint of Grand Central Publishing. The Forever name and logo are trademarks of Hachette Book Group, Inc.

The publisher is not responsible for websites (or their content) that are not owned by the publisher.

Library of Congress Control Number: 2020938830

ISBNs: 978-1-5387-0303-8 (trade paperback)

Printed in the United States of America

LSC-C

Printing 1, 2020

To my lovely dad, Len Lierens
Who was evacuated from Stepney, London to Hinckley, Leicester.

Keep the home fires burning
While your hearts are yearning
Though your lads are far away
They dream of home

Lyrics by Mrs. Lena Guilbert Brown Ford
Music by Ivor Novello

CHAPTER ONE

1939—Now

In August, two women wearing hats and holding clipboards come to do the room count. They are in the house for all of one minute. They trot straight upstairs and push open the doors, then, before I've had time to put on my lipstick, they are back down again. All that morning's cleaning, baking and wiping was in vain. They thank me kindly for my time and I am still thanking them kindly for their efforts when they are gone.

I can't leave it like this.

I swing open the front door and follow them down the path. Never mind my tartan carpet slippers; if I don't speak out, Edmund will give me what-for.

"Excuse me, I say—excuse me!"

They turn wordlessly.

"Our spare rooms are not actually spare rooms," I explain.

The smaller woman raises her eyebrow at me but it does not feel like an invitation to continue.

I continue anyway. I am in for a penny, in for a pound.

"My husband needs one. It is for visiting family members."

Taller woman looks at me disapprovingly. "That still leaves one."

"Dressing room?" I say and as the words come out my mouth I know how stupid they sound. Not just stupid—these days, such words could even be treasonous.

She tilts her clipboard at me to have a look. "We've put you down for one," she says, pointing at our names: *Mr. and Mrs. E Lowe. Three Bedrooms.* "Just the one. You'll manage."

The smaller woman leans toward me. "It might not amount to anything."

But I know it will come to something. I know it will because it did last time when no one else thought it would. It's all very well saying "It never came to anything in 1933, or in 1937" but it did in 1914, a fact people conveniently like to gloss over.

Still, I stand there hesitant on the garden path. The women carefully open and shut the gate—no one could say they are not thorough—and I open and shut my mouth like a goldfish in a (one-bedroom) bowl. They trot off to number six, where Mrs. Dean appears to welcome them in warmly.

Mrs. Burton comes out of number two, next door—they were at hers just before mine. I note she is holding a dishcloth and a mug in her hands and one fat, pink curler dangles precariously over her forehead. Who am I to judge? Standing in my slippers for all the world to see?

Mrs. Burton and I have been neighbors for eighteen years but I can count the conversations we've had on one hand: gutters; trees; Christmas greetings. And the two times her dogs got out. Edmund hasn't encouraged friendships. He doesn't like people knowing our business (even though as far as I know we have no business).

She sees me and nods. She is a mild-mannered, gentle woman. I imagine she is about my age, but she looks older in that way that women with children often do.

"Didn't take too long, did it?"

"No…"

"Wish we had the room," she says pleasantly.

"Oh yes."

"Be nice to do our bit."

"Do our bit, absolutely." I hesitate. "It probably won't amount to anything though, will it?"

Mrs. Burton's house is also a three-bed but she has two nearly grown daughters. One girl is bold, leans out of the window and waves at people in the street and the other always has her head in a book. Mrs. Burton has been put down for zero. She laughs, but wistfully. Says she would have liked to have nine or ten come to her. "You just want to *do something*, don't you? Help the children escape the bombs."

I do, I do, but there are so many things stopping me. I don't.

Mrs. Burton is about to go back into number two when she reconsiders. "Why don't you come over for a pot of tea, Mrs. Lowe? You look like you could do with a brew."

Mrs. Burton's house is identically laid out to ours, but its decor and its furnishings are much shabbier. The kitchen wallpaper is peeling in parts. The ceiling shows signs of a leak. The cream surfaces are now brown. I decide that there is more love here. Less love for accrued items means more love for the people. I don't know if that's true, but it feels true.

My house is very tidy.

Mrs. Burton is worried that her dogs will worry me. They are two large hairy dogs and I don't say it, but these are particularly unattractive specimens. It seems odd to me that out of all the dogs in the world, she has chosen these. I tell her they are fine, and when they jump up and paw my skirt, I pretend it's charming. They turn their attention to my slippers and I try to nudge them off. The dogs, that is, even though I am appalled at my slippers too.

The visiting billeting women have thrown me. I want it known that I am not the kind of lady who would usually venture outside in her slippers. The dog mounts the armchair and proceeds to maneuver its hind parts up and down over the cushion there.

I blush. I am not used to dogs and I don't know if this display has been put on for me alone, or if everyone who enters the house is the recipient of such a show. Maybe the dog is trying to tell me something?

Mrs. Burton asks if I've been allocated an evacuee and I reply wearily, "One, just one, but my husband…" and I am thinking, *Can this really be happening? Since when was one* just *one?*

Mrs. Burton finally drags the dogs outside and asks if I've got anything for him or her, and I stare at her mystified.

"I mean for the evacuee?"

Still nothing. Edmund says I can be very slow sometimes.

"Toys?"

Toys! Of course. I didn't think of that. "No, nothing." Pity the poor child coming to my house. Not a rocking horse. Not even a teddy. I have such a lot to learn. I can't help feeling excited, but then quickly tell myself, *It's not going to work, don't get your hopes up.*

"I might be able to help you there," says Mrs. Burton, and even as I am saying, "No, no, Mrs. Burton, please," she has rushed upstairs, leaving me alone in the kitchen at the table with the ticking clock. It is five minutes fast. Or am I five minutes slow? I wish I weren't so awkward. Mrs. Burton has lace doilies of the type my sister used to hate. I look at my nails. My nails at least are clean. There is a newspaper on the other side of the room but I can't get over to it and it's not one of the terribly informative ones anyway.

Finally, Mrs. Burton staggers down the stairs behind a full cardboard box. With an "oof" she places it down between us, pulls things out one by one. Pens, books, crayons, marbles, football, stamp-collecting album and, just in case, a skipping rope—"Only let 'em do it in the garden, mind. I lost three of my favorite ornaments with that—boy on the piano, girl with the violin and the goatherd."

I don't know if I'm expected to select one thing, or the whole lot, but then she shoves it across to me. "It's all yours, Mrs. Lowe."

"I don't think it's likely—"

"It'll make the little one feel at home, won't it?"

Oh dear Lord, is this really happening? So much for it *not amounting to anything.*

Mrs. Burton tips sugar into my tea. She is so eager to make life sweeter. She is sunshine, and I am rain.

I fumble in my pocket, wondering if I should make a payment. Mrs. Burton laughs incredulously. "You'd do the same if it were the other way round, wouldn't you?"

"Absolutely no way are we having an evacuee here," Edmund says over the chicken and leek pie with mash. Admittedly, the gravy is not my best work—I'm not getting the consistency right recently. I'll add it to the long list of inadequacies that dogs me. The carrots are also perilously overcooked, but Edmund prefers them like that. Even his own crunching annoys him.

"It might not come to anything," I say. "I don't think there'll be another war, do you?" I add nervously. "No one is that stupid."

Everyone is that stupid.

"I'll not have screaming kids running around here."

"Why would they be screaming?" I always try to remain civil over dinner with Edmund. It's twelve minutes out of my day, that's all.

I imagine numbers one, two, three, five and six—our neighbors, normal-appearing people—excitedly getting everything spick and span for London children who need to escape the bombs. I imagine they all have their husbands' blessings.

I continue cutting my pie. The knife squeaks for mercy against the plate. Edmund winces.

"Don't want filthy city kids smearing their fingers over our walls."

"Why would they do that?"

"There are plenty of families who can take them."

A pause.

"Edmund, we're a family who can take them."

"I meant the ones who have children, they *know* children. They'll be better at looking after feral city kids than us."

Than me, Edmund means. He thinks *I* can't look after a child. The second he rests his knife and fork on the plate, I whip it away, scrape the remains in the bin, take the plate to the sink and scrub it clean. He is still sitting there, staring into the distance. Together time is over.

Three weeks later, German armies are amassing by the Polish borders and Hitler has gone and signed a peace treaty with the Russians, which is not what we want at all. Britain is in uproar. *Not again.* The Nazis have got to be stopped—but really, does it have to be us who do the stopping?

I read the government leaflets on how to protect ourselves from bombs. I buy and hang material for the blackout—every window must be covered, not a chink of light may give us away. The streetlights don't come on any more and Edmund has even unscrewed the lamp from his bike. There's talk that rationing will be brought in sooner rather than later because everyone agrees that last time it came in too late. "Lessons have been learned from the Great War," pronounces the minister ominously on the wireless.

Not that many lessons, I think.

When the postman brings the anticipated letter, I leave it for a bit and in my head, it ticks like a bomb on the kitchen table.

Edmund goes to the living room to tune in to the next installment of bad news. They tell us what we have already guessed: Operation Pied Piper—the mass evacuation of children from London—is going ahead.

I clean the already-clean kitchen, avoiding the letter. Eventually, I open it, read it. So, it's true. We have been allocated one, just the one. I am to go to the village hall tomorrow and collect him or her. The hall is only five minutes' walk away, so I can't complain about that. Everything is only five minutes away in Hinckley.

I bake an apple pie because this is a national emergency. And what could be more welcoming to a little traveler than a slice of pie? We are more than halfway to war—there's no going back now—and children will be delivered from London. I think it's a bit like the stories we were told when we were little: about the stork that brought the baby, only I used to think it was "stalk" and the baby grew from a root and then was plucked from a branch.

While the pie is in the oven, I go up to look at the spare room, the one I'd told the billeting officers that family use when they come to stay. The only one who ever used to come was my sister, Olive, and the last time she came to stay was over fifteen years ago.

The walls of our house are bare. I sometimes remember the chaotic beauty of Olive's friend Mrs. Ford's house in Warrington Crescent: there was barely a space not covered by art—not just the walls, but the chests of drawers, the tables, the display cabinets, every surface was hidden with a carefully selected lamp, statue or ornament from Christie's. Mrs. Ford was known for her excellent and transatlantic tastes. When we first moved here, I planned to put up pictures everywhere but Edmund said he didn't want to spoil the plaster.

The spare room is the only room where the walls are spoiled. On the wall behind the headboard is a picture that Olive drew. It lives inside an elaborate golden frame that doesn't really do justice to the simplicity of the pencil-drawn portrait inside. It was one of her many sketches of me. She had done a series to support her application to study art at Goldsmiths College, which was accepted. In the picture, I'm looking out of the drawing-room window of our old family home. I find the way she captured my face both familiar and unfamiliar: all my features are there, all rendered in their correct proportions, but they are arranged in an expression of optimism or perhaps enthusiasm. Not my habitual look. I was nineteen when she drew it. She was seventeen and a half. That half was always very important to Olive.

This picture wouldn't be strange for a young child to have in their room, would it? Should I get something else? What do children like to look at? Pretty cottages? Ponies?

I take the pie out of the oven and let it cool on the side. Then I go to bed. Edmund is outside, in his shed or somewhere else. I don't know where he goes.

I can't sleep.

A child.

One child, just one, may be coming to live with us!

CHAPTER TWO

1914—Then

Everything was shaky, everything was blurred. It was our generation's chance to prove ourselves. This was it! Excitement was overflowing like an unwatched pan. I was nineteen, Olive had just turned eighteen. Richard and Edmund were both nineteen. Christopher was twenty. We thought we knew everything.

Smack bang in the middle of the street, stopping all the traffic, the newspaper boy had jumped onto a stool and was shouting aloud from the paper. At each point he made, the crowd cheered and he extravagantly threw his black cap up in the air and then deftly caught it on the down. I found myself quite mesmerized.

"*Britain Prepared for War!*"

"Hoorah!"

"*Shipbuilding Yards Working at Full Pressure!*"

"Hoorah!"

"*Asquith Still War Minister!*"

"Hoorah!"

The war woke us up. It was as though we had been sleepwalking until then. Suddenly we were full of adrenaline, full of whizz, bang, fizz, crammed with possibilities. They called it "war spirit" and it was everywhere, contagious as measles.

The Saturday after war had been declared, Father, Olive and I were invited to Aunt Cecily and Uncle Toby's for a special luncheon party. I don't think it was a celebration, but it came pretty near.

Edmund, his brother Christopher and their parents were coming to join us after lunch. Their family and my aunt and uncle were exceedingly close and there was rarely a family do without them making an appearance.

I always dressed with care, but that day I gave it extra attention. Long navy skirt, white blouse, lacy collar. Was it frivolous to be interested in my appearance when we were at war now? Father was still interested in making a profit, Olive was still interested in making art, Aunt Cecily was still interested in hosting parties and no doubt Uncle Toby was still interested in malt whisky and expensive cigars. It must be acceptable.

I tried a different style for my hair, and then another and another. Edmund had never expressed a preference, but a stranger had once stopped me in the street to tell me that the nape of my neck rivaled the beauty of the *Venus de Milo* and I wondered if maybe everyone felt like that about my neck or if he was just a lone chancer.

Olive was wearing an old dress; the paint stains had come out of this one, but it still looked worn. I tried not to be disapproving but it was difficult to do. It didn't look fit for an occasion and I dreaded to think what Edmund's mother would make of it, but then Olive never made an effort and she had got worse since going to art school. That is, her appearance had got worse—admittedly, her mood had markedly improved. She had just started her second year and she adored just about everything about her studies (although she was now scared that the war would bring all her enjoyment to a close). I explained that was unlikely. Everyone said the war would be over by Christmas. I had decided it would be over by the winter solstice—the shortest day—because I thought that would be very fitting indeed.

That Saturday though, Olive was in one of her dark moods again, mostly because her friends, the Fords, were also having a gay old afternoon and she would much rather have been there than at our altogether-more-staid family gathering. The Fords lived in Warrington Crescent, a road as attractive as it sounds, not fifteen minutes from ours in Portchester Terrace. The Fords were American and bohemian. Mrs. Ford was an art collector. Her son Walter didn't do much but he was devastatingly handsome and enviably popular. Their house was always full of the most talented and interesting people, who Mrs. Ford collected.

Aunt Cecily's and Uncle Toby's gatherings were more restrained and predictable. However, duty still prevailed. Olive was a free spirit, but she was not *that* free.

My father always dressed very appropriately and that day he was in a fine-fitting suit with shoes so polished we could almost see our reflections in them. He was more proper than most gentlemen. He believed strongly in a smart appearance but, equally, he didn't impose his views on Olive or me—an attitude that was quite unusual at the time and something I only came to appreciate later.

We walked across the park to our aunt and uncle's house in Cottesmore Gardens as it was a pleasant summer's day and my father had decided at the last minute it wasn't worth hailing a cab. The sunshine was so bright that you couldn't see much ahead of you. The heat created a hazy film across the trees and the houses. I saw horses stop to drink noisily. Suddenly, I envied Olive's comfortable shoes, although I remained embarrassed about the silly beret she had popped upon her head at the last moment. Typical Olive.

I didn't mind hiking across London, I just didn't want to look like I had. As we turned into Kensington High Street, we had a shock. Great crowds of people were milling around.

"Ah," said my father quickly, "there is a recruitment office around here."

Olive insisted we stop to look. She was like that. Always observing things. She told us that people nowadays don't see enough: "It's all rush, rush, rush, busy, busy, busy." She said you have to see what you see, not what you expect to see. So we all stopped and tried to see. Even Father. What a jolly lot of men they were—there wasn't one who wasn't in high spirits. It was clear these men were looking forward to giving the Hun a good thrashing. They were so cheerful, you'd have thought they were off to Southend for teacakes and a paddle in the sea.

And another thing that stood out immediately was something that was maybe obvious but was, I thought, interesting: the men were all shapes and sizes. You had beanpoles, and you had short ones, you had the chubby ones and you had the streaks of water. They also wore very different types of clothes: there were shop assistants, office clerks, postmen and farm boys among them. *How wonderful it would be to see them come together and transform into a unified British army. It would take your breath away*, I thought.

And then I noticed something else. I nudged Olive.

"They're not all eighteen, are they? They can't be. They look so young."

"Some of them will be. Some of them will pretend to be."

"They won't send *them* though, will they?"

Olive put her arm through mine. She was always the more libertarian of us. "If they want to go, why not?"

"Richard was right!" declared my Aunt Cecily as soon as we had crossed the threshold. She didn't normally answer the door herself. This was another sign of the times. "Hello, darlings." She was flushed with excitement. Her gray hair was falling out of its bun. Her collars uneven. Her great skirts were even more voluminous than usual.

Even Uncle Toby came out to the hall to greet us. "Richard knew!" he said, shaking each of our hands triumphantly, as though he'd won a bet. "And he'll be better equipped than most."

Richard was our only cousin and growing up, we spent most, if not all, of our free time together. Olive and I used to make him wear our bonnets and dresses and perform plays: he was a malleable, easy-going boy and he made an excellent Lady Macbeth. His collapse on the floor into madness made us squeal with laughter.

As we grew older, and he started to refuse dress-up, we played endless snakes and ladders, chess and backgammon. Richard was one of those people who always wins a board game. In his nursery, which was rather better equipped than ours, there was a row of stuffed bears on the window seat and a rocking horse, and on it I would rock, patting down Dotty, as I called her, while Richard would repeatedly and infuriatingly kick a ball against a wall and Olive would sketch. As we got older still, we would do the same thing out in the garden, only I would chain daisies instead of rocking Dotty.

Earlier in the year, our darling Richard had read an article in *The Times* that suggested that war was imminent. This had spurred him into action and, without telling anyone first, he had raced off to a recruitment meeting at London's Hotel Cecil. Naturally, that impressed us all for The Cecil was really rather grand.

"What happened?" we had urged him on his return. Richard played nonchalant. "They asked me all about cricket and rugby."

"And?"

"And then…" Richard shrugged modestly. "They said they'd take me on."

Of course they had. Our Richard was brilliant. It would have been unreasonable if the 23rd Battalion, 1st Sportsmen's Royal Fusiliers *hadn't* snapped him up. That was in May, and there was a luncheon party to celebrate then too.

While the parents had debated the likelihood of war, I had asked him if he really thought it would happen, and he took me aside and shook his head knowledgeably. "Vivi, those people who say it will never happen need to study history more. Then they will understand: it can, it will and it has."

"You're too thin," my aunt declared of Olive, as she usually did. It was a kind of dance they had. Olive was always thin: she was pale and indoorsy-looking, with dark crescents under her eyes, but she was not *too* thin. Olive laughed. We loved our aunt very much.

"Feed me up then!" she said, which always stirred my aunt and never failed to make her feel important.

After a starter of chicken liver pâté on toast, we raised a glass to our darling Richard just as we had when he had left three months earlier. "To King, God and country." Then we tucked into the main course of venison. Aunt kept hovering by Olive—"One more bite, dear girl"—like she was two years old again. I half expected her to pretend to be a steam train with the mash on a spoon.

The war had put us in good spirits. The time had finally come. Our mettle would be tested. Uncle Toby poured more sherry and, caught up in the thrilling atmosphere, I probably drank more than usual, even though I tried to limit myself. I didn't want to be silly when Edmund and his family came. I suppose we were all feeling relief in the thing being decided, the uncertainty being over. And if all the troops were led by men like Richard, our honey-colored, athletic gentleman, then the Hun didn't stand a chance. Or, as Uncle Toby proclaimed, "They don't have a hope in hell," and Aunt Cecily, hand over heart, whispered, "God help them all."

"Anticipating war is worse than war itself," pronounced my uncle, smacking his lips. "Now we know, now we know."

Olive smirked. Recently, she found everything Uncle Toby had to say very amusing. She told me he "epitomized the capitalist pig with his snout in the trough." I had protested that was unfair. Aunt Cecily and Uncle Toby had always been very generous to us. Certainly, they had some opinions you probably wouldn't want paraded in public, but wasn't that true of many of the older generation? The important thing was that they were good, loving people, wherever they put their snouts.

*

Edmund and his parents arrived just as the maid was clearing away the rhubarb crumble. He stroked my back in greeting and this sent an excited shiver down my spine. I couldn't help it.

Even from an early age, it was clear that the Lowes didn't feel Olive and I were good enough for their children, but Richard was inseparable from us, and since everyone loved Richard, they eventually had to get used to us too.

After they discovered that Olive and I were not *so* badly educated—we actually spoke more languages than Christopher and Edmund—the Lowes let their guard down a bit, and when they learned I played the piano, Mrs. Lowe became *almost* accepting. We weren't parasites on Richard's coat-tails any longer, we had things to offer too.

Mrs. Lowe desperately wanted Edmund to learn piano. When we were about twelve years old, she tasked me with teaching him whenever their family came round. But Edmund did not want to learn, so he just used to sit on the stool gazing out of the window in the hour allocated for us. We devised a game that meant I would play the piano with my right hand, holding his fingers over the keys with my left, while Christopher, Richard, Olive and all the parents chatted in the garden obliviously. These were my favorite times. Eventually, Mrs. Lowe realized Edmund was not making progress and we were released from the drawing room, but I missed those days and thought about them still. I knew Edmund thought about them too because occasionally he would mention them and when he did, it made my face grow hot.

Today, Mr. and Mrs. Lowe were filled with their usual grumbling assessments of the modern world—had we seen the men joining up?

"Yes," we replied with animation.

"Such energy," began Olive. "Such verve!"

"I've never seen so many—" started Father.

"What a bunch of ne'er-do-wells," huffed Edmund's mother. "If this is the best the country has to offer..."

"It *is* a worry," I agreed, although it had never crossed my mind before.

Olive nudged my ribs so that I could see that she was raising her eyes to the capitalist pig chandeliers.

Edmund's mother, with her fine-boned figure, her marble skin and her symmetrical features, was everything I aspired to be: a beautiful, opinionated matriarch, adored by her husband and sons. Her approval was everything to me. The harder it was to receive, the more I worked at it. We Mudie-Cookes weren't aristocratic or connected or even particularly talented—we were certainly less so than Uncle Toby or Edmund's father—and these were points that went against us. The fact that Father—however amenable and well-off he was—was self-made was always humming away in our background. I couldn't help feeling that in fine company we were "tolerated"—but whereas Olive loathed that fact, I was grateful for it, and tried my very best not to stand out.

Even when we were children, Olive never liked Edmund or his family very much and she still maintained that he wasn't good enough for me. She always said "With a face like yours you could have anyone, Vivi," but she was wrong. We didn't have the right background, and all I ever did was work for Father and play piano passably. I didn't amount to much, but what probably irked Olive most was that I didn't have plans to change either. I didn't have big ambitions like her—I simply hoped to marry and have my own family one day. Olive declared my goals were terribly bourgeois and tsked, "What about Paris? What about New York? Don't you want to go there?"

That was the thing: I didn't particularly want to go anywhere. Travel isn't important to everyone. Olive never understood that.

Edmund was studying philosophy at Cambridge and had an eye on the Indian Civil Service. His older brother Christopher was doing the same.

I once used to dream that Olive would marry Christopher and I would marry Edmund in an adorable Jane Austen–style wedding.

These foolish thoughts didn't last. Olive and Christopher couldn't stand each other—and not in the Jane Austen style of not standing each other either. Olive loathed Christopher and Christopher loathed Olive. Admittedly, even *I* struggled to get on with Christopher and I got on with almost everyone (Olive called it an irritating skill of mine). But Christopher was more pompous than Uncle Toby and his own father combined. Fortunately, that Sunday afternoon Christopher was not gracing us with his presence: he was at the races. "He's with a nice set of people," his mother told us. I don't know if it was her intention to make it sound like *we* weren't a nice set of people (Olive would have said it was).

If Edmund and I did marry, and if he did join the Indian Civil Service, then I imagined I might have to go overseas—but I didn't count that as travel in the way that Olive meant. She had ideas of wandering around Europe with just a Baedeker's travel guide, gallivanting between the sights. In any case, there were a lot of bridges to cross before Edmund and I got as far as marriage.

Bridge one was the fact he hadn't asked me to marry him.

Bridge two was the fact that Britain had just declared war on Germany.

Bridge three was his mother. I had to win her over first.

Edmund's mother was talking about Lord and Lady Baker. They never minded dropping lords and ladies into the conversation. She had already told us twice about the wonderful party they'd attended the day before: "Oh, the champagne!" and "Who do you think was there? Only the Duke of Norfolk, that's who."

Edmund's mother had black and white opinions on everything, but that afternoon her main bugbear was the Jews: a house in their street had recently been converted into a synagogue. They declared it was manageable when the Jews stayed in their patch of east London but now that they were spreading to the Midlands and the north... Who could think it was acceptable?

It was hard to tell which was worse in Edmund's mother's mind: Germans or Jews. "There are lots of Jews in Germany," she pointed out in that knowing way she had.

"Christ-killers," Edmund's father added gruffly. He was a man of very few words and those few words were invariably miserable. It was just like him to be annoyed about something that happened two thousand years ago.

"I thought the Romans did it," replied Olive, always ready for a quarrel.

"Judas was a Jew," chimed in Edmund's mother.

"So was Jesus."

Our father joined in. He would always serve up an anecdote at a party; he worked hard to be agreeable. This time, he mentioned an incident with a Jewish customer who hadn't paid. I had done the accounts: we had plenty of non-payers, but this one had evidently stood out for him.

"They don't do business fairly," he decided.

This made Edmund's mother even more furious. Spittle flew from her mouth. "I don't see why we don't go to war with *them*!"

Aunt Cecily didn't like this kind of talk, I could see it from the pursed sulk of her mouth, and Olive also was chewing her lip mutinously. I got out the dominoes and asked my Aunt Cecily to play. I was aware Edmund was watching me and that made me clumsier than usual. My aunt won three times in a row and accused me of not concentrating.

I thought the dominoes might cheer her up but instead she became quite tearful. She said I wasn't a patch on Richard and it was moments like these she missed him the most.

I patted her hand and promised her I would get better with practice and that I would play her whenever she wanted until the day Richard came home.

*

Later, Edmund asked if we would like to take a stroll around the garden. He asked both Olive and me, but I didn't want Olive to come and she knew it. I wondered if this was the moment he'd ask for my hand and, from the look on Olive's face, she did too. I could never tell what was going on in Edmund's handsome head though.

"So, this is it," Edmund kept saying, but I don't think he meant the "it" I was thinking about.

"Will you join up, Edmund?"

"I don't know," he said. He seemed quite uncharacteristically anxious.

He sat on the low step. I awkwardly hovered, and then placed myself next to him with as much grace as I could muster. *Look at things carefully*, I thought, gazing across the lawn. There wasn't a weed to be seen. Edmund put his head in his hands. I might not have been there for all he cared.

The day before he had left us, Richard had whispered to me, "Edmund's a hard nut to crack. Take care of him."

"I will," I promised. I took care of everyone, after all.

"He loves you…"

I flushed. "He hasn't said as much to me. Has he said anything to you?"

Richard had idly flicked at my collar. "*Everyone* knows it, silly."

I watched pretty bundles of clouds as they moved across the sky. After they'd made some distance, Edmund spoke. "I don't know what to do."

I felt disappointed. The step was also painful on the derrière. It wasn't that I expected him to ask there and then but some sign that I was on his mind was long overdue.

"What do you think I should do, Vivienne?"

"Ab-out?" I asked.

He looked up, startled. "Do *you* think I should join up?"

I shook my head. I really had no idea on that one.

"Whatever you do, we'll all be right behind you," I said. I hoped that sounded supportive enough. I had wanted to say *I* instead of we, but feared it would be too much.

When we went back in, Olive was standing up dominoes in lines, a sure sign that she was bored. I would always knock them with an errant sleeve or a fat thumb, but she could make them wind their way across the low table. Walking past with a plate of cake balanced in one hand and cup and saucer in the other, Aunt Cecily nodded approvingly at Olive. "Ooh, is that a train?"

"It's a snake," my sister said, raising her eyes once again at me. At the Fords', someone was more likely to be able to dance on dominoes, or to produce one from behind their ear.

"Marvelous," said Aunt Cecily absently before wandering over to join Uncle Toby.

"How did it go with Edmund then?" Olive whispered.

"Very well, Olive, thank you."

"You were *ages* in the garden."

"We were admiring the rhododendron."

"Of course you were."

She rummaged around in the drawer next to us; I'm not sure what she was looking for, but she found nothing there.

"Any news on the marriage *question*?" She and Richard always called it that. Pressing issues became *questions*: The Balkan question. The suffragette question. The marriage question.

"Shush, everything is up in the air now—"

"Is that what he said?"

"No, it's what I'm saying. I don't want to talk about it any more, Olive. Thank you."

My sister flicked the dominoes so one by one they toppled over. They kept their shape as they went down. It was quite impressive.

"I'm leaving now, are you coming, Vi?"

The cheek of her. "You can't go *now,* Olive. It's far too early!"
"Course I can," she said. "I told everyone, they said it was fine."
I stared at her suspiciously. My aunt and uncle did not take kindly
to people leaving before the cheese course.
"What on earth did you tell them?"
She smirked. "I said it was for the war effort."
"You're such a... such a *liar,* Olive."
I think she was startled at my choice of word, I certainly was,
but still she shrugged, stood up and made for the door. It wouldn't
be the last time I would call her a liar either. I suppose it shouldn't
have bothered me that she was leaving—after all, Edmund, Father
and all the others were still there—but it *did* bother me terribly.
For one, Olive got to have all the fun, and for another, a room was
always smaller and duller without her in it.

CHAPTER THREE

1939—Now

Hinckley is abuzz with all the theories about the "evacuation question." The London children will come up on one train—no, two trains, three trains—then donkey and carts, or maybe busses would bring them to the village hall. How many carts? How many busses? Nobody knows. It would give us a big clue as to the numbers involved. One bus could be eight kids. Three busses could be ninety. We'd have to wait and see.

"Are you taking any, Mrs. Lowe?" A tall, worried-looking woman walks over to me. I rack my brains to remember her name. *Mrs. Fellows, could it be? Married to the vet?*

"Course she is," says the milkman, who has crept up behind us, as stealthy in the afternoon as he is when he delivers at 5 a.m. "Why wouldn't she?"

I think about the time in the Hinckley pet shop many years ago. I had brought a rabbit home and it lasted three days. I cringe as I recall the return trip—*Mr. Lowe has allergies, you see.*

"I have been allocated one," I say awkwardly. "But I'm not sure..."

"I'll put you down for an extra bottle, shall I?" The milkman grins. I'm not sure if he's being serious.

"I like children, but I couldn't eat a whole one!" says Mr. Shaw from the post office. You can't post a letter without a "Knock knock, who's there?" from Mr. Shaw and his sweet-natured wife.

"If they say you're getting one, you'll get one," says Mrs. Fellows insistently. "God knows what I'll do. There aren't enough hours in the day already."

"But they'll want to place them with big families first, won't they?" I ask, thinking of Edmund's expression when I came home with the rabbit.

"They'll want whoever they can get to look after the children," she replies confidently.

Mr. Shaw interrupts. "One out, one in!" and I'm not sure what he means initially, then I realize he's talking about his own boy, tousle-haired and freckled Simon Shaw, who has gone and signed up early, the day Chamberlain came back from Munich, flashing around his white papers.

Just like my cousin Richard last time round; but of course, I don't say anything. No one wants to talk about last time round, even though it was little more than twenty years ago.

The milkman nudges me, says "I bet Simon Shaw gone and done it just to get away from his father's terrible jokes."

We stand in the back of the hall as the children troop in. It's like we're at a play and instantly I am back, remembering the recitals and the piano performances at the Fords' house during the Great War. I shake it away. I am remembering that time such a lot lately. I thought I had put it all to bed, but now with all the talk of fighting and bombs, it feels like it's been released, yanked out in the open, roaming the countryside of my mind.

The hall is chilly in all weathers but especially so today. Poor children. Big ones and little ones. Large ones, thin ones. Straggly hair, cropped hair, curls...

Someone, whose name I can't remember, says to me, "I didn't think I'd see you here," and I reply nonsensically, "I'm just having a look," which is what I always say to the shopkeepers of the dress stores in town.

"Haven't you been allocated one?" she goes on and I remember with a dread feeling that it's Mrs. Carmichael, the doctor's receptionist. I hate seeing her.

"Oh yes," I say, "but we'll see... Who knows?"

The mayor couldn't make it. He never can. He has a reputation for being "too far up his own backside" if you'll pardon Mr. Shaw's French, so the deputy mayor does everything the mayor should do. The deputy mayor is an older man with a striking ginger mustache and a freckly forehead. I try to steer clear of him. He says he's only going to say a few words, but we all know when he says that, he's going to get into the hundreds.

"Mr. Hitler hadn't reckoned on the good people of Hinckley!" he exclaims, and we clap, even though we are holding teas, which makes it rather awkward.

He says everyone should step forward and get to know each other.

"Shall we...?" says Mrs. Carmichael, smiling nervously.

"Go ahead. I'll wait," I reply, although I don't know what I am waiting for. I stand back and pretend to sip my tea. I'm shaking so much I can hardly keep hold of the saucer. This is excruciating. The other villagers don't hold back. They swarm forward like it's a cake show and the ones with the fancy icing have caught everyone's eye.

I wish my neighbor Mrs. Burton had come. We've formed quite the friendship in the last three weeks. We're making up for the eighteen years when we didn't speak. I know that her two girls are Ethel and Sally, although I'm not sure which is which, and I know her two dogs are called Laurel and Hardy, even though Laurel is female. I've almost got used to them now. Mrs. Burton throws something at Hardy when he does the humping and it seems to stop him. She found them as strays, heartbreaking they were, she told me, and couldn't leave them. I like that Mrs. Burton is someone who takes in unwanted dogs.

A pretty and composed-looking girl is standing at the front of the group of children with a suitcase in front of her. Goodness, she looks like a female version of Edmund with her careful smile and long, athletic legs. She will likely be more popular than the tubby lass with chocolate smears around her mouth, but who knows really. Both girls are being roundly interrogated by people, including Mrs. Carmichael (she'll go for the leggy blonde, surely).

A boy in shorts with scabbed knees is talking to Mrs. and Mr. Dean.

There are a pair of sisters—are they twins? One is definitely bigger than the other, but they are identically velvet-ribboned, small darting eyes, holding each other's hands.

A London teacher is talking earnestly to Mr. and Mrs. Shaw. "Yes, two, but they are so tiny, they don't take up much space."

A tall, strong-looking boy stands out. Farmer Jones—flushed, but no more flushed than usual—has collared him, naturally. Poor kid. He'll be up at 4 a.m. every day, plowing the land. *The farmer wants his boy.* Thinking of the nursery rhyme, I smile to myself. But this boy is no pushover.

"I'm supposed to be looking after Pearl Posner," I hear him say uncertainly. "I live next door to her in Stepney and I promised her ma I'd look out for her."

Farmer Jones huffs. He asks, "Where is she then?" and he is directed to a scrunched-up little thing who has decided to sit on the floor instead of a chair and whose face is obscured by a...I was going to say a bear, but I think it's a grimy flannel. I see her through Farmer Jones's eyes. *She will not suffice. She's too small to operate machinery.*

"I'm only supposed to take one of you. She'll find someone else to look after her, son." And the boy, frankly, looks relieved to be free of his burden. He whispers something to the girl, who shrugs back at him, then rolls over on to her side. I presume it's the mothers who are friends, not these two. The sturdy boy is off with Farmer Jones over to the officials—Jones promising him a nice joint. "Do you know what lamb is, son? It's God's own food."

Most of the boys go first. Or the pretty, older girls who look like they know how to do a bit of spit and polish. Some of the pairs have separated: not everyone is attached to their cousin, but some pairs have refused to split and mostly those are in the eight or so who remain unselected. There is a young boy with hair that won't settle, and a snotty-nosed kid, even smaller, who is trying to meet everyone's eyes. I try not to meet his. Imagine Edmund's face if I brought *him* home! The walls would be smeary in no time. Mrs. Beedle, the butcher's wife, takes him. I think it's a match. She *has* to be the tolerant type, married to that Roy Beedle.

"You'll be a help, won't you, sonny?"

The boy grips his name badge and says loudly, "I'm not Sonny, I'm Keith." And everyone laughs and Mrs. Beedle smiles indulgently; she thinks the best of everyone. Her expression says, *Looks like I haven't done too badly after all.*

Then there is just the one child left, the girl on the floor. Pearl Posner. I see now she has dark blonde hair and purple shadows under her eyes, thin as a string bean. She is snotty too, and her sleeve is damp and ragged like she's been chewing it. She must be about five years old. I look at her and I see shades of Olive. A lighter-haired, olive-skinned, more exotic version of Olive, but the Olive *type* nevertheless. I am now one of the only adults in the hall without a child. This girl is the only child without an adult. Everyone else, it seems, has paired off.

Mr. Pilkington nudges me with his corduroy elbows. Usually, Mr. Pilkington is striding across the fields in his flat cap and knee-high boots, carrying a shotgun, but he obviously wanted to see what was happening today. He winks at me.

"Jews are always chosen last," he says, smiling serenely, like he is saying something profound. "She'll clean up, after a bath."

I ignore him. Heart in my boots, I go over and squat in front of the girl on the floor. She doesn't raise her eyes straight away, she leaves me waiting. When eventually she does look up, I see her eyes are brown, flecked with green. Her pupils are huge and black. She reminds me of something familiar, I'm not sure what. Her face is mucky, but nothing a wash won't fix.

I hold out my hand.

"Hello, I'm Mrs. Lowe."

"I'm Mrs. Lowe," she parrots in an exact mimic of my voice.

I laugh nervously. I turn round to see if anyone has noticed us. I don't think anyone has. Mr. Pilkington has gone. The butcher's wife, Farmer Jones, the Shaws, the Carmichaels, the milkman—all home with their catches. I take a hold of the poor little thing's name tag—I don't know whose idea this was, to label the children like pots in a shop.

"I think you're Pearl Posner."

She laughs too, a small squeaky sound, then suddenly grabs my outstretched hands. The shock of it nearly makes me topple over backward.

"Are you my one?" she asks quietly and I want to giggle at the phrasing but she is so sincere, it would be rude.

"I think so."

I do the paperwork at the table where there's usually flower-arranging on a Monday, and all the time I am ticking the boxes I am thinking: *How on earth am I going to cope with this vulnerable little thing? I, who can't even look after Edmund's shirts?*

She thinks I'm a grown-up. She thinks I'll take care of her, but I'm eminently unqualified for the job. I'm the last person to be able to do this.

She is not five. I was a long way out (another thing that doesn't bode well!). She is seven, nearly eight. Female. Date of birth: 22 September 1931. She has two little brothers. Not here. Back in London.

We walk all the way from the village hall, me carrying her battered suitcase. It's not heavy but it's awkward, and it knocks insistently against my knees. At each painful clunk, I think: *Please let Edmund be out, please don't let him be at home.*

I proudly show Pearl the lavatory. We have one upstairs and one down. She says she doesn't have an indoor one at home but seems less excited about our multiple lavs than I might have been. As I show her the spare room, I call it "your bedroom." Surveying the room through her eyes, I see now that it is distinctly lacking atmosphere. There's a single bed, with a single blanket. A wardrobe and a table with a chair. I always pretend to myself it's a work in progress but actually it's an empty shell with limited prospects. The box of Mrs. Burton's toys is on top of the wardrobe. Maybe they will help cheer up the place? I thought it would be bad luck to get them out too early, like getting a cradle long before the baby's born.

Pearl seems quite taken with the picture on the wall though. She reaches out and gently slides her finger along the gilt frame and I think she is going to ask if it is real gold or something (it isn't). But she is looking closely at the actual picture.

"It's you, isn't it?"

She's sharper than she looks. "A long time ago."

I tell her my sister drew it.

"She's clever."

"She was, yes."

I think, *I need to find out what she likes doing. What are her hobbies?* "Do you like drawing, Pearl?"

"Mm, ye-es..." she says mildly.

"Or music?"

"Hmm."

She glances back at the picture. "You look like a film star here. Like Ava Gardner."

Ahh. "Do you like films, Pearl?"

"Yes!" she says keenly. "We go every week."

I'll have to see what I can do. I haven't been to the cinema for a few years now, but Pearl could be a reason to go again.

I help her open her suitcase and we start to unpack. There isn't much to it. There's the gas mask, underwear, nighties, plimsolls, socks and some washing items. I find all her things charming: the scuffed black shoes are adorable, and I have to scold myself for being sentimental—*she's not a doll.* I open the wardrobe for her and she gazes into it, wide-eyed, like she is looking into the depths of a cave.

"All for me?"

I have taken out my wedding dress and Olive's clothes. They are now in the trunk at the foot of my bed. It's silly but having them there makes me feel like they are defending me, like a suit of armor. I should have moved them ages ago.

"All for you, yes. Do you think you'll be happy here, Pearl?"

She nods. Her dark, dark eyes have long lashes and she has a small mouth. I have never seen anything so sweet. She *is* a little Olive all over again. But I won't muck it up this time.

I am nervous, but Edmund stays out that evening doing whatever it is Edmund does. I don't know if the other host mothers will be tucking the children in tonight, but I relish it. As I plump the pillows and fuss over the folds of the blanket, Pearl tells me about her brothers—"the baby and the new baby," she calls them. Mummy spends most of her time feeding them, "from her boobies"—she looks at me uncertainly, as if checking it's an acceptable thing to say. I nod. When we are finished talking, I try to remember what happened next when I was little.

I get on my knees at the side of the bed.

"Shall we pray now?"

She mimics me, with her fingers, her eyes wide.

"Our Father..." I begin.

She is staring at me blankly.

"Don't you... you don't?"

"I've never..." She blinks up at me helplessly. She reminds me of a small woodland creature. She whispers, "Sorry, Mrs."

I flush. I feel terrible.

"That's all right, it was just an idea, to keep you in your routine, if it was your routine. And please call me..."

What the devil should she call me?

"Aunty Vi."

I back away. It seems absurd that she is here. That the "stalk" finally grew a little girl for me.

I potter quietly around the kitchen, scared that any noises I make will wake her. I check she is asleep. *Dear God, what if she should die in the night?* I check on her at eleven and twelve. Slightly after one in the morning, I hear Edmund come in and I freeze in bed. What if he checks her room, goes mad? But he doesn't. I hear the lavatory flush and the taps run but then he goes to his own room.

At two o'clock Pearl is still asleep when I check, but I must have dropped off because at three o'clock I wake to the sound of my bedroom door opening. I snap upward. "Who's there?" A small silhouette of a girl and her flannel can just be made out in the door-frame. I take her back to bed and then clamber up to the box on the wardrobe where I know there is a teddy bear. She grasps it greedily, but still wakes me every fifteen minutes or so until around five o'clock, when I give in. "Come on, you may as well sleep in mine, just for tonight though."

I don't sleep. I watch her, her tiny perfect features.

At seven, I wake her. She stretches and groans and looks very much at home. When I ask if she is hungry for breakfast, she nods several times, very fast.

*

Toast and marmalade, two slices, cut into triangles because everyone knows that triangles are more fun. Pearl, munching, crunching, tells me that her mother sings. *Lovely*, I think, *to the baby and the new baby.*

"What does she sing?"

"She sings what they tell her."

I laugh. "Who?"

"The customers in the Dog and Duck."

This doesn't quite fit the image I had formed of Pearl's mother, and for a moment, I think Pearl must have it wrong. *A pub singer? Really?* Pearl continues obliviously. "Daddy is overseas."

She explains she has two grandmas, one grandpa and three uncles; one is a favorite who calls her Pearly Girl. They look after her when "Mummy is doing the songs."

"A big family then."

She nods with satisfaction.

That's what I had wanted. That's what I dreamed of.

As we are eating, Edmund walks in. Double-takes at the sight of us. "What's going on?"

"This is Pearl Posner—from London," I add unnecessarily. I have already realized that Pearl can be a girl of few words—when she wants to be—but I still expect her to say hello. Instead, she ignores Edmund completely, her finger on her toast. I will have to talk to her about manners (I can't imagine how *that* conversation will go).

"You haven't—" he says thunderously.

I hiss, "It'll just be for a few weeks, Edmund."

"Mummy said just a few days," pipes up Pearl helpfully.

He shakes his head at me and leaves the room. Within seconds, he returns. "Can I have a word, Vivienne?" His eyes are bulging. *Oh Lord.*

Pearl puts her toast triangle into her mouth all at once. I go out, wiping my hands on my apron, staring at my slippers. I don't want Pearl to hear. I don't want Pearl to think she isn't wanted. She *is* wanted. Maybe not by him, but by me.

"What could I do, Edmund? It's compulsory. They insisted!"

"If they thought the rooms were in use they wouldn't have allocated—"

"I couldn't lie to them. Anyway, we'll get money for her."

"It's not about the money." Edmund runs his hands through his hair; he still has hair. People still call him handsome.

"No, I know." I say the one thing that might move him. "But it's about doing our bit, Edmund, you know that."

After breakfast, I take Pearl beyond the churchyard to the small, scrubby patch of land there, with four crooked swings. I am expecting to see several evacuees playing there, but we are the only ones. I don't know what the others can be doing and I am worried I have missed an instruction.

"Have you been on a swing before, Pearl?"

She narrows her eyes at me. "Um, yes?"

Hup, hup she goes and I push her, but she doesn't need me; she kicks out to make herself go higher, and it is painful to watch: why does it hurt to see her soar like a bird, her head thrown back? Is it because I used to imagine coming to this place, these swings, before?

"Who was that man?" Pearl asks, interrupting my reverie. "In the kitchen."

It is as though the swinging has loosened something, emboldened her.

"Oh, that was Mr. Lowe…" I pause. "My husband."

She crinkles her nose. "Really?"

"Yes!" I say. I feel this is an insult, but I'm not quite sure who she's insulting: him or me.

She nods slowly. She brings the swing to a wobbly still, then surveys me. "He has a very nice car."

I laugh. "You noticed it then?"

She does the fast nodding again. "Can I go in it?"

My heart sinks. Edmund's Ford Prefect is his pride and joy. He won't even let me drive it and I know exactly what he'll think about Pearl's fingers smearing his clean leather seats.

"We'll see," I say.

Walking back to the house, she tells me she was expecting us to keep chickens. Surprised, I apologize for their absence. I had got it into my head that the London children wouldn't know their chickens from their herons or their geese. But Pearl is very knowledgeable about a lot of things. At home, they call her "clever clogs," she says. She tells me about a neighbor's dog. She imitates the noises he makes: a varied symphony. Charmed, I tell her, "What a coincidence, our neighbor here has dogs."

I know, we will go and meet Mrs. Burton's dogs!

I have never called on Mrs. Burton before, she usually comes to invite me, but she always tells me to drop by whenever. Now is the time to test it. We knock and Mrs. Burton greets us with surprise but also with warmth. She has cake, she has stories, she has all the right maternal instincts.

And of course, Pearl is a natural with Laurel and Hardy. They lick her face and roll over and she tickles their tummies while Mrs. Burton makes us a brew. Mrs. Burton teaches us to say "sit" to them, then "lie down," and they do, they really do! Pearl and Mrs. Burton are laughing, and when Laurel comes to sit at my feet, I feel that maybe, just maybe, I am part of something again.

CHAPTER FOUR

1914—Then

Those first lazy August days at war, Olive and I often went out walking in the sunshine and although we didn't say it, we were trying to spot what was changing. We were sniffing out the war on the ground. Olive said some men had already left Goldsmiths to fight. The engineering students were joining up at quite a pace. She said a professor of fine art with a German name had "disappeared." She also asked if I'd heard that the suffragettes had ceased their operations for the time being. I thought this was a relief. Some of Olive's suffragette friends were a rum gang and I didn't want her locked up and force-fed for slashing paintings in the National Gallery. Instead, it seemed to me that everyone was working together, putting their backs into the war effort. It gave you a nice feeling.

There were only two other girls doing the fine art degree like Olive. In the mornings, they had assembly and prayers like at school. There were no women's lavatories in the art school building so she spent most of her lunchtimes over at the trainee teachers' block and that's where she found out that a lot of boyfriends and brothers were joining up too.

I was working in Father's office, not far from our house. Some two years earlier, Father had employed a Mrs. Webster to assist me. Unfortunately, Mrs. Webster proved highly capable and, rather than helping me out, she took over. The filing system she created was so competent, and her note-taking so efficient, that I was left with very little to do. Father used to say Mrs. Webster was a short-term measure, and when we were all ready, she would move elsewhere and I would take over, but secretly I doubted any of us thought that was likely any more.

Very little had changed in the office since war broke out, although my father kept talking about disruption to the "supply chains." Mrs. Webster, who inclined toward morose at the best of times, was inclining further that way now. She had a nineteen-year-old son, Harry, and was worried he'd be called up. My suggestion that the war would be over before the winter solstice did nothing to allay her concerns.

Olive loved posters, any posters. Before college, she had gone through a huge Toulouse-Lautrec phase. Naturally, she was thrilled with the recruitment posters. The sign men must have been working overtime for they seemed to be everywhere and there were different posters every few days. You couldn't walk down a street without passing three or four pasted on the walls.

Britons need you. There he was: Lord Kitchener depicted bold as brass, with that mustache you could sweep the fireplace with, the piercing eyes, like the strictest headmaster, the most merciless grandfather shouting, "Go to your room without dinner!"

"Just look at those hands," Olive said admiringly. Olive had always struggled with hands and disproportionately admired those who could manage them. I always told her to cover up the hands she did with a cup or a handbag, but she wouldn't. She *had* to see a thing through. She didn't cut corners, not artistically anyway.

She was right though: these hands were impressive. Clearly, Reginald Leete, the artist, had no fear of hands—Lord Kitchener was the owner of an enviably perfect and pointy index finger.

Soon we saw a new one: Britons want you. Join your country's army. God save the King.

"They needed us last week, they *want* us today," I pointed out.

Olive stared at it, drinking it in: she obviously reveled in its forcefulness and admired everything about it. "Be hard to say no to that," she said. I agreed. That was the point. There was something almost hypnotizing about it. Olive told me about a lecture she'd attended where they'd learned about the "infinite spark"—the "God-light." "An inexpressible something in a picture that makes it hard to look away." That was what she chased. That was what *all* artists chased, apparently.

Someone stopped behind us, breathing heavily, too close to our backs.

"I don't think they want you, girls, they want big strapping lads!" he jeered. I turned round, smiling nervously, but Olive wouldn't take that lying down. Olive wouldn't take cheek from anyone.

"You joining up then? Big lad like you..."

He blushed into his collar.

Olive linked her arm with mine and as we marched away, she imitated our Uncle Toby: "Now we know, now we know..."

A few days later, Olive said that some injured soldiers would be coming in to King's Cross station. This threw me. Soldiers were injured? Already? We'd only been at war for a matter of days! It made me worry for our cousin Richard. For the first time, I wondered if we were getting the full picture from the newspapers.

"We ought to go then," I said stoutly. "Show our respect."

Olive agreed. She was always looking for ideas for new things to paint.

We bought flags off a street seller who cheerfully admitted the war had given him a roaring trade. We joined the crowds of people waving flags and clapping; a happy bunch we were. Then the men—or patients, I suppose—started coming out. At first, I felt embarrassed to be looking, but then I leaned over to Olive and said, "They don't look *too* bad."

Some waved right back at us; one man with a bandage wrapped right round his head did a jolly little jig. Other men looked down and seemed to be pretending we weren't there.

"In fact, they look rather relieved," I whispered to Olive.

"They'll be patched up and sent right back again!" she said, then shouted heartily like we were at a rugby tournament, "Go on, boys!"

One woman pushed through the crowds and gave a soldier a red rose. I don't think she knew him, she just wanted to do something.

"Thank you, boys, for all you've done," she called after him. I admired her spirit.

In the background were starched nurses, concerned and facilitating, checking that the men could walk. Olive nudged me.

"Wish we could do something like that, Vivi."

"Wha-at?"

"Don't the nurses look *wonderful*?"

I laughed. Olive could be such a dreamer sometimes.

Then came the worse ones. Some on crutches with actual missing legs. Several men in wheelchairs. One man was pushed through with his head lolling uselessly over his chest. As he went past us, I heard him babbling like a baby. It reminded me of Richard performing Lady Macbeth. What on earth was the matter with him?

I thought, *it's possible he was always like that*. Surely, no one could descend into that state in a mere two weeks? He must have had something wrong to start with.

Every night at supper, we raised a toast, "To Richard" and "For God, King and Country," before we tucked in. But that evening, I don't know why, we forgot our new routine and it wasn't until we had all taken a bite of beef and ale casserole that I remembered. I just burst into tears—I couldn't get the image of that poor creature in the chair out of my mind.

Father and Olive stared at me.

Stuttering, I explained, "We forgot our toast! What if something terrible happens to Richard?"

I looked up just quickly enough to see Olive rolling her eyes and Father continuing to put his fork to his mouth.

"I'm just being superstitious," I added apologetically.

Uncharacteristically, Father shouted back at me across the table, food still in his mouth, "You don't think anything would happen to that boy, do you?" He chewed angrily. "He's only nineteen—damn nonsense!"

"Sorry, Father."

Father backed down immediately. I saw he had tears in his eyes. "He'll be fine, Vi, you know Richard."

Olive put her hand on mine. Sometimes she could read my mind. "Don't worry, Vivi, Richard won't be coming back in that state, I promise you."

The next day, Olive showed me a sketch she had done of the flag-waving crowds. She was very pleased with it. She had drawn a cheering little girl with curly hair and a shouting boy with a plaster on one cheek (hands in his pockets). It wasn't Olive's usual style; in fact, you could say it was quite twee, but I thought: *War brings out different sides of a person.* And I knew Olive wanted to do something good with her patriotism. She wanted to use her passion for the better. I could see these images embroidered on handkerchiefs or drawn onto china plates one day and I told her that.

"What are you going to call it?" I asked.

"What do you think?"

"How about *Before the Victory*?"

She pondered for a moment and then said: "*War Spirit*."

She never used my suggestions, however good they were.

"And what will you do with it?"

"Show it to the Fords, of course," she said. She grabbed her coat. "Actually, I'll take it there right now."

"Olive?!"

"War effort." She smirked. "Just doing my bit."

CHAPTER FIVE

1939—Now

Her first Sunday in Hinckley and Pearl seems to think she is coming with me to church. I don't like to say no to her, not yet. I wonder if she is perhaps scared of being in the house on her own. Or with Edmund. That's understandable. But Edmund is out most of the time anyway. Our house does creak and sigh sometimes, like it's elderly and trying to get back on to its feet. I remember Olive used to hate an empty house too. I tell Pearl that I am playing the large organ at the front of the church, so she'll have to sit on her own in the pews.

She stares at me with her saucer eyes. "*Orangutan?*"

Laughing, I correct her. "Organ—it's like a piano with pipes."

"And what's a pew?" she asks. I love that she is curious and such a quick learner. Because she is so tiny and hesitant, you might think she is feeble, but she isn't.

I know what it's like to be underestimated.

As we walk there, I feel proud to hold her little hand in mine. People wouldn't know she was an evacuee; they might well think she is my daughter.

I wonder where Edmund is again. It's awkward when Pearl asks and I have to admit I don't know. She sees some friends—other evacuees—in the churchyard. They are clambering over headstones. I don't know whether I should tell them off. Children don't usually listen to me. I say, "Why not play round the back, where the swings are?" and I am surprised when they head off.

Pearl stares longingly after them. I nod, and whisper, "You can go and play too, if you like."

Should I be letting her go off alone? I don't know what I'm doing. I *should* know what I'm doing. I'm forty-four. They've let me in charge of a small child. Without even an interview or an exam.

Today I play "All Things Bright and Beautiful"; the vicar likes to keep things jolly. As I thump the keys, I think of Pearl, falling out of a tree and screaming. I think of her skipping into the woods, picking poisonous mushrooms, eating them; of her little tongue furring up. I think of her finding the brook. I don't even know if she can swim. *How could I not know this?*

> Each little flower that opens,
> Each little bird that sings,
> He made their glowing colors,
> He made their tiny wings.

When we get back home, Edmund is there, grim-faced and drinking whisky. It's been on the wireless: war has been declared. This is it. Now we know. There's no getting out of it.

"Oh God," I say. We knew it was coming but still it is a shock. I flop into an armchair, sniffing back tears. Edmund pours himself more whisky. Pearl surveys us both, terrified.

"I want to go home!" she cries out. Her eyes are wider than ever. I jump up.

"I can understand that, Pearl," I say. I realize quickly that I must cover my feelings. It is my duty. This is what the adults do. "But London is not safe. Come and help me in the kitchen. Let's make a nice stew."

She chops and slices as she should, but her face is mutinous, and she refuses to speak.

*

The photographs in the newspaper make me shiver. The Nazis hate everything, but mostly they hate the Jews. You can see them at their massive meetings—rallies, they call them—with their arms out in a salute and their armbands. I think they look pathetic. And he's such a little, horrible-looking man too, that Adolf Hitler. With his stabby voice and that shabby mustache—a horrible, spoilt little emperor. The Germans I met during the Great War—patients or prisoners—were well-mannered and so *sensible* somehow. They'd help you out if you were struggling to carry someone or if someone was having a nightmare. They wanted the war to be over as much as we did—and yet, look at that blighted country now! How have they fallen so hard for Hitler? What has he promised them? Sometimes when I read about the Nazis, I find it hard to breathe.

I try not to think about Sam. What would Sam be thinking now; how would he be feeling? I know one thing: he wouldn't be *that* surprised.

That night, Pearl is inconsolable.

"I don't want you, I want my mummy."

I stand by the door uncertainly. I don't know how I am supposed to mend this.

"I don't want a stupid war!" she shouts. She kicks the wardrobe—which I can understand—and then her own suitcase, which I can't.

"None of us do," I say, but that seems to make her worse.

"Mummy said it was a holiday. She said. She SAID."

I can't think of anything to tell her, but that *I'm sorry. I am. I truly am.* She cries herself to sleep and I watch her, the most useless woman on earth.

CHAPTER SIX

1914—Then

It was cooler in September and it rained little but often. I kept getting caught out. Pointless to worry about how to wear one's hair when the drizzle turned your style to frizz, or a downpour plastered it to one's head.

I thought often of dear Richard on the continent. Having him over there felt like we had a very personal link to the war. I knew our link was tenuous—other girls had brothers or husbands who had gone—but it *was* authentic. I pictured him repeatedly throwing that ball against the wall of his nursery. I would never complain about that never-ending thunk again. I thought of him in his uniform, how he had looked so different suddenly and how he came over all shy. He had chuckled and pulled at his epaulets: "I'll get used to it, girls, don't you worry." Typical of him to want to reassure us above all else.

We loved Richard very much. I supposed it was natural that we were very worried about him.

Ever the good boy, Richard wrote to my father as well as to his own parents and to us. Olive suggested he had a lot of time to write letters—a good thing—but I didn't think he did, I think he just prioritized us.

On the surface, his letters were chirpy and upbeat, but I sometimes detected fear and uncertainty in his words. He quoted the chaplain often and I wondered what Richard—a non-attender at our local church—would be seeing the chaplain for.

Richard promised to be home for Christmas—we spent most years at our aunt and uncle's—yet he begged us for knitted socks that went up to the knees. *It's going to be a harsh winter.*

"Why, though," I pondered, "if he's coming home for Christmas?"

"Don't fret," said Olive simply. She said I was reading too much into it. "If he says he'll be home, he'll be home."

Richard wrote a lot about food too. He seemed quite obsessed. And just like the talk of chaplains, this seemed like a Richard I hadn't met before. Cans, tins, biscuits, scones and clotted cream occupied his mind, and *please, please, send some chocolate, anything to keep the cold at bay.* He keeps mentioning the cold, I thought, startled. Well, of course it was cold, but... *The nights are long. And my boys are suffering.* Now he signed off his letters: *if anything happens to me, I know you'll look after Mother. You and Olive have always been like sisters to me, more than sisters.*

But then he would be back to his cheery self:

Now, send me some news about Edmund and Christopher! What larks are those chaps getting up to? And Vivienne, do you have anything on the marriage question to report to your big cousin?

His letters meant the world to me.

At the end of every term at Goldsmiths they held exhibitions, and it was at the big end-of-year exhibition in year one where Olive had first met the Fords. She did tell me the story of how, but the tale was so long and meandering that I lost the thread of it, and even if I hadn't, I felt sure she was missing out the more pertinent details. Apparently, Mrs. Ford didn't believe Olive had made her pictures herself. They were *that* good! And Olive didn't believe Mrs. Ford was the famous art collector. It seemed *that* unlikely! When they realized their mistakes, *Oh, how they laughed!*

Mrs. Ford, her mother Mrs. Brown and her adult son, Walter, lived all three generations of them together. Mrs. Ford was divorced, something that I found quite shocking, but even more shocking perhaps was the fact that she would talk openly about it. Her ex-husband was a doctor, and "one hadn't experienced boredom until one spent an hour in his company." Mrs. Ford had shiny black hair and glossy red lips. Her mother, Mrs. Brown, was growing poorly with age, but Mrs. Ford looked after her with good humor. And Walter, well, Walter was a good-time boy: he'd just come from the States and it was as though he were brimful of both California sunshine and New York literary events.

Right from the beginning, I presumed Olive had a "thing" for twenty-one-year-old Walter. Not only was his hair like his mother's, blacker than coal, and his lashes long and pretty, but he wore clothes with such panache, he ought surely to have worked in fashion. Yet there were many handsome young men at the Fords' house. The Fords were the most sociable people I'd ever met—I didn't know if it was because they were American or if it was just their style, but their house was always brimming over with guests. There was the piano player, David, and his charming wife; there was the trumpet player, Clive, and James who played the banjo. Rod who wrote something called "science fiction" and Frank who wrote ghost stories. Johnny was a singer, over six foot three—an ogre, a giant, but when he sang, he could produce tenderness you would never believe someone like him would be capable of.

I visited on occasional Sundays with Olive and although everyone was unfailingly kind to me, I sometimes felt as though I were being handled with kid gloves. This was a very different social milieu to the one I was used to. Everyone was eccentric or glamourous or talented. Even if you weren't, they'd encourage you to find a way in which you could be.

"I help at my father's business," I said, pretending to myself that Mrs. Webster didn't exist.

"A beautiful girl like you?"

"Well…" Praise was given out freely at the Fords', like confetti at a wedding.

"I would have thought you were a goddess by trade."

I chuckled.

"Or an artist's muse, maybe?"

I thought about muses in history. *Didn't they all come to a bad end?*

"Oy, she's *my* muse," interrupted Olive possessively and everyone laughed.

Mrs. Ford loved art, and she adored artists, but her own particular talent was for songwriting. She'd had a few minor successes in the past. She told me the titles of some of the songs but I didn't recognize any of them. Now, she was hungry for more.

"There's nothing like it, Vivienne," she explained to me, "hearing people *sing* the words you wrote. No greater thrill! *Nothing* compares."

She slapped a laughing Johnny on the knee. "Not even *that*!"

She was working with David on a song. That's what they did virtually every single day: he'd come round with his charming wife, and they'd be drinking and laughing and playing the piano.

Apparently, David was writing the music and Mrs. Ford was doing the words.

One Sunday, after they'd been hammering at it for hours on end, David turned, and singled me out. "Vivienne, is it? Do *you* like it?"

Was it my imagination or did the room go silent? Everyone was waiting for my verdict.

And I felt in a flutter, because David was another one who was terribly handsome and dangerously bright. I croaked, "It's a little like that song 'Bleak Midwinter,' isn't it?"

He clicked his fingers at me, then said loudly so everybody could hear: "Lady, *you* have a very good ear."

"And a very good face," murmured Johnny and I went as pink as the rose in his buttonhole.

One day, after some of the younger men had left to go to another party, and there weren't many of us left, Olive said, "I think Johnny might be falling for you, Vivi."

Some women like to have men tripping all over themselves for them. I didn't. And I certainly wasn't interested in Johnny, or any singer, artist or writer. I wanted a regular, conventional man. A man from a good family, and who would *make* a good family. The kind of man who was seeking a role in the Indian Civil Service. I remembered Edmund's hot hand in mine at the piano and the sweet strokes he gave my back when no one was looking. Poor Edmund—he didn't know what to do about the war.

Mrs. Ford lit her cigarette and exhaled. It felt like an age passed before she gave her verdict. "Johnny is a nice chap."

"I'm not interested," I said more firmly. I felt they were ganging up on me.

"Oh, that's right," said Mrs. Ford in her amused tone that left the younger men breathless. "You have someone, don't you, Vivienne? Edward, is it?"

"Edmund." I was embarrassed. "I don't know."

"Loyal girl."

Olive said to Mrs. Ford in a strangely jolly voice, "Vivienne is loyal to Edmund, but is Edmund loyal to Vivienne?"

"How do you mean?" I snapped.

"Good God, Vivi!" she retorted. "It was a joke." She raised her eyebrows: "Sensitive subject."

Mrs. Ford was a diplomat, unlike my bandit sister. "Bring your Edmund here some time, Vivi," she drawled. "Let me have a look at him. I'm a good judge of people."

I couldn't for a moment imagine Edmund mixing here, but I said I would. To do otherwise would have been rude.

As the war continued relentlessly toward October, it began to gradually dawn on us—to dawn on everyone, I suppose—that we were in it for the long haul. The newspaper reports were not as positive as they had been in August. Victory seemed to be moving

further and further away. People were dying horribly in Belgium
and France. Villagers were fleeing. The Germans were massacring
civilians. It wasn't what anyone expected. Antwerp fell and we dug
in and hardened. We were going to have to get used to this. Even the
musicians and entertainers at Mrs. Ford's were in a quandary about
what to do. Some days, Johnny said he wanted to fight the Bosch.
Other days, he wanted to go out and entertain the troops.

"Better than *being* the troops, eh?" said Olive archly.

He winked at me. "We can all help the war effort in different
ways, right, Vivienne?"

Yet it was always a gay atmosphere at the Fords'. To be on the
winning side is not a terrible place to be—and despite the dark clouds
gathering, that's where we thought we were. We were so puffed up
with our own self-righteousness and importance that we couldn't see
the wood for the trees. The piano kept playing, the drinks kept being
poured and the guests kept coming. On any given Sunday, Olive could
be found pontificating about the artist Percy Millhouse—her most
recent obsession; Mrs. Ford might be laughing about the politician
David Lloyd George and Walter could be arguing about men's breeches.

Sometimes, I would sit there among them, and just watch and
wonder.

It was clear that Olive was, inexplicably, trying to wean me off
Edmund. Yet the more she tried, the less I wanted to. I knew Edmund
didn't have talents or "mystery" like so many of these characters, but
that didn't necessarily mean that he was as dull as Olive suggested
he was. On our latest visit to Aunt Cecily's and Uncle Toby's, he had
played footsie with me under the table, all the while expounding on
why the Belgian and the French armies weren't half as good as ours.

One day, a new gentleman came to visit the Fords. Olive took his
elbow and made a beeline for me. This man was thin, curly-haired
and handsome, but I felt instantly he was not for me and I was not
for him. He sat by me though, and chatted contentedly about his
little sister, Mairi, who was out nursing in France—no, Belgium,

oh, he couldn't remember where she'd bloody got to—but anyway, she was a fearless trouper. "She's only eighteen," he said admiringly, "but what a daredevil! You should see her ride a motorbike. Not like me," he went on, rubbing his chin, embarrassed. "I don't know what the heck I should do with myself."

He got out a silver coin. "Heads I go to the Caribbean and become a sugar farmer, tails I join up?"

He threw the coin up in the air: It came back tails. He shuddered and looked at me beseechingly. He had lovely wet eyes.

"Best of three?" he suggested.

"Where is the Caribbean anyway?" I asked.

"The other side of the world..."

"Best of three," I agreed.

The living room, where we all gathered, had a large open fireplace, and as the weather grew cooler, Mrs. Ford would send the men out to the garden for some wood-cutting. It was all great fun: everyone had such a zest for life. They all wanted to try out their strength, but you couldn't help but note that Walter, with his cape flying around his broad shoulders and his strong arms, was the best chopper of them all.

"Be careful!" we'd call out, especially after one of the men had a near miss on the out motion, almost embedding the ax in his nose.

Then we'd bring in the logs and Mrs. Ford would light the fire. Gorgeous it was to watch the flames dance, heating up the room.

Sometimes, Walter Ford would appear with an actress or a singer with a face full of makeup. I would always look over to see if Olive was watching. If it were me, and if it had been Edmund, say, I didn't know how I would bear it, but Olive seemed accepting to the point of oblivion.

And sometimes, she would drink too much and stay over, and one time I did say to her, "Should you, Olive? It's not seemly." I couldn't imagine what Edmund's mother would say if she knew what went on. Olive thought that was hilarious, which wasn't my intention. "Oh, Vivi, you can be so bourgeois sometimes."

"What does that mean?"

"It means don't worry about me, darling."

Edmund refused to come to Mrs. Ford's Sundays. "It's just not for me," he told me at Aunt Cecily's, and although it was irritating, I admired his steadfastness. Edmund was solid and unwavering. He didn't have to conform with the nonconformists, did he? The Lowes were known around town, and one time someone at the Fords' said to me, "Oh, you know the Lowes? Well, I never! Top-class family, aren't they? *Very* flush," and I felt a burst of pleasure that we were such close associates. I could see I went up in people's esteem, just because of the connection.

Another time though, I was in the garden as the men were chopping wood and I don't think they knew I was there. Someone said, "I saw that Edmund Lowe again at the Windmill. I know they're rich, but how he affords it night after night, I will never know..."

"What's the Windmill?" I whispered to Olive.

But she just steered me away inside—pretended she was cold or had a cold or something.

"They're just being sillys. Ignore them."

"But what is it?"

"It's nothing,"

I persisted until she admitted, "Oh, Vivi, it's just a men's club..."

"And?"

"Where they watch ladies dance with tassels on their you-know-whats..."

"It wasn't Edmund," I said bluntly.

"I'm sure it wasn't," she said but her expression wasn't as confident as her words.

She began talking about what she had been working on at college that week. "It's awfully hard, it's all lines and triangles this term, not really my thing," she said.

She was trying to distract me, I knew it. She was great at lines and triangles.

"Poor Edmund is extremely conflicted about the war question," I went on. "He doesn't know whether he's coming or going." I was determined not to let this slide.

"I can imagine," she replied.

The song that Mrs. Ford and David were working on together grew better each time I heard it. One Sunday, David thumped it out on the keys and Johnny took it seriously for once and sang earnestly this time, with the actual words that Mrs. Ford had written. We all stood around, the wine flowing.

David stopped playing suddenly. He looked around at us all and said, "It's coming along nicely."

Bizarrely, Johnny burst into tears. He said he'd never sung anything so lovely, and what a privilege! Everyone made a big fuss of him—*it's the stress of the war, see.*

While cuddling him, Mrs. Ford looked around over his shoulder, then charged me with a responsibility. She wanted me to copy the lyrics out, ten, maybe twelve times, if I wouldn't mind, that is? I was always delighted to be charged with a task and availed myself of the study, where I could fulfill my work in silence. It was a lovely job and I was as careful and neat with the writing as I could be. The sun was low in the sky when I had finished. I re-entered the living room boldly, feeling, I imagine, like St. Nicholas delivering all the treats at Christmas. "Here, I have it, everyone!"

They were summoned from the hillside
They were called in from the glen,
And the country found them ready
At the stirring call for men.
Let no tears add to their hardships
As the soldiers pass along,
And although your heart is breaking
Make it sing this cheery song

When everyone had a copy of the lyrics, we sang it, all of us together, as David played. I felt myself becoming tearful, thinking of Richard and how he'd heard the stirring call.

David and Mrs. Ford couldn't agree on the title. They were arguing good-humoredly, but neither would back down. They asked each of us: Olive and me, Uilleam Chisholm—the curly-haired boy Olive had introduced me to—Walter, two actresses, Johnny, Frank and Clive, to raise our glasses for a favorite title.

"Keep the Home Fires Burning" got just two votes: only Uilleam and I chose it. Everybody else preferred "'Til the Boys Come Home." Uilleam and I laughed: "That told us, then!" he said.

Mrs. Ford snuck an arm round us both. "Actually, it's for the publisher to decide. It could well change yet."

David went around the room shaking everyone's hands, thanking them for their contribution and saying, "I daresay we've got a hit on our hands."

But Mrs. Ford had to outdo him. "David, darling, it's going to go down in history!"

Mrs. Ford was nothing if not ambitious. We all clapped each other on the back once again. We were so excited. We felt like on this piece of paper the war was won.

We were so naive.

CHAPTER SEVEN

1939—Now

There is going to be a welcome party for the evacuees in the church hall. Pearl Posner has no party clothes: there is nothing shiny or pretty in the wardrobe. Either she is a functionalist like Olive, who once threw clothes out of the window in a fit of pique against capitalism, or she is very poor. I suspect the latter.

I decide to take Pearl to the shops in town and we set off excitedly. The upset of the other night is all forgotten, thankfully, and instead, she chats breezily about the markets back at home: the barrels of salted herrings, the performing monkey who wears baby clothes and the rows of purple cabbages. It sounds like a different world.

A shopkeeper comes out to tell me that he's already seen three evacuees this morning, and they've all got head lice and "What's the matter with them from London? Don't they wash?"

I don't even know this man, but I don't like his tone. He expects me to agree with everything he says. What a shock he'd have if I didn't.

I steer Pearl away and along to the next dress shop, where I know kind Mrs. Purnell will cluck over the wooden counter and compliment Pearl. Mrs. Purnell is a soft touch. Once, at a bus stop, I heard teenagers say that "if you want to get your hands in the till, Mrs. Purnell's shop is the best one."

But after the doorbell has announced our arrival, we find Mrs. Purnell is not there; instead, it's her daughter taking care of the shop, the newly married Mrs. Fraser. Mrs. Fraser swings over to us, her high heels clattering on the floorboards. Her skirt is tight and her blouse, with its pussycat bow, is immaculate. She looks dressed for a dance. I don't know Mr. or Mrs. Fraser, but Mrs. Burton has warned me that "Mr. Fraser is not half so good as he thinks he is."

"You got one then?"

"Uh huh."

Mrs. Fraser licks her lips. "She looks Italian. Is she Italian?"

"I don't think so," I say, wishing I could make us both invisible.

"I went to Italy a few years ago," she says. "Rome, Venice, the lot. I'll tell you this for a fact: the Vatican is overrated."

I imagine Mrs. Fraser at the Coliseum, making mincemeat out of the lions.

Pearl waits patiently as Mrs. Fraser examines her.

"Is she a Jew then? They sometimes look Italian, it's all in the nose." She taps her own, mysteriously.

I wince.

Mrs. Fraser says, "What?" quite sharply.

I'm a coward. What can I say? I mumble, "Sorry, I've had this headache since yesterday... can't seem to shake it off."

I wonder how kind Mrs. Purnell ended up with a daughter like this.

Pearl is reluctant to choose anything at first. Then, after some cajoling, she selects a navy cotton pinafore—she is smaller than the size small but Mrs. Fraser says her mother will take it in. I say, "Don't worry, I'll do it." Mrs. Fraser wants to argue and for a moment, I fear we are going to get into a tug of war over the alterations, but she glares at me for a while and then backs down.

"If you insist."

"I like sewing," I say, more to myself than anyone else.

I buy a little matching cotton blouse to go with it, sized for ages 5–6 because Pearl really is small. She will look a dream.

"She's malnourished," barks Mrs. Fraser triumphantly. "That's what they do, you know."

Outside, Pearl doesn't seem disturbed by Mrs. Fraser. She is concerned only with her pinafore. She declares it's the prettiest thing she's ever seen and when Hitler is beaten, can she please take it home to London?

"Of course, love," I say, mindful of her tears the other night. "And that won't be too long, I'm sure."

There is cotton bunting along all the walls of the church hall. The triangular Union Jack in umpteen rows—sixty, seventy of them. Lest we forget which side we're on. Then there are signs written on a bed sheet: *Welcome Children* and *Hinckley Hearts London*. Most of the adults from London are going back tomorrow. They have homes and families to attend to. The teachers are tall, quiet women: it feels strangely appropriate that these teachers are taller than the rest of us. Pearl goes to join one of them who is reading *The Tales of Peter Rabbit* to a small group of children.

Mrs. Burton arrives laden down with tins and trays, apologizing for being late even though she isn't. She doesn't have a horse in this race, but she has been cooking and cutting and primping for us all. It's nice to have a friend here and I go and help unpack her cakes.

The adults are all talking about Mr. Hitler and how, "silly bugger, he came back for more. Didn't he learn his blinking lesson the last time?" I get chatting to my neighbor, Mrs. Dean, who has also taken a London child, a ten-year-old boy. Out of nowhere, she says that she worked as a nurse during the Great War, in the Somme. I don't know how she knows that I was in France too—the village grapevine, I suppose—but she does. She murmurs, "Brings it all back, don't it?"

I nod wordlessly.

"Lose someone, did you?"

"Mm," I say. She puts her hand on mine. I am only just getting used to Pearl laying her hands on me like I'm a piece of furniture; I'm not ready for other people to do it yet.

I squirm and she relents.

"It won't be like last time, Mrs. Lowe," she advises. She speaks with complete conviction, and even though I admire it, I think, *How does anyone know what it will be like?*

There are sandwiches in ever-decreasing circles on trays.

"All the C's." Mr. Shaw nudges me, and as usual, I'm not sure what his joke means. He explains. "The sandwiches." He says it like *Sam-Witches.* "Cress. Cheese. Cucumber..." I point out there is also ham, hating myself as I do so.

The other Stepney boy, Nathan, comes over to say hello to Pearl. He tells us he is living on the farm with Farmer Jones and his wife and for some reason, I pretend I don't already know that. He tells me he has just had his fifteenth birthday; they got him presents and a cake and everything. He is the cat who's got the cream—but he's a well-mannered boy, you can't begrudge him. He reminds me of some of the younger Tommys we used to transport in Belgium—and I'm not surprised that Mrs. Burton's noisy daughters fall into awestruck silence at the sight of him.

"Would you like a sandwich?" I offer him the tray. He looks through them carefully, then warily selects the cress. He looks at me with troubled eyes.

"Farmer Jones gives me pork," he says in a low voice. "I'm not supposed to eat pork."

"Have you explained that to him?" I say. My heart is beating fast as I think of Sam. I can imagine he was like this boy once.

"I have."

"What did he do then?"

"He fried me some bacon instead."

I don't know if he is upset or not.

"It's fine," I say eventually, for he seems to think I know about these things. I try to be wise. "How about you eat pork here, but not when you're back home? Would that be okay?"

He nods.

Eating the sandwiches, Pearl advises me that she doesn't eat crusts. I'm not sure where I stand on the crust question. I don't know if one pushes these things? I know my father would have insisted I eat them up and I know fear would have swallowed them down for me. But I also know Olive used to slip her crusts under the plate.

I say, "Pearl, they will make your hair curl," and she scowls at me.

"But I don't want curly hair, I want wavy hair like yours."

She drinks her blackcurrant cordial very fast and it leaves a little purple mustache. I don't know why but that reminds me of Edmund, in 1914, before he went to France.

I must stop living in the past.

I wait for Edmund to join us at the party. I told him about it yester-day; I even left a pleading note. *It will be good for us.* I suppose I knew deep down he wouldn't come. It's painful seeing some of the other host fathers here. There are host grandfathers and grandmothers too. Why can't we be more like them?

A small blond boy with a plaster holding his glasses frames together stands in front of me and laboriously recites: "Hitler has only got one ball, the other is in the—"

I shush him gently as he points to a group of sniggering bigger boys. "They told me to say it."

"Did they now?" I try to look disapproving.

He leans in, whispers, "What does it mean anyway?"

"Maybe it means Hitler likes football?" I shrug.

"Or tennis!" he agrees happily.

"Oh yes, but silly Hitler, he keeps losing his equipment."

Pearl splutters into her cordial. "Even *I* know what it means, and it doesn't mean *that*."

The vicar asks if I wouldn't mind playing the piano. I feel irritated for an instant, because I'm not the entertainment, I'm here as a host mother, but then everyone else is in cozy groups, and I'm not. And I like the vicar; he's always been kind and never made me feel like an outsider. Brightly, I ask, "What, now?" and he says, "Well, I don't mean tomorrow, do I?"

He's another one who tries to be funny.

While I am playing a favorite—"Tiptoe Through the Tulips"—the deputy mayor wanders over and sits too close to me on the bench. Some time ago, he asked if I could concentrate if he talked while I played. Stupidly, proudly, I had said that I could. Now, whenever I play, he plants himself beside me and talks at me.

"How do you always look so well turned out, Mrs. Lowe?"

What can I say to that?

"This shows off your lovely shape. I bet you had all the suitors back in the day. Mr. Lowe is a lucky man."

I concentrate on the tulips I am tiptoeing through.

"What's your one like then?"

"Fine." I plonk onwards, looking across the room for "my one."

Pearl has pulled her coat over herself and is lying across two chairs. I think she may have fallen asleep.

"If you want to swap or get rid, just say the word." The deputy mayor puts his freckled hand on my knee. "I'll sort you out. No need for payment." He scratches his nail into my stockings and I play a crashing chord, like a cry for help.

Everyone looks round. "Sorry!" I call. Pearl sits bolt upright, squinting at me. The deputy mayor stands up quickly.

"No offense meant," he says, stroking his mustache.

"None taken," I reply, not looking at him.

The vicar comes over, even more pleased with himself than usual for he has gathered some song requests. Top of his list is "Keep the Home Fires Burning."

I knew they would ask for that. I don't play it any more. I tell him I don't remember the tune and go straight to second one down: "The Biggest Aspidistra in the World."

CHAPTER EIGHT

1914—Then

The telegram came to the office the morning of 24 November. *Dear God. No. The very worst news.* Father and I hugged each other tightly, then he said he would away to Aunt Cecily's immediately. He was weeping as he ran out into the street.

He had told me to stay behind until Mrs. Webster arrived, but I had to do something, I couldn't just sit there, so I locked up and took a carriage soon after he'd gone. I had only ever been to Goldsmiths for the end-of-term exhibitions, never when it was a normal working college. But I needed to go now: I needed Olive.

Voice shaking, I urged the driver to go as fast as he could, and he told me, "Keep your ruddy hat on." I slumped back in my seat, shamed. Then he seemed to soften. "Is it an emergency, Miss?" and I told him, "Unfortunately, it is," and he took me a back way along the cobbled side streets. I was shivering like it was the depths of winter.

At the college, the sign for the arts department seemed to be deliberately small and hidden. Relieved not to have missed it, I turned my trot into a skirt-holding gallop. As soon as Olive saw me, she would realize something was wrong. Things could not have been more wrong. I couldn't think about *that* yet though. I had to get Olive.

There were men, men everywhere. I didn't know how Olive could stand it. Soon I found my destination, a studio B, but she wasn't there, and so I was sent upstairs, up to the third floor. I knocked on a door, heard a deep voice, a rumbling like an underground train. "Enter."

The first thing I saw was a man, lying on a chaise longue, wearing nothing at all. Stone cold naked. I saw his thighs, a nest of hair and his penis. When he noticed me, he dragged a towel over his private parts but not as quickly as he might have, and to make matters worse, he winked. He had terrible teeth too, terrible. I looked away sharpish. *How could that be right?* I knew Olive had fought quite a battle to get into the life drawing classes. The college thought it was inappropriate for female students. Now I found myself siding with the college. Was *this* what she had fought for the right to draw?

Edmund's mother would have a fit if she knew about this.

Anyway, I didn't have time to debate the merits of debauchery in an arts education. *Where could my sister be?*

A small, red-headed man with a beard looked at his pocket watch. He must have been the teacher, unlikely though it seemed.

"Miss Mudie-Cooke? Yes, she *should* be here today"—He gazed around him, pulled his lips down and shrugged—"but she doesn't appear to be."

Outside the college, I hailed another taxi—*dear Olive, what a wild-goose chase*—and ordered it to Warrington Crescent. Perhaps Mrs. Ford knew where my sister had got to? Again, I asked the driver for the quickest route but this one blew his nose on his filthy kerchief and declared there wasn't one. I sat back on the bench, tears in my eyes, feeling quite defeated. I was desperate for Olive. I could have waited until she returned home but it wasn't yet eleven and she usually came back about six in the evening; that would mean waiting eight hours. I couldn't not let her know. Not when I knew. Little made Olive more furious than inequality of information—she had a younger sibling's fear of being left out.

I told the driver to pull over, not at number sixty-three, but near Kensington High Street. I suggested it would be easier for him, but in truth I wanted a moment on my own to collect myself. Then I ran past the station, my black cape flying, past the news-seller, past the postboxes, past the *Britons Want You!* posters and Kitchener's exceptionally good hands.

And I tried not to think about the naked man I had just seen, reclining on the sofa.

I had hammered on the front door several times before I noticed the shiny brass bell. *Of course.* I rang it with varying rhythms before keeping my finger on it.

And breathe, I told myself. *Breathe.*

No one answered.

Then, eventually, a noise, footsteps on the stairs, the front door slowly opening. Olive was standing there, disheveled. She was shocked to see me, and I was shocked to see her too. I was expecting Mrs. Ford, not Olive, and why was she turned out so badly? No shoes, no socks. Almost as bad as the man on the sofa—*no, no, not that awful.* Dress unbuttoned, hair half up, half down. I remembered her hair was definitely up when she left the house, because I'd watched her from the window. I often did. There was always something charming about watching Olive striding off down the street on her way to change the world.

"Darling?" she said, clapping her hand over her mouth in surprise. "What on earth brings you here?"

"Wha-at? Where is Mrs. Ford?"

"She's upstairs," she said. "Do you want me to get her?"

I tried to edge past her. For once, number sixty-three was quiet— eerily quiet, it seemed to me. There was no Walter, no music and no piano. None of the usual crowd was here. No David, no Johnny, no pouting actresses, no Uilleam…Well, it was ten o'clock on a Wednesday morning; even those without a job would have the temerity to pretend they were working.

"No, it's you I wanted anyway. You're the reason I came…"

Olive steadied my arm. It must have been clear what an abject state I was in.

"What is it, darling? Talk to me!"

"It's Richard."

I thought she would understand straight away, but she didn't. She stared at me, bewildered.

"Oh, Olive…" I continued. I could hold myself together no more. I finally cracked into great terrible sobs. *Our darling cousin.* "He's dead."

Olive told me, "Wait, wait here." She ran up the stairs two at a time and disappeared into one of the rooms off the hall. I was distressed at how long she took, even though it could only have been three minutes at most. I tried to collect myself but part of me felt like simply bashing my head against the wall. *Oh, Richard, Richard, please don't let him have suffered.* I couldn't bear to think of him frightened. I couldn't bear to think of him in pain or yearning for us. *Let it have been instant death, unawares into oblivion.*

"What *is* going on?" I asked when she returned. My voice was stern, but I couldn't care less. I just wanted to get out of there and over to Aunt and Uncle. The excursion to Goldsmiths—the reclining man on the couch who I could not get out of my head—had been a waste of valuable time.

"Nothing," she insisted. "Sometimes I come here for a nap, that's all. If I'm not feeling well."

"Aren't you well? What is it?"

Olive said, "I'm fine now." She worked her fingers into her coat. She tweaked her stockings. "The nap helped."

"Mrs. Ford doesn't mind?"

Olive snapped, "Why would she? Oh, poor Richard, I just can't believe it."

Poor, poor Richard. It was inconceivable that our sweet cousin was no more.

Olive slipped on her shoes but left her time-consuming laces undone. Then, with a shout, "I'm off!" we left the house and I determined to leave my confused feelings there also. There was no time for strangeness, we had to concentrate on Richard, Aunt Cecily and Uncle Toby now.

As we traveled, Olive fired questions at me. Was I sure? How did I know? And how did they know? And how could anyone be certain?

The tram was busy and I kept my voice low so that people wouldn't hear. There were men in uniform, old women with shopping bags, a young woman shushing a baby. I was still shivering and Olive told me to stop as though I were doing it voluntarily. I looked into her eyes, just to check what was there, and they were filled with tears. "Oh, Vi, I can't believe it."

And it felt suddenly like we were different from everyone else around us. Removed. Apart. We knew death and they didn't. We had a higher consciousness somehow, we knew something they didn't know. I looked at all the people and thought, *You don't know what we are carrying inside us. This is how it feels. This is what it is.* I felt as though the stuffing had been knocked out of us.

And as we raced toward Cottesmore Gardens, I saw the posters again, pasted on the walls: Kitchener's finger, his stern expression; and I had to look away, so painful did their exhortations seem to me at that very moment.

My uncle and aunt had proudly put up a round red disk at their window that read *NOT at home. A man from the house is now serving in His Majesty's forces.* They were delighted with their disk and had said that several neighbors had called to ask where they might get one too. As we stood waiting for the door to open, I tried not to look at it. *Not any more, he isn't.*

Even the maid was loudly sniffing. "Oh, it's the Mudie-Cooke girls!" she muttered, more to herself. "What a morning, what a day… The poor boy, what a terrible shame."

Everyone loved Richard. My father used to say he could charm the birds out the trees. Father would have done anything to recruit him to work for his company but everyone knew Richard was destined for greater things than carpets.

I was worried Father would be annoyed that I had come instead of holding the fort at the office, but instead he looked relieved. He did not rise to an emergency but tried to sink into invisibility. He greeted us both gratefully: "Terrible news, girls, can't believe it."

A few other people were in the living room, milling around, talking quietly. I saw Edmund's mother and I waved "hello," regretting it instantly. This was not a day for waving. She was serene in a long black dress that seemed to have been designed with a stylish grief occasion in mind. My uncle was sat in his usual leather armchair, but he seemed to have shrunk to half his usual size. Normally an imposing figure, he had become little more than his own shadow. A man was talking earnestly to him and Uncle was nodding but you could see his eyes glazing over. He wasn't listening to a word.

As I approached, I saw the person he was talking to was wearing the white collar of a vicar, and I heard his words of consolation: "For his country. The greatest sacrifice."

Kneeling at Uncle's feet, I said, "I'm so sorry, Uncle, we all loved Richard so very much."

Uncle Toby cleared his throat. "He was a good boy, wasn't he?" I knew he was asking this for the audience, for all the well-wishers who didn't know Richard as well as we did.

"The *very* best."

Was it because we had forgotten him in our prayers that night at dinner?

The vicar nodded at me approvingly. "He is with God now."

And I thought of my godless, adorable cousin and wanted to ask the vicar if that would be all right, would there be a place for him in heaven? But I couldn't, not today, not in front of my uncle. What if the answer was no?

The staff were in one room, weeping. A couple of men—Richard's school friends, I think—were in another, talking about joining up. One of them kept punching his palm.

"I'm not going to let them kill our finest," he said, thumping harder each time. "The Hun is not going to get away with this."

Edmund's mother gripped my arm and we agreed how very awful it was. I was determined to make a good impression on her, so she might tell Edmund what a helpful person I had been on this, the bleakest of days. She asked for a sherry and I raced to get her one. After that I didn't know what to say. She suggested I look for my aunt. She said, "Poor Cecily, she doesn't have the comfort of a daughter," and I realized I hadn't seen my aunt since I arrived.

I went upstairs. Olive stayed in the drawing room with Father, Uncle and his friends. The doorbell kept ringing; more people were coming in and shaking my poor uncle's hand. *Terrible business. Shocking.* "Richard was unlucky," they decided.

I had never been in my aunt's bedroom before. I peeped in, and realized she wasn't there. The window was wide open, and the curtains fluttered insouciantly. For one foolish moment, I had a ridiculous idea that Richard was going to fly in. Like *Peter Pan* maybe. Like the Lost Boys.

I called out softly for her. There was no reply. Then I heard a moaning from the lavatory next door. I edged across the room, pushed tentatively at the half-open door. She was lying on her side on the black-and-white checked floor.

"I can't stop," she said. She was weeping. I had never seen her so undignified. She pulled herself up and retched, then retched again and again. Ineffectually, I patted her broad back and held the stray hairs away from her face as she vomited. Occasionally she pulled her face away from the basin and wept, whispering, "Whatever am I going to do without him?"

When finally she had stopped, I guided her to her bed and drew back the covers. She leaned heavily on me, I could smell a sweet, acrid smell. I rang down for a pan. I tucked her in like she was a small child. She used to come and do that for us in the early days after Mother died. I loved my Aunt Cecily very dearly and I regretted that I had perhaps neglected her recently, what with Father's work, spending time with the bohemians at Warrington Crescent and thinking up new ways to make Edmund propose to me. She apologized over and over, and eventually she fell asleep. I didn't know whether to perch on the side of the bed or go downstairs. But then my aunt smiled in her sleep, where Richard wasn't dead, and I thought it best to leave her to it.

CHAPTER NINE

1939—Now

The holidays are over. Pearl goes off for her first day at our small village school just beyond the church. Usually, I clean the house on a Monday afternoon, but Mrs. Burton has invited me for tea after lunch. In her kitchen, Mrs. Burton bakes biscuits, puts them in a tin and rattles them at me to help myself. She is a proper baker, not like me—I bake only out of a sense of duty. Mrs. Burton feels strongly about rising yeast and room temperatures.

Mrs. Burton's oldest daughter Ethel is not the *easiest* of children and Mrs. Burton tells me she is fed up with it. Ethel has got so much attitude—and now she wants to go out and stay out until goodness knows when.

"And Sally?" I ask about the timid younger sister who walks around with her nose in a book.

"Sally could do with going out a bit more." Mrs. Burton sighs. "What can you do?"

We bite and crunch and I stroke the dogs, who I have become increasingly fond of. Mrs. Burton says she's heard the Prime Minister is poorly. "Where will that leave us?" I ask.

"Doubt it'd make much difference," she says, then laughs shyly. We try to avoid getting too political—we both know how those old tribal loyalties can come between friends—but it's clear she doesn't respect our Neville Chamberlain.

*

I meet Pearl at school at the end of her first day. Partly to get away from Mrs. Burton because, much as I enjoy her company, it's slightly overwhelming—I'm not used to such attention—and partly because I can't wait to see Pearl again. Also partly because Mrs. Burton told me that everyone thinks the Germans might be parachuting in any day now and I'll be damned if Pearl has to fight them off all by herself.

Only one other host mother is at the gate, and she is there for her younger two children anyway.

"Yours won't walk by herself?"

"She's only little," I say. *Why shouldn't I meet her?*

The woman says her children are behaving better with the evacuees in the house. She says she's heard of others where it's the other way round. Kids have started spitting, swearing—*oh yes, the London children know all the words*—or throwing things. But not hers. Charlie and Kate are good kids. I feel sorry for Pearl that she is not with this woman, in her capable hands. She is all knowledge and efficiency.

The relief on Pearl's face when she sees me makes the wait worthwhile. I take her bag and coat. None of the real parents do. I am faux-pas-ing all over the place. She can't remember if she's had a good day or not. I don't push the question, I know not to do that at least.

The teacher introduces herself as Mrs. Bankhead and, in the next breath, says she has been teaching at Hinckley Primary for twenty-three years.

"Nothing fazes me," she adds, as though I am about to attempt to faze her. "Not even the arrival of twenty-two London children. At short notice. Some of whom can hardly write."

I ask how Pearl did.

"Pearl Posner can be a silly sausage but she isn't one of the worst at reading or 'rithmetic."

"Well done, Pearl! You're going to do really well here," I say proudly. Mrs. Bankhead narrows her eyes. "We don't know how long they're staying yet," she reminds me.

Pearl fills up the house: her coat on the banister—*It goes on the hook there, oh never mind*—her shabby little shoes, her swollen school bag. *Her.* I peel off the skin of her apple snack, making it coil like a snake, and she squeals at my magic.

Mrs. Burton told me about Vera Lynn's "Goodnight Children, Everywhere" message on the wireless. It's for the evacuees to listen to and feel comforted while we wait for Hitler to bomb the cities. So, a few evenings later, Pearl and I snuggle up on the armchair to give it a go. I've got one ear on the wireless and one ear out for Edmund coming home, asking where his tweed jacket is or wanting his trousers ironed.

Vera's calming voice washes over us:

Sleepy little eyes in a sleepy little head
Sleepy time is drawing near
In a little while, you'll be tucked up in your bed
Here's a song for baby, dear

Pearl feels my hair. It is not a gentle head massage though, it is more a search, a dig, an excavation. I take a sharp intake of breath and pull at her wrist, suddenly annoyed.

"That hurts, Pearl! What on earth are you doing?"

"I'm looking for horns."

I grab her hands, pull her round to make her look me in the eye.

"What do you mean?"

"Looking for horns?" she repeats.

A chill runs through me.

"Horns?"

"They did it to me at playtime," she says brightly. "They say Jews have them—like devils? I don't *think* I have them though, do I? I just wanted to see if you've got any."

I won't charge up to Mrs. Bankhead at the school to complain, not yet. Not yet. Mrs. Bankhead has twenty-three years of experience; no doubt she's got this under control. The world is at war, everything is topsy-turvy and we are all being blown about like autumn leaves, we are all changing colors; we have to sit, watch, and reconfigure. *Don't rush. Don't panic. You don't make an omelet by not cracking eggs.* I know all the phrases.

I tell Pearl that the people who talk such rubbish are idiots or nasty or both. They don't understand people who are different. Maybe they've never met different people before. I spell it out: *You are Jewish but you don't have horns.*

"No one has horns."

"Not even a bull?"

"Maybe bulls. But not humans. Not Jews. Not Christians. Not anyone. Do you understand? If they say it again, you tell me, and I'll . . . I'll sort it out."

God knows how.

She gives me a look. Pearl has an array of expressions that I am just beginning to decipher: the puzzled, the disbelieving and the dopey. This one is clear: she wants me to shut up.

CHAPTER TEN

1915—Then

People were getting engaged left, right and center but not Edmund and me. Our relationship hadn't been formalized—yet, in early 1915, I was more positive than ever that we were edging toward a conclusion of some kind.

The first time I saw Edmund after Richard had died, he clutched me tight, and I felt his warm breath in my hair. We had never been so close. He muttered, "I'm so sorry," over and over again, as I stroked his shoulders dizzily. "I know."

I remembered that one of the last things Richard had ever said to me was that Edmund loved me, so I waited, and I girded myself to wait for as long as it took.

Richard's death had left us all feeling wounded. We didn't trust as easily or laugh so freely. Dreams were just that: dreams; all our plans seemed unlikely now. They certainly didn't bring us as much joy as they used to. Everything was gray and unremarkable. Many a time, I'd arrive at the office to find my father staring out of the window, and if I said anything, his jaw would slacken and he'd mumble, "I miss that boy so much."

"I know, Father, but we have to get on. It's what Richard would want."

Not only was Edmund devastated by the loss of Richard, but he felt it highlighted his cowardice—his words, not mine—in not joining up straight away. He kissed my hand and nuzzled my wrist, then said, "I've never lost anyone before. It's such a horrible thing."

"You mustn't let it make you afraid to love again," I said softly. "Richard wouldn't want that."

I had suddenly become an expert on Richard's wants.

For once, Edmund met my eye. "I know you're talking sense, Vivienne, but it's very hard."

It seemed to me the marriage question was every bit as complicated as the Balkan one. Another awkward thing was how close Olive was growing to the Fords—and, perhaps, Walter Ford in particular—and, it had to be remembered, *I* was the older sister. It stood to reason *I* would marry first. Everyone knew this. And even though I knew conventions were breaking down all around us at quite a pace, I didn't want this particular convention to break down. Olive should not get engaged until I had. Clearly, I should go first.

"You could have anyone, Vivi," Olive often said with a sigh, but it wasn't true. Most men skirted around me. They chatted to Olive and although they may have looked at me from across the room at Mrs. Ford's, they rarely made an approach. And anyway, even if they had, Edmund and his family were the ones I had set my heart upon. I don't think anyone realized quite how single-minded I could be. Part of that single-mindedness meant that I definitely did not want to ask Edmund about being sighted at the Windmill. People behave strangely in strange times; I was sure that was what it was.

It wasn't just us, by the spring of 1915, everything was changing. Even Mrs. Ford had stopped holding her bohemian parties, and instead opened her house to sick and injured soldiers. Number 63 Warrington Crescent was now listed as a convalescent home by the Home Office. Admittedly, that didn't stop Olive going there for her naps, but the Sunday frivolities were over.

Johnny had gone to Malta. David and his wife were in America and David had changed his name to Ivor—Ivor Novello—which apparently would make him stand out from the crowd. Harry was touring with his band. The singers were touring in Spain or Portugal. Even Walter, party-loving Walter, had joined up and was training in Cheshire.

"How do you feel about Walter being away?" I asked.

"I feel fine about it." Olive shrugged.

Another thing Olive felt fine about, more than fine about, was Mrs. Ford and David's—that is, Ivor's—song. It was just about everywhere and with the title "Keep the Home Fires Burning." That in itself made me smile. Uilleam and I had won in the end!

You couldn't walk by a public house or a music hall without hearing the chorus being belted out. Every time I heard it—whether it was a group of schoolgirls trying to raise money for the war effort, or a carousing drunk man on a park bench—I would tell Olive to pass it on to Mrs. Ford. It had certainly caught the *zeitgeist*.

But in general, we were getting more and more fed up with the war. Cargo ships weren't getting through the Channel. We were anxious about shortages of food. I was unsure how we, as an island, going gung-ho into war, could have failed to anticipate that.

"How can I create art when I just feel so useless?" Olive complained. She refused to do uplifting or supportive paintings any more. She had thrown her *War Spirit* into the fire at Mrs. Ford's. "It took ages to burn. If I ever paint again, it will be as a pacifist. I am a pacifist now."

She was always an -ist or an -ette. Why wouldn't she just be Olive?

And then, about five months after Richard died, Olive came home from college and before she had even removed her coat, she was on at me. Had I ever heard of the FANYs? The First Aid Nursing Yeomanry?

I hadn't.

Olive's eyes were shining as brightly as they had the day she got her letter of acceptance into Goldsmiths. We went back in the drawing room, where I continued my desultory practice of "Für Elise." I had been at Father's office, but Mrs. Webster had everything under control as usual and I had come home feeling unsatisfied. The newspaper's stories were harrowing—as was the new usual. And on the way back, I didn't know if it was my fraught imaginings, but it seemed to me that there were an increasing number of men in wheelchairs in the street.

"We can't sit on our hands any longer, we should go and help."

I stopped playing. "Go and help?"

"YES! We must go to France."

"France? What? Why?"

"The FANYs need drivers, and stretcher-bearers, and tea makers and...we can do it, Vi. I know we can."

"Oh, Olive, where has this sprung from?"

Olive knelt at my knees. She gazed up at me beseechingly. "Darling, imagine men like our dear Richard suffering."

I bristled. I had no need to imagine Richard's suffering; it was something I mulled over nightly.

"They're all someone's brothers and sons. We can go out there and make things better."

"But, but...what about Father?" I asked dully.

Olive looked disappointed. She stood up and brushed herself down. "Oh, Father will be fine," she said dismissively. "What do you say, Vivi? Isn't it time to do our bit?"

I doubted that Father would be fine. I wasn't thinking only of the business, but of the way, emotionally, he had always leaned on us.

"He's only forty-nine," Olive pointed out. "That's not *old*, Vi. Molly will clean and cook every day. Mrs. Webster takes care of everything." I blushed. Mrs. Webster and our division of labor was a perpetual source of embarrassment to me. "I've already spoken about it to Aunt Cecily, and she promised to visit him at least three or four times a week—"

"You spoke to Aunt Cecily before you discussed it with me?"

My sister nodded. She didn't even have the good grace to look guilty. "Aunt needs the distraction more than ever," she said decisively. "She welcomes the chance to help."

"I don't know," I said. For me, of course, it wasn't *just* the question of Father. The fact was, I didn't really want to leave home. I didn't want to travel and I didn't want to go to France and I couldn't see how I could make things better. I was all for the quiet life, and although I may have complained about our mundane existence, I liked it. Olive had adventures and I watched. I was happiest watching.

"Father, Aunt Cecily and Uncle Toby all *wanted* war . . . *this* is the consequence," Olive explained.

This didn't strike me as fair.

"We all *thought* we wanted it," I said, even though, immediately, I thought of those I knew who hadn't: Mrs. Webster, for one; her son Harry hadn't and neither had Uilleam Chisholm from the Fords' house. And neither did one of the carpet delivery drivers, who, to my mortal embarrassment, had cried in front of me. But then he was a special case—he had fought in the Boer War and couldn't understand why we were "going back for more."

"Nobody thought it would last this long."

"Nobody thought enough at all," said Olive crudely. "Well, it has, and it is, and the men need us. The nurses are being run ragged. We have skills."

"What? Your sketching and my piano playing?" I snapped. "Are you planning to pencil the Hun to death?"

She ignored me.

"We have languages. Sturdy constitutions."

"Sturdy?" I smirked. "No one's ever called *me* that before."

Olive ignored me. "The poor nurses out there are having to do the lot. Transporting and cleaning and goodness knows. If we go out, we can help alleviate the pressure on the professionals so they are free to nurse and we can contribute in other ways."

"But, Father..." I repeated doubtfully. Already I knew this was an argument going nowhere (which was always the case with Olive). She had already won it. And then with a flourish, she dealt her trump card, or her final domino: the double six that she always kept up her sleeve. Peering slyly at me, she muttered, "You know, you don't *have* to come, Vivi, I could easily go without you."

She knew I'd never let her do that. We were a team, she and I, team Mudie-Cooke—always had been, always would be. From when the "stalk" grew us, it was always us two sisters against the world. When our mother died in childbirth, even though I was too young to understand anything much, I had understood that I was to do everything in my power to protect this little baby.

And another thing: might not this be the way to show Edmund that I was the girl of his dreams? Mightn't it spell out to Edmund's mother that, despite my lowly birth, I was of good stock? I was industrious. I was patriotic. Our father might be self-made, but we were not entirely un-made.

"All right," I said. "I'll find out more. But you must promise to tell Father—"

"Oh, I'll tell him it's for the war effort." She looked at me, satisfied. "It *is*, this time."

Olive nearly didn't reach the five foot two minimum requirement. At the interview with the FANYs, she stood on tiptoes in her stockings, her smile rigid, every pore in her body propelling her northwards: *I am tall enough, I am, I am.* Imagine if she were foiled by a mere inch!

"We also lay carpets," said Olive. She looked at me.

I thought, *Good grief, she is keen to go.*

"We don't have much call for that in France," said one of the two women interviewing us without a smile. The other had that marvelous ability to raise only one eyebrow, a talent she was putting to excellent use right now.

Olive fired back haughtily: "I merely use it as an example that we're not afraid to get stuck in."

"What about driving?" the eyebrow-raising woman asked, now examining her own nails.

"We both drive," lied Olive shamefacedly. I coughed.

The non-eyebrow one laid down her pencil. She looked at the other skeptically.

"How unusual!" the other said. "Pray, tell us. What do you drive?" I thought we had been found out and judged guilty and would be sent home with a flea in our ear.

"Cars," said Olive brightly.

I licked my lips. I had to support my sister. I knew Olive: if we didn't go to France with the FANYs, she would just wangle another way to get there. At least this way seemed to be mostly legitimate and structured.

I remembered Walter once leading us outside to admire Johnny's latest speed-wagon. "We learned in a friend's Silver Ghost," I lied. (Johnny would rather have died than let me behind the wheel.)

"The Rolls-Royce?" asked eyebrow woman sharply. She did it again now. *Hup*: one eyebrow nearly at her hairline.

"Yes. Um, a Rolls-Royce Silver Ghost. It is a beast," I said, which was exactly the word Walter had used, "but I think after you've driven that, you can drive just about anything!"

Olive smiled at me gratefully and I smiled back at her. *So, I was in this now. Properly.*

We moved on. When the women heard that we spoke three languages, their demeanors changed. It was like the gaslights being switched on at dusk. Suddenly, we could all see.

One looked at the other. "*That* could be useful."

"My sister speaks five," Olive boasted. "Latin and Ancient Greek, too."

"Olive! I don't *speak* Latin or Ancient Greek," I explained apologetically. "I just... studied them for a time."

A very short time.

"The height rule is just a recommendation," eyebrow woman said. "When can you go?"

Olive and I looked at each other.

"When do you want us?" Olive said.

We filled out the paperwork.

I still thought it wouldn't happen. I thought it was just another fantasy of Olive's. She had these ideas twice a year, usually just before the end-of-term exhibition. They didn't usually come to anything life-changing.

The khaki tunic is to have four pockets with FANY buttons and badges and made with plain sleeves. There will be a Red Cross circle on each sleeve, the center of the cross to be seven inches from the shoulder. The bottom of the khaki skirt is to be ten inches from the ground and for footwear, khaki puttees and brown shoes or boots, or long brown boots, are to be worn.

Olive read out the letter, which arrived the Monday after our meeting. My hands were trembling too much to do it.

"Oh, gracious me," I said. "So, it's really happening."

"And I've just bought new *black* boots," she complained.

"Take them back to the shop," I said, but I wasn't interested in her black boot woes: they weren't really woes, she was delighted with her boots; and anyway, I was growing apprehensive about telling Father because Olive still hadn't done it and it looked like that too was going to fall to me.

I did have another big reservation though:

"What about driving? I wish we hadn't lied."

"How hard can it be?" replied Olive.

CHAPTER ELEVEN

1939—Now

Early October, when Pearl has been with us for just over a month, Edmund comes home at lunchtime. My heart sinks when I hear his car pull up, then the scrabble of the key in the lock. He stomps into the kitchen and I wonder if it's German parachutists. It has to be a major crisis to pull Edmund back here at midday.

"You have to send her back."

"What? Who? Do you want a sandwich, Edmund? Cress?"

"No, I'm not staying. The *child*. You need to take her back."

Take her back? Like she's an item from a shop? Like the unfortunate rabbit?

"My parents need to come here. It's not going to be safe."

"I know, but Pearl is staying here because it's not safe."

"She can't. We need the room."

We have a three-bedroom house. We are three people. Now in a normal marriage, three rooms would be more than enough. In a normal marriage, Edmund could come in with me and we would still have one spare.

"She has to go. I'll speak to the billeting officers," he says.

Over the next few days, I fret and fret. How can I let Pearl go back to London? Or should I inquire locally whether someone else would

have her? Perhaps Farmer Jones? I could go to the deputy mayor…
But no. I don't want to lose her.

Finally, I give in and talk to Mrs. Burton about it. What a joy
it is to share something, a pleasure I have been denied for a long
time. Mrs. Burton is such a good listener, and she also has plenty of
problems of her own; knowing this somehow frees me up. Of course,
I don't tell her the long sorry story of my marriage—the short sorry
version will suffice. Edmund doesn't know where to put his parents.
He thinks we should get rid of Pearl.

"What's *wrong* with him?" she ponders out loud. We are waiting for
the tea. Mrs. Burton won't serve her tea before it's perfectly brewed.
The kitchen might need a good tidy, but she's a tea perfectionist.

"He wasn't *always* like this," I say defensively, Laurel on my feet.

"The Great War?" she asks.

I nod even though if I think about it really, it's not the *only* truth.
Did I ever know what Edmund was like? Was he an affectionate man
before the war? Did he ever love me? I realize that, for a long time, I
have been hiding behind this idea that it was the war that damaged
him. I am going to fight this. I am not giving her up, not for him.
I've given up enough things for him.

Yet when he returns home that evening, Edmund has had a change
of heart. Later, I find out that the billeting officers convinced him:
it doesn't look good to reject a child for no reason. And my dear
husband is all about looking good.

"I'll find out if there's a place nearby my parents can rent."

And there *is* a place they can rent. Mrs. Harrison's boys have gone
away to fight. She has turned her large house into an old people's
home. There are four old people there already and Edmund's parents
will round up the number to a perfect six. Mrs. Harrison was a nurse
so she'll take care of medication, which is grand because Edmund's

father had a stroke two years ago, and he takes a lot of pills. Edmund's mother, of course, is in great health. (Sometimes, I think of what Mrs. Ford used to say at the end of a long Sunday afternoon when the flames of the fire were dying, and the mood was turning melancholy: "Whom the gods love die young.")

Mrs. Harrison will put them up and make them breakfast every morning. "Nothing fancy, mind." She'll do eggs and they can "like it or lump it."

They will lump it.

"Can we at least take on Charles?" Edmund says, as though I owe him a big concession.

I am going to say: "For God's sake, Edmund, no, not your parents' tortoise, remember how you made me return the rabbit?" But then I think... *Pearl. Pearl Posner likes animals* and so I agree.

Edmund travels down to London in the car to fetch his parents. When they arrive, Charles is sitting in a cardboard box in the back, regally chewing a lettuce leaf. They have all reinvented Charles as Edmund's brother's tortoise, even though as far as I can remember the only thing Christopher ever said about him was that he regretted the family didn't call him Percy, after Percy Shelley, a joke that took me a while to get.

I greet them at Mrs. Harrison's because it's the right thing to do and I don't want people gossiping about the Lowe family not getting on. Edmund is paying some local boys to unload—"mind that box, it's very fragile"—so we go inside to Mrs. Harrison's sitting room. The armchairs are tired and their sides have been clawed by a cat. Still, there is a gas fire, a wireless, a table and the now-ubiquitous blackout curtains. Mrs. Harrison talks to me about how it's a nightmare in the dark: the old folk roam around, crashing into things, and she's worried someone's going to break a hip.

I don't have to look at Edmund's parents to know what they are thinking: *Common* or *Couldn't they find us anything better than this?*

Mr. and Mrs. Lowe are riled up about the war and I imagine they haven't had much of an audience to offload their opinions on recently.

"The Huns had to come back for more," says Edmund's father. "Didn't we show them what we are made of last time?"

Bile in my throat. I think, *You didn't show them anything.*

"Filthy, rotten good-for-nothing—"

"Where's the evacuee?" Edmund's mother abruptly asks me.

"School," I say.

"Oh, she goes to school then?"

"Yes."

Edmund's mother puts her hand on mine. "All the upheaval is awful, isn't it?"

Tears come to my eyes at this unexpected kindness, but I pull my hand away because I have never forgiven her. And I'm not going to now.

CHAPTER TWELVE

1915—Then

My aunt and uncle used to love holding dinner parties but since poor Richard's passing, they hadn't had the heart. Edmund's parents invited us to theirs instead. It was going to be a farewell lunch for Edmund and Christopher because, belatedly and reluctantly, they had decided to join up.

Perhaps it wasn't excellent timing, but Olive and I decided that this would be the perfect occasion to tell our father about our joining up with the FANYs too. Our admittedly convoluted rationale was this: we thought being in public would check Father's response—whatever it turned out to be; we weren't sure what to expect—and it would at least ensure he maintained a modicum of self-restraint. Our father wept copiously at Beethoven's symphonies and Monet's paintings, whereas Uncle Toby and Edmund's parents were great believers in the stiff upper lip. Olive decided that, for once, their company could prove an advantage.

But first, I waited impatiently for Edmund to get me alone. He was at the front, back and sides of all my thoughts and now that he was going away, and I was going away, this seemed to me the last chance we would have to cement our relationship for some time. I imagined announcing to our families that we were to be married, and the glorious images in my head were so realistic that I had to remind myself that they hadn't happened yet. I wanted more than anything in my life to be Mrs. Edmund Lowe and to be Edmund's mother's daughter.

When we arrived, Edmund stroked my back again, in that intimate way he had, and he raised his eyebrows at me when Olive and his mother argued over some point—the Irish, I think—but I didn't get a chance to speak to him alone before lunchtime. I wondered if maybe I was being foolish about wanting a declaration. It was suddenly so obvious that we would be together, that we would marry, why did it need to be made public? I smiled at him and he smiled back, and I thought, *Well, there it is. It's happening.*

He, Christopher, their father and Uncle Toby talked military strategies and laughed at the Italians and smoked cigars. I watched the hands of the grandfather clock hardly move. It was like it too was struck with a lethargy.

Aunt Cecily eventually asked for a tour of the garden with Edmund and said I must come too. When we had reached the back fence, she suddenly announced she would go back for her scarf.

"We'll wait," said Edmund.

"I've changed my mind," she said, tearing off toward the house. I tried to make my face say *I knew nothing of this trap*—which I hadn't—but I knew I was as pink as anything in the flower beds.

Edmund and his brother Christopher had kept a tortoise since they were small and I saw it rooting in the garden now. I couldn't say I liked it much. They used to claim it was related to Darwin's pets, and I never could tell if it was a joke or not. Naturally, it was known as Charles.

"Look at old Charles," said Edmund, his voice muffled. "Oblivious as ever. He'll outlast me and everyone here, I expect."

I knew that tortoises lived a long time, but this seemed morbid.

Edmund and I walked a little, and then we came to the bench and I sat, averting my eyes from Charles. If he did outlive us, then it wasn't his fault, of course, but what a shame. Of all the things to be outlived by in the world, it had to be an ugly creature whose main interest in life was cabbage.

Edmund hovered for a while, then perched next to me.

He took my hand and, as his smooth palm pressed against mine, I couldn't help but think, *Is he really going to go in the trenches with these soft hands?*

He said, "We used to hold hands while you played piano, do you remember?"

"Of course I remember!" My voice sounded high and squeaky. "It was...fun."

"It was," he said nostalgically.

We didn't say anything for a while, and then desperately, I blurted, "I'm not sure your mother likes me, Edmund."

He made a puzzled face. "I've never heard her say a thing against *you*."

The way he said *you* seemed to suggest that she had said things against someone, and I guessed that was Olive.

"I see," I said. "Well, good." More daringly, I added, "I'm very fond of your whole family, Edmund. They are all such wonderful people."

Too much? I wondered. But Edmund didn't seem to be listening anyway.

"I don't know about anything now," he said throatily. I looked at him, alarmed at his despair. "On one hand, I feel ashamed I didn't join up immediately, but on the other"—he continued but his voice now was so low, I could hardly hear—"I still wish I hadn't gone and done it. Oh, Vivienne. I wish...I wish things were different."

He told me he had had a long discussion with his vicar. He had never told me about his church visits before and I was thrilled to be privy to such information. "He said I should do my duty." Edmund choked. "In every way."

Caught up in the excitement, we kissed, very gently, very slowly, on the lips. I wasn't sure whether to close my eyes or not. I kept them open and noticed Edmund had a rash around his collar.

Then he withdrew. He said, "I'm sorry, Vivi, everything is so up in the air right now. I can't..." He paused.

Out of the corner of my eye, I could see Charles the tortoise munching some vegetable or other. It seemed to me that he was gloating.

"I know it is," I reassured him. I was good at that. And I loved it when Edmund called me Vivi. I was usually a Vivienne to him. "I know and I don't demand anything of you, Edmund."

I could hear the snip, snip, snip of hedges being pruned in the neighbor's garden. Perhaps one day they might accidentally snip poor old Charles, and he would buck his destiny.

Edmund looked helpless. He nodded. "If only I could be more certain about... everything."

And it seemed to me he was saying, *about you.*

"It's fine," I said. And it was. It was going to happen one day, I knew it. It didn't have to happen now. I could still feel his kiss on my lips and it felt like we had made a leap forward.

"It is, isn't it?" He grinned nervously at me. "You're a special person."

Back inside, Edmund's mother looked closely at us both. She said we had stayed out so long, weren't we afraid of catching a chill? Greatly encouraged by what had just happened, I burst out that it was a simply wonderful day. The marriage question was not so much a question any more but a statement of fact.

I wasn't sure, but I think Aunt Cecily gave me a cheeky wink.

Olive and I were just about to tell Father our news, when, I don't know exactly how, the conversation turned to Russia and then moved on to the Jews there and how very awful they were. On and on Edmund's mother went. Her latest revulsion was the curly sidelocks that she had seen one man wearing while walking down the street. To be out in public... *like that.* So brazen! Didn't this tell you how much they hated the British way of life? *They will not mix.*

"You can see what's going to happen in Russia," said Edmund's father, and although I couldn't—my psychic abilities did not extend to political questions—I agreed heartily.

"They've got no loyalty to anyone!" I was in high spirits and this was something I'd heard Edmund's mother say countless times before.

Olive was annoyed. "*Who* should the Jews be loyal to?" She was addressing me, even though Edmund's mother was the worst offender. "The Tsar, who sends his Cossacks to rape and pillage?"

"Well, I don't know an awful lot about—" I started to admit.

"So why did you have to say anything at all?" Olive snapped. "If you have no real knowledge, why are you so insistent on giving your insubstantial opinion?"

I flushed. To be humiliated like this, in front of our family, especially when I was feeling so positive about Edmund, really wasn't on.

"Everyone says so, Olive," I carried on. "The Jews are only interested in money. They're a self-serving bunch."

Olive threw down her knife and fork. You'd think I'd insulted *her*.

My father used to say Olive was always the champion of the underdog. When she was little, she would bring him crabs she had "rescued" from the seaside, expecting them to live long, happy lives in our garden. She was not practical, she was not a realist.

Father told her so then and Olive got up and left the room. Moments later, I heard the front door slam.

Edmund's mother laughed as if to say, *point proven*. Aunt Cecily and Uncle Toby both raised their eyebrows. Olive had a reputation for volatility—and seemed to enjoy living up to it.

"She spends too much time with the Fords," Father muttered.

"They're not Jews, are they?" asked Edmund's mother with a look of horror on her face. Everyone turned to me anxiously.

"No," I said, feeling important. Mrs. Ford and her mother attended church—I wasn't sure who was the keener but I knew they went regularly. As for Walter, I was certain he worshipped only his own reflection.

Father chewed an after-dinner mint. "Perhaps it would do Olive good to spend some time away from them anyway."

I took this as my cue to tell him about the FANYs; with Olive gone it was clear that this was up to me now. "Interesting that you should say that, Father... I have some news."

On the surface, Father seemed to deal with it well. He said he had suspected some secret shenanigans between us, and he said it was right, it was proper, that we did our bit—if that's what we wanted. Once he had given us, or rather me, his blessing, Uncle Toby came over and kissed me and Edmund's parents looked at each other with, I hoped, approval.

"For God, for King and Country!" I announced, then more quietly, "And for our dear Richard."

Aunt Cecily tearfully squeezed my shoulder. "That's the spirit, girl." Then Edmund came over and whispered, "But why didn't you tell me you were leaving when we were in the garden?" and I didn't know how to respond to that, so I just said, "I was going to, but Charles put me off," and Edmund gave me a peculiar look. He could be very dour sometimes. And then I fretted that I had lost my chance. If I had told him, maybe he would have proposed to me. But deep down, I didn't think he would have.

As we walked home, my father grew anxious, which was exactly what we hadn't wanted to happen, so I said, "I'll look after Olive, Father, of course."

"I know you will, Vivi," he said. "You've always been a good girl."

Three days later there were two suitcases, two handbags, two hats, two pairs of boots: twin everything except for one pair of binoculars (Olive had recently expressed an interest in birdwatching), all lined up in the hall. It was an impressive selection of luggage. But just as we were about to take the carriage, Father lost his stiff upper lip—he lost all his stiffness—and he broke down. "I can't lose you, girls, not after your mother. If anything happens to you, I will kill myself."

He clutched us toward him, snorting back tears.

It was pitiful. It made me waver but Olive, champion of the underdog, was not champion of *this* underdog. She impassively patted him on the shoulder.

"Father, we love our country, we want to serve."

Father tried to collect himself as Olive and I gazed at him apprehensively. He retrieved a handkerchief from his pocket and blew his nose loudly. *Please don't collapse*, I was thinking, *please, please*.

"God bless you," he said, wiping his teary eyes. "So proud of you both."

We carried our suitcases outside. Olive was beaming.

"I can't wait to get drawing," she whispered, as though that's what we were setting off to do.

CHAPTER THIRTEEN

1940—Now

"I'm thinking of doing some things for the war effort."

Mrs. Burton has done so much more than just think about it. She has been attending meetings, she has been getting directions and in the living room, she has gathered ten neighbors and friends. "The WVS," she tells me, so delighted that you can see her dimples. "The Women's Voluntary Service. Are you in, Mrs. Lowe?"

I pause. As ever my first thought is *What will Edmund say?*

"There will be cake…"

I burst out laughing. "How can I turn that down?"

Mrs. Shaw is here because she is trying to take her mind off her Simon, who is somewhere on the continent—they won't tell you where they are exactly—and Mrs. Dean is worrying about her two lads, who are twins, born only twenty minutes apart and now in the Navy on some whacking great warship.

In the kitchen, making tea, Mrs. Burton says quietly to me, "Sally and Ethel may be rascals, but I can't help feeling glad I didn't have sons." I smile and don't make a sound, I just quietly pat Hardy's long fur, and Mrs. Burton looks up like she suddenly understands. "Sorry, Mrs. Lowe, that was insensitive of me."

"Not at all," I say heartily. "It just didn't happen for me. I was sad for a time, but not any more."

"Good."

*

The plan is we will turn clothes into other clothes. "That's this week's task, anyway," explains Mrs. Burton, brightly. "Next week, it might be something else...we'll do whatever is needed."

The vicar is going to pick everything up and arrange distribution. They have sent us knee-high socks (I am reminded of Richard's appeals for them) and we must turn them into polo-necked jumpers for shivering sailors.

"Who here is good at sewing?" asks Mrs. Burton. Laughing, we all agree we are just about good enough.

"We will work our socks off," says Mrs. Shaw and we laugh again and tell her that's a joke worthy of her husband.

Soon we are meeting most days and Mrs. Burton's living room has been taken over by socks, rolls of material and sewing machines. We're low on wool now—low on wool already; there's none in the shops— so we spend a lot of time unpicking old clothes and re-forming them.

Apparently not only does Mr. Burton not mind—although he did holler once when he sat on a knitting needle—but he wholeheartedly supports it. Mr. Burton isn't home very often and, silly me, I had thought he was like Edmund—another mysterious, prowling cat—but no, he works assembly lines during the day, car production, which has now been turned to military production—and since the war broke out, he's also doing air raid precaution, patrolling the streets of Coventry.

"He is frustrated—he's too old to enlist," explains Mrs. Burton quietly.

Last time round he fought in Salonika. He and Mrs. Burton met when he was home on leave and she was working in a munitions factory.

"All this *busy, busy, busy* takes me back," says Mrs. Dean. "Oh, I had *all* the boyfriends," she reminisces. "That's what the war was, a great big game of matchmaking."

I flush.

"Not for everyone, of course." She pats me tenderly on the arm. "You and Edmund were childhood sweethearts, weren't you?"

I don't say anything. Sometimes, I feel like I have done everything wrong. The mistakes I have made seem to line up to give me a good kicking.

"Good times," Mrs. Dean continues, still nostalgic. She looks around guiltily. "I mean, terrible times, but some positives came out of it."

Five more women from the streets behind ours join our WVS group, including the doctor's receptionist, Mrs. Carmichael.

When I first see her, I retreat into the kitchen. I don't want to be in the same room as her. But Mrs. Burton isn't having any of that, of course, and soon I have to go back and sit opposite Mrs. Carmichael with her deliberately enigmatic facial expression.

Everyone is chat-chatting and Mrs. Dean, in a conspiratorial tone (she *is* a gossip), asks Mrs. Carmichael if she knows everyone in the village's medical history.

Mrs. Carmichael says quickly, "Not at all, please don't." Then she adds, "Even if I did, I've got a memory like a sieve."

She doesn't look at me when she speaks.

A few days later, her shifts at the surgery change and she can only do one hour a week with us.

Mrs. Fraser from the clothes shop also joins us once but decides that "it isn't a good fit" for her. She'll go with the other women volunteer group the other side of town. "They're a bit more"—she pauses—"respectable."

Mrs. Burton already knows all the other evacuees' stories—how, I don't know.

Farmer Jones is walking on air with his Nathan. Solid, strong, works like an ox and then some. The Caseys have got themselves a bed-wetter but she has *wonderful* table manners so it's swings and roundabouts. Mrs. Gibbon is not displeased with hers. The girl can sew. And Mrs. Wiley is not complaining either, although the child—a prolific letter-writer—costs a fortune in stamps.

But Mrs. Morley says her boy moans about the food. *Can you imagine?* To Mrs. Morley, who prides herself on her kitchen and her fried liver! And Mrs. Clements, who's not long recovered from "ladies' problems," is regretting the twin girls already. *Is she strong enough to manage, that's always the worry, isn't it?*

"How is your little Pearl getting along?" Mrs. Burton asks.

How are we getting along?

My washing load has doubled. I now spend the early hours of the morning scrubbing tights and jumpers, hanging out, folding, putting away. Our food bill has certainly gone up. Not that Pearl eats much more than a sparrow, but I still have to offer her a full plate of something nourishing (and somehow, she manages to get most of her dinner down her front!). Although I go to the post office and get my regular reimbursement and joke from Mr. Shaw, the money the government gives isn't going to cover the half of it.

It's not just the extra cooking, the extra washing, the extra drying and the extra ironing though. Or the ration system and the queuing. Or the fact that everything has to get done before the blackout darkness. There's homework too. And the *worry* about the homework. Who knew I was so poor at arithmetic? While her comprehension is good, Pearl's spelling is abominable and if I hear the history-class ditty "Divorced, beheaded, died, divorced, beheaded, survived" one more time, I will...well, I don't know what I will do. Meanwhile, I'm trying to keep everything smooth in the house with Edmund. I'm pretending nothing has changed. The war hasn't changed *his* workload at all.

Yesterday, Pearl stuffed something down the toilet she shouldn't have. She has smashed a vase with Mrs. Burton's damned skipping rope. She has a store of moldy apple cores under her bed.

The poor mite is sickly, she gets headaches; she is not what I imagined.

"You *had* to get the runt of the litter," Edmund told me.

She doesn't sleep well, and these days she doesn't even call out or whisper for me. She just slips into my room and into my bed, flannel in hand. It happens so often, I eventually say, "Do you want to start out the night in here?" (*please don't let her mother hate me*) and she nods delightedly, *yes, she does.* And of course, Edmund has no idea.

I am already dreading the thought of her leaving.

By the end of October, Mr. Hitler still hasn't launched an attack; there have been no bombs, so some of the children *are* going back to London. What starts as a trickle—the twins, the boy who didn't like liver, the bed-wetter—soon becomes a stream of returnees.

The government doesn't want the children to return to the cities. Posters go up to keep them in the countryside. *Keep them out of harm's way.* The children can't help but feel divided. But for some, the separation from their families has proved too hard and they can't wait to get on the train back home.

There is no word yet from Pearl's mother, so I presume Pearl is staying. She writes to her mother twice a week, chewing on her pencil, and I always leave the room because otherwise, I would be so tempted to pry: *What are you saying? Do you want to go back to Stepney?*

At the end of November, hesitantly, I ask Pearl if she has heard any plans. She says, "Oh, I think Mummy can work more if I'm not there."

I ask her if she is all right with that. She shrugs. She doesn't give me the reassurance I humiliatingly crave, but I know that it's all right: Pearl does not have a desire to leave. I also know it's not *particularly* because of me, but because she has her sights on the school nativity play.

The nativity play is a big deal this year. It will be at the church in front of three hundred people, and Pearl thinks she should be Mary.

"That's quite ambitious," I say.

She looks at me as though it's self-explanatory. "Yes. Mary is the main character."

"Right," I say, admiring her self-belief. "Well, let's try and get you the part then."

I help her plan her audition speech. She does "The Owl and the Pussy-Cat" beautifully, and I can't help feeling it is more age-appropriate than her other choices, but after much prevarication, she decides on Wordsworth.

> I wandered lonely as a cloud
> That floats on high o'er vales and hills,
> When all at once I saw a crowd,
> A host, of golden daffodils;

There is something charming about a tiny city girl reading this grand ode to nature—but it isn't just that; the transformation that comes over Pearl as she reads is something wonderful to behold. One minute she is a wee skinny girl with dark shadows under her eyes, the next she is a tower of strength. It makes me think of Olive and what she could do with a paintbrush.

CHAPTER FOURTEEN

1915—Then

Only two weeks after our Paddington interview, Olive and I were posted to Lamarck Hospital in northern France, near Calais. We would join some FANYs already there. Our main task was transport: we were to transfer patients from wherever they were to the hospital or wherever they were designated to go.

If only Edmund had just have asked me to marry him, I thought as Olive and I caught the train to Dover. I certainly wouldn't have stayed in England, but I would have felt as though everything was settled, that we had something to look forward to and that I was someone important. Vivienne Lowe had a nice ring to it. But Edmund hadn't made his move, and although I was surer than ever that one day he would, I still couldn't wait for the uncertainty to be in the past.

The other FANYs came out to greet us and I couldn't help noting that they were posher than us. They were about the same level of posh as Uncle Toby and the Lowes. (When I told Olive, she laughed, saying I was obsessed with class.) They were Daisy, Enid, Agnes and Dorothy—or "D.E.A.D.," as they explained.

"Well, now you're DEADOV," said Olive and they laughed.

"You're going to fit right in," the one in spectacles—Agnes—said.

They showed us round, explaining that the medical staff stayed on the third and fourth floors of the hospital and patients made up the rest of the building.

Olive and I looked at each other in surprise.

"So where are we staying then?"

We were in huts in the grounds of the hospital. They used to be the sheds and garages.

"Home for the next few years!" said Daisy, who, I gathered, was the loud-mouthed one.

I guessed Olive was thinking the same as me. *Years?!*

Our boss, Mrs. Fielding, was squat and short-haired and, to my shame, I thought she was a man when I first met her. Who *her* boss was, I had no idea.

At 6 p.m. we went out in our work clothes to the courtyard to one side of the hospital for our first night on the job. No time to settle in for us—things needed doing. It had already grown dark—it was a starless sky—and all I could see was the silhouette of these great lump-like machines. Drawing closer, I realized that these were our ambulances.

"Girls, in you get," Mrs. Fielding ordered Olive and me. "This is yours."

"Good luck!" called out Daisy. Agnes shouted, "Just follow us," as she got into hers.

The engine and the driving area were up front, in a cabin of their own; the back was just material over a frame or cage, I think. The cabin was high and had three steps to get up into.

I stared at it. "They'll send us home if they find out," I whispered to Olive.

We clambered in obediently. I had landed, unintentionally, behind the wheel side, Olive next to me. I waved at Mrs. Fielding as if we were about to go. I slowly put on my hat and my gloves and sat there. I didn't know what to do. I waved again at Mrs. Fielding. She had her arms crossed. I couldn't make out her expression—it was too dark—but I expect it wasn't friendly. She stalked away, her boots making irreverent splashes in the mud.

"Just start it up," said Olive. *She* could talk.

I tried to think of the time Walter and Johnny had driven the beast, but they were messing around, singing and waving whisky bottles. God knows how they'd done it.

"For goodness..." I said. "I have not the faintest clue how."

"Ask one of the others," hissed Olive.

"Why don't *you* ask one of the others?" I snapped back.

But it was too late. One by one, the other ambulances had pulled away: Agnes and Daisy. Enid and Dorothy. Black exhaust fumes, puttering, stalling—Charles the tortoise could probably have given them a run for their money, but off they went nevertheless.

"It might be the handle at the front," I decided. "You jump out and try it."

Olive did. Nothing happened. "I can't turn it," she hissed. "It's not this..."

We stayed there, stranded, like a little rudderless boat in the middle of an ocean. It wasn't long before Mrs. Fielding reappeared. If I had thought she looked intimidating before, now, pulling on her tea-cozy hat and long military coat, she looked furious.

"Girls!" she said. "What are you waiting for?"

"It's not a type I'm familiar with," I said weakly. I turned to Olive, resignation on my face. "If we're sent home, we're sent home. You can't say we didn't try."

Olive looked at me. "I'm *not* going home."

Mrs. Fielding had climbed up next to me.

"Budge up," she said and we shuffled along the driver's bench. She glared at us both, then shook her head, laughing. "I admire your confidence. You *do* speak French though?"

We nodded. "*Oui*," said Olive to prove the point.

"Good. Then, you'll find the driving's the easy part. Watch and learn."

That first night, Mrs. Fielding drove us to pick men up from the meeting place near the front. The men were waiting on the ground on stretchers; even so, they were surprisingly chirpy. They'd been near an explosion but the worst ones had already gone with our colleagues. We put them into the ambulance. I heard Olive telling them, "You're my first."

Once they were in, Mrs. Fielding said I should try to drive us back to the hospital. My heart was in my mouth. I don't believe I had ever been so afraid. I could scarcely see anything ahead of me. You couldn't see creatures, you couldn't see soldiers. *It might be a trap*, I kept saying to myself, *it might be the Hun*. There were three patients in the back, Mrs. Fielding and Olive next to me, and I was responsible for all of them.

"You'll get used to it," encouraged Mrs. Fielding. It took about fifty minutes in all. When eventually I saw the golden lights of the hospital, I could have wept with relief. Some orderlies promptly came out and whisked the patients away, calling, "Thank you!" and "*Merci!*" as they did so.

Mrs. Fielding followed them, leaving behind a crumpled map for me.

"Well, that wasn't too bad, was it?" I smiled weakly at Olive. I meant, *that was horrendous.*

Olive was laughing.

"What?"

"Vi! You know we've got to do it again, and again, and again..."

I tried not to look too aghast.

All night long, I drove the ambulance into the darkness, that same route, and sometimes there were flashes and explosions near us, and sometimes there was nothing to guide us but blackness, and it was hard to tell which was worse. The later it got, the less I could see, but I suppose gradually the roads became more and more familiar to me, and by the third or fourth time, I knew when to expect a bump or a sharp turn.

The fifth time we arrived at our meeting point, it was to a scene of some horror. There'd been another explosion; several lives had been lost and the people waiting were in a terrible state. Fortunately, Daisy and Enid were there and we coordinated our efforts. We picked up one poor soldier together and put him on a stretcher. Olive ran alongside us, holding his face together.

When we got back into the ambulance, Olive was weeping softly. "I didn't expect it to be so bad," she breathed.

I couldn't comfort her. I had to get us back to the hospital as fast and as smoothly as possible.

The next afternoon, I tried to teach Olive how to drive. She hesitated, prevaricated and squealed every time the ambulance moved. She said she wanted to cry. When it came to it, at six in the evening in the courtyard, with her shoulders slumped, she said, "I just think we've got to face it, you're much better at it than I am."

And so, although Olive did eventually learn to drive, mostly I drove the ambulance while she navigated. Or, if we had men in the back, she would stay with them to soothe their brows or give them water. She sometimes got them to sing "Keep the Home Fires Burning" with her to cheer themselves up, and she would always tell them that she knew who wrote it, whether they were interested or conscious or not.

CHAPTER FIFTEEN

1940—Now

At three o'clock every day, I go down to the school and stand just beyond the gate. There is just me now; I am the only parent there. Some of the children recognize me and say, "Hello, Pearl's host mother," as they walk alone from the school building.

Sometimes Pearl is at the front of the queue, sometimes at the back. Today she is at the back.

It's the day of the casting. The nativity question. I shouldn't ask as soon as I see her, but I can't control myself. This is important to Pearl so it has become important to me. Perhaps more important. Forget the war, this is life and death.

"Did you get it?"

"I'm going to be a sheep," she says. Her face crumples and she is in my arms in tears. They have chosen Helen, a tall, leggy local girl, instead. A girl who doesn't even want to be Mary, one who gets stage fright. They have chosen her over my Pearl. Apparently, Mrs. Bankhead didn't think Pearl would look "right."

But that night, as I unpack the satchel like a good host mother, I see that Pearl is not *only* a sheep, she is also Mary's understudy—at least that's what the letter says.

I read it again and again. *Didn't Pearl understand?* I wonder. I lie in bed and I can't sleep. I know that all over the country, mothers, fathers, politicians are worrying about the war and here I am, worrying about a sheep. But it's not just a sheep. I ask myself, *How will this affect Pearl's self-esteem?*

Next morning, at breakfast, I tell her.

"You know, you're Mary's understudy."

"What is that?"

"It means you're still in with a chance, Pearl," I say.

At Mrs. Burton's, the dogs roam around the kitchen, tails held high, and I scratch the top of Laurel's furry head as I offload to Mrs. Burton. "And even worse: I've got to make a sheep costume! Have you ever heard such a thing?"

How can I make a costume when we are running low on wool? But actually, more importantly, how can we continue to be the WVS if we can no longer knit for the soldiers?

Hardy woofs at me and then rubs his face against my leg. It's like he is trying to tell me something. Mrs. Burton and I stare at each other.

"You know what?" asks Mrs. Burton hoarsely.

"Are you thinking what I'm thinking?" I reply.

We look at Laurel and Hardy and then at each other.

"There's no reason why dog hair can't be made into yarn, same as wool," Mrs. Burton says.

"Absolutely," I say.

And that is how we founded the WVS first dog-hair unit.

We brush the dogs in the kitchen, just Mrs. Burton and me, for the other members of WVS tend to prefer knitting or making toys. One of us gently holds the dog down and whispers sweet nothings into its ear, the other combs his loose fur off him. Then we send the fur to be spun in the town of Ashby, some fifteen miles away.

The first time we do Laurel and Hardy, we give the dogs half a sausage each as a thank-you. We've gathered so much from them. "Unfortunate timing, it being winter," says Mrs. Burton.

"They might get cold—but what a good pair they are, they've done their bit too."

As a special treat, I go back home and fetch my slippers, and give them one each. They are over the moon.

We call in all the dogs in the area. The vets and the pet shop are a terrific help (I feel like I have more than made up for the awkwardness over the returned rabbit). We see about seven or eight dogs a week. We are so busy we even have to turn some away. We have our eyes on Mrs. Carmichael's fluffy Golden Retriever and Farmer Jones's Newfoundland for a while before they let them over.

I am amazed at myself. I have become someone who handles dogs with ease. Someone who thinks nothing of hauling a Collie or an Afghan Hound over my lap and telling him or her to stay still. When I tell Edmund about it, *why do I still tell him things?* he can't stop laughing. He says it's the most hilarious thing he's heard all week, in months even. I say we've got the support of the WVS and the government right behind us, and he stops laughing pretty sharpish.

Pearl and I take the role of understudy seriously too. Throughout November, I ensure she memorizes Mary's lines *just in case*. In my opinion, the Mary in the script is a particularly verbose Mary. She is in nearly every scene and she is full of backchat. Is it wrong of me to think, *Well, it would have been quite hard for Pearl to remember all this?* This is a job for four actors, not one. This Mary makes great friends with the angel. She chats with Joseph. She is the star—no, she is not *the* star, the star is also great friends with Mary. When the innkeeper turns them down, she has to huff, she has to say, "I really should have called ahead."

And then, only two weeks before show-time, we learn that poor blonde Helen has scarlet fever and is going to be put in a sanitorium for a few weeks.

Pearl is Mary!

We prepare every afternoon after school at home and at Mrs. Burton's.

"Action!" I say. "And…cut!"

We pretend to be film stars. Pearl knows her lines, no problem. Even as we knit, Mrs. Burton balances the script on one knee. Mrs. Shaw reads "narrator." My next-door neighbor claps and nudges me: "Ooh, I wish I was at her school."

Pearl can't speak without a Mary-ism. My favorite is the way that in the stable scene, she puffs: "The baby is coming," then staggers around as though she's been shot.

But all the rehearsals, all the tickets, all the costume-making is in vain, all is wasted, because there is "no risk to London" at present and so they've decided to return the evacuees for Christmas. They've decided there mightn't be a real war after all.

Do we celebrate that Hitler hasn't yet attacked? Twelve are going back. Five are staying. A few have disappeared already.

The butcher's boy and Mrs. Dean's boy stay. The farmer's Nathan stays—he is part of the family!

Pearl is one of the twenty who goes.

I wave off her peaky face. She is wearing her favorite pinafore and the pretty blouse, and a coat I bought her from the lovely Mrs. Purnell. The children are desperately excited and singing Christmas carols. If I hear what "my true love sent to me" one more time I might scream. Pearl says very little. I want to tell her something profound, something to convey what she has brought to me for these few short months; how I don't think I've been this happy for a long time—since 1917, in fact—but instead, all I can say is:

"Take care, Pearl."

"I really wanted to do the Mary," she whispers.

"I know you did," I say. "I know."

*

The house feels quieter than ever but it's worse than before, much worse. I have seen what I might have had. Edmund eats dinner, then pushes the plate away.

"Perhaps it's for the best," he says, gently. I look up in surprise, but he leaves the room before I can respond and soon, I hear the Ford Prefect purr away. Pearl never even got the chance to ride in it. I keep the glassy-eyed toy bear she used to hold next to me on my pillow. It had been wonderful while it lasted.

I must be an evil person because secretly I want a very gentle and friendly un-killing kind of bomb to wash down over London and for everyone to leave again.

The next day, I box up the toys and take them next door, but Mrs. Burton says, "Keep them just in case" and "You never know."

And I shake my head. *I will not cry, I won't.* Not in front of anyone. Olive would have, I won't.

Mrs. Burton takes my hand. She knows I'm heartbroken. "We've got knitting, sewing, brushing and organizing to do, Mrs. Lowe," she whispers. "Don't give up now."

I go into the living room, where the ladies are. We've got uniforms now, we're official—the WVS at your service—and although I feel bereft, I join in. No dogs today. In three weeks, we've taken fur from over thirty of them and we're sewing dolls for orphaned children now. I grab some scissors and start the pattern.

At Christmas, since there is no Mary—no one could have been expected to learn all those lines in just a few days—Mrs. Bankhead, flushed with embarrassment, stands in for her. I imagine she regrets extending the role now. Loping around the mock stable at the front of the church, she holds the script in trembling hands. *Pearl should be doing this*, I think resentfully.

"You're an angel." Mrs. Bankhead delivers her big line without enthusiasm to an angel less than half her size.

I don't know whether to send Pearl a Christmas card. Foolishly, I mention it to Edmund who, now we have resumed normal service at home, is his usual sniffy self.

"Why would you? She's a Jew," he says flatly and then when I give him a look, he shrugs. "Do what you like. You always do."

The very next morning, a card arrives from her. It shows a fireside scene, stockings and presents.

To Mr. and Mrs. Lowe,

I am surprised she calls me Mrs. Lowe, and I am surprised she has mentioned the Mr. I imagine someone who didn't know anything about us had helped her write this.

I hope all is well. I have seen three films. You could have been in them all. I am currently with my grandmother in her house in Watney Street. My favorite uncle will be here for Christmas and he will have a surprise for me!

On Christmas Day, Edmund and I and his parents chew overcooked chicken quietly in the dining room. That's how they like it. They still can't understand why we don't have staff.

"No one does any more," Edmund tells them. Which is as good a cover for we-don't-have-enough-money as I've ever heard.

"Anyway, Vivienne manages." He nods curtly at me. And this is as good a compliment as I've ever had from him.

"We're fine!" I say brightly. "There's just the two of us, after all."

Edmund's mother watches me steam the plum pudding. She is very proud of the pudding that her last maid from London sent for her. You'd think she slaved over it herself the way she goes on. We tuck into it silently. Edmund's father finds the coin hidden inside and says angrily, "Almost broke my tooth on it."

"It's good luck," I say.

"We're going to need it when Mr. Hitler decides it's time."

"Well, hopefully by then, we'll have built up our defenses a bit," Edmund comments. Edmund might be an idiot, but he's usually spot on with politics.

"We're going to sign a peace agreement before too long," his father retorts.

"I sincerely doubt that," says Edmund. "I don't think it's peace that Hitler wants."

Edmund's father doesn't like anyone disagreeing with him. He slams down his cup. "I don't care what that bloody man wants."

Finally, they go to listen to the wireless and leave me to start clearing up. From the kitchen, I hear them say that Edmund doesn't visit enough, and he offers for me to go more often. *That's good of you, Edmund.*

I can hear Mrs. Burton's next-door noise through the walls: a party; Mr. Burton's brothers have come, the girls have their friends, there are grandparents, and I wish I could be anywhere but here.

Evacuate me, I think, as I stand by the sink.

CHAPTER SIXTEEN

1915—Then

Some men were shocked by us FANYs. We would be loading up some poor fellow into the back of the ambulance and he might cry out:

"But you're a lady!"

"And you're a man," I liked to reply sarcastically.

Some of the soldiers liked a laugh and joke, despite their misery.

"Oh, I thought I might have been in heaven!"

"Not this time, we're taking you to the hospital."

Or the serious type might say, "Thank you for being here, Mrs."

"No, no, thank *you*," I would say, as I said to all the men. For they had given so much. The conditions they endured were inhumane and yet everyone I met was stoical and steadfast.

While driving, Olive and I still managed to bicker just as much as we did at home. Once, we picked up a man in a dreadful state—his arm had blown right off. In between yelps of agony, he was still in good enough spirits to tease us.

"Sisters, are you?"

"How can you tell?"

"S'obvious. Arghhh!" he shouted. "No, it's all right, it's just—arghh!"

"Do we look alike?" I asked. Although no one could accuse us of that! We had always been chalk and cheese, or as Olive liked to say, "paintbrush and Madeira cake."

"No, it's the arguing. You're just like my girls at home."

"She thinks she's the boss," Olive replied playfully.

"I *am* the boss," I said suddenly. I think that took Olive by surprise. It certainly surprised me. But I could feel myself growing in France; I was transforming into something stronger. I had a natural affinity for the roads. I quickly learned mechanics. I liked being around the men. I loved doing my best for them.

In England I was so used to being with Father and Mrs. Webster, or the dull customers talking about weaves and shades, that I hadn't realized I could ever be daring or interesting. This life was a world away from wrapping myself up into knots, trying to anticipate what Edmund or his mother would think of me. For the first time, I felt like I was truly myself.

For Olive, it was less easy. She would always be my wonderful sister, but she didn't see herself as wonderful here. She couldn't help but cover her eyes if a man was spurting blood. She was rendered speechless if someone was in terrible pain. The other FANYs liked her but she was indifferent to them, and I quickly realized that out here I, for once, was the more popular one.

Olive said all she wanted to do was draw or paint and she admitted she resented time spent away from her canvases. Oh, it was fine when we were rescuing people, but all the waiting around?

"Such a bore," she said.

It wasn't all work. We sometimes walked to watch the ships pull in to the port at Calais. And one time we went bathing in the sea. Olive stayed on shore, sketching, but even she was eventually tempted to dip her toes in the blue. We visited Paris a couple of times too: I sent postcards to Edmund *and* his mother, and I was careful to describe the sights in an informative way that couldn't be interpreted as boastful. *Such a fine line!*

Daisy wanted me to go on a double date with her. A Canadian patient had seen me in the hospital grounds and wanted to take me to town to hunt for some cake. We FANYs weren't allowed out alone on dates, but we *were* allowed on a double date, strangely. We were also allowed to date in the afternoon, but not of an evening.

I explained to Daisy that I had someone back home.

"But you're not engaged?" Daisy was nothing if not persistent. "You can still come? I'm sure your Edmund wouldn't mind."

But I thought that even if Edmund wouldn't mind, Edmund's mother certainly would, so I'm afraid I rather conned Olive into going in my place. I had noticed she barely wrote to Walter and indeed had hardly heard from him, so it seemed to me that she was now a free agent. She said she would love a walk to town, so she set off with Daisy and the two soldiers, quite oblivious to the fact that it was, in fact, a date.

She was still oblivious when she returned.

"Did you like him?" I inquired.

"Oh yes, he was very interesting. A botany student before the—"

"No, I mean, did you *like* him?"

"Not like that," she said, bewildered. "Anyway, it's you who should be going on dates, not me!"

"How do you mean?"

"Because I'm not looking for anyone," she said as slowly as if I were a simpleton.

"But *I'm* not looking for anyone, I have Edmund," I huffed. "You *know* that."

She scowled. I continued. "I didn't know that you and Walter were still a thing. I'm sorry. I shouldn't have fixed you up."

She made a face.

But after that, I noted she put her London letters under her pillow. And when Agnes came round to our hut with her new Brownie camera and I said, "I would like a photograph for Edmund, if you wouldn't mind?" Olive piped up, saying that she supposed she must have one taken for someone special back home too.

*

About a month after we'd arrived, we were waiting in our ambulance at a railway sidings. The wait was routine, but this place was new. We were to collect our assignment, put them in the ambulances, drive to the hospital, same as usual.

You never knew what state the poor men would be in. It was with some relief that I found our three that day weren't bad: all were coherent, with wounds to the legs and arms, nothing to the chest; the chest was so much trickier.

But we were under fire. Our trucks were being sniped at. Shells were coming over at us. You couldn't see the enemy, there must have been a trench just the other side of the railway tracks. While everyone else ran for cover, Olive and I stayed with our charges, our charges who couldn't move. For once, she let me hold her hand like when we were little girls: I think it was more for my benefit than for hers. *Oh dear God.* A whizzing, a buzzing, a terrible screeching sound. It was petrifying. *If we die, we die*, I told myself. I thought of Father, Aunt Cecily and Edmund and his mother. *We can't die. Not yet. Not yet.*

The ambulance next to ours was shelled. It collapsed.

We sat sheltering in the back with the two men, who couldn't move.

"Get shelter," one groaned. The other man just lay there, his lips trembling. He was repeating something, I thought from the Bible, but when I leaned in closer, he was saying, *Mum, Mum, Mum, Mum.*

We hadn't been there long enough to know the rules. Both of us knew we couldn't leave them, though. We couldn't leave them defenseless.

The first told me his name was Frank. Frank Bollingham, reservist.

"Don't want to die, Miss."

"No, we mustn't die," I murmured to Olive. "Father will go nuts."

Olive's eyes were gleaming like a madwoman's. "This is strangely exhilarating."

"It isn't, Olive," I whispered.

I've never had much of a voice, Olive neither. But we met each other's eyes then and started to sing and even poor frightened Frank and the other fellow joined in.

Keep the home fires burning,
While your hearts are yearning,
Though your lads are far away
They dream of home

And then, about thirty minutes later, the shelling had stopped, everyone raced back and we drove away with what was left of our sorry convoy.

"You should have left them to get to safety yourselves," announced Daisy as she climbed into the driving seat. The threat was over. It was their ambulance that had been destroyed. She and Enid would return with us. They'd go back for the bodies tomorrow.

"Next time make sure you get to cover," snapped Mrs. Fletcher when we returned. "You're no good to us if you're dead."

It was growing light. Pink and orange streaked the sky. Olive staggered off to bed, but I stayed back to do maintenance on our van. I felt very affectionate toward it suddenly, as though it were a loyal pet. *Take care and reward it.* Kneeling down by the tires, greasing the engine, I tried not to think of the carnage we'd just seen. We'd got lucky. *Very* lucky.

I went into our hut. I tried to describe it to Olive the next day, but I couldn't find the words: it was just indescribably lovely to see her lying there, mouth open, snoring and alive.

And from then on, everyone in the hospital canteen seemed to know about us. Olive and I had gained a reputation for being heroic. It was both flattering and unsettling. I knew you were only as heroic as the last thing you'd done. I didn't know if I could carry on being brave. I didn't know if we *had* been brave. *Are you brave if you're unaware of just how much danger you're in?*

*

A few days after our ambulances had come under fire, Mrs. Fielding caught me going back to our hut.

"I want to take you and Olive to King Leopold II first thing. Courtyard at five."

Olive was already half asleep but since this was big news, I woke her up.

"We're going to meet the King tomorrow!" I called urgently. I wondered what I could wear that might make me look a little more feminine. I wondered if he'd heard of our steadiness under fire. A medal would be a fine thing. The Lowes did not impress easily, but a medal would surely stir them. I could only dream of Edmund's mother clucking over it. "*And then I told Lord Astor about your meeting the King…*"

Olive sat up. Her hair and her face were mussed. "Wha-at?"

I started undressing quickly.

"We're meeting the King of Belgium tomorrow." We would only have six hours' sleep. Dear God, I didn't want to look ruined.

"The King?"

"Yes. We're meeting King Leopold II."

But Olive only threw back her head and laughed.

"What?" I said, now annoyed with her.

"It's a bloody ship, you nincompoop. The *Leopold the Second*. It's another way of bringing casualties in. Agnes told me. They sometimes use the ships and canal boats if the men's injuries are so bad, they don't think they will be able to withstand the bumpy roads."

"Oh," I said, pretending not to be disappointed. *Of course it was.*

Daisy had tricks she could do with cards. She could guess the card you'd seen. She could make a card appear on the other side of the room. She said at home, she could pull a rabbit out of a hat, *yes, a live rabbit.*

"Why can't you do it here then?" Agnes jeered.

Daisy responded that she could cast spells on people, so they couldn't speak any more, and she'd do it to Agnes if she wasn't careful. She turned the whole card deck into red, then black, then mixed again.

One time, she said, "I've another. I'm going to analyze you." I looked at Enid, Agnes and Dorothy. They shrugged. Dorothy said, "I've already been done…"

She threw a coin about five meters in front of her. I waited.

Everyone stared at me. I stared at Daisy's bright gray eyes, which were giving nothing away.

I watched the copper coin as it shone on the floor; I could see it clearly. *Was this about my eyesight?* I waited. Or perhaps Daisy had glued it to the floor? I had seen her do a trick with glue once—you spent ages trying to unstick yourself. I didn't want to look like a ninny. I hated showing myself up. Everyone was giggling now. I couldn't tell if I'd done the thing—whatever it was—wrong or right.

Suddenly, Daisy had her arms round me. "You're all right, Vi! You're not a Jew."

I felt a cold wave wash through me, but I was delighted at the same time. I'd passed the test. That had to be better than not passing, didn't it? I had been quite tempted to pick the thing up too.

"Ha, brilliant," I said.

Olive arrived next. She'd been drawing in our room. She was working on a lovely little cartoon. It was three pictures in a row: *What a VAD does in Theory. Popular Fiction. Practice.* In the *Theory* picture, the volunteer is well-turned-out and smart, standing by a shining automobile. In *Popular Fiction*, she is having a jolly time of it; soldiers are holding mistletoe over her head, she is slender, radiant as a bride. It is only the third VAD that I recognize: the one who is overwhelmed, rained on, carrying a leaky oilcan.

I couldn't wait for her to show it to everyone. I wished they could all see how talented she was.

Olive came and stood next to me and asked what was going on. "We're doing a thing!" I explained vaguely, letting Daisy take over.

"Let's find out what you're made of, Olive!" Daisy made it sound quite ominous.

She threw the coin higher this time, and it rolled across the ground. I thought of something the Canadian soldiers had told me the other day: "Things can turn on a dime."

Olive had no compunction about walking over to the coin. I tried to tell her with my face, "No, don't do it," but either she didn't get my message or she ignored it. She squatted down, stared at it for a second, then picked it up. She came back with her arm outstretched and tried to return it to Daisy, who refused it.

"It's yours," Olive said, confused.

"Oh, dearie me," said Daisy. "This is not good, Olive." Everyone laughed.

Those months with the FANYs in 1915 passed faster than a blink of an eye. Edmund was in Belgium now, and sometimes I wondered if I might one day have to transport him to a hospital or if we would be reunited in some railway siding or waterfront. I remembered him as tall, lean and handsome but I couldn't quite picture the *details* of him and this made me ashamed. I couldn't conjure him up. There were just fragments of him: an ambitious, intelligent man who wanted to be in the Indian Civil Service. A somber man with his hands in the pockets of his coats. A man who needed to be left alone.

All will be well, I reminded myself, *when the war is over and we're back in England.*

Edmund hardly wrote and when he did, it was usually a dry old message of the kind I sent to Aunt Cecily. (Olive had read one over my shoulder once, and her expression said everything!)

As for Olive, I noted, she now wrote more to Mrs. Ford than Walter. She explained Walter wasn't great with words. With that, I could sympathize.

"Do you miss him though?" I asked her.

She paused. "A little," she admitted. "It would be...invigorating to see him chopping some wood in the garden," she added mischievously. "He was rather adept at that."

CHAPTER SEVENTEEN

1940—Now

Debates in Parliament, "the Norway question," rationing and more rationing. Churchill is now our prime minister; we race to listen to his stirring voice on the wireless. British Summer Time is back, which helps a bit as there is more daylight. No Germans have managed to parachute themselves in to Leicester—not that I know of anyway—but news elsewhere is unrelentingly grim: France has capitulated as Edmund always said they would.

The Nazi occupation of France is heart-rending news. I think of the brave French soldiers I knew in the Great War. Trying to make light of their wounds in the back of my ambulance. Singing "La Marseillaise" in the railway sidings. The frazzled doctors and frantic nurses. How had things come to this? Europe was going through this turmoil again, just one generation after it had fallen apart.

Two soldiers made it home to Hinckley from the hideous events at Dunkirk and we WAVs talked about holding a party in the hall, but apparently, they were too exhausted and there wasn't much of an appetite for one among everyone else.

I had no appetite for anything any more. Not even Mrs. Burton's biscuits.

And then, toward the end of summer, bloody Hitler finally turned his attention to us. *It was our turn now.* They called it the Blitzkrieg. Blitz, for short.

"Lightning attacks?" I think, *They love a new name for old things.* The way the newspapers report it, it's as if it's the first time England has ever been bombed. Of course, it's the first time it's been this ferocious, but it is *not* the first time. I know this.

The dramatic things we feared last September are now happening. The voices on the wireless grow ever more somber. The Pathé film clips show soldiers less cheerful, more fatigued. The phoney war is over. Down go the buildings and the town centers. The pictures in the papers start to look like wastelands. People are dying. We, the civilians, the innocents, are under attack.

How can London stand it? Poor London. I want to wrap it up and bring it here. But it's not *just* London. It's all the industrial towns. Sometimes it's good to live nowhere special, in an in-betweeny place like Hinckley.

I desperately miss my Pearl-in-London. I am so worried about her, I lie awake at night, willing her to stay safe. I hear of children crushed or burned alive. Won't her mother please send her back to me? I don't think I can bear it for much longer.

Mrs. Burton's husband, Ernie, who I never see much of despite spending so much time in his house, appears in our street, driving a mobile tea canteen. Gleaming silver it is, fully fitted and purpose-built.

"Present for the WAVs!" he calls, hooting the horn.

The tea canteen is for us to drive to wherever needs tea. Outside railway stations, hospitals, community events . . . but we know its primary purpose is to go to the site of anywhere that's been bombed.

We gather round, admiring it. It is state-of-the-art inside too. It's got all its bits and pieces in the right places. Loaded with china cups and saucers. Sacks of sugar. Milk. We can pour sugar in if they like it sweet. If it's cold, if it's bad, we will. Milk in the cup first.

"Who's going to drive it then?"

No one volunteers. Mr. Burton suddenly looks anxious. "Oh no...
What? Can none of you drive?"

I put my hand up slowly.

"It's been a while but..."

Mrs. Burton looks at me, and chuckles. "Dark horse."

"It was a Ford Model T ambulance, actually."

Mrs. Burton and I take it out for a run. We pass by Edmund's parents'
home and, spur of the moment, decide to stop there. I hoot and the
residents who can walk come out and admire it.

"It's a beauty!" says one old man, sliding his hand along the side.
"Amazing what they can do nowadays."

Edmund's father stays indoors, huddled up to the wireless.

"It's a wagon." Edmund's mother sidles up to me. "You'll look like
a gypsy in that."

I hate you, I think suddenly. My ferocity, after all these years,
takes me by surprise.

CHAPTER EIGHTEEN

1915—Then

Olive and I went home for Christmas 1915. The first thing I saw were children carrying wreaths and mistletoe through the street and I felt a great surge of hope.

As soon as she could, Olive raced over to see the Fords. Walter was away, training in Oxford, so I couldn't understand her great hurry to get to Warrington Crescent but she said to me, "You want me to stay in with the capitalist pigs and the crashing bores? No thank you."

In civilian clothes, Olive looked muscular and blithe, her hair pinned back in her cap emphasizing her pointed chin. She had struggled in France, we both knew that. And we were both surprised that I had not. But Olive was determined that once we'd done with Christmas, we'd return together to Lamarck Hospital to do our best. I loved her determination and commitment to our team and to the men. It occurred to me that we were closer than ever before. That's what driving into blackness, with death all around you, can do for you.

"We're the Mudie-Cookes," she whispered with a squeeze. "And we're not doing too badly, are we?"

On Christmas Day, it was just Father and me who went over to Aunt and Uncle's—and since it was our first Christmas without dear Richard, naturally it was a somber occasion. We tried to have good cheer but it was impossible to hold back the tide of missing him.

Aunt Cecily told me that Edmund had applied for leave but not been given permission. This seemed desperately unfair. The likelihood of us getting leave at the same time seemed to be narrowing but we all had to do our duty and I understood, after the things I'd seen.

I was glad when Edmund's parents came over. Aunt Cecily and Uncle Toby weren't as convivial as they used to be and I was nervous that the Lowes might have moved on. Their being here showed that they were good, loyal friends. And they brought with them Christopher, who *had* been granted leave, and I had to admit, he was much warmer to me than he used to be. They also had brought with them a rich fruit cake that Mrs. Lowe was very proud of.

When his mother asked, "Is it really as bad as people are saying?" Christopher said, "No, Mother, it's far worse. Am I right, Vivienne?"

I nodded. Strange to be on the same side as him for once.

Christopher was an officer. At dinner he speared his carrots merrily like he was playing a violent game with them: "To be honest, I'm not having too rough a time of it," he confided, and I noticed his throat was spotty against his collar. "But I know plenty who are."

Edmund's mother sliced her food into tiny pieces. She soon returned to one of her favorite subjects: skivers and whingers.

"The problem with the world today is it lacks backbone," she said.

I smirked, thinking of what Olive would say if she heard that. *The world lacks backbone? How is that even logistically possible?*

Christopher asked for seconds, especially of those fine roasted potatoes, and his mother looked embarrassed. "And a little more meat?" he continued obliviously. When Aunt Cecily admitted there wasn't any and asked didn't he know about the shortages, he too blushed, and said, "Not to worry, it was just a joke." He turned to me and asked if I'd heard the news that he was getting married to a girl he called Pigeon.

"No. I didn't…I didn't hear that." Silly, but I felt flooded with resentment. Edmund and I had been close for a long time. Where had this Pigeon come from and how had she suddenly overtaken us?

It occurred to me that since Christopher was older, it might be that Edmund was waiting for him to marry first: he might have felt it was inappropriate for him—for us—to jump the queue.

I stared into my plate. The thing was, I didn't know if I wanted anything to happen between Edmund and me any longer. Since I'd missed him so little while I was in France, I wondered if maybe he and I were just habit and not the real thing. Maybe we weren't as compatible as I once thought. As if he knew what I was thinking, Christopher laid down his knife and fork and looked at me seriously. "War intensifies everything," he said. "You know that. It accelerates. It amplifies. Chin up, Vivienne. Edmund will come to his senses."

Timidly, I smiled. "That's just what Richard used to say."

He winked at me. "Edmund's lucky to have a loyal girl like you."

He picked up his cutlery again and asked if he might, just might, grab the Brussels sprouts I had left.

CHAPTER NINETEEN

1940—Now

I write to Pearl. She writes back and her tales leave me goose-pimpled with fear. This is a terrible time. *Another* terrible time. How can we stand it again? I am glued to the wireless as it reports on the devastation— it's not just London, oh, Mr. Hitler is intent on caning the whole country—but my heart is in London for it's London I know best and it's London where my loved ones are.

Pearl hid in the Anderson shelter at the end of Nathan's parents' garden. They live by a railway track so it's classified as a dangerous area—especially at risk. She walked to school the morning after the bombs. Two of her classmates were squashed, sheltering on the steps of the Underground. Her mum was talking to someone else, but Pearl heard her describe it. *Squashed like beetles.* Nowhere is safe, she writes cheerfully. People are getting crushed by their own ceilings.

I want to cry with frustration. *Send Pearl here!*

One morning, while I am listening to the wireless in the kitchen, Edmund comes in. Taking his sandwich for lunch, he stands next to me for one moment, listening to the estimates of the numbers killed.

"It's terrible," I say. Briefly, he puts his hand on my back, in the way he did in the old days, only he doesn't move it to stroke me, and I daren't breathe.

He goes over to the bread bin, but instead of lifting the lid, he picks up the whole container.

He holds out something: a grimy envelope covered in crumbs.

"When did this come, Edmund?"

I turn over the paper and look at the stamp. I can see for myself: two weeks ago.

"Why didn't you tell me?"

"If you'd ever bothered to lift the bread bin to clean underneath, you'd know, wouldn't you?" he says as he walks off.

Mrs. Dean, I think. *Mrs. Dean is who I need.* I run over to her house with a sixpence, clutching the letter from the Raines Foundation School, London, tightly in my fist. I'm not losing it now.

"May I use your telephone?" I cry breathlessly. Mrs. Dean is always glad when someone needs the phone for she has not made as much use of it herself as she had imagined. She hovers by me as I make the call, pretending to dust the cobwebs from the picture rail.

What if Pearl has been bombed? What if she's in hospital? What if she's already gone to some nasty house where they feed her bacon and feel her head for horns every day?

"Please, let them know—we have a place for Pearl."

CHAPTER TWENTY

1916—Then

The first months of 1916 were even more difficult than those months preceding. Endless dark shifts. Freezing rain. Driving from the train to the hospital. Hospital back to train. Port to hospital. Hospital to port. Holding hands with bloodied men. Terrible injuries. Heartbreak. We dealt with men who had been gassed. Men who had been blinded. Men who called out for their mothers, their sweethearts. Sometimes I wondered why the doctors battled to save them; they must have known there was no hope...

One side of the hospital became the place for dead bodies. I went there two, three times a night, either to pick up or to deliver. You tried not to think about it too much.

One brutal night, we had done about six runs and I was growing desperate for a break. There had been explosions, shootings, smoke and we had lost two Frenchmen in the back of the ambulance around midnight. By four in the morning, I was seeing to an English Tommy, who was very dignified despite his dreadful predicament. We decided Olive would stay in the back with him. Then a second patient was loaded in, and he was shrieking about something, flailing about, and the Belgian stretcher-bearers grimaced, "Sorry, ladies, it's only his thigh...but I don't know, he won't let us look."

The patient had a crazed look in his eyes, but you can't turn people away.

"The hospital will deal with him," the stretcher-bearer continued. "Maybe give him a jab or something to calm down."

I was just leaning over to give the first man some water when I felt something smack hard onto my back: the second patient had leapt on me. I buckled under the weight of him and, desperate to avoid hurting the first man, twisted away from him and fell down, smack, onto the ambulance floor.

"You German whore!" he was shouting as he pulled my hair.

I struggled hard. He was out of his mind. I pushed him off me as brutally as I could. I could hear Olive screaming. She was tugging at him, trying to pull him off me. He got up again and started yelling at both of us, "Hun! Bitch, Bosch whore!" As I clambered up, he came for me again, but Olive clonked him over the head with a petrol can and he fell to the floor, dazzled.

"Help!" She leaned out the ambulance. "Over here. We need help!"

I had taken a nasty blow to the head against the floor of the van. I rubbed my cheek and pulled at my hat. Useless tears came to my eyes. My body hurt. I would be purple with bruises. I leaned over my first patient. "I'm so sorry…"

Two British officers came in and dragged the attacker out. They were full of apologies. Then the Belgian stretcher-bearers from before came and apologized too. They didn't know what else to say.

"Just keep him away from my sister!" Olive barked. I could tell by her voice she was very frightened.

I stroked my elbow. I would be okay.

Our poor first patient raised himself up. He held out his hand to me. Tears coursed down his cheeks. "I'm so sorry I didn't help."

I knelt by him. "It's not your fault."

"He whacked you pretty hard."

"Nothing compared to what you've been through."

"He'll be court-martialled, I should think."

I nodded. It gave me no satisfaction; in fact, I couldn't bear to think about it. The whole episode felt shameful. Olive still looked agitated, but she didn't say anything. We were all still in shock, I suppose.

The next day, I still had a bump the size of an egg on my forehead and felt like throwing up whenever I thought about it. I felt so vulnerable, it somehow took my breath away. If Olive hadn't been there, I might have been... and by one of our own men. He had overpowered me; he could have hurt me very badly. And I felt so sad for him too: how diabolical the war must be to turn a man into that.

I was still going over the incident in my mind when, about a week later, a telegram came from Aunt Cecily:

> *Christopher is very poorly in hosp. If pos come home. Lowes need support.*

I thought of how Edmund's mother didn't have a daughter, and Aunt Cecily would be desperately trying to be a good friend but feeling so much grief after losing Richard that she might be devastated all over again, and I knew immediately that returning to England was the right thing to do. The Lowes might not have been my family, not quite, but we were close, and this was their hour of need. Not so much pigs with their snouts in the trough, but worried parents wringing their hands.

I still had a few days' leave owed to me, but Enid and Agnes were on long-awaited leave at that time and if I left too, our team would be short. I consulted Olive, but she just stared at me uncomprehendingly. "You'd waste your leave on *Christopher*?"

I thought this was both a disturbing and an unkind response and told her so. She scowled. She was in quite the doldrums lately. Our

Christmas trip to England hadn't cheered her up in any way—quite
the reverse. If I inquired, she would simply snap, "I miss the Fords,
that's all, can't you understand?" as if I were the unfeeling one. She
had cut her hair quite short and was wearing an enormous sheepskin
coat like some of the soldiers did. She looked like a buffalo. She
looked like someone trying to appear as unfeminine as possible.

I asked Daisy what she thought—about my returning to England
so soon after my last leave—and she told me I must ask Mrs. Fielding.
Mrs. Fielding would know what to do. I didn't want to hear that. I
don't know if Mrs. Fielding deliberately made herself unapproach-
able, but I was always nervous speaking to her. That day, she was
preparing an ambulance.

"Nasty business, what happened."

"Yes," I said uncertainly. It took me a moment before I realized
she was talking about the incident with the violent patient.

"Some of the boys...their minds are destroyed." She paused. She
gave me a sympathetic look. "I've never seen anything like it."

I hesitated.

Daisy and Enid laughed at Mrs. Fielding sometimes. They called
her a *sapphist*— a word I had never come across before. I thought,
she doesn't seem that bad.

She asked if she could do anything to help. Surprised, I said, "I
was thinking maybe a few days in London..."

She agreed immediately.

"It's difficult," she said sympathetically, "when your own turn on
you. I know that. Try not to think all humanity is bad, dear, the
soldiers are suffering terribly. Take your time to recover."

I nodded. I felt guilty that she thought that was the reason I was
going, but it seemed easier to go along with it.

"Olive going with you?"

"No, she...no."

I don't know what Mrs. Fielding must have been thinking but she
put her hand on my shoulder and squeezed.

"Very well, off you go. And don't worry about Olive, we'll keep an eye on her."

Early the next morning, I found myself green-faced on a packed ship in choppy waters. A queue of men offered to get me water or cigarettes before their sergeant shouted at them to "Leave the poor woman alone!" and "Give her some bleeding air!"

Then I was on the train to London and it was so tightly cramped that again, I found I could hardly breathe, but a soldier, who was as pale as I was, insisted I take his seat.

"Just a little bit longer and I'll be home," he said. "I can manage…"

It turned out to be a lot longer than a little, because someone jumped on the line in front of the train. We took in this information and waited. I offered to swap my seat with someone else, but they too said it was all right.

"Always liked sardines," he said wryly.

We had been waiting for about an hour when the soldiers broke out into "Keep the Home Fires Burning," and I could just imagine Olive's face, her proud chin jutting forward, if she had heard: "Did you know the lyrics were written by a friend of mine? Her name is Lena Ford."

And I found tears filling my eyes as I sang along.

> There's a silver lining
> Through the dark clouds shining,
> Turn the dark cloud inside out
> 'Til the boys come home.

I thought longingly of those sing-along Sundays at the Fords', watching the boys chopping wood in the garden, full of vim and vigor. Where were they all now? How could things have changed so quickly?

I tried to focus on Christopher and Edmund. It had now been over a year since I'd seen Edmund. I hoped he'd kept something burning for me. His occasional letters were masterpieces of brevity, but then Edmund was never good at keeping still.

Then, some people on the train started up on a very funny version of "It's a Long Way to Tipperary" and the mood changed from painfully sentimental to something jolly. By the time we pulled into London, I was almost shaking with laughter. Oh, it did me good to laugh.

CHAPTER TWENTY-ONE

1940—Now

One week later, she is here: my Pearl, back from London. She has been re-evacuated! Only a handful have returned, and then there are the five who have stayed here all along.

"What about the other children?" I ask. "Aren't they coming back?"

Pearl shrugs. *Oh, how I've missed that shrug!*

"They'll stay with their mums," she says, an indecipherable expression on her face. "Some are going to America on a massive ship. Mummy asked if I wanted to go."

"And what did you say?"

"I said I'd much rather come here."

I try not to smile but I can't help it. I grab her round the waist and plump a kiss on the top of that pretty head.

We go straight to the swings and there—while she is flying, suspended in the air—she tells me about the bombs, the shelters and the shivering in the underground. She says they sang songs to keep cheery and one time she recited "The Owl and the Pussy-Cat," and everyone applauded. An old man with rheumy eyes and gnarly hands said, "How do you know all that, Pearl?" and she had told them, "My evacuation mother taught me."

Back in our garden, helping me hang her tiny clothes out to dry, Pearl nods toward the shed.

"Is he still in there?"

"Who?" I ask wearily. I don't like the way she talks about Edmund, and yet, and yet... she's not *entirely* wrong.

"Your husband. The Mr. Lowe."

"He's at work," I say. I *think* he's at work. "You'll be able to say hello later."

She raises her eyebrows at me. Pearl has no interest in saying hello to the Mister.

Seeing her socks hanging in the breeze makes my heart zing with pride. *Look at us, Mr. Hitler,* I feel like saying. *We're happy.* And then I feel terrible because I know, all over the world, people are suffering and there is something obscene about being this delighted.

Pearl tells me that, despite the bombs, she went to the London picture house every Saturday morning—it was only a penny—and she saw this film and that film and they were *all* brilliant.

I ask, "Aren't they too old for you, Pearl?" and she responds haughtily, "I'm nine now," and I laugh and say, "Only just..."

She says, "You should do your hair more like Lauren Bacall."

I say, "We'll go to the picture house together soon, if you like?" and my Pearl shrugs again. "S'all right, I just like being here with you."

Charles the tortoise has acquired an unfortunate habit of turning over onto his shell and not being able to right himself again. I wonder if it's an old age thing. The first couple of times he did it, I felt sick. It brought back dark memories somehow. But now I blot them out and Pearl and I race to restore him.

"Silly Charles," she scolds. "Why does he keep making the same mistake again and again?"

"That's life," I say lightly.

"It doesn't have to be," Pearl says, collecting leaves for his snack.

*

Sometimes I take Pearl to Edmund's parents' home. At first, it was mostly so Mrs. Harrison didn't remark on the fact that I hadn't been to visit. But as time has gone on, I go there because we have a good time and Pearl thinks the old people—not Edmund's parents but the others—are brilliant.

There is the man who gets up every time someone speaks on the wireless: "Stand up," he orders us, his knees wobbling. "Show some respect. There's visitors here."

There is another old boy who everyone says is sweet on me. Sometimes we play dominoes, but his eyes are fading, and he thinks all the two-spots are four and the four-spots are eight. Sometimes, he throws the six across the room and says it's a cheat.

Sometimes the elderly people will make a comment about the Jews, but Pearl and I manage to ignore them, and nowadays, mostly it's the Germans, the French, the Russians and the Japanese who get their ire. I try to explain that some of those are allies but they don't listen or they don't care. One lovely old woman folds paper into tiny boats and swans for Pearl. We listen to the wireless and commiserate about the poor people and the dreadful bombs: Newcastle, Leeds, even Cardiff. *What did poor Cardiff ever do?* we wonder.

CHAPTER TWENTY-TWO

I went to see my father at his office first; he was surprised, then delighted to see me and then saddened when I reminded him of the reason. He wanted us to have lunch together, but self-importantly, I said I didn't have time and instead took a carriage to the hospital.

Once I found the ward, it was easy to recognize the back of Edmund's pretty golden head. And then I saw Christopher. Even from a distance, I knew he wasn't in a good way.

I stood at the end of the bed. "Hello, Christopher. Edmund."

Edmund spun round at my voice.

"Good Lord, Vivienne, you are the last person I expected to see here!"

I didn't know why he'd said that. Why should I be the last person here? I ignored his outstretched hand and leaned over Christopher.

"Christopher," I said. "It's me, Vivi. Are they keeping you comfortable?"

He said, "Vivienne? Well, well, well," and then he started laughing and then coughing. "I told you, Ed. There, what did I say?"

Edmund stood up uneasily. He was in full uniform, down to his socks, and very handsome he looked too. Aunt Cecily used to say, *Edmund would look dashing in a paper bag*, and it was true.

He said, "How did you know we were here?" and when I explained, he swallowed and said, "Mother and Father will be pleased."

"I'm pleased," said Christopher, coughing. "And when this poor girl's Casanova wakes up, he'll be pleased too."

Edmund scowled at his brother; I asked if he would prefer I left them to it, but he shook his head, then stalked off to get me a seat. "It's a shock, that's all."

It transpired that Christopher had been in a motor accident and ended up upside down in a ditch, stabbed in the chest by his own steering wheel. He'd been operated on, more than once, but there was nothing they could do about his lungs. It was a question of "wait and see."

Christopher asked me to talk to him. Conscious of Edmund next to me, I told him about the other FANYs, and I told him about my mistake over the *King Leopold*. I wanted to make him laugh, poor fellow, for he was in deep discomfort.

Edmund kept raising his eyes to the ceiling and I wasn't sure if it was exasperation or perhaps anxiety about Christopher's condition. I reminded myself: *Edmund does not behave emotionally, but that doesn't mean he doesn't feel emotions.*

And Richard had said, *He loves you, everyone knows it.*

But as I talked, I began to feel an overwhelming sense of shame. I was intruding on this most private of family moments. I had made assumptions and now it was clear I shouldn't have come. *What was I thinking?* I couldn't help but blame Aunt Cecily. She might be the sort to open her arms to anyone, but the Lowes were not. Why had I been so foolish? It was arrogance to think they needed me. I dreaded seeing Edmund's mother. I couldn't stand to think that she might be offended that I had come.

Then a vicar came, and at once, Edmund rose up and looked more invigorated. The vicar spoke kindly with Christopher, who was half-dozing again, and then turned to me. I saw that under his overcoat, he wore a uniform and that there were several medals lined up on his chest.

"Vanessa, isn't it?"

"No," I said. "It's Vivienne. Vivienne Mudie-Cooke."

I didn't look at Edmund. It seemed like he had not even talked to his favorite clergyman about me.

Pigeon arrived. She was a tall, heavyset girl from Cheltenham. She kept saying to me, "I knew Christopher and I should have got married, I knew it. He wouldn't have taken any risks...," which didn't seem to make any sense, but clearly meant something to her and I knew that this was the way it is at the bedside.

Pigeon had never met Edmund's family before and I thought, *what an initiation*, but try as I might, I couldn't warm to her much. She was as haughty and cool as Christopher was, or used to be. Her real name was Beryl, she said, but everyone called her Pidge. *I* must call her Pidge. I feared I wouldn't be able to.

She said she volunteered at a hospital near her home. Five days a week. She was very particular about that. "You should see the men," she said, shaking her head at me. "You wouldn't believe some of the sights." She clearly thought I was a woman who did nothing.

The vicar said he had connections in Cheltenham, and they talked animatedly about their shared acquaintances, the Searles and the Mongers.

It all felt too much with poor Christopher just...just lying there, groaning, looking awfully poorly and left out, what with us all sharing our life stories.

I touched Edmund's arm. "I'll be out in the corridor," and this time he turned round, and grasped my hands: "Thank you for coming." I was so surprised, I took a step back. He brushed his mouth to my ear. "I do appreciate it, Vivienne, I really do."

Nurses clipped by me in the corridor, focused on their duty; it felt as though they saw me, but did not see me. They were carrying jugs of water and rolls of bandages, wheeling trolleys. The pace was slower here than at Lamarck Hospital, but no less intense for it. I felt slightly better after Edmund's effusive thanks. Funny how just one kind word from him could allay my fears. He *was* pleased I came. Everyone was pleased I came. Maybe things wouldn't be so much up in the air from now on.

I watched a family come in, mother, father, two children, all clutching their hats, and the nurse—a young thing in a stained apron—awkwardly trying to warn them:

"He might look very different."

They nodded eagerly. "That's fine."

"He might not be able to talk." The nurse glanced at me.

They looked at each other; still nothing. "That's all right."

"They told you he lost his sight?"

Silence.

Next time I went back in, Christopher didn't look well at all. He kept getting panicky. I said to Edmund, "Is he getting worse?" and he said, "No, I don't think so. He's the same as before."

I talked to the nurse—maybe I was overstepping my place—but she agreed: we would tell Edmund he needed to call his mother and father now. He looked bewildered. "But they are coming this evening, isn't that soon enough?"

I whispered, "I don't know what's happening, an infection maybe, but to be...safe...let's tell them to come now."

Christopher stopped writhing at one point and suddenly seemed amazingly lucid. "You should marry, Edmund!" he called out. He patted the mattress for someone's hand, and I gave him mine. "Life is short. Women like Vivienne, well, they don't grow on trees."

I leaned over to him and wiped his brow. I was used to being among the sick and I found I could do it far more easily than Edmund, who mostly stood there in disbelief.

"Do you want me to get Pigeon?" Pigeon had gone back to her lodgings and wasn't coming back until Wednesday.

Christopher shook his head. "Not now, Vivienne. Don't tell anyone but being near her is really...exhausting."

Edmund's eyes were suddenly full of tears. How frail he looked then, even in his smart uniform, even with his broad shoulders. He was all cheekbones and shadows. I called the nurse over again and this time, she agreed she would call for a doctor.

"Good-good," I said for Edmund's benefit. As if the doctor was the panacea. We were pretending a cure was on its way.

Christopher continued to twist and writhe. Edmund now held his hand, but any time I made to go to the bathroom, or offered to go to the tea stand, he whispered, "Please don't leave us, Vi. I can't stand it."

It wasn't until about six that Edmund's parents managed to get there. There had been a mix-up or something. They were all dressed up. Somehow, the effort they had gone to—the lipstick, the hair, the keeping up appearances—made me want to weep. Edmund's mother greeted me warmly but formally. "You needn't have come, Vivienne," she pronounced thickly.

I said it was the least I could do, and she said accusingly, "Hmm," and "But your sister didn't?" And it seemed I was in the wrong for coming, and Olive was in the wrong for not.

"Olive sends her love."

Christopher raised his hand very lightly. "Olive is nuts..." he murmured, and he and Edmund laughed loudly and although usually I'd be annoyed at such an insult, I laughed too. "She speaks highly of you too, Christopher."

Edmund looked at me gratefully.

Edmund and I walked outside to give the parents some time alone with Christopher, and he was more effusive than ever. I couldn't help but think: *This might be the making of us.*

There was a tea van outside; I told him it was a similar make to the ambulance I drove in France. I bought us both a cup of tea from a woman with no teeth, not a single one, in her mouth and Edmund said, "Well, she doesn't look an inch like you, that's for sure," and I think it was a compliment.

The sun was setting and it was a beautiful evening, cold but bright. I imagined Olive readying herself for her shift in France. I hoped she would be all right without me. A million nasty incidents could befall her. What a time we were having: if we could only bring some good to those suffering around us, what more was there to life?

We weren't out for long before Edmund wanted to go back in, so we did, and he took off his coat, because he felt suddenly warm in the building, and I said I'd sit out in the corridor for a bit—for privacy—and he kissed me. It was only on the cheek, but it was spontaneous, and it felt heartfelt.

"Thank you."

I waited in the corridor with his overcoat slung protectively over my knee. Ridiculous I know, but I thought of Charles, the tortoise, and if it really was true that he would outlive the lot of us. I thought of his shell-y back and his slug-like face and I thought, *Well, perhaps there has to be some compensation for looking like that.*

When the next set of nurses had walked past, I pushed my fingers into the woolen warmth of Edmund's pockets and felt them press against a card. I pulled it out.

I found a picture. It was of a woman. She was naked except for a black fur stole round her shoulders. Oh, and high-heeled shoes. She was kneeling on the floor. Must be cold on her knees... *who was she?* No girlfriend would ever pose like that. No photo studio would let her. I slipped it back into the pocket. I thought to myself, *Just ask him,* but at the same moment, I thought, *I will never ask him.*

My heart was racing. I wished I could unsee what I had just seen. I tried to think of Charles the tortoise again, but that didn't help.

Edmund came out, not three minutes later, and the first thing he said was, "I'll take my coat, Vivienne."

"It's fine," I said clutching it tighter to me. I knew his game.

Ignoring me, he scooped it up. Once it was on, that tightness around his mouth reduced. "So cold. You know hospitals."

With Father, I ate fried egg on toast. Father wanted to do more than that—he couldn't help wanting to celebrate having me home—but I couldn't manage it, and he quickly understood why. I was waiting for news to come in the night, but it didn't and I slept through seamlessly. I hadn't been in such comfort for a while and the feather pillows and the fresh sheets that Molly had prepared felt like a balm to me.

I left the house at first light, while the shops were still pulling up their shutters, and the milk cart was doing its round. You might think that all was still normal in the world. As I walked past the station, though, I thought of the poor person who had thrown him or herself onto the tracks, and wondered what sad story preceded such an action.

I was going to do my best. That was all I could do.

Christopher was still hanging on. His parents were there. Edmund noticed me first and gave a watery smile and a kind of hopeless shrug. I nodded, went back to the corridor and waited. Again, I wasn't sure what I was doing there. I didn't want Edmund to feel alone, but maybe I should have stayed in France.

About two hours later, Edmund came out, shaking his head, and I understood. His shoulders had turned in, his cheeks had hollowed. My heart went out to him.

Edmund couldn't meet my eyes. "Thank you so much for being here, Vivienne. I don't know what I'd do without you."

"You shouldn't have to go through this," I said.

Suddenly he crumpled and threw himself toward me. "Oh God, Vi, it's so awful, I can't bear it."

His shoulders were wracked with grief; he heaved up and down. And I comforted him and I thought it was for this—the traveling, the uncertainty—that I had come, so I could do this for him.

When he pulled away, he said quietly, "I saw six men die last week, six men! And now I have to bury my own brother. For God's sake, Vivienne, it's agony."

"I know," I said, "I know."

Blinking, we went out into the bright sunlight. The mobile tea van was still there but with a different person at the counter.

The hospital grounds made an unexpectedly pretty scene. Drooping leaves and branches and blossom on the ground. I remembered how it was when Richard died and the shock that the world went on without him. There was a bust of a person I didn't know in the garden; there were bird droppings on its shoulders and I couldn't stop thinking of Christopher lying there in his hospital blues, with his sad, sad face.

"Something good should come out of all this," said Edmund and I clutched his hand and said, "It will, it will."

"So...what do you say, Vivienne?"

Was this it? The marriage question? I turned, confused. Behind us, someone was arguing with the tea person because their tea was too strong, and how come he couldn't have his money back?

"Shall we get married then?" he continued.

"You mean..." I asked tentatively, "after all this is over?"

He nodded. He looked suddenly relieved. "We could do it sooner, if you wanted?"

I was trying to catch my breath. This is what I'd wanted but the wait. And the picture. That picture.

"Thank you, Edmund. When the war is over will be fine."

"Do you want me to ask your father?"

"I...no. It's fine."

"Good," he said.

His parents came out, gray and shattered. Everything had been wrung out of them. Edmund's mother, usually so beautiful, looked like a damp, gray dishcloth.

"We've decided to get engaged," Edmund told them. "We're engaged to marry." Afterward, I thought, *engaged to marry? What else would one be engaged to do?*

They nodded meekly, distractedly.

"Well," said Edmund's mother. I think Edmund and I realized, very quickly, that perhaps this wasn't the best time for an announcement.

I walked back home to Father's, and every step was filled with sadness. I couldn't help wondering if Edmund and I had somehow sealed a terrible mistake.

CHAPTER TWENTY-THREE

After Pearl has left for school, and if it's not a day for queuing at the post office, the butchers or the grocers, and if Charles is the right way up, and if I'm not playing the organ for a church service, I go to Mrs. Burton's. We are proud to call ourselves the home front. The Women's Voluntary Service: we do whatever is needed. Toys for the poor children who've lost everything in Hull. Jumpers for our boys in the mountains of Italy. Brushed wool from the dogs packaged up and sent to be processed.

We reminisce about the foods we can't get any more—"I haven't seen a banana for months"; "Cheeky!"—and save up those which we know the others particularly like. "A cauliflower for you, Mrs. Dean, sent from family in Warwickshire!"

We worry about recipes and give each other tips on how to make a stew go further. Our cooking is no longer about taste, but eking it out. It suits me; I never made anything particularly tasty anyway. And Mrs. Burton is generous to a fault, and people are generous to her because they know she is. They give her the fatty bit, the bit extra, the baker's dozen, the *oops, now, I've overfilled it.*

We keep the home fires burning.

Some of us, the ones whose husbands are away or perhaps the ones who like our husbands less, meet in the evenings and carry on with our making and mending. They heat the village hall for us, which saves heating our houses. Sometimes, I bring Pearl and she

sits poring over her homework. (She is not a silly sausage.) If we're
at home, we listen to the wireless while I sew or knit, but sometimes
she says, "Play with my hair," and I do that instead. I contort her
unruly mane into funny styles to make us laugh.

Pearl is doing well at school. She has friends there, she says, but
seems disinclined to see them out of school, which suits me.

"They are all the same, all the townies," Mrs. Bankhead, the teacher,
explains one day.

"Townies?" I ask, mystified.

"That's what we call the children from London. It's townies versus
locals."

"Versus?"

Mrs. Bankhead looks shifty. "I didn't mean *versus*...there's no
malice. Some of the London children are quite different, that's all.
Especially the..." Her voice trails away.

"Especially the?" I repeat.

"Different ones," she says and turns her back on me.

In October, we WAVs organize a dance and everyone says we do
the town proud. The church hall looks sparkling and anyone who
can brings cakes. I watch the Burtons whirl around the room
together alongside the Deans, the Shaws and the Pilkingtons and
wish Edmund had come. There are more women on their own now
though, more than ever—the younger ones whose husbands have
joined up or the ones with husbands doing the ARP—so I don't feel
as lonely as I used to, and the deputy mayor is away in Bournemouth,
so I don't have to worry about swerving his octopus hands.

Mr. and Mrs. Fellows and their grown son Cyril are there. He is
trying not to be awkward in his unfamiliar uniform, all starchy and
solid. He is going away the next day and everyone is shaking his
hand and saying, "Good lad," or slapping his back. I did notice Mrs.
Burton's Ethel slip outside with him and the huge smile she had on

her face when they came back in, but I am still surprised the next morning when, as we're clearing up, Mrs. Burton tells me Cyril and Ethel got engaged. Sweet Cyril called round and asked for Ethel's hand before the dance yesterday. They are *madly* in love. Pearl slides her finger along the plates for left-over icing. I sweep the floor. Mrs. Dean is looking for a missing tablecloth that, of course, is her favorite.

"The man in the green uniform? With the red hair?"

"That's him. What do you think—romantic, huh?"

"*I* don't think so," says Pearl. She says she is not interested in love. Mrs. Burton and I chuckle.

Mrs. Burton has not given up on Pearl yet though.

"What would you say though, if Ethel said she wanted you to be her bridesmaid?"

I think, *Woah, that's a commitment,* but Mrs. Burton eyes me reassuringly. This has evidently been the subject of an earlier discussion.

Wrinkling her nose, Pearl says she would have to think about it, but she might say yes if there is a promise of a nice dress?

We laugh.

I'm under the impression that Mrs. Burton is walking on air about the engagement, until Pearl takes the plates to the kitchen and we're alone. Then she makes a pained expression at me, her hand pressed over her heart.

"He's a lovely boy, that Cyril. I just hope he gets through it."

CHAPTER TWENTY-FOUR

1916—Then

Just as I had suspected, Olive *couldn't* look after herself. In the six short days I was away in England, she had only gone and shattered her ankle.

I had just arrived back in Lamarck when Enid called out to me, "You heard, did you?"

I was full of the story of Christopher and my engagement. On the boat over, I had already practiced my lines on some officer intent on making lady friends: "Edmund is backward at coming forward, he will be heartbroken at his brother's passing, but together we will get through it." (The officer had quickly realized that I was a lost cause and had moved on to a couple of Belgian nurses.)

"Heard what?"

"Olive's had an accident."

"Oh, gosh!"

I ran to our hut, dragging my suitcase through the mud. There, I found a strange sight: Olive sitting in a deckchair—I didn't know where *that* had appeared from—pencil and sketchbook in hand, a glass of strange-colored liquid and a newspaper at her side and one bandaged leg stretched out in front of her on a table.

"It's not as bad as it looks. Don't fret, Vivi," Olive said immediately on seeing my expression. She explained: it was the consequence of a foolish dismount from the back of an ambulance—she would insist on jumping rather than using the steps—followed by an agonizing wait on the ground.

Relief filled me. *Thank God it was nothing worse.* Dear Olive; I had had quite the fright. I began to unpack my things. I wanted to give her a right telling-off, but I knew that wasn't fair, or reasonable.

"How is our dear friend Christopher?" Olive asked presently.

"Dead," I said. She had the grace to look sorry.

"Oh, Vi, how terrible!" She waited a while, and then when a decent amount of time had passed, she raised an eyebrow. "So how is Edmund coping?"

I suddenly felt deflated. I couldn't tell her the whole story because I wasn't sure what the whole story was. I thought of Pigeon and the photo I had discovered in Edmund's pocket. Everything was moving so fast, and I was so slow to catch up.

"Yes, he's fine." I took a breath. "Stout fellow." A pause. It was now or never. "We're actually engaged."

Her expression was unreadable. "I supposed that would happen. So, are you happy?"

"Yes," I said. "I couldn't be happier."

She held out her arms for me to give her a hug, and I went over to her, awkwardly, for although we were close, we were not great huggers and neither is a deckchair conducive for one. I found it easier to return to the subject of her leg.

"So, what does this mean?" I asked, pointing to the bandage.

"Three weeks out of action," she explained.

"Oh no!"

"Tedious, isn't it? To tell the truth, I'm just so relieved it's only my leg and not my sketching hand."

I would have thought a leg would be much worse, but you never knew with Olive.

"I'm so glad you're back, darling. Could you get me some apples?"

"You're hungry?" I felt a sudden fury at our colleagues: *they weren't feeding her?* I should have been here. *I* would have taken care of her.

Pointing at her notebook, she laughed.

"I need something scrumptious to draw."

CHAPTER TWENTY-FIVE

1940—Now

Pearl's mother is to visit. She and some other parents are coming up from London on the train. I don't like to tell Pearl until it is definite because we have had false alarms before, but Pearl hears everything at school anyway. She is so talkative the Friday before. She can't wait to show her mum around. She doesn't know whether to wear her newer clothes or her London clothes. I can see the dilemma.

The plan is that the mothers, and some fathers, will spend the afternoon in the village hall. There will be a light lunch there—all lunches are light nowadays, and made by us WAVs, of course. I'm off the hook for the piano, thank goodness, because the vicar will bring in his gramophone. We've all gone crazy for Glenn Miller's "In the Mood." We listen to it five, six times in a row.

Saturday morning arrives and it's bucketing down. *What a day for a trip*, I think as the rain batters at the window. Pearl springs awake next to me, big grin on her face. She doesn't care a jot about the weather, she is going to see her mother.

Don't be jealous, I tell myself.

"Today is the day!" she chirrups.

"Let's get you ready, darling."

*

We're doing cheese sandwiches and egg this time. The eggs are powdered so we add curry powder to them. Mrs. Dean is too heavy-handed, though, and the ones she does end up so spicy, they'll blast you off to Mars. Last year, Mrs. Burton—with great foresight—dehydrated lots of apple rings which we have turned into a large and tasty apple cake.

At the village hall, Farmer Jones's wife looks happier than ever with her Nathan, bronzed from his outdoor life, in a crisp white shirt, on her arm. Mrs. Dean has her boy, who is best friends with Keith, the butcher's boy. Mrs. Cope is not here. Mrs. Burton told me that whenever the poor boy she took in complained, he was put in the understairs cupboard. Poor mite. They sent him elsewhere.

We wait and wait, and then, just after twelve, the Londoners pour in, no doubt glad to be out of the rain. Pearl is one of the first to shout out: "Mummy, Mummy!" Pearl's mother has dark hair, dark, wary eyes, rosy cheeks and the plumpest lips I have ever seen: she looks like she's been punched in the mouth, yet the effect is awfully pretty. She is carrying a large baby and holding the hand of a little boy. At first, I don't see much resemblance to Pearl but, perhaps, there is something in the sloping shoulders, in the slender legs in black stockings when everyone else is wearing tan. I think, *She sings in a public house,* and then tell myself to put it right out of my snobby head.

Pearl charges over so fast, I fear she might bowl her mother over.

I walk to them both slowly, aware of each step. Pearl's mother wrinkles her nose at the babies and says apologetically: "I had to bring them, sorry."

Pearl clings tightly to her. *This woman has three children,* I think to myself. *Three!* And she is so young and attractive. She makes me feel... elderly.

We smile at each other. *So,* I think, *so.* I feel like someone has joined up all the dots. I want to be a person who is good with children, so I squat down beside the older child. "How do you do?"

I ask. A pumpkin-shaped thing with dark eyes and dark hair, he has two streaks of grime under his nose.

"Want toilet," he says.

Pearl's mother says: "This is Max, this is Leo, and I'm Mrs. Posner. Please call me Eleanor." We shake hands. Her palms are surprisingly cool.

"Eleanor? That's not a Jewish name," I say.

She stares at me. I realize belatedly this isn't a great thing to begin with.

She squints at me. "It is my name. Pearl, stop squeezing Max."

I want to tell her, *I have several Jewish friends*, but I have heard Mr. Pilkington say that before, and I fear this will make it worse.

Anyway, it's not true. I don't have a single Jewish friend.

The new baby is cute, except for a peculiar bald patch at the back of his head that reminds me of medieval monks.

She is still staring at me, weighing me up, judging me, analyzing me, and eventually she remarks, "Pearl told me you were beautiful."

"Pearl is very kind," I say. Pearl gives me her *shut-up* face.

"Is your husband here?"

Pearl answers for me. "He's never here, Mummy. He lives in the bottom of the garden. In a shed."

Eleanor gives me a quizzical look. I give a hearty laugh. *Aren't children hilarious?* "How funny, Pearl. No, he doesn't live in the shed or the garden. He's not—" I look around, hoping no one is listening—"a gnome."

Eleanor is unaffected by this information anyway. She is still studying my face. She puts her hand up as though she wants to make a point in class, then lowers it, embarrassed.

"You know, I'm sure I know you."

"I don't think so."

"Your face is familiar. Have you ever been to the East End? Whitechapel? Stepney?"

The Dog and Duck?

"Never in my life," I say firmly. She recoils slightly, as though sensing my revulsion.

"I need to change him," she says curtly, and I hasten to tell Pearl to show them to the bathroom. I expect Pearl to stay with her there, but she doesn't. She comes back and stands next to me; her face is unreadable. I think suddenly, *She is torn, poor girl; she feels like King Solomon having to choose between mother and host mother*, and I say, "Go and help Mummy, there's a dear."

Keith's London mother is just as lively as he is. She throws a ball to him and he heads it back to her to do again and again.

"Sorry, I can't help myself!" Keith's mother calls out. She is wearing trousers, an energetic woman who is full of beans. The ball goes flying toward the table but with some excellent footwork, she gets it back.

"Control, Keith! Have you forgotten everything I taught you?"

Mrs. Beedle, the butcher's wife, draws her lips into a tense smile. I can't help thinking it probably mirrors my own.

We all sit down at the trestle tables that we covered earlier with long white tablecloths. There is more bunting, more even than before. I count a hundred Union Jacks in ten rows across the beams. It looks a treat but the hall smells damper than usual.

Pearl sits between Eleanor and me. The baby sits on Eleanor's knee, the older boy on the other side of her. He kicks the table legs, making the table and its cloth shake. I think Eleanor knows this but has decided to ignore it, so I shall too. It's hard to know my place, especially when I know how Mrs. Dean slaved over the decoration. Across from us, Nathan's mother and father are hugging him. Both his parents are short and rounded and it amuses me to see Nathan have to stoop to cuddle them. He looks very happy.

"That's my boy!" Nathan's father keeps calling out and slapping him on the shoulder. Nathan says, "Shhh, Dad," and his father shouts, "I want the whole world to know how proud I am of you!"

Farmer Jones and his wife don't know where to put themselves. "You've not still got that silly flannel, have you?" Eleanor says suddenly to Pearl.

Pearl nods, flushing. Eleanor shakes her pretty head at me disapprovingly. I squeeze Pearl's knee, say nothing.

Once we've all sat and even Keith and his footballing mother have stopped still, the deputy mayor taps his glass with a spoon and we all hush. He starts his speech. You'd think that Hinckley, Leicestershire, was the only place in the world accepting evacuees from the way he talks about us. It's important to have some *civic pride*, as he calls it. "We're a town with a big heart," he says.

"And a big head," mutters Mr. Shaw subversively.

The sandwiches, the C's of cheese and curry, are all gone. No one is blasted to Mars. The apple cake is a great success; I see Mrs. Burton standing beyond the hatch in the kitchen and she returns my sly wave. It's strange to be on the in, and not on the out.

Eleanor Posner is a neat eater and unlike Pearl, she eats all her crusts. She takes the larger of the two slices of apple cake I offer her.

"Ravenous," she says, "haven't eaten since yesterday. Do excuse me."

"Go ahead," I say. I admire her honesty.

The gramophone is on. A few of the children are playing marbles under a table, but some of the girls can't help but spin around to "Chattanooga Choo Choo." Some of the parents have pulled up chairs to chat. I see the London mother of one of the girls who, Mrs. Burton has told me, lost her husband and youngest son in the Woolwich bombings. She is crying silently as she watches the dance.

The deputy mayor likes the look of Mrs. Eleanor Posner. I thought he might. He stands beside her, fiddling with his gold cufflinks, fiddling with his expensive blazer, and spends a while gazing down at her exotic red lips. I hear him telling her that we are all in the same boat. Eleanor doesn't look *entirely* convinced.

Then he taps his glass again and Eleanor looks away, quietly amused. This time, he announces that in twenty minutes there will be a demonstration of country dancing.

"The children have got awfully good at the do-si-do," he says. "Our heritage, our values…"

Pearl's lip curls; she is not awfully good at country dancing. As the deputy mayor drones on, Pearl's mother gently, but somehow with great authority, rests her dainty fingers on my arm.

She says, "I say, would it be awfully off, would it be a gross infringement if…I would dearly like to see where Pearl is living so I can *imagine* how she lives, you see?"

Pearl is delighted but I think, *This isn't the plan.*

"What about the country dancing?" I ask and they both burst out laughing. Eleanor lifts her mouth to my ear and whispers conspiratorially, "I don't think the do-si-do is Pearl's thing." I take a look out of the windows, about to say something else, but Eleanor gets it in before I do. "I think the rain has stopped."

Edmund *is* out, thank God. Pearl wasn't wrong about him, however much it displeases me to hear it out loud.

Eleanor eyes the kitchen and nods at the pictures Pearl has done that I tacked up over the counter only this morning. *Other than that, there isn't much sign of life here*, I think. I am almost ashamed at how tidy it is. I am tempted to put on the wireless to make some noise, but that seems a peculiar thing to do.

"Do you want to show Mummy your room?"

Pearl nods delightedly. They troop upstairs together, Eleanor with the new baby in her arms, alarmingly, leaving me with the bigger child in the kitchen.

The little boy—is it Max or Leo?—crawls under the table. He just sits there, sulkily.

"You can go upstairs if you like," I say, although I don't know if he can do stairs. I don't know if he can understand me either. I feel like I'm talking a foreign language. His lower lip juts out. I think of Mrs. Burton's box of tricks, but it is upstairs with Pearl and her mother and I have an inkling they don't want to be disturbed.

I have an idea: I get the old coppers I keep in a jug on the windowsill. I say to him, "They can be an army...if you want." I need only say this once. He is delighted and grabs at several of them with his chunky fists. I sit under the table with him; I just about fit under there. I imagine he's used to it, sheltering from the bombs.

"These are Nazis and these are the British," I say, lining up coins in two neat rows.

"I kill them," he snarls. He scrabbles his hand through my efforts. He looks very pleased with himself, so I forgive him.

"That's it." I stack them up into towers this time. Maybe he will prefer that.

"This is a fort," I say. "You do a castle..."

I go to collect some more coins, because this is fun, this is working, I am entertaining the boy, but when I turn back, I see his face is pinky-white and his eyes are suddenly huge. His arms are going like he is a puppet pulled by strings.

"What is it, Max? Tell Aunty Vivienne."

Aunty Vivienne? He probably has no idea who that is.

He is coughing and spluttering. He can't speak; I'm not sure, but I don't know if he can breathe.

...He can't have, can he?

"Where did you put the coin, Max? MAX?"

He is turning redder and redder. He is red and round. His eyes are rolling back. Tears come down his chubby, heated cheeks.

I slap him hard on the back, once, twice, three times. Nothing happens. Did he put a coin in his mouth or am I whacking him needlessly: "Eleanor?" I say, but not loudly enough to be heard; I am too timid, too confused. *God no.*

One more strike, I do it hard and fast, and to my horror and relief a coin flies out, then does a show-offy spin in the middle of the kitchen floor.

Thank the Lord.

Max coughs and coughs and coughs. I sweep up all the coins with my arm and brush the evidence away.

After about ten minutes, they still haven't come down. Perhaps Pearl is telling Eleanor that she hates it here with me. I feel humiliated. *She wouldn't say that, would she?* I remember that night that war was declared. *"Mummy said just a few days!"*

I trudge up the stairs, holding Max's wet hands. I feel friendlier toward him now, even though he has returned to his earlier unimpressed-with-me state.

Eleanor is standing in the room, staring at Olive's picture. She really is a beautiful woman and I imagine, even if she sings like a yowling cat, she must get a lot of tips in the Dog and Duck.

Pearl is sitting on the bed, with the new baby wrapped in a blanket. His eyes are closed and his mouth wide open.

Eleanor doesn't turn away from the picture when I come in. She says, "*This* is how I know you."

"The picture?"

She nods. "Not this one though."

Now she turns to survey me.

"You don't look very different. Remarkable."

I laugh with nerves. I don't know what she can mean. She takes Max, who seems entirely unaffected by the coin incident—thank goodness he doesn't speak much—and rocks him to her.

"I would have recognized you anywhere."

CHAPTER TWENTY-SIX

1916—Then

Since Olive's leg had temporarily put her out of action, I was paired with Daisy—Daisy who liked to sing tunelessly and swore like a fishwife despite claiming she was a distant relative of Princess Mary! She was a strapping lass, twice the size of Olive, and twice as loud. Every week, she declared she had sworn off men but then she was always mooning after a stretcher-bearer, doctor or patient or another.

Olive laughed when she heard. "I can't believe they've put you two together." Neither could I. Enid, Agnes or even Dorothy would have been a better match. Daisy hated driving in the dark and I hated driving in the rain, so I said I'd do the dark, she could do the rain.

It didn't rain once in the entire two weeks we were together. That was when I started smoking in earnest. One of the doctors told me it was good for stress relief.

The day before Olive was due to start her shifts again, I took her out for a short drive. We parked up near a railway station, then walked out to a field, where we ate a picnic of tinned peaches and crackers and I relieved my stress, cigarette after cigarette.

Olive and I were stretched out on the long grass, watching the clouds move. We were playing, "What can you see in the clouds?," which was a game we used to play with Richard when we were young. Olive could always see old men with cigars, young girls in flamenco dresses, unicorns or a man doing a running race in profile. Richard could see cricket lawns and rugby balls or a face. Compared to theirs, mine were always so mundane:

"A tree, that one looks like a tree, Olive!"

She sat up abruptly. "There, that looks like a plane."

Such a rare thing to see a plane! I had only seen one three or four times in my life, and each time I had been overwhelmed by incredulity that it was managing to stay up there. This was definitely a plane, but it was making a buzz, a hum, of unnatural noises: it was a struggling plane. A wing on fire, *actual fire*. Was it a British plane or a German trick, a deceit? Olive almost laughed with surprise. She shook grass out of her hair. Transfixed, we stared skywards.

It took a few moments to realize we had to move—we had to move fast. The airplane was on its final descent, clumsily; someone was trying, someone was steering it. I felt the draft as it whooshed above us, and *down, down*. But Olive was glued to the spot. I can remember thinking, "Everything's up in the air" as I dragged her arm and pulled her twenty yards or so into the trees. It felt like the longest distance.

"Wait," I commanded her fiercely. "Do *not* move, do you hear? Wait."

And the plane was down now and I was running toward it, praying Olive was not behind me. The leg rendered her useless but mostly, I had a responsibility to our father to keep her safe.

I was scared about what I'd find, but I didn't hesitate.

Pilot, smashed windshield—he'd been shot in the shoulder and made it back from goodness knows where.

The man behind him was dead.

I reached in and tried to free the pilot. He *was* British; it was not a trick. He cried out. "I'm stuck, I'm stuck, I'm stuck!"

His eyes set on mine and a sudden lightning went through me.

"Leave me!" he yelled. "Go. GET AWAY NOW. I order you, Nurse."

I was all fat fingers, a thousand useless thumbs and clumsy hands— *don't paint them, Olive*—I was clicking at a buckle, clicking at a harness, *it's stuck, he's right…*

He was pushing me off, shouting that the plane would explode. I ignored him. The belt was clicking. I juggered and jiggled, and juddered and juggled and fumbled, and *pulled*, and I heaved myself in, bit the frayed rope in desperation.

"Save yourself…"

"NO."

And finally, he was undone but he still didn't move. He was motionless, frozen, still stuck, and I was grabbing at his uniform, frantically, at all his limbs, his parts, his anything, trying to free him from this tight seat, because if we took too long—never mind the plane exploding—I knew Olive would be coming toward us.

And then I had him, I had him. He was out, and I clutched my arm round him. I couldn't lift him. I was telling him to run but his legs were like jelly, sopping jelly legs—half pulling, half shoving him toward the wood.

I pushed him to the trees—that extra falling, frightening feeling— where Olive was standing, her hands over her wide-open mouth in a silent scream.

Do I go back to get the dead man? Save the body for his family? I knew what a difference a body made but in those two namby-pamby seconds, the wishy-washy hesitation, my question was answered by that feared boom, as the flames licked the petrol tank: it was all over.

We were surrounded by people. I didn't know where they'd come from at first, but then I saw two ambulances had pulled up nearby. They must have followed the plane's descent. Olive was right in front of me, thumping my arm. "You were amazing, Vivi, amazing." I couldn't catch my breath. I thought of the man on fire trapped in there and I felt that I was as far from amazing as was possible to be.

Noise of explosions, people shoving and shouting. And throat-constricting smoke.

The survivor was put in our ambulance. *Who was doing it? I wanted to be with him.* Olive was peering at me.

"Vi, you need to drink something."

A rough gray blanket was wrapped round me. Someone was saying I was in shock. "I'm not in shock," I said, surprising myself with how loudly I spoke. "How is he?"

"Go and sit over there," one of the men said, ordering me back to the trees.

I ignored him and instead crept into the back of our ambulance. You couldn't keep me away from him. As someone—a doctor?—was giving him a going-over, I waited breathlessly. He too was wrapped in a blanket; we were dressed the same, like subdued twin children. He raised his eyes to me, smiling weakly.

"It's you."

"It's me."

"You're the one who saved my life."

"I'm so sorry about the other man."

It wasn't a doctor, it was another ambulance driver. He squinted dispassionately from me to him. Then he said to me: "We're expecting several injured in on the next train. Could you wait for them?"

"Wait?" I felt discombobulated. "How long for?"

"We'll get them out to you quick as we can."

I looked over at the poor pilot and his wounded arm. "We need to get him to the hospital."

"Won't be too long. As you're already here, it'll be a good help."

"But he should be seen..."

The pilot shrugged, rubbed his cheek. "It's all right with me," he said, his eyes lowered. "I'll last."

Olive poked her head into the back of the ambulance. She asked if I wouldn't mind if she went and rested up front for a bit. Her ankle was still giving her gip. I said fine—we were being made to wait for more casualties anyway.

"He's all yours," the driver said to me as he jumped down.

After all the shouting, the frantic running, the flames and the explosions, it was just me and him in the quiet. He was shivering, and I was shivering. We smiled at each other; it was like an expression of recognition somehow. I poured him some water without him asking and he gulped it down greedily. Then he ran it all over his face, and he rubbed his cheeks, his nose, his lips. All the grime that had been there disappeared, and I could see him properly. It was like when you clean a window that has been all smeary. He was nothing like...he was nothing like anyone I'd met before. We couldn't stop staring at each other.

Olive shouted back from the front of the truck. "Let me know if you need me, Vivi!"

"I'm fine!" I called back. I turned to him again.

"I'm so sorry about your copilot. You must be devastated."

He twisted his hands, then looked at me.

"Can I tell you something? We didn't get on at all. Not that I'm glad he died or anything like that, but..." He stared into space. "Don't feel sorry for me."

"I don't."

"I'm a terrible person," he said eventually. "I'm sorry, I shouldn't have said anything."

"No, no," I said, "you're being honest." I racked my brain to try to change the subject to safer topics. "So, do you have any brothers?"

"Two *and* a baby sister," he said proudly. "My poor mother."

Him and me. Me and him. We talked for two hours while we waited. Life stories shared. I didn't know my own life story until

I heard it coming out my mouth to him. How sad it was that my mother had died. How lucky though to have a nice Aunt Cecily. How terrible it was that Cousin Richard had died. How lucky I was to be so close to my sister. She was an artist and I was a... well, I played piano and worked for my father and here I was.

"Here you are," he repeated incredulously. "And I'm very glad you're here."

He was a tailor before the war. A *tailor*! He loved art and music and writing too. *If the war hadn't happened, you know.* He could have gone to night school. Maybe university. Who knows?

He had dark curly hair, even teeth and a smile that lit up the back of our dingy ambulance.

He had cigarettes in his top pocket. I said he could have mine, but he said he couldn't take anything else from me. I got out the packet for him, because his arm hurt. He asked me for a light, I leaned over with my match. I had to cup the flame to keep it from being extinguished by the wind. The curtains behind us and the driving area opened, and Olive was there. Her dark eyes were on me, staring at us both. A look that contained something, I didn't know what exactly... not concern, not pleasure or displeasure exactly, but something I hadn't seen before.

She narrowed her eyes, then looked away again.

He said he wasn't in pain, but he must have been. I told him that if he wanted to sleep, *don't mind me*, but he said he felt too wound up. I understood that. He said he might just close his eyes, but I had such a beautiful voice, would I mind talking to him while he did? I had this wild thought that he had dropped from the sky expressly for me.

Not long after that, there was the rumbling sound of a train coming in and then Olive was back at the gap, murmuring that they were coming.

The stirring outside turned into a commotion. The new load arrived. Two men on stretchers, one young lad on foot. And another on someone's back. They'd already been checked over. They were loaded up and then some doctor patted the side of the van like it was a horse, and said, "Off you go, ladies."

Olive sat next to me, but I found myself longing for silence, too shy even to say anything to her. I had never felt like this with Edmund. In Edith's *Tatler* magazine, they were always talking about "A bolt from the blue." People kept getting hit by them when they least expected. Edith laughed that they were more destructive than bombs.

When we were back at Lamarck, Olive and I unloaded our three men. The pilot was asleep. I whispered that I would be in to see him tomorrow but although he mumbled my name, I don't know if he heard.

As we changed for bed, Olive said she had never seen anything so picturesque as the two of us in the back of the ambulance. She had been staring for ages, *didn't I realize she was there?*

I said I hadn't.

"His name is Sam," I told her. I suddenly wanted to talk about him. I could have talked about him endlessly. "Sam Isaac."

She smiled at me triumphantly. "I've never seen you like this over *anyone*, Vivi!"

I didn't ask what she meant.

The next day, I didn't wake until near midday. For a moment, I was soaked in a feeling of tranquility, then I remembered the day before and my emotions churned. Olive was already awake, sat up, sketchbook resting on her knees.

"You should have woken me!"

"You were so peaceful there, sleeping beauty," she said before returning to her paper. Her legs were bare and her toes were sticking out, just like back at home. Olive never seemed to feel the cold.

I thought of my conversations with the pilot, Sam. *Would he remember the things he told me? The things I told him?* Perhaps he was delirious all along. Perhaps I had dreamed it all.

"What are you drawing, O?"

"New picture," she said, but she rolled back the paper deliberately, so I couldn't see it, then said we should go and get breakfast.

In the canteen, Enid and Agnes had just arrived back from leave and were distributing chocolate. I could hardly believe only two weeks had passed since I'd seen them. So much had happened. When they saw Olive, they called out, "Bad luck, O, shame about the ankle," and when they saw me, they called out "Congratulations!" and I thought that was unusual: we help people all the time, maybe not out of burning planes, but still. Then Enid passed me a card:

Congratulations on your engagement! Don't forget to invite us to your wedding!

All the FANYs had signed it.

They were talking about Edmund. Edmund Lowe. My fiancé.

I could feel Olive's eyes drilling into me.

CHAPTER TWENTY-SEVEN

1940—Now

"It is *you*, isn't it?" Pearl's mother sits on Pearl's bed, holding the framed picture on her knees. I feel like bursting into tears. It must be the stress of the Max incident. *What on earth was I thinking, giving copper pennies to a toddler?*

"I... Maybe. I don't know. What picture?"

"The one of you. You're in the back of an ambulance—you're holding a flame."

I breathe.

"How do you know it?" I need to sit. I place myself on the bed next to her.

"I saw it once," she says, mystified, as though the question is ridiculous.

"Yes," I say. "But what? I mean... how?"

I have so many questions, I don't know where to begin.

She bites her lip, puts the baby on her other knee. He shakes his scrunchy little fist at me. His arms look as though elastic bands have been applied to the creases.

"Do you know Sam then?" I whisper. Is *that* what she means? She knows Sam. *My* Sam.

"Yes."

I can feel my insides drop. The baby clutches his knuckles to his mouth. He's got no control over his hands.

"How?" I murmur.

Baby on hip, Eleanor Posner goes over to the wall and replaces the picture back on its hook. It's lopsided, like a ship on high seas with its bow pointing to the ocean floor, but I don't care about that, not now. I wait, my heart beating out of its cage, thumping a tune. *Don't be his wife, don't be his wife.*

"Sam's my big brother."

CHAPTER TWENTY-EIGHT

After all the noise and disruption of the plane crash, there followed a quiet few days. A lull in activity. "The Bosch is licking his wounds," Daisy said. And I, who usually hated a lull, because it meant doing nothing, was delighted, because this lull meant I could visit the pilot in peace.

I did leave him for one day. I knew he'd have surgery on the arm, but I also felt shy and didn't know what the right thing was. I could hardly wait to see him. He was in a cramped ward of thirty, maybe forty men—we'd had a big delivery of Australian wounded—but he had the end bed and, by some trickery, no one was in the next one. In this busy place it felt private.

"You came!" he said, his eyes alight.

As we talked, I felt the same ease, the same connection to him as I had done in the back of the ambulance. *It's just because you saved him*, I told myself. *It's because you are invested in keeping him safe. That's war. It's probably what Christopher meant by "intensity."* I told myself: *Of course, I mustn't confuse this with the far deeper and far more permanent feelings I have for Edmund.*

When Olive was working on something, she became obsessed. And the next morning, and the morning after that, she was obsessed. I spotted that dangerous glint in her eye. She was devoted, single-minded. Sometimes, she threw her pencil across the room.

"Gah, the proportions aren't right!" Sometimes, I would wake up and she would be wide-eyed, sketchbook on her knees, drawing wildly, chewing her pencil.

"Don't interrupt me," she would say as soon as she saw I was awake. Sometimes I would wonder if she was coming down with some kind of sickness.

"I won't!" I would reply, disgruntled. I would pull on my uniform while she sketched up to the very last minute.

"You won't like this one," she said. I laughed. Olive could be so silly sometimes. With my uniform on, I got back down under the covers. We still had twenty more minutes until breakfast.

"Why won't I like it?"

"You just won't."

And then she got out her paints, and once she opened them, the room smelled of oil.

I didn't visit Sam the next morning. Nor the next afternoon, since Olive and I unexpectedly had to transport some cheery boys to the port. The next day, though, I went. I told myself, *I owe him a quick visit, that's all. What's the harm?* But he wasn't there and I filled up with this horrible panic that he might have died alone of an infection and no one had told me. But then I found the ward sister and she laughed: he had only gone outside to watch badminton.

Sam was sitting in the sunshine outside one side of the hospital, where we played. As I approached, I watched his kind, worn face. It seemed to me he looked much older than his twenty-six years. When he saw me, he gave me a broad grin and waved with his healthy arm. I walked over, feeling that curious mix of self-consciousness and delight he evoked in me. At the same time, I saw Olive limping out with her deckchair, shading her eyes against the sun.

Sam's dark eyes were on me. "Are you going to play?"

"No," I said but then Agnes called for me to join her three. "Please, Vivi!" they called. "We're short."

"Go on," said Sam. "It looks fun."

So, I played with Agnes, a doctor and a patient who had just a stump for his left arm, but was full of determination. We exchanged volleys. Neither Olive nor I were interested in sports, but I wasn't bad when I put my mind to it. The four of us were evenly matched. The doctor whacked it, and Agnes yelped: "Out!"

The shuttlecock had fallen next to Olive. As I went to pick it up, Olive said in a low voice: "Your pilot hasn't taken his eyes off you."

I gave a small shrug, pretending I was unaware, or I didn't care— I'm not sure which.

"I'm engaged to Edmund, O."

Saying the words aloud made them feel more real.

Olive picked up her chair and placed it to the side of Sam's. I knew they were discussing me. I pretended to myself that I didn't care what they were saying, but I was desperate to hear what it was. Olive clapped when I returned a tricky shot. I blushed beet red but kept on playing.

Daisy and Enid were both looking at me from the side and talking behind their hands. When the game was over—Agnes and I just about won—I went to get water and Daisy smirked at me. She gestured toward Olive and Sam, still deep in conversation.

"*Oy vey*," she said strangely. "I didn't think *he* would be your sister's type?"

I stared back challengingly. "This is the gentleman who was in the flying accident the other day. He is not Olive's *type*, nor mine, we merely feel responsible for him."

They nodded, and I felt proud of my dignified response. *That made sense*, I thought.

*

Quiet evenings, I played piano in the hospital canteen. "Keep the Home Fires Burning" was always one of the most requested. Sam sat near me at the piano with Olive.

"Our friend wrote the lyrics," said Olive, as usual.

"Do you have to tell *everyone*?" I asked, laughing.

Olive was deadly serious when she replied, "Yes, otherwise it will be forgotten. Women are always being written out of history."

Diplomatically, Sam said, "It's a beautiful song... I love the idea of having someone waiting back home."

"You don't have anyone waiting for you, then?" Olive asked. She could be such a busybody.

He didn't look up. "Not really."

"Olive won't admit she is in love with the son of the *woman* who wrote 'Keep the Home Fires Burning,'" I interrupted. Their conversation was making my stomach flutter.

"Not a girlfriend or a wife?" asked Olive, ignoring me.

I grimaced at her. Sam smiled to himself. "No wife or girlfriend. I'd like someone special but I'm waiting for the right one."

The next few days, there was a big push further along the line and many casualties. Badminton and sing-alongs were abandoned. We worked and we slept, with little time even for eating. While the days were warm, at night the temperatures plummeted unseasonably. One night I drove for over twelve hours straight in the sleet and I had run out of cigarettes after three hours. You couldn't tell if it was thunder overhead or the roar of the guns. I think it was both. *Acrid smell. Dying men. Petrol and blood.* When I arrived back, blue-lipped, fingers rendered useless by cold, I was shaking so much I thought I'd never warm up. But of course, this was nothing to what our poor boys out in the battlefields were going through.

*

It's silly, but I thought Sam might be annoyed that I hadn't visited for a while, but when I next saw him in his ward, he said he'd heard it had been rough and was I still fine?

"Always fine," I said, smiling. It occurred to me that was exactly how I felt when I was with him.

He was in bed writing a letter, leaning over a pocket-sized book. "What's that?"

He blushed. "Elizabeth Barrett Browning. Poetry is my escape." He grinned at me: "It's not quite 'Keep the Home Fires Burning,' but it's not bad."

I smiled at his kind eyes. "I'd like to read some."

"Do."

"Carry on with your writing," I told him. "I'm happy watching."

He explained that he was writing to his brother but he was nearly done. I leaned over to see rows and rows of equisitely written words. It was so tidy, so *lovely*, it took my breath away. I followed the consistent swirls on the page, watched the gorgeous progress of his pen. It's funny—beautiful handwriting was not something I had particularly valued before that moment.

I leaned in. "*G-d*? Why have you written that?"

"That's what some Jewish people do. It's so God is not represented on earth."

"Really?" I hadn't heard that before. "But why have *you* done it, Sam?"

He screwed up his eyes. "Why do you think?"

I was completely clueless. "I don't know."

"Because *I'm* Jewish, Vivi."

My belly contracted. I thought of what Mrs. Lowe used to say about them, what Father said, what *I* said. I looked at him askance: Sam was a *Christ-killer*?

"Really?" I wondered if this was a joke, some *ha-ha* concocted between him and Olive maybe, but then I thought of Daisy's comment, and even the driver's attitude that first night. It seemed to ring true. Plus, why would he lie?

"Uh huh."

"I've never met a Jew, uh, a Jewish person before," I admitted. I wondered where his curly sidelocks were. "What does it mean... I mean, to you?"

I felt silly but he reassured me. "Good question," he said thoughtfully. "This brother"—he waved his paper at me—"is religious. I'm not. For me, being Jewish is more of a cultural thing, I suppose. Shared history, community, values, food even." He laughed to himself, but then looked pained. "Things are very difficult for the Jewish people. When times are hard, those who are different are often blamed or scapegoated. We seem always to be at hand for that."

We sat in silence for a minute or so.

"What about your family, Vivi?" he said. "You're an Englishwoman through and through?"

"Yes," I said. Then, remembering, I said, "Actually, my father used to say we Mudie-Cookes may have Spanish blood a long way back... that would account for my darker skin."

Sam bites his lip. "You do have extraordinary skin."

"Thank you."

"And that's your surname, is it? Mudie-Cooke? I like it."

I snorted. "I used to secretly think Olive was muddy, I was the cook."

"You're good at cooking as well as rescuing pilots in peril? Is there no end to your talents?"

I laughed. "Only compared to O. She would make King Alfred look like an expert pie-maker!"

"Come here," he said suddenly, and even though we were close already, I leaned further toward him and he pulled himself up and kissed me. It took me by surprise but at the same time it seemed a perfectly natural and unshocking progression.

"Sam?" I hesitated, but then I kissed him back. My questions faded away. My answers were all here. I felt the ground beneath me shift.

*

Some weekends, touring drama groups came from England to cheer up the patients. I expected to see Walter, Johnny or David—sorry, Ivor Novello—turn up one evening with a pile of ukuleles or wigs. (That was unlikely: Walter was in Cheshire, Johnny was in Gallipoli, Ivor was in America, Frank and Clive were in Belgium and no one knew where Uilleam Chisholm had got to.)

The Friday night of "the kiss," a group came to perform a comedy, *Chu Chin Chow*, which had been a hit show at His Majesty's Theatre in London. I asked Sam if he wanted to go. He said, hmm, he had several other invitations to consider... He was joking: *He would be delighted to come.*

At seven that evening, I went to the canteen to look for him. The nurses had rearranged beds and there were wheelchairs, and some of the walking wounded at the front. Sam was on his own toward the back.

Olive had been in our hut before I left, so unfortunately, I wasn't able to dwell before the mirror as long as I would have liked to. It's silly, but I could tell from Sam's eyes that he approved. I thought of our kiss earlier. I was yearning for the chance to repeat it. After the show, I decided, we could go outside under the pretext of a cigarette.

I was desperately not thinking about Edmund, but had an intuition that all would be well there. The bridges that lay between us were endless after all and it seemed to me evident that Edmund and I had grown apart. I hadn't had a letter from him since I returned, and I figured that anyone who wanted to wait until the war had ended to marry was not *entirely* keen.

I read Sam the story of the play.

In Baghdad, the bandit chief disguises himself as a Chinese merchant, Chu Chin Chow, to gain access to the palace. But his identity is revealed by his slave, who pours boiling oil on him and then finishes the job by stabbing him to death.

"That sounds cheery," Sam commented. Giggling, I read on.

The show in London was a lavish spectacle, scantily-clad slave girls and a chance to forget the Great War's trenches.

"Well, I'm certainly looking forward to it now," Sam said.
"I can't imagine there are scantily clad slave girls here."
"Maybe they will improvise," he snorted.

There *was* a scantily clad slave girl, but she was at least six feet tall and complete with luxurious beard and mustache. Sam laughed loudly. And when he laughed, I wanted to as well, and when only two, three minutes in, he took my hand, it felt like the most natural thing in the world. I flushed from my cheeks to my toes, and my heart was racing. What if anyone saw? What would they think? But I *couldn't* take my hand away. I couldn't. I wanted us to be joined. His fingers were locked in the spaces between mine, and mine found the spaces between his. *Is there a word for that space, a biological word for the dip between one finger and another? I should know about hands, I've analyzed them for long enough with Olive.* I knew about the ring, the middle, the little finger; I knew about the little one who went *wee wee wee* all the way home…

Olive was in the back of the ward during the interval, again scrutinizing me. She was helping distribute water.

"Enjoying the show?"

"It's interesting." She looked up at me with doe eyes. "There's a letter for you, back in our hut."

"Oh?"

"I think it's from Edmund's mother. I recognize the handwriting."

"Thank you, Olive."

Edmund's mother? What did she want with me? She'd never written to me before. I suddenly felt nervous.

"Aren't you going to get it?"

I thought, *Here is someone who knows how to take the shine off a lovely evening.*

"Not right now."

She raised her eyebrows at me.

"We've got twenty minutes before the second half."

"I *know*, Olive."

One of the actors came on to introduce the second half. He was wearing a bow-tie and I stared straight ahead at him as though my life depended on it. The curtains swung back, and I let out a wild laugh, I don't know why. I could not tell you what he said about the inhabitants of Elephant and Castle in London. I couldn't tell you what observation about the West End made the crowd roar. I couldn't tell you why a man came on wearing only a sheet. I could only tell you about the heat creeping over me, and how hard it was to breathe in there.

I just feel responsible for him, that's all.

When the actors were bowing for the finish, Daisy came over and I'm sure she noticed that Sam and I were holding hands. Under her gaze, I felt suddenly tearful, as though everything was breaking apart in front of my eyes. I detached my fingers from his and stood up. I'd never not opened a letter from England immediately before.

I hoped maybe Olive was confused and the letter was from Aunt Cecily or even Uncle Toby instead.

"I had better…"

"Of course," he said politely, his eyes on mine.

"You don't mind?"

"It's fine." *I* minded though. I wished we had gone out for a cigarette during the interval.

"Goodnight, Vivi. It's been wonderful."

I fled the ward, feeling his concerned eyes on me.

*

Dear Vivienne—or do you prefer to be called Vi?

I didn't get to tell you last month, but thank you, so much, for coming to England and for your subsequent cards. It didn't go unnoticed or unappreciated. You are a credit to your family.

Christopher is forever in our hearts.

Belated congratulations on your engagement to Edmund. We are very proud to welcome you to our family. I don't think I ever made a secret of it, but I have always wanted a daughter. And now, please—you, Olive and your dear father—you are part of us now.

Let us plan the wedding for as soon as possible. Please don't wait on our account. These are terrible dark times, but it does us good to have some brilliance to look forward to.

One small thing, Edmund begged me not to tell you—he doesn't want you to leave your post so soon after Christopher— but he is in a hospital in Sussex. Please don't panic, he is making an excellent recovery and we don't expect him to be here for much longer than a few weeks.

I will ensure that he writes.

Yours lovingly,
Mrs. Lowe—Evangeline

CHAPTER TWENTY-NINE

1940—Now

Pearl and Eleanor are waiting for me. It's time to go back to the village hall. I have come back upstairs under the pretext of tidying my hair. I have put on fresh lipstick. I am nearly running out of it, and goodness knows what I'll do after it goes—but this seems an occasion that warrants it. I feel like Sam is watching me. I rub in some rouge even though I am red enough. I am still sweating hot and cold. Trying to put a face on it. I had thought Pearl might be emotional today, but I didn't expect that *I* would be.

Eleanor pulls on her coat. Her heels are too high for our uneven and now puddled roads. Her stockings already have a tiny ladder over her calf. It draws the eye somehow. I still have four pairs left. *If I were a better person*, I think, *I would offer her a pair.*

This is Sam's baby sister.

I could ask Eleanor not to tell him. I could tell *her not to tell him. I could say we had a promise...*

What will I do if she tells him she's met me? What will he do?

We walk back to the village hall. Clippety-clop, her heels go. It's like walking with a horse. A truck passes, then a car slows down to ask directions. I try to help but my mind is not really on it.

I am desperate to ask more questions, but Eleanor talks about the London bombings and how they sleep crammed in the Underground, like sardines, and that feeling when you emerge from underground to see what has been destroyed and what hasn't.

"It's so quiet here. It must feel like the war is just a...a distant dream. You must be able to forget it's even happening."

"I served for three years in the Great War," I say quickly. "I don't forget easily."

"Of course," she replies gracefully. "I know you did. I didn't mean anything. I know you saved my brother's life."

Pearl gazes seriously from me to her mother. She says, "Mummy didn't get to meet the dogs."

Lightly, I say, "Next time," and she nods.

Pearl and her mother aren't too emotional in the hall. I think they already said their goodbyes back at home. Pearl is subdued with the baby and Max. She kisses the crowns of their heads.

We wave and wave, and Eleanor and my eyes lock, and I hope mine say, *I'll take good care of her*, which is part of what I'm thinking, but I'm also thinking, *Sam. What is she going to tell Sam?*

CHAPTER THIRTY

1916—Then

The last time I saw Sam Isaac was a gray-skied September morning, 1916. Men were piled in the back of our ambulance like rolls of carpet. Some of them were singing: *Pack up your troubles in your old kit bag.* I was driving, and Olive sat next to me, with her concerned expression: "Don't you want me to drive?" Her ankle still wasn't strong enough though, so it irritated me that she kept asking.

When we arrived at the port, I helped dismount those who needed help, and bade them farewell. Sam carried one man by piggyback to the gangplank even though it must have hurt his shoulder. Then, gruffly, he said he was heading over to the tea van. He didn't directly invite me but I followed him anyway, and when we were there, he bought himself and me a black coffee.

I had spent the last two days going over and over what to do. I had written him a brief note saying I regretted "giving him the wrong impression" and asked Olive to deliver it. She visited him often and was growing increasingly annoyed with me.

"It's because he's a Jew, isn't it?" she said one time.

"No," I said, hurt that she would think that of me. Maybe that was part of it, but it wasn't the *main* reason.

Olive looked unconvinced, but then she had never liked Edmund and sometimes, I think, she liked to imagine the worst of me. Maybe it made her feel better about herself?

But Edmund was in hospital now! This was enough to stop any girl in her tracks. My fiancé was poorly. But with what and why? I had read and reread the letter from his mother, but however many times I went over it, I could never find a clue as to what had happened—or how bad it was. The way his confinement had been perched on the letter's end, almost as an afterthought, surely suggested it couldn't be *too* serious. But then, if it *wasn't* serious, why had he been sent back to England? I didn't know a great deal about army protocol, but I knew they did not let their officers go off sick easily.

I had written to Edmund's mother immediately, but she had not yet replied. I wrote to Aunt Cecily but she knew nothing and was shocked to learn that he was in England at all.

Every month or so in Lamarck, I might transport a soldier with a wound in an unlikely place. Invariably not life-threatening, these were known as "Blighty wounds"—injuries self-inflicted to gain passage back home. It was perhaps mean of me, but Edmund's mother's phrasing seemed so opaque that my imagination was left to fill in the gaps. I pictured Edmund stuck in some trench on the Western Front, anticipating the dreadful going "Over the Top." Well, who could blame anyone for a little slip of a rifle?

If it *were* a Blighty wound, I knew that I wouldn't be expected to stand by him—no one could be expected to tie themselves to a coward. But what if it wasn't that: what if it were simply a case of appendicitis, a broken femur, a spell of the measles? You couldn't walk away from a promise for those.

Sam and I moved over to a bench where we could watch the ship—the ship he'd return on—be loaded up with its cargo of men with their rich variety of injuries. Men leaning on each other, men with stumps where their legs once were, men with bandages over their eyes, men being stretchered in.

It was such a commonplace view, but at the same time, you couldn't see it and think it was anything other than deeply shocking, absurd and wrong.

Sam must have been thinking along the same lines, because he said: "Look at Europe, tearing its young people apart. How we have let ourselves down. And for what?"

I nodded, thinking of the excitement in the streets in 1914. "I could never have dreamed war would be this ugly and people would hate each other so. What have we become?"

"Vi," he said quietly, and I knew, painfully, he was going to try again. "We could be different. We could...make it work. I know we can."

I shook my head, drained my cup.

"Please change your mind, Vivi," he said softly. "Give me a chance: love, marriage, children...together, there's no reason we couldn't make each other happy." Then, his voice trembling, he said, "I don't believe you feel about your fiancé the way you feel about me."

Yet still, I couldn't speak. Every part of me was crying out for him but I knew it couldn't be. I had decided my future many years back and I just couldn't shift myself from that path. Edmund and I were finally moving toward our goals: his being in hospital was not a mystery or another bridge to cross, it was simply a timely reminder of where my heart should be. I was the good sister, the kind cousin and the loyal person. I *would* take care of him.

"Don't write then," Sam said flatly. "Unless you change your mind."

"I won't," I replied.

"I won't get in touch either."

"That's for the best."

But then, I'm not sure how it happened, I was in Sam's arms, safe in his arms, and his lips were on mine and mine on his and I pulled his coat to be even closer to him. I had never been kissed like that before. Kissed so that the rest of the world ceased to exist. For a moment, I didn't know where I was. I just clung to him, his mouth joined to mine, and I felt an incredible whoosh of incredulity that I was capable of being so...so primal or animalistic. I had never seen myself as a passionate person before.

"Are you all right?"

"I'm fine," I whispered back. I wanted him to swallow me up, and he did, he kissed me again and again.

And then he let me go. He was walking away, hauling his bag, out toward the wooden gangway to be swallowed up by the ship. I couldn't let him go like that.

I cried out, "Sam!" and he looked back, shaking his head at me.

"I won't write," I repeated.

"Nor will I," he replied. And then the ship blew its whistle and he hurried away.

The sea was as gray as the sky. It was choppier than it had been for some time, and I felt sorry for the ship's passengers because it mightn't be a peaceful crossing. Already I regretted my promise to Sam and wished he might write; just the once would do, to let me know that he had arrived back on English soil safely. I drove slowly back to the hospital, straining to listen to the chirrup of the birds over the rattle of the engine and the clatter of the wheels. Olive knew better than to try to engage me in conversation.

I couldn't leave Edmund Lowe. Not now. You couldn't leave a sick soldier during a war, could you? What kind of monster would that make me?

Four days after Sam had gone, Olive called me into our hut. She was grinning widely, happier than I had seen her for some time.

"What do you think?"

She turned the picture she had been working on to face me.

She had done it. She had created the God-light: there was something about this piece that meant I couldn't look away. It was compelling. Even the hands were perfectly executed. I looked radiant, somehow, Madonna-like. There was patriotism, but there was realism too.

"Olive," I whispered. "What have you done?"

She laughed. "I think it's the best thing I've ever made."

I had always encouraged Olive to do art. Always. As a little girl, she used to draw on rough gray paper Father brought home from work, and then when she'd gone through those, she'd sketch on my textbooks. She defaced portraits of kings and queens with mustaches, beards and glasses; not only that, she would cover over the writing with pictures of her own—but I didn't mind.

I remember when her favorite subject matter was elephants, especially their ears like the number three; rabbits with cotton-fluff tails; fat toddlers with bottles. For a short while, when we were very small, I had the steadier and the less smudgy hand but soon her elephants outranked mine and I still didn't mind. I adored my little sister. I made up drawing competitions for her and let her sweep the board of prizes. *First, second, third and a billion runners-up!* I invented new categories she could enter: *Best Adult, Best Toddler, Best Elephant Ears, Best Dogs.* I taught her to treat her tools, her coloring pencils, then paints (and eventually, my books!) with respect. When she got upset about her failure to do realistic hands, I told her: "If you really can't do hands, even after you do plenty of practice, then maybe it's a sign to avoid them," which I took to be a great philosophy, not just of art but of life.

Even here in France, I had taken on some of her tasks—washing her clothes, care of the ambulance—just so she could have time to draw.

"I need thinking space," she often complained. Sometimes, she said she was creating even when she wasn't. "It's part of the process, Vi. It may look like I'm doing nothing, but actually, I'm fermenting ideas."

She *couldn't* say I didn't support her.

*

"Why would you do this, Olive?" I exclaimed, once I was over the shock. "You can't show this to anyone."

"What do you mean?" She gazed at me disbelievingly. "What on earth is wrong with it?"

"You can't. It's . . . you know what's wrong with it. I can't . . . look like that."

"You *did* look like that," she said, shaking her head at me. "You still do when I mention his name."

"No, I can't look like that, with . . . with a man who is not Edmund." *I shouldn't have to spell it out to her. What was wrong with her that she couldn't get what I was trying to say?* "I'm an engaged woman, Olive!"

Olive sighed. "You're engaged, not enslaved."

"What's that supposed to mean?"

"It means that I don't see the problem."

Olive could never, ever, see the problem.

My voice was shaky. "I have to put my future husband and his family first, not you or your art. You're going to have to get rid of it." This was the one time I had asked her to do something different. *The one time.*

If Edmund saw it, what would he see? If Edmund's parents saw it, what would they say?

You realize he's a Jew?

I always knew the Mudie-Cookes were no good.

"I worked extremely hard on this," Olive muttered.

We glared at each other. Finally, she sighed. "I'll make it look less like you, if it's that important to you!" When I said nothing, she added, "And I will make sure no one sees it. All right?"

I backed down too. "Thank you, O. Yes, that will probably do."

CHAPTER THIRTY-ONE

1940—Now

There is, of course, no word from Sam. I am a fool to think there would be. As though Eleanor would forget the bombs and devastation all around her, put her singing job at the Dog and Duck on hold, get babysitters for her small children and rush to tell him the news. "You'll never guess what! Remember that woman you met in the First War, the one who turned you down for her fiancé in hospital?" As if Sam would stop his job as a tailor, or whatever it was he was doing now. As if he would dash to Leicester to declare he has thought of me every single day...

What would be the point of him getting in touch anyway? I'm Mrs. Edmund Lowe now. Not Vivienne Mudie-Cooke.

I sit with the WVS group in Mrs. Burton's living room. Listening to their chatter, I feel a million miles away. We are all experts on foreign policy now. We have learned who is doing what and where, we know the names of shouty leaders, dictators in far-flung places, we know the names and colors of air forces and towns in Turkey and Malta.

Mrs. Burton is concerned. Not about the assembly line of wool and the assembly line of toys, which are running with a streamlined efficiency Mrs. Webster could only have dreamed about, nor about our tea van, which is out today with Mrs. Dean and Mrs. Beedle at the wheel, but about me.

She tries to get me on my own in the kitchen. I stare at the kitchen scales that her mother and grandmother used before her, and the silver cake slice that has given pleasure from so many thousands of cakes. I hear strains of bad news from the wireless in the other room. We wait for water to boil. She is gazing at me.

"What's happened, Vivi? You seem so out of sorts recently. Is it Mr. Lowe?"

I shake my head. *Not this time. Won't the kettle ever boil?*

"Is it Pearl?"

Mrs. Burton looks worried and distractedly offers me an empty biscuit tin. I pretend to take one, and she apologizes.

"You haven't been right since Pearl's mother visited. Did something happen?"

"The only thing that's wrong is that you keep asking me what's wrong," I say wryly. The tea takes forever to infuse, and we sit in silence, both gazing at the pot as though it holds all the world's secrets.

"You can talk to us. You're among friends here, Mrs. Lowe," says Mrs. Shaw when I head back into the room, tea cups balanced precariously on the tray, and everyone murmurs agreement. I am mortified. They've been discussing me, and it feels like they pity me. I can't bear that.

"Mrs. Burton is on her way!" I say brightly. "Who's for a brew?"

Churchill is on the wireless. Sometimes he reassures us, sometimes he puffs us up ready for the fight. Sometimes his speeches move me to choking, hot tears. We are going to get through this, like we did the last time, we the ones who've been through it before say. But I am frightened too. Fear is a constant background noise. I think I was less afraid last time, even when I was in the thick of it—that's the horrible thing about growing older. You know how precarious it all is.

What will we do if they invade? How bad might it get? We no longer fear parachutists dropping from the sky. It's goose-steps on the Dover coast that is our new nightmare.

"Will I have to wear a yellow star?" Pearl asks out of the blue when we are queuing for stamps in the post office.

"If you have to, I will too, and so will everyone else, love," I say. This is what the brave people did in Denmark to protect their Jewish friends and neighbors.

I try to imagine Edmund and his parents marching up to the village hall with the six-pointed yellow star on their coats to protect their Jewish friends and neighbors, and I think, *Oh God, it had better not come to that.*

The old woman in front of me turns round. She looks timid in an expensive-looking wool coat and she is wearing glasses, which don't seem to help for she is squinting madly at us. She smiles first at me and then at Pearl.

"That's right, chicky," she says encouragingly. "We all stand together. Don't you worry." She strokes Pearl's cheek while saying to me, "Your daughter is lovely."

"Evacuee," I say quickly.

"Of course," she says. She squints into my eyes. "Lucky you."

When it's my turn, I pass over our letters to post. One for *Eleanor Posner, 5A, Watney Street, London, England, The World, The Universe,* from Pearl. One for Mrs. Cecily Thompson from me. "Keep calm and carry on," Mr. Shaw says solemnly.

"Sorry, what?"

"It's from the new posters," he says. "Haven't you seen them, Mrs. Lowe? They're everywhere."

How could I not have noticed the new posters? Olive would have spotted them right from the off. She would have been disappointed at my narrow vision. Again.

CHAPTER THIRTY-TWO

1917—Then

Not long after our disagreement over the painting, Olive decided to go off on her own. She had long wanted to go to Italy, where the war was being bitterly fought in the mountains and civilians were being pushed from their homes in their thousands.

Olive's Italian was better than her French. She wasn't the best at driving—she would do anything to get out of it—but she was a wonderful linguist and a friend of a friend of a friend needed someone to help translate. In Italy, she would be helping to coordinate relief efforts there.

I watched as Olive pulled her suitcase from under the bed. She still walked with a slight limp but if I worried about it, she grew agitated. "Don't fuss, it's fine." It was another subject best avoided; we could have made a long list of them by now.

She took great care packing her art papers—I was always surprised how careful Olive could be, when she wanted—but then she rolled up her clothes and chucked them on top haphazardly. She still had her ridiculous hairy sheepskin coat and an array of frightful berets. I hovered nearby, wishing I could do something, but she wouldn't let me. I was frightened at being left alone out there, but also relieved in a way that she was going. I realized she hadn't been a part of the gang of Daisy, Enid, Agnes, Dorothy and me for a long while now, even before her accident.

"Do you want to come?" she asked, blowing her hair out of her eyes.

"I'm fine here at Lamarck," I said.

"Thought so."

I was still worried about the picture of Sam and me. She had titled it: *In an Ambulance: a VAD lighting a cigarette for a patient*. I told myself, *Don't be stupid, how would anyone know it's you?*

I thought of my initial reaction to "Keep the Home Fires Burning" or "'Til the Boys Come Home." I had had no idea how quickly an idea, a work of art, a song, can catch hold and become part of the national fabric of the time. It sounds ridiculous, melodramatic maybe, but I had an intuition that *In an Ambulance*... also had the potential to be that fabric too.

I had to ask Olive about it. "Did you change it then?"

"I said I would, didn't I?"

"Thank you. And what will you do with it now?"

"I got rid of it," she snapped.

I paused. I could never quite trust my sister.

"How, though? Have you sent it to Mrs. Ford?"

"This is not your business, Vivienne."

Despite our recent altercation, I wanted to get Olive a gift, a reminder that I loved her. In Calais town one afternoon, I had found a strange tiny shop selling pipes. Among them all, hanging from the walls like the pipes of a church organ, a slender silver pipe with a fine swirling engraving caught my eye. I told the gentleman at the counter that "*C'est pour mon fiancé*," blushing scarlet as I did. I didn't know how he would have reacted if I said it was for my sister. Some people have an aversion to seeing women with mannish things.

I gave it to her then, unwrapped because I could not find any good paper. It was a beautiful thing.

"I know you wanted one, Olive..."

Her eyes filled with tears. She hugged me tightly. "I'll think of you every time I smoke it."

CHAPTER THIRTY-THREE

1940—Now

One morning, there is a knocking at my front door at 6 a.m. I race down, with a presentiment of horror, but also half-afraid Edmund might wake and be put in a worse mood than normal.

It's Mrs. Burton, but my relief is short-lived. *Had I heard? Coventry had it terrible last night.* Coventry? I knew Coventry was where the not-often-seen Mr. Burton did his ARP.

"We need the van."

"Oh, yes, of course."

Her girls will give Pearl breakfast and take her to school. She says it all quickly. It tumbles from her mouth—the scheme, the plan. *She is a woman*, I think admiringly, *who thinks on her feet.*

I race up to dress, heart pumping. It's like the bad old days in France, winding up the ambulance ready for a rescue. Never knowing what grim horrors you'd find there. Whispering, I wake Pearl and instruct her to go straight next door when she's ready. She nods. Her hair is all wild, sleep in her eyes: "Next door...yes, yes, bye-bye, love you..."

"I love you too, Pearl."

We're off and there's nothing much on the road yet. I'm driving. I know I can do this. I've done this before.

"Any news from Mr. Burton?" I ask Mrs. Burton, nonchalantly, as though it's not the main thing on our minds.

"Not yet," she says cheerfully, but her lips are in two straight, stern lines.

The van is the fastest thing I've ever driven. We're at 40 mph and it doesn't mind, it would happily do more. It has a windscreen and wipers that you operate by hand—not that we need it; it's a beautiful November day. The moon is still in the blue sky. You wouldn't believe there had been a bombing.

The closer we get to Coventry, the more vehicles there are on the road; there are ambulances and police cars, and some routes are entirely blocked off. And in the city, we are met with destruction. Where buildings were, now only bricks and rubble lie. I can't look at my friend. She speaks with a policeman and he directs her to a good place to set up. He says he'll be along for a pick-me-up, soon as he can.

"We'll go through the sugar ration today," she says perkily. "Glad I picked up that sack last week."

People start queuing before we've had time to put on the urn. They tell us the names of the factories and department stores that have been wiped out. Gone up in flames, burning all through the night.

"You should see the cathedral," they say. "It's still on fire."

Tea always goes down well. I make sure Mrs. Burton remembers to have one, for she is looking more ravaged as every minute passes. I hope Sally will remember to take Pearl to school. Course she will. And if not, what's one day off school? The kids here aren't going to school today, that's for sure. They've lost everything.

Mrs. Burton has even thought to put a bag of soft toys in the back, made from old jumpers from the retirement home. *How does she think of everything?*

She's also brought a bag of socks.

"Clean socks and a cup of tea," she says. "That'll fix it." She is so pale I worry she is about to faint. I tell her to sit on the wooden stool we keep at the back. It's hard to convince her to rest.

"I don't need to," she says.

"Just for a minute, Mrs. Burton. I can keep us going." Filling, heating, pouring, stirring, waiting. It is tea but it is more than tea, it is a symbol of us. Of hope and survival.

What if Mr. Burton is not coming back?

It's not *just* tea. They're still finding people dazzled and distressed. They're still pulling people from the rubble. A police officer shouts for us, explains that there are no ambulances at the moment.

"We'll take them," I call. "Won't we, Mrs. Burton?"

We shut our window and pull the poor souls in. They're in quite the state. Mrs. Burton sits in the back to hold shaking hands. The nearest hospital is too full, and they send me to another, five miles away. It's like I'm in France all over again. For a moment I imagine Olive by my side and I take a deep breath to steady myself.

Precious cargo delivered, back we go. There are more walking wounded waiting for a lift.

"Squeeze up," I say, and we take two more up in the front. "What a night!" they say. One of the babies cries until Mrs. Barton gives her some sugar from her finger.

After that, it's back to the urn, and news of us must have spread for thirsty tea-seekers are coming from far and wide, and thank goodness for one woman, who jumps up: "I can't bear just sitting around. Give me something to do!"

We get her to rinse the cups.

We have been there twelve hours, we have done four hospital trips and we have run out of milk three times. The people of Coventry and the emergency services won't stop drinking our tea.

"It means we're alive," I say to a fireman. I regret it instantly when I see Mrs. Burton wiping tears away.

The sun is setting when we see an outline or silhouette of two men in long black overcoats, helmets and boots.

"ARPs?" I ask. I don't want to give her false hope, but it looks like Air Raid Patrols to me. Covered in dust, head to toe, they look like the contents of an ashtray have been dashed upon them.

Mrs. Burton rises onto her tiptoes, squints out into the setting sun.

"Ernie?" she calls in a tone I've never heard before. It's a rumbling sound of fear and longing. "Ernie...Is that you?"

The dust-covered man's mouth twitches.

"Who else would I be? So, old girl, do you like my new look?"

"Hmm, I don't think so." Mrs. Burton hangs onto the counter to steady herself. I make the tea.

"Haven't you got any biscuits?" He shakes his head in fake disapproval.

Mrs. Burton's hands are shaking as she hands over the cup. "Didn't get a moment to bake today..."

He grips his tea. Drinks it, and his face, almost imperceptibly, relaxes.

"You all right, my love?" Mrs. Burton whispers.

"Tell you about it when we get home."

"Good man," she says indistinctly. "Good work."

He leans against the side, pulls his helmet low over his face and closes his eyes. She lowers herself back on the stool with her head in her hands. I warm through the teapot for the next round.

We go back to Coventry four days in a row. We're not just doing tea, we're an ambulance service, a clean-sock service and a listening, cuddling service too. On day three, Mrs. Burton finds out I've been putting in one extra spoonful for the pot and we have a mild altercation about my wastefulness costing lives, but her heart is not in it. Despite that, we are a great team. Secretly I think she would have been a far better partner for me than Daisy—who was so rude—and Olive—who could be so tearful—in the Great War.

The people of Coventry are brave, stoical and grateful for every hot drink or kindness. We all agree Winny Churchill is going to get us out of this fix. Old Adolf is getting desperate—he must be.

Edmund complains that his dinner is not on the table. I queued up two hours for some brisket at our butchers but didn't have time to fry it over. In Coventry, I pick up some salted cod—they get more fish in the towns—and prepare it late at night when the house is quiet. No one's going to like it much, but it's good for our health. I prepare an egg and bacon pie one morning, and when I'm back late in the evening, it's all gone. I'm too exhausted to question it. I think of all the families in Coventry, in London, in Hull, still waiting for news, living in church halls or sleeping on the floors of relatives: I can't complain.

Pearl goes in to school with Susan or Ethel. I suspect some mornings she arrives after the bell, but I don't say anything.

"When are the Nazis going to stop bombing?" she asks at dinner. We're all asking ourselves that.

"We'll beat them soon," I say.

"How?" she despairs.

"We're bringing planes down all the time."

I remember the planes coming over Calais last time round and I find that I'm holding my breath. Edmund, for once, is surprisingly helpful. He reassures Pearl that planes have come along a lot since the olden days. She says, "Oh, interesting!" but it's cars Pearl loves most, not biplanes.

"Thank you," I mouth to him, over her head. Solemnly, he nods.

CHAPTER THIRTY-FOUR

1917—Then

Sam was a man of his word. He didn't write. No letters came from Edmund either, although Edmund's mother wrote regularly, letters that were full of words but with surprisingly little substance. Aunt Cecily also wrote regularly. She meticulously detailed her regime, the food shortages, the walks she took. She was knitting and would send mittens that I didn't need but I gave them to patients.

My dear aunt was petrified of being caught up in an attack in London. Living as I did only five miles from the front line, where explosions, shellings and shootings were a daily occurrence, this seemed absurd to me. But Aunt had worked herself up about it. She described zeppelins, the black shadows, "as long as your dad's warehouse," then the explosions. "Poor beloved Croydon," she wrote, a phrase I never expected to hear. Apparently, Uncle Toby was annoyed that "he missed the show."

I thought hatefully, *So they're getting a little taste of the suffering we see daily out here.*

I remembered Mrs. Fielding saying how easy it was to lose our humanity, and so I wrote back especially kind words to make up for the blackness in my heart.

Some time later, my aunt wrote to ask if I knew what was going on exactly with Edmund. She said that the Lowes were "keeping very quiet about it." It was she who put a new idea in my head. She wrote:

They don't want me to visit him in Sussex, and they refuse to elaborate on his injuries. I am beginning to wonder if he's not in hospital at all and instead is doing some kind of military intelligence. Is he awfully hush-hush with you too? Uncle Toby thought he might be with the War Office now?

Military intelligence, I thought. Something about that phrase rather pleased me. It would be right up Edmund's street too and it would explain a lot. Not *everything*, but a lot. But still, my doubts remained. And the more I thought about it, and the less I heard from England, the more they grew. I had ultimately dismissed the idea of a Blighty wound; it wasn't Edmund Lowe at all—for all his initial reluctance to fight, Edmund was a team player. Also, he was in mourning for his brother; it was not possible. I was sure whatever had happened to him, it was something that he had no control over.

I remembered his despair at the hospital: the pained way he told me, "I saw six men die, six." He had lost his only brother, for goodness' sake; things do not get much worse than that.

And although I did not want to remember it, I recalled the attack I had sustained in the ambulance. Mrs. Fielding's unexpected kindness toward those who were suffering "diseases of the brain." I remembered watching the first casualties of war arriving in London: the drooling man who had horrified me so.

Wasn't the more likely explanation for Edmund's sojourn in hospital that he had lost his mind?

CHAPTER THIRTY-FIVE

1941—Now

One time, in spring, I pick up Pearl from school and we go to the Harrisons' because Edmund's dad isn't doing too well; the doctor is coming at four, and Mrs. Harrison has asked if I could be there too. Edmund long ago delegated care of his parents to me—so I find out who the doctor is, and since he isn't mine, I agree.

The doctor's fancy car pulls up and, as no one else seems about to, I go to open the front door. As he comes in, he greets Pearl heartily and she asks him if that is his car, and he replies, "She's a beauty, isn't she?"

He asks Pearl what she wants to do when she's older, and she pauses dramatically. She is getting better at speaking to strangers, but she is still by no means fluent. "Films, maybe?"

"A little actress?" he says with his eyebrows raised at me. I shrug.

I show him to Edmund's father. Edmund's father doesn't look at all well, but the doctor's verdict is "An infection—keep him warm" and "plenty of fluids."

Back in the living room, about twenty minutes have passed before I realize I haven't seen Pearl for a while.

"Where are you, Pearl?" I call out. Domino man and wireless man look bewildered. She's not with them. Could she be with the folding paper lady? No, she isn't. Surely she's not with Edmund's mother? (That would be a first.)

"Pearl!" I run through the house, checking the kitchen, checking the "best room." I hammer on the toilet door. She hasn't gone upstairs, has she? I throw open all the bedroom doors, frightening an old lady who has retreated to her bed for her afternoon nap.

"Pearl?"

Edmund's mother finds me. Gripping my arm, she hisses, "They can't be trusted, Vivienne."

"What?"

"See what else is missing. I bet she's gone through my purse."

I shake her off, the hateful, hateful woman. "Pearl! PEARL! Where are you?"

She is nowhere to be found. I have never felt this desperate in my life. Not even in Calais during the war. *I can't lose her, I can't, I can't.*

I want to cry, *Help me, Olive. I'm so sorry for what I did. Olive. Please forgive me.*

Out in the garden, Mrs. Harrison is slowly pruning pink roses but she is on her own. "What's happened, Mrs. Lowe?"

I run out into the street, calling out Pearl's name, my own ugly voice echoing in my ears. I'm screeching "Peeeearrllll!," surveying each suspicious tree, bush and streetlight, and then I'm back indoors again, circling the place like a frenzied dog.

The old people gaze at me like I've arrived from Mars. Mrs. Harrison's cook comes out to see the commotion. Trying to keep my voice steady, I beg for information but she too doesn't know anything; she tries to settle everyone down. I want to sink into the ground and be disappeared. I just want to die.

I cannot deal with this. I cannot. Not again. Pearl, please. Please be safe, please.

My fears are bounding ahead unleashed: *the phone call I will have to make to London from Mrs. Dean's. Mrs. Dean's ears flapping, the way she gets excited when she is the first to hear a terrible tale. "Is Pearl there? No? I'm so sorry, I seem to have lost her. Yes, that's right. I've done it again."*

And suddenly the doorbell chimes.

The doctor is standing there. Back again, like he's never been away. Back with a big smile on his usually serious face, his bag at his polished shoes.

"Come and see."

Little Pearl is curled up asleep in the back seat of his sedan.

CHAPTER THIRTY-SIX

1917—Then

We were still at war. It was so cold that winter in Lamarck that it took twenty minutes to get the ambulances going, men's hands froze to their guns and I learned everything you could ever need to know about frostbite—quite the innocuous word for something so heinous. The roads were churned-up mud or rinks of ice and morale among the men was lower than it ever had been. The English Army did not revolt—but if someone had told me they had, I wouldn't have been surprised. Conditions were *that* bad.

Agnes went home to take care of her sick mother, but Daisy, Enid and Dorothy remained: a hardy core. There were other FANYs in northern France and we met them occasionally. We met the girls who drove shower trucks for soldiers to wash in—Daisy was most envious of them. And girls who drove food trucks near the front line for soldiers to have some hot cabbage soup—Enid thought that sounded great. But I thought that we, the transport mules, had the best deal. We were neither at the war front or the home front but somewhere in between.

We were visited by some very high-up army bigwig, and he was highly complimentary. "You girls are neither fish, flesh nor fowl," he shouted, his monocle popping, "but you are thundering good red herring!"

Mrs. Fletcher turned as red as a herring at that and we FANYs delighted in calling each other herrings for some days afterward.

Sometimes, I could hardly recognize myself as the timid daughter and office clerk I had been in London. The girl who had been so shocked at the sight of a man's privates in an art class. And although I missed Olive, it was nice to move out from under her shadow.

I thought about Sam Isaac a lot. Obviously, I knew I shouldn't have but he had had a huge impact on me. I was just an ordinary woman but he had made me feel extraordinary. I shouldn't have let him kiss me, that was clear, but I was glad I had. To know what a passionate kiss was like, to feel completely loved and desired, was part of life's rich tapestry, I told myself. It was an *educational* experience. Silly things reminded me of him: airplanes, sewing, poetry, writing, badminton... and I was amazed how often the words *Chu Chin Chow* came up in conversation.

Before Christmas, I wrote to Edmund asking if I might visit him in his hospital over the holidays. I knew hospitals well enough to know that the nurses would run themselves ragged to provide a good time for the men: wherever he was, he would be cared for, especially at this time of year. But the thought of him alone in some dreary ward, trying to join in with the carol singers, made me shudder.

I didn't get a reply from him, but in the new year a card came from his mother saying she had seen my letter, and "not to worry, Edmund still wants to marry you, more than ever, Vivienne dear." I was too embarrassed to tell anyone about it.

Finally, toward the end of that long winter, just as the driving rain was beginning to, if not stop, but at least feel warmer on an exposed neck or cheek, I got a letter from Edmund. He was still in hospital, he wrote, but would go straight back to his regiment out in Belgium. He wanted to thank me for all my letters, my sweet cards and most of all, my patience. He missed me, I was a darling woman and he was so proud that one day he would call me his wife.

It was the kind of letter I'd hoped to receive all my life. So why did it confuse me so much now?

Edmund's handwriting was even, his grammar and his spelling were as they should be. There was nothing in the content that should have raised suspicions and yet... I didn't quite recognize it as Edmund's voice. It was more flowery, more *emotional* than the Edmund I knew. Was this the work of someone with a severe case of shell shock perhaps? Had he spent the last few months basket-weaving?

While I was still puzzling over it, a telegram came from Aunt Cecily. She was dreadfully sorry to bother me, but Father was ill. Could I possibly come home? She wrote that she had sent for Olive in Italy too. She had been right about Christopher last time; I had no doubts she was right about Father too.

I tried to organize it so Olive and I came home at different times, to spread the care, but it didn't work out like that. We both took a month's leave with three weeks' overlap. It was the middle of March. As she hugged me goodbye, Daisy laughed and said, "Beware the Ides of March" and I agreed that I would.

Olive got back first. She swung open the front door to greet me. It was the first time I had seen her for over a year. Her hair was short at the back and over the ears and her eyes were sparkling. The limp was gone! Italian coffee and wine had fixed her. And the spaghetti! *Thank heavens for spaghetti*. She said she adored *la bella Italia*. Italy at war was better than Britain at peace.

"*Ciao, bella!*" she called and tackled me to kiss me once on each cheek. She spoke with a strange hybrid accent—she said she couldn't help it. She told me that she was "extraordinarily susceptible to the foreign tongue." I stared at her, mystified.

Once I managed to calm her down, I asked how Father was faring.

"Oh, Father..." she said in a bored tone. She thought he might be "on his way out."

"Is that what the doctors say?"

"Well, no," she admitted, "but he's not eating so . . . Anyway, if he's going to go, it must be within the month," she added. "I have to go back to Milano."

I hadn't known she could be this heartless.

I leapt up the stairs to our father's room and there I found him, sat up in bed, pillows propped behind him, flicking through a notebook.

"Father!" I called out.

"You're home too?" he said. "I must be in a very bad way."

I had always been slightly afraid of my father's room. Silly, really; there was nothing to be scared of. Just old oak drawers, a wash jug—it was a simple room with a man's smell. That day, the window was open and you could hear the ringing of bicycle bells, the starting of engines outside. As soon as I came in, I asked him if he wanted the window shut, but he said no, he liked listening to the signs of life outside.

I sat down and tried to hold his hand, but he was too preoccupied.

"Can you help me make sense of these numbers?"

"I must say, I thought you'd be worse."

"Oh, you know Cecily."

"It wasn't just Cecily."

"Olive too? Well, she is an alarmist, you know that. She *will* keep smoking that pipe in here though. Makes me cough."

Later, he put down his notebook and looked me in the eye.

"So, tell me, Vi. How is my future son-in-law?"

"Not too bad," I said shortly. My father looked at me, worried. He knew me well. I told him I hadn't seen Edmund since I was in England over a year earlier, when Christopher died and we became engaged. It was strange in that while in France it seemed like only a moment or two had passed, back here it suddenly seemed to be an *abnormally* long time. Other couples managed to visit each other in hospital or take leave together. Other couples managed to write more. Once the word "abnormal" had entered my head, it settled there. I shook myself. I was being cruel. *Poor Edmund. Losing his men, losing his brother...* He wouldn't want to lose me.

Abnormal Edmund.

"He's been in hospital in Sussex. Poor Edmund," I said.

"He didn't get himself shot, did he?"

"I'm not entirely sure," I said slowly. It was humiliating to admit I still didn't know his whereabouts or his whatabouts, even if it was only to my own father.

"We-ll! What's wrong with him?" asked my father, puzzled.

"I don't really know."

Father was fit to explode. His cheeks puffed up. "What... but what do you think?"

I busied myself cleaning the bedside table. There were three half-full glasses there, and Father's spectacles, and a book.

"Aunt Cecily thinks he may be doing hush-hush intelligence work."

"But you don't?"

"I suspect, maybe he had an illness of the mind."

My father winced. "Edmund? Is he the type?"

"I don't think there is a type, is there? It's afflicting an awful lot of—"

He pulled a face again, then got back to his numbers.

Olive and I didn't overlap as much as I'd hoped. She spent much of her time with Walter, Mrs. Ford and Mrs. Brown. She asked if I would like to come to Warrington Crescent, but I felt I shouldn't and instead, I spent most of my time with Father. The first week we were there we found him in the type of nightgown that even Scrooge himself would have found old-fashioned, so first thing we bought him new pajamas. He battled us over them at first, but once he relented, he was very pleased.

I asked if the Fords' house was still being used as a convalescent home and Olive laughed—"No, that didn't last long" and told me, "The poor injured were moved to somewhere more somber."

When I asked after Walter, she shrugged. "Walter is here and there."

Our father was not as poorly as everyone had feared. After a few days of eating very little, he rallied and tucked into a watery chicken soup and crackers. From then on, he had a raging appetite for anything. The food shortages were hitting England hard by now, harder than I'd realized back in France, where portions had been meager for so long, but we fed him porridge with honey and toast and he began to look brighter by the hour.

One evening Aunt Cecily and Uncle Toby came round and we shared the bottle of red Italian wine that Olive had brought home with her. Unfortunately, we had nothing but crackers to eat with it, and Uncle Toby grew quite melancholy.

"Who would have thought things would turn out like this?" he said. I remembered his exultance, his jubilation, in August 1914.

I shook my head at Olive: "*Now we know*." And it felt good to see her smile like in the old days.

Edmund's family invited us all for supper, and seeing as our supplies were so low, we agreed. I didn't expect Olive to join us, but she was in great spirits that afternoon. She said her paintings were going well and she was looking forward to going back to Italy. She preferred working there, she explained. She felt like she was making more of a difference than she had in Lamarck.

Tentatively, I asked if we might see the pictures she was working on. She glanced at me briefly, then said most of them were at Mrs. Ford's.

"But they are *bellissimo*!" she said, laughing to herself.

What are these affectations? I thought. Olive used to hate things like that.

"I'll bring some tonight, if you like, to show the Lowes?"

"Wonderful, I'm sure they would be pleased."

I was always curious about my sister's love life, or the absence of a love life. Since it now didn't seem as if she was concerned about Walter, and since she was in such a pleasant mood, I dared ask if she had met anyone "of consequence" in Italy.

"Gosh no... the only people I met were Americans who think they're dashing, and Italians who know they're dashing, and neither are my type at all. No, no, no!" She said that half the ambulance drivers dreamed of being artists, writers and poets. She laughed at that. "Who wants to get into a relationship with one of those?"

This seemed to be a joke, but I wasn't sure what was so funny. Still, as I gazed at her, I could tell there was no secret sweetheart in Italy.

It was her turn to ask the questions.

"And how about you, Vi? Did you ever hear from Sam again?"

"No."

"Really? No communication at all?"

"What would be the point?" I responded sternly. Really, Olive was incorrigible. "Edmund and I are engaged and that's that."

"I thought you had strong feelings for Sam."

I was scarlet. "Well, I didn't."

"He certainly had strong feelings for you."

"Enough, Olive, enough."

Edmund's mother and father were very welcoming to us all that evening. It wasn't just that Edmund and I were engaged; each time I saw them, I found myself liking them more and more. *They might come across as snobbish, but that's just their exterior, they're soft and vulnerable inside.* They clearly wanted the best for everyone, even Olive.

We ate a starter of broth, then a course of lamb and potatoes. Edmund's mother was terribly apologetic. They had been expecting more vegetables, but unfortunately their "source" had the dates wrong and they wouldn't be with them until Saturday.

"Too late for you girls, although"—she turned to our father— "would you please join us then? We need to build you up a little."

Father agreed. He was feeling a lot better now and regretted very much pulling us away from our important work overseas. Both Olive and I assured him that we had been delighted to come home, and were even more delighted to see he was on the mend.

"The war sometimes just has to wait," said Olive. She was very kind to Father's face.

The Lowes did their usual showing-offs about their lord and lady friends and their dances (there may be a war, but lords and ladies still have to dance), but inevitably, they were more subdued than they used to be.

And then Olive showed them the drawings she had done in Italy: ambulance sidings and huts. Empty fields.

I could see Edmund's parents didn't think much of them and I felt stirred and defensive. I tried to explain what Olive was doing.

"'They're not beautiful, but they are true. That's how things look out there right now. Not many people get to see the war from this perspective."

The Lowes nodded and considered. Then Edmund's mother said, "I liked that one you did ages ago, was it of the grapefruit?"

"It's fine," Olive said coolly. "These are not for everyone. I understand that. Some people prefer art like that of Percy Millhouse."

I smirked. I knew that, these days, Olive regarded the artist Percy Millhouse as a talented sell-out, no matter how respected he was.

The Lowes served coffee with slabs of dark chocolate they'd managed to get from goodness knows where, and Olive produced yet another bottle of Italian red she'd smuggled home. Then we turned our thoughts to dear Christopher and how missed he was, and we talked about Edmund and I turned pink, because I could see, perhaps for the first time, how proud and pleased everyone (except Olive!) was for us to be marrying.

The parents wanted to know what plans we had, the marriage question, and I said, "We'll wait until this war is over…" and Edmund's father gruffly said, "Damn war," and patted my hand paternally, and Edmund's mother didn't even pick him up on his language.

I said whatever was happening, I knew that Edmund would be making the best of it. Edmund did well whatever he did. He gave everything his all.

Olive raised her eyebrows at me cynically, but my father nodded. "He's a sensible one, make no mistake."

. I smiled at Father, grateful for his support. Edmund's mother wiped away a tear. "I always knew you were a loyal girl."

Before I left, Edmund's mother gave me a bracelet—it was a chunky gold bangle with a horseshoe design on one side. She explained it was one of hers, given to her by her own grandmother. She wanted to pass it on to me.

"And we'll plan the wedding. Soon?"

"Very soon," I promised. For the first time ever, I felt as though Mrs. Lowe were talking to me as an equal, a family member, and it was mesmerizing. I felt confident then that the thing with Sam was just a silly dream, a fantasy, for who really would fall for a man who had fallen from the clouds? My destiny was, as had always been written in the cards, with the Lowes.

Richard knew it, Aunt Cecily knew it, Father knew it and now Edmund's mother and father knew it. The only one who didn't seem to know it was Olive and she was probably jealous or something.

I had trained my mind to think of Edmund when it slipped to dream of Sam. I thought of Edmund hugging me outside the hospital; the first—and last—kiss we shared in the garden under the watchful eye of the tortoise. If my imagination ran toward his doubts and reticence, or the picture he kept in his pocket, or his startled "Good Lord, Vivienne, you are the last person I expected to see here," I quickly tuned them out. It was like playing the piano: *just avoid the wrong keys. Nothing to it.*

It was about eleven o'clock and we were in the taxi on the way home and I was still overawed by Edmund's mother. Had she really said, "We'll plan the wedding soon" about our wedding? I touched the bracelet she had given me. Admittedly, it wasn't to my taste—a horseshoe? On a bangle?—but it was a Lowe family heirloom. I couldn't think of anything sweeter. It couldn't be denied: this was a welcome and a half to the Lowe family. It seemed I had won them over at last.

I leaned my head against the carriage side, smiling. I thought of the tortoise—Charles!—and the hare. *Nothing wrong with endurance*, I told myself. It's a quality prized too little these days. I ignored my father passing around the mints, and that was when we first heard the noise: it sounded like a terrifically loud swarm of bees, a sort of buzzing and groaning from the sky. You knew straight away it was incoming: we all gazed at each other, horrified. The driver said, "Not again..." and stopped the cab. The whole street had stopped. Everyone stood still, frozen.

And then it came, a massive boom, the ground beneath us shunted, followed by another crashing, banging explosion. And then nothing. A terrible silence. It was very close, I knew that. Maybe one street away from where we'd parked, no more than that.

"Oh God," Father mumbled. "How can this be happening here?" Horror was etched on his pallid face.

"Wait," I said, like he was a small child. "Don't move, Father."

I told him to stay in the carriage. I pushed some coins into the driver's hands and then, without speaking, pulled Olive's arm. We slipped out into the street. There was dust, dust everywhere, blinding, choking. I could hear emergency bells ringing.

We ran toward the chaos. We knew what to do.

There was a policeman already there. "Bombs!" he shouted. "You can't go that way."

"Where, where are we? Where did they hit?"

"Warrington Crescent."

Olive and I looked at each other.

And for a moment, in a shameful thought that I would never confide to anyone, I thought, *Phew, isn't Olive's painting of me at the Fords?* It would never survive the bomb—never be displayed in public, thank God. I would never have to betray Edmund's mother or to explain how I came to be so cozy with a man who was not Edmund, a man who was a Jew.

But in the next moment, I registered the fire's intensity, the rising smoke and the thunderous noise. My experience kicked in immediately.

"Just how bad is it?" I asked unnecessarily.

"Get back, get back!" the policeman shouted, not only to us, but the other people who were getting out of their carriages behind us and were standing, astonished spectators in the street

I said that we were nurses. I was so frantic, so desperate, I would have said anything, but I didn't need to. He let us through.

Dusty air, gray vision, red eyes. Olive and I ran forward in the dark, stumbling over rubble where rubble shouldn't be. Half the street was destroyed. I couldn't work out where I was at first, and then I got my bearings. "Over here!" I shouted to Olive and she galloped after me. It was hard to say for sure, but I thought about six houses must have been hit; the Fords' would have been somewhere around the middle of them. I counted madly, using a surprisingly bold house number on the other side of the street to guide me.

"Here, here, it's this one!" I should have known it sooner.

Where the Fords' house had been was now mostly bricks, beams and rubble—but piled high, as high as a room itself. Olive went one way, I went another. Hard to believe this was where the parties were held, the piano played, the artwork displayed. *Was it really this one? Gone in an instant? Gone without chance.* I couldn't believe this was London. I was experienced at the aftermath of an attack, but this was something entirely different. This was my home, my people. "Mrs. Ford?" I shouted, "Walter?" and I could hear Olive shouting too.

I ran over the top of the rubble. The house had collapsed: inside was out, upside was down. The lovely paintings Mrs. Ford was so proud of collecting, all wasted, all disappeared. Her good taste... and yet one side of the room was almost intact. *How can that be?* The randomness of it was shocking. *Which side of the house were the people in? Direct hit or—*

A noise. Human. Or animal? *Not sure.* I proceeded further. I had completely lost Olive by now, and was wondering if perhaps she had found something, and if maybe I should gather her up, go to Father and get everyone home. I was thinking that it was a good job the house was no longer a convalescent home. Then there was shouting, and then a whistle blew for quiet, there was a "Shhhhhhushh" and everyone was quiet as night, and we listened as hard as anything, straining to hear, and then someone caught it, a groaning, a groaning, and they found her: Mrs. Brown, Mrs. Ford's elderly mother, and she was pulled up. She emerged, and she was dusty yet whole. I heard her speak: "The others?" and it was a miracle, and this gave me heart and courage. It wasn't useless! We *could* get them out. They must have survived. If Mrs. Brown, old and decrepit, could...

Then there was a sound of digging, excitement, and a man was leveraged out. I didn't know his face—a visitor maybe? And then I saw Olive freeze and bend, and I too could see what she was looking at: Walter's shoe and Walter's leg. And she knelt there in the bricks.

I continued on my path. I had an intuition Walter and Mrs. Ford wouldn't be far from each other, and they weren't.

I saw something, pinky-white, in the rubble. A lone hand. I followed it, and I found that she—I thought it was Mrs. Ford—was pinned down, maybe in her bed. The fallen masonry, the bricks, were like blankets; it was like she was a princess in an odd sort of fairytale. I threw off the poles that held her down and the plaster that obscured her face.

Yes, it was definitely Mrs. Ford and I knew immediately, despite the light in her eyes and the fact that she was sitting up, that it wasn't good.

"Hang on, Mrs. Ford. We'll get you out."

"No…"

"It's just your legs," I lied. "We'll have you free in a jiffy."

Then I saw. Her head was covered in blood, misshapen, shattered. She looked stunned. "We've just got your mother free," I said breathlessly, trying to contain my horror. "She's going to be fine."

I found her hand and squeezed.

"Get my Walter out," she whispered. I don't think she recognized me. "Help my boy, please. Walter."

I had known her for over four years as a glamourous host, an entertainer, an art collector, a songwriter, a freethinker and as a fiercely respected, beautiful woman. But now, for the first time, I saw Mrs. Ford as a mother: her concern for her son was as fierce as any mother's could ever be. That was all she cared about at that moment: the safety of her boy—he could have been three or twenty-three. What I saw then was pure biological, fundamental, maternal love and fear.

"Make sure they save my boy," she insisted. "My son. His name is Walter. Walter Ford."

I looked over my shoulder. I could see men carrying a figure and Olive following. I recognized the black trousers, the distinctive purple cloak. The kind of clothes no wallflower would wear.

"They're working now, they'll get him out, you just need to hang on for me."

"Promise."

"Yes."

"He's alive? My Walter?"

I nodded.

Her voice changed. "Thank God. Thank God."

I held on to Mrs. Ford. I knew she was going then. I knew it. She asked me once again about Walter and again, I lied: "He's safe," I said.

Her face finally relaxed. All her tension evaporated. "So long as he is." A holding, a crushing, a joining... and then a nothing. Her fingers eased their grip on mine. There was not one single moment when she was here and then not—it was a series of moments, a number of steps downward that I hadn't realized I was on until I hit the ground, and then there we were, and I could feel she was gone. My hand held hers but her hand no longer held mine.

It must have been only four minutes since we'd got there. Ten minutes since Father was offering mints around in the cab. Things can change on the turn of a coin.

To this day, I don't know if I did the right thing or if I committed a terrible crime by lying to her, if it was immoral or unfair. She was a mother who died thinking her son was alive. Was that a gift or a curse?

Twenty seconds later, I scrambled out into the dark. Dust everywhere. People sneezing in torchlight.

Olive was shaking me, balancing on rubble: "What's happened? Where is she? Where is Mrs. Ford?" When I told her Mrs. Ford was gone, she let out a terrible animal cry.

The policeman shoved us out back into the road. "Out, out!" he bellowed—we were doing no good, we were obstructing—so we stood there, bewildered, among the arriving cars and fire officers dashing. Then, when I looked to where Olive had been next to me, she had gone.

*

The driver had decided to leave. He had told my father to get out of the carriage and had left him there, frail old man he was, abandoned in the street. I saw Father stood at the edge of the rubble, his hands up in fear and despair. I went over to him and wrapped my coat round him. He was shivering and bewildered.

"Can't we go home now?" he begged.

"I...wait...Olive will be...just give her a moment."

"There's nothing we can do," he kept saying. His nostrils flared, his eyebrows meeting in the middle. He looked ancient suddenly, a man from a different era.

"I know."

"Oh, when will this lousy war end? Let's go home and let the police deal with it."

Finally, Olive rejoined us. Her hair was white with ash. I shepherded her and Father down the street. I was saying, "There's nothing we can do," to her, and "We'll find another carriage, don't worry" to Father, over and over again.

And we did find a way home; it was our only bit of luck that evening. A horse and carriage pulled up. There were others in the back, huddled and frightened too, and the driver said he'd take us wherever we needed, free of charge, because *what a terrible night, terrible. You wouldn't think it would happen here, would you?*

"Did she ask after me?" Once we were inside the cab, Olive asked me repeatedly. She was saying it so often: "Did she say my name? Did she call for me?" that I grew exasperated with her. You wouldn't have known she had been in the FANYs, or had been working in the mountains of Italy; she was like a timid little girl again. The other occupants of the cab were looking at her nervously. Father had buried his face in his hands. Finally, I snapped. "For God's sake, Olive, stop asking! There wasn't time. She didn't even recognize me, she just wanted to know if Walter was all right."

She paled. "Of course she did," she muttered. Her eyes looked dark and wild. She tilted her pointed chin upward, which made her look suddenly haughty. I felt abruptly, absurdly frightened of her. She had always been unpredictable but never like this. She looked at me, whispered harshly, "So what did you tell her then? When she asked after Walter? What did you say?"

"I told her he was fine," I choked. I felt like hell. My eyes were stinging. My throat was on fire. I deserved everything bad: *What a terrible, terrible lie.*

I shook my head and sobbed then and Olive began to sob too and from behind me, I could hear my poor, ancient father begging us: "Please, girls, let's go home."

I woke up to find my Aunt Cecily leaning over me. It was a shock. Her face was too close to mine; her breath smelled milky and it made me wince.

"To think, you've been all round the world and you got bombed in London." Aunt Cecily was awfully upset. I supposed everything went back to Richard, a reminder of her greatest loss. I lay there for a moment, trying to understand what was going on. I felt weighed down by responsibilities, and wished I was in France, where at least every death was anonymous, we were untroubled by family or backstory, and you could sing songs, put your foot down on the accelerator and keep a defensive barrier around you.

"Your poor father," she added. "What a thing for him to see! We came as soon as we heard. Poor Uncle Toby is famished."

"Is Olive all right?"

"Still asleep," Aunt Cecily said.

I doubted that. I hastily pulled on my clothes and galloped downstairs. Father and Uncle Toby were in the drawing room. He had picked himself up and brushed himself off and was now regaling Uncle Toby with stories of our lucky escape. Last night he had been in the pits of despair, but now he seemed almost elated. I couldn't tell if he was putting it on for Uncle Toby or if he was genuinely bursting with survivor's euphoria. I had seen that enough times at Lamarck.

"They say an Irish girl was calling 'bejeezus… bejeezus,'" Father was cheerfully recounting. "For a moment, we could have been in the ghettos of Dublin. They pulled her out. Thank bejeezus."

Uncle Toby was joining in. "Bejeezus indeed. And I heard that there was a soldier in there who survived. And do you want to know how? They think the carpet saved his life!"

Father was saying, "Now that is interesting." I could only imagine what was going through his whirring brain. A new way of advertising the carpets? *Lifesavers against bombs. Wrap yourself up in a Persian rug. Match your furniture and survive the Hun.*

Chortle, chortle, ha ha ha. Bejeezus.

"Good morning, Father, Uncle Toby," I said and they both pretended to be concerned.

"Your uncle brought some pears." Father had the good grace to look embarrassed.

"Least I could do," said my uncle gruffly. "Terrible news… I think Aunt Cecily is arranging some toast for us."

The bomb had hit too late to get in that day's newspaper, thank goodness. We'd have to wait a few hours before we could relive the deaths of our friends in print.

I read about U-boats and Father and Uncle talked about the racing.

Then I spotted Olive. Hovering like a ghost in the doorway, she was wearing a white nightgown and her short hair was stuck to her head like a helmet. When he finally noticed her, Uncle Toby did his best to look sympathetic; he whipped the jocular look off his face and walked over to her, palms outstretched.

"Olive, good to see you up."

She ignored him. "I'm going there now."

"What? Back again?" Father was horrified.

Olive explained that she would walk all the way to Warrington Crescent, if necessary. Uncle Toby wearily caved in.

"I'll get my car, Olive, least I can do."

As we walked out, he hissed at Aunt Cecily, "I didn't even get my breakfast."

Uncle Toby's driver was not a smooth driver and the vehicle bumped and juddered all the way there. I wished we had made our own way— I didn't know if I could deal with Uncle Toby *and* Olive. There was something dead-eyed and vacant about her this morning. I hoped she wouldn't take out what had happened on Uncle Toby. That wouldn't be fair. He might be annoying, but he wasn't to blame.

My poor sister. I held her hand. I tried to imagine how I would feel if I had heard that Edmund had died, but I couldn't think I would be as devastated as this. *And yet, it had hardly seemed like she was fond of him...*

"You all right, Olive?"

She nodded.

I talked with the driver about the car. He said it was a Daimler and a pleasure.

I said that I drove a Ford Model T in France and Uncle Toby said: "You don't really drive though, Vivi, do you?"

"What do you think I do out there, Uncle Toby?"

Perhaps it was me who would take it out on Uncle Toby. He shrugged. "I have absolutely no idea."

Olive had begun to sob copiously next to me, face in her hands, making her fingers wet with tears. Until that moment, I don't think I had realized how much she loved the Fords—how much she loved Walter. I supposed they had been perhaps making plans for a life together. Now that I saw it, I clutched her close.

"My dear girl."

*

The whole road was closed off now. There were visitors and reporters within the lines, and crowds without. Uncle Toby said in an excited voice, "Isn't that the Princess Mary?" And Olive made a whining sound, and I said, "Sssh," and grabbed her hand but it was as much to keep her under control as to soothe her.

This was a major event. London had been targeted before but never so successfully. Flags were at half-mast, and little wreaths of flowers had appeared.

The Irish girl who had been pulled free had later perished in hospital. An entire family had been wiped out. It was as bad as anything I had seen in Lamarck.

Olive half-walked, and I half-pulled her, through the rubble where the houses had been. I found it hard to breathe. Horrible, distressing discoveries everywhere. A shoe. A magazine. A gymslip.

"You *will* be all right, Olive," I told her firmly.

I didn't hear her reply at first; I had to ask her to repeat it. She did, wearily, loudly.

"What other way is there to be?"

It wasn't until that evening, as I packed to return to France, that I realized with horror that the Lowe family bracelet had gone. I must have lost their precious heirloom in Warrington Crescent, somewhere in all that mess.

CHAPTER THIRTY-SEVEN

They are talking about Pearl Harbor on the radio now. They don't have exact numbers for casualties, but they believe it to be in the thousands. *Thousands* dead. A number too big to contemplate. My Pearl listens attentively at the breakfast table, rapidly spooning the porridge into her mouth because I always tell her to do it quickly before it gets cold. The heat disguises the fact that it's disgusting without milk: we've had hardly any recently.

"What's happening?" she asks, petrified. "They keep saying my name."

"Oh, darling, it's nothing to do with you," I reassure her. "It's a very different kind of Pearl."

I should switch it off, to shield her, but I am mesmerized by the announcer's words. I am both attracted and repulsed by the horrors unfolding.

Isn't this what we wanted? America would surely enter the war now! But not like this. So many dead. Sons, husbands, fathers.

We talk about it at Mrs. Burton's. On big news days Mrs. Burton keeps the wireless on and we speculate about what it means.

More enemies. The other side is winning.

Trust Winny Churchill, we all agree. *He'll keep us going.* We all have faith in him. I can't quite work out if it's because of him, or because there is no one else around. Maybe the reason doesn't matter.

But ultimately, I remember Pearl Harbor Day not for Pearl's confusion or the cold porridge I couldn't scrape out of the bowl, but for the unmistakeable sight of Mr. Shaw, dragging himself up to the Burtons' front door as I gaze out of their front window. I so rarely see him outside the post office and, at first, it's difficult to comprehend that he is here.

"It's Mr. Shaw!" I call brightly. "What's he—"

But Mrs. Burton has opened the door. Mrs. Shaw is leaping up, running to the hall, and has collapsed into his arms.

CHAPTER THIRTY-EIGHT

1918—Then

I saw out the rest of the war at Lamarck. I was the number-one driver, even Daisy conceded that. I missed Olive dreadfully, but was happy to get frequent letters from her.

The Vivi who worked in her father's carpet business and dreamed of being a civil servant's dutiful wife was now long buried. This Vivi drove wounded men for hours and dreamed mostly of a gin and soda and a cigarette at the end of a long shift.

And then the war ended and, as quickly as we had got stuck in, we were sent home.

Father said it was like we'd never been away. Olive and I looked at each other. Maybe it felt that way to him, but for both of us, everything had changed. Olive had maintained her strange accent, but she was more placid than she used to be. She went out less—*where would she go now the Fords were finished?*—and I thought she was less interested in her appearance than was seemly.

I thought Olive should go back and finish art school—hadn't she been her happiest at Goldsmiths?—but she was surprisingly averse to the idea. She didn't fit the place any longer, she said. It was like a pair of stockings she'd outgrown.

"All the new ones coming through, with no idea about what we did and what we saw. The war affects everything. You can't even paint a pear without it being there in the background. But the new ones, they don't know about all that."

Aunt Cecily had arranged voluntary work for Olive just one day a week in a recuperation center for wounded soldiers near Liverpool Street station. She did "creative arts" with the men, which as far as I could work out meant anything from weaving and sketching to working with clay, from basket-weaving to paper-folding. She admired her students awfully.

"You should see them, Vivi. Painting with their fingers, feet. One of them even puts the brush between his teeth. These are brave, determined men and their pictures, you know, they're really not all that bad," she said.

Olive seemed lost in other ways though. Restlessly looking for something to do, looking for something to pin her down, yet railing against anything that did. When she painted there was harmony in the house, but she said she had lost her drive for it.

Three mornings a week, I was helping Father with the carpet business. *Is this what family is?* I pondered. To sit here in this windowless office with a notebook and pen, checking Mrs. Webster's figures? Once, I found a rare error. Gleefully, I raised the alarm but, of course, it was later revealed that it was a miscalculation of my own, and not the fault of the impeccable Mrs. Webster.

It was odd to be spending so much time with my father. We had always had a tender, open relationship, I had thought, but now a wall of resentment seemed to have built itself between us. It was difficult to explain why. Perhaps I couldn't help but remember his former support for the war and the way he used to talk about foreigners. This was completely unfair because I had talked that way too, but I suppose I had lost some of the respect I once had for him—and for myself.

Edmund's unit were involved in clear-up operations in France and Belgium so he wasn't demobbed until spring 1919.

I read up on derangement, the thousand-yard stare, shock and madness. *Violence is rare*, the encyclopedia assured me, and I shivered, remembering what had happened to me in the back of the ambulance in France. In fact, those who suffered were more likely to be the victim of violence! I leafed through the encyclopedia, looking for chances of recovery. No one seemed to know, but it suggested that love might work.

I decided I could do that.

Our reunion took place at the Lowes', on the first of April, in front of everyone. Everyone laughed fondly as I walked in and called out: "Oh, Ed!" I'd never once said "Ed" in my life, nor even thought of him as an Ed, but the "mund" just wouldn't come.

He didn't get up from his chair. He was thin, his hair wispier, but he hadn't lost his good looks. I was used to transporting soldiers with no teeth—and no hair—and compared to them, his teeth were impressive.

I stared at him. I wanted a sign that my waiting, my sacrifices, had been worth it. I *needed* a sign.

He did look grateful to see me so I began to feel relieved. It was going to be fine. He had a stick, but he didn't really need it, he just loved the design, he said. It had a little owl carved at the end. He asked if we'd all been looking after Charles, and everyone laughed. *Trust Edmund!*

As lunch went on though, and he talked more to his parents and to my father than to me, my heart sank. This was not what I remembered or had hoped for. I felt like I was performing, I was performing delight at the return of my fiancé when I was feeling rather dead inside. Did he have an illness of the brain? Now I had seen him, I doubted it.

Perhaps it had been military intelligence after all.

Relationships can be hard work, I reminded myself. *We can do this. Think of our families.* I had never been afraid of hard work in France, and I wasn't going to be afraid of it now. That night, I would remember that it was April Fools' Day, but I thought nothing of it.

*

However impressive or not their war record was, it was very tough for the returning soldiers. Mrs. Webster's son, Harry, was now profoundly deaf, but he had found work as a carpenter. Of course, Edmund was cushioned more than most, but his parents were not as wealthy as they used to be—something about stocks and shares—and neither were they generous people. He had to do *something*. His long-ago ambitions of a career in the Indian Civil Service had faded. I tried to be positive, but he darkened at the mention of old dreams.

"They won't want me now," he told me, and when Edmund shut a conversation down, it was well and truly finished. And anyway, he couldn't go away because of Christopher—"How would my parents cope?"

Fortunately, Uncle Toby came up with a job for Edmund managing a bank and so we celebrated, but it was only the Lowes, Aunt Cecily and Uncle Toby, Father, Edmund and me (Olive was occupied at the recuperation center) and it felt like a thin party. Everything that once seemed solid now seemed insubstantial. I felt like we didn't have much to hold onto.

Edmund didn't touch me in those months of our long engagement— well, how could he? We were most always with the parents. Occasionally, we walked alone in the garden, but not often and not for long. If we sat on the bench, there might be a hint of his suppressed passion, but he would always push me away.

"When we're married," he promised. I suppose that, much as it annoyed me, I also quite admired his restraint. Edmund was a gentleman, a churchgoer. He was a man of desire—yes, I knew this from the picture I had found—but he knew how to behave appropriately. *One day*, I told myself, *it will be appropriate. One day, we will be husband and wife and mother and father.*

My father caught the flu, not too badly, then my sister, then finally I went down with it. It was called the Spanish flu (Edmund's mother said, "That figures."). It was going around everywhere, but in a bizarre twist, it didn't seem to hit the feeblest or the elderly—its main targets were the strong. The Angel of Death passed us over, but Olive lost two friends from art school who'd both been struck and died overnight, foam on their lips, and a colleague of Edmund's became very ill and barely managed to pull through. Edmund didn't catch a thing.

Olive told me that the newly formed women's work subcommittee at the new Imperial War Museum wanted to display her paintings. She flushed, explaining they had been in touch before—quite regularly, in fact—but she had been determinedly ignoring them for some time.

"But Olive, this is wonderful," I began. "Your art in a museum? What an honor!"

"I don't know...I don't have anything very good to show."

"Of course you do!"

My darling Olive was losing her confidence, and I couldn't understand what it was. I knew she had lost some of her favorite paintings at the Fords', but there were others that she loved that hadn't been there. Her work in Italy, for instance—that had been at the Lowes' the night of the bombs—even her cartoons.

"What about the one...you know the one I mean?" I asked shyly. *Please don't display it, please don't.*

In an Ambulance: a VAD lighting a cigarette for a patient.

"It's gone."

"I see." I squeezed my hands together. I wanted to know if it had definitely been destroyed by the bomb at the Fords' that night, but I couldn't bring myself to ask.

Finally, Olive agreed to meet the committee, but only if I would come along. It was a hot summer's afternoon and there were too many flies. The committee were, as you'd expect, all keen and persuasive and they loved Olive's work. I couldn't identify the exact source of Olive's reticence, but eventually, she agreed that her work would become part of an exhibition of women who'd served in the war.

Olive wouldn't go to the opening party, but she did greedily read the newspaper reviews of it.

"A controversial selection. Wastelands. Uncompromisingly bleak. If you are looking for solace—" Olive snorted; *perish the thought*—"you won't find it in Olive Mudie-Cooke's unrelenting landscapes."

One critic wrote: "It is the exact opposite of celebration. In no way could Mudie-Cooke's work be described as glorification. These pictures portray tragic waste. A warning might be helpful for those less stout-hearted."

With glee, Olive pored over the coverage. "*Bellissimo!* Not bad for a girl who didn't get to finish college."

Sometimes, it felt like Olive was fine, everything was *bella*, she was the same old Olive Mudie-Cooke, the same little sister. Other times, during that first hard year of peace, it felt like she was slipping away from me. I couldn't put my finger on it. She was retracting more and more into herself. I'd ask her a question and she'd take an age to answer. I'd point something out and she wouldn't comment. Sometimes, she would airily say to me, "Do you remember that man with the disease of the lungs?"

"Yes..."

"I think about him sometimes."

Or, "The man who cried for his daughters, do you remember him?"

"Yes, O."

"He visits me every night."

"Perhaps the doctor could give you something to help you sleep?"

She smiled at me, a curiously unhappy smile. "Do you think I'm going mad, Vi?"

"No," I said sternly, "I don't."

I had enough on my hands worrying if Edmund was crazy. I didn't think I could cope with her too.

I didn't tell Olive, because I knew it wasn't the same, but I felt
like I saw Sam everywhere. I'd see men in a similar uniform, the
same height or head shape, and I'd have to catch my breath. Once, I
followed a delivery man down the street until he looked up, frowning
quizzically. "I'm sorry," I murmured. "I thought you were someone
I used to know."

It's grief and it's normal, I told myself. I distracted myself by sewing,
but every stitch brought me closer to Sam. I dreamed I was wearing
a skirt and I asked him to fix it and he made me stand on a stool,
pins in his mouth, and he folds up the hem and...But Sam was
most likely dead and I and everyone else was grieving. *Lost family,
lost friends, lost dreams.*

And that's what Olive was feeling too, but at the same time her
grief did not seem normal. Or it seemed normal, but with a bit
extra on the side.

I didn't know what it was.

About six months after her exhibition at the Imperial War Museum,
Olive and I went to the National Gallery to see John Singer Sargent's
brand-new painting. It had only been on display for a few days
and already there were reports of fainting and wailing among the
terrified onlookers.

"Excellent way to stir up a crowd," Olive said cynically.

We had to stare at it from behind a rope, and although it was only
9 a.m., there were a good thirty or forty people already there. My
sister wasn't cynical once we were in front of it, though. We stared
at it open-mouthed for a good few minutes.

"Oh God!" Olive sank down onto the cold stone gallery floor. "I
don't know whether to curtsey or bow."

"Get up, Olive." I looked around quietly. Had anyone noticed her
behavior? A couple in black shuffled away from us. The woman
was shaking her head angrily.

Yes, I'm afraid they have.

"It's a masterpiece, isn't it, Vi, can you imagine?"

"Yes, but get up, darling, it's embarrassing."

It was called *Gassed* and showed an army of men, each with their hand on the shoulder of the next. It called to mind the artist Bruegel. Such suffering, pain—incomprehensible.

Outside, despite the chill in the air, we sat on a bench and we couldn't stop talking about it. I said that although it was a brilliant representation of what we had seen, it wasn't realistic-looking. Olive was pale-faced. First, she argued that it *was* realistic, and then that it wasn't.

"Sod realism!" she shouted, waving her program around. "*This* is more honest." She looked around at the people coming down the steps. "This is the truth, you know that. Dirty, ugly, desperate truth. Such a waste, a tragedy."

There was a tea van, and I went over to buy us some. I said it was to warm ourselves up, but mostly it was to give myself time to regroup my thoughts. I couldn't decide if Olive coming here had been a good idea or not. It certainly seemed to have set her off.

"To think," she kept saying, "I thought I was making an artistic contribution."

"You are, O. Your contribution is important."

Her chin jutted out angrily. "I didn't do much. You were always the better ambulance driver."

"You're the far better painter, darling." I laughed. She could be ridiculous.

A massive man crammed into a modern-fitting suit came toward us. I thought he was going to tell us off, maybe make a point about how unladylike Olive was—people did so much like to point it out—but instead, he shook our cold hands enthusiastically:

"Remember me? It's Johnny, Johnny Wardle . . . I saw you admiring the Singer Sargent. So impressive, isn't it?"

"Johnny!" we both called out. How delightful it was to see a face from the old days. Could it only have been five years ago? Five years of tumultuous change.

"I haven't seen anyone for years. How the devil is everyone? Walter, Uilleam, David—or should I say, 'the world-famous Ivor Novello'?"

Olive paled. I probably did too. He didn't know what had happened.

"What?—Who?"

Olive shook her head slowly. "Walter was killed."

"Oh no." He paused. We all stared at the floor. "Where?"

Olive hesitated. "In London. It was a bomb."

He rubbed his head in shock. "Here in London? Well, I never... his poor mother must be devastated. I never knew a woman more beautiful than Mrs. Ford, inside and out. I will go and see her as soon as—"

I interjected. Olive was shaking her head but seemed unable to say anything else.

"I'm sorry, Johnny, she was lost too."

He shook our hands once more and went off, considerably less sprightly than when he had arrived.

CHAPTER THIRTY-NINE

1942—Now

In Mrs. Burton's living room, life goes on. We WAVs knit and make and do the accounts for the tea van. We talk about how the butchers are so low on quality meat now, and about the best things you can make with turnips and parsnips and the blackberry bushes near Farmer Jones's, perfect for a crumble. Replacing things is our skill; working out the things we can do without. The things you get used to. We wonder if the Russians will halt the Germans—surely the Russians will halt the Germans! The fighting at Stalingrad is brutal, we hear. Horrendous.

Mrs. Shaw is quieter than she used to be. We make sure she knows she is always welcome. She can talk about her Simon, who is missing after his ship was sunk in the Mediterranean, whenever she feels up to it.

Ethel Burton has just turned eighteen and is raring to do her bit. She has joined the Land Army and is delighted to be stationed in Norfolk. She thinks anything is better than working in munitions.

I go over on her last morning at home. Mrs. Burton is still upstairs, packing for her. (Mrs. Burton doesn't know how Ethel will manage living on her own.)

Ethel shows me her pretty engagement ring. They're saving everything they can for the dress. And they've come good on their promise: Pearl *will* be their bridesmaid. "This time next year."

All being well.

"You must miss Cyril," I say.

She nods vigorously. She's a glamourous young woman and I wonder how she'll manage on an isolated farm. "I hate that he's away, I get so lonely." She smiles shyly at me. "But it's a bit like that song you all used to sing in the old days, 'Keep the Home Fires Burning.'"

"Mm," I say. I feel suddenly tearful at this optimistic young girl starting out on adult life.

"That's what I'm going to do for Cyril."

CHAPTER FORTY

1920—Then

The day before my wedding, Olive was jittery. She had the same vacant expression she sometimes had when she was immersed in a picture. She was wearing her painting clothes all the time now too. I didn't like seeing her so disheveled. It was awkward.

She said, "I've got something I simply must tell you, Vivi. It's exceedingly important." And I led her upstairs to my room, because important things didn't belong downstairs where people could hear. I wasn't too worried though—Olive and I had always had different ideas of what "important" meant. Important to Olive was "there's an exhibition at the Royal Academy and I will die if I can't go."

"I don't think you should marry Edmund."

"What? Olive! Why do you have to do this?"

"He's no good for you."

I had to tell myself to breathe, I had been holding my breath for so long. *Out and in. That's how you do it.* She was gazing at me. No one gazed like Olive.

My dressing table consisted of three white drawers and three mirrors arranged in a kind of horseshoe shape. I stared into the mirrors. My face was reflected back hundreds of times and in each image, I looked disappointed and aloof. I didn't *feel* disappointed or aloof, but I did feel anxious. Olive was so unpredictable these days that she had that effect on me. I thought, *she's not going to mention his visits to the Windmill, is she? Please don't, Olive.*

"Do you remember that time that plane went down in the field?"

I nodded. I knew she sometimes thought I was slow and simple, but did she seriously think I would forget Sam just like that? She must have known how I had felt about him.

"And then you became friends with the pilot...and I painted you."

I frowned. I didn't know why she was saying this unless she was intending to be cruel.

"*That's* the man you should marry."

Oh God.

"Olive, is this really the *exceedingly important* thing you had to tell me?"

"Yes," she said defiantly.

My mistake was to try to reason with her. "O, I haven't seen him for...so many years."

Three years and four months.

"So?"

"So, if he wanted me, he'd come."

Don't write. Don't call. Don't speak to me.

Olive was shaking her head vigorously. She hated to be wrong. "I bet *he* thinks you don't want him, Vivi. Go and see him, go and find him today before it's too late."

"The wedding is *tomorrow*, Olive. Be serious. You want me to call it off, just because—" my voice cracked—"you imagine I'll get on better with someone else."

"It's not just someone else though, is it? You loved him. You don't love Edmund."

"You're being ridiculous."

I must stop thinking about the way he kissed me. Olive doesn't know anything about that.

I clipped on my earrings. A present from Aunt Cecily, they had been Mother's originally. I hadn't told Olive where they were from and I was scared she would ask. That afternoon we would have tea with Edmund's parents. All of us. The families together. Olive had better come along. Her hatred of convention never ceased to amaze me. She would destroy us all if she carried on like this.

The earrings were too tight, and my lobes began to turn a distressing shade of lobster. I didn't know whether to change the subject or persevere.

"You don't love Edmund Lowe. We both know that."

"Even if I did want to be with Sam, which I don't, it's too late now," I told her. "He's probably dead."

"I would have heard if he was dead!" she exclaimed.

"What? That's ridiculous. And anyway, I wouldn't know where—"

"I'll be able to find him!" she shouted excitedly. "I *bet* I could. I know what synagogue he belongs to, it wouldn't be—"

"No!" I said. The word synagogue sent ugly shivers down my spine. "No, I'm marrying Edmund. I can hardly let him down now, can I?"

It wasn't just Edmund I was marrying either. This was what Olive didn't understand. It was *all* of us marrying *all* of them. We would become one big family. I thought of the cake that Aunt Cecily was slaving over. When she'd told me she was baking three tiers, I had inexplicably thought she meant *tears*. I thought of the bunting being sewn by Edmund's aunt. I thought of the guest list: *Lady this, that and the other. Lord and Lady Mosley.* The gentry were coming. Even Father had been rendered speechless at some of the names. "That's my girl," he'd said finally, tears in his eyes. "We *are* going up in the world."

Even Pigeon was coming. Edmund's mother said that that girl was desperate to get her claws into someone and a wedding was as good an occasion as any, even if it was your dead fiancé's brother's wedding.

Edmund's mother had bought my dress. "Because of how you were with Christopher," she said. "I'll never forget that." And we would marry in the church where Christopher was buried and the vicar was the one who had buried him.

Christopher was never far from our thoughts.

Edmund's mother had wanted to buy Olive a silk dress too. *"We can't have her turning up in one of those smocks. Really, Vivienne, you know I think some of them are starting to smell."*

Now, Olive stared at me venomously.

"You can't *love* Edmund, Vivi, you just can't. He's so…" She paused, I wondered what sneer she would find to say about him. She twisted my lipstick round so it rose majestically out of its container. "Unlovable."

"He's fine, O."

"Fine? Could you sound any more tepid?"

"He's a good man and he's been through a lot."

"Everyone has."

"No, Edmund has more than most people. Not only did he fight bravely in the war"—I said this although I had no idea how brave he had been, or if he'd been brave at all—"he's also been very sick. You don't think I can just drop him now, after all that?" I hissed. "How would that look?"

She gazed at me, shook her head, then stomped out of my room.

"Sam," I breathed. I let my hands go to my earrings and I took them off. My ears felt gloriously free again. I had to say it out loud: "Sam."

I had wanted to marry in June; I had fancies of being a June bride, but it was one of those compromises you make. Lord and Lady Mosley were going to Australia in June, so if we wanted them there… Besides, what was the use in waiting? Edmund and I had known each other for over twelve years; we had been engaged for three, reunited for one. No one could say we were hasty. We weren't like all those "intense" and foolish war couples. No one could say I didn't know what I was getting into. So, on 24 May 1920, I took a deep breath and hoped for the best. And didn't Edmund look handsome in his uniform, with that impressive row of medals? Everyone agreed. Later, I heard people say, "He almost outdid the bride."

*

Throughout the ceremony, I couldn't help thinking, *What would Sam say if he could see this?* I hated Olive for putting him back squarely into my head when I had worked so very hard at getting him out.

No, it wasn't her fault.

I wanted to know how she was so confident that she'd know if Sam were dead, but I didn't dare ask.

Edmund's father gave a long speech about how Christopher should have been there, and talked about Edmund's war service too. He breezed over his illness. He said, "We nearly lost this boy too. Thank goodness we didn't."

Edmund's father didn't mention my war service at all. My years in France with the FANYs seemed to have been erased from history.

Then my father stood up. This was unexpected because he was a man who hated formality and speeches, and he knew he was a fish out of water here; but he too wanted to reference Edmund's "commendable" war service. He mentioned our dear cousin Richard and I saw Aunt Cecily cover her face with her handkerchief. And how, at the beginning of the war, there were two brothers and their best friend: Christopher, Edmund and Richard, and now only one of them stood before us, and how proud and grateful he was to be his father-in-law. He wasn't just saving the country but building the future, the *right* kind of future.

Then my father made a joke about rolling out the red carpets—he'd do it himself—and everyone laughed, even Edmund's parents, although I guessed they were thinking "*nouveau riche.*" Or perhaps not "*nouveau riche,*" because it was French—perhaps only "*newly rich*" would do. I wished my father would sit down. Everyone was hungry and we had lords and ladies there, although, *surprise, surprise,* not all of them had turned up.

And of course, as is tradition, the bride didn't say anything. Only, it didn't feel like tradition somehow; I felt like a gag had been placed over my mouth. I tiptoed that day even though there were no tulips, only white carnations.

Pigeon came over, and then she and Edmund were giggling about something.

"What is it?"

"Private joke," she said, but I guessed from their expressions it was about Edmund's déclassé in-laws.

Then there was the dancing. Olive was soon flying about the room, looking hot and bothered, but not letting that stop her. Pretty and pale, she was in a dark navy dress. She *did* get attention, but she didn't *keep* attention, for she never responded and men swiftly transferred it to girls who looked like they might be less challenging.

We had an extraordinary band. One of them was a blind man playing on the trumpet. I asked them to play "Keep the Home Fires Burning," and when they did, O rushed over to me and hugged me and we danced together, my wonderful, terrible sister and I.

"I love you, Vivi. You're the best."

"I love you, O. Don't ever doubt it."

I had wondered and I had worried about my wedding night. I suppose the fact that I thought it was *my* wedding night, not ours, says something. Obviously, I didn't have a mother I could ask questions of, although I don't know what questions I would have asked even if I had the chance. I thought Olive might know some of the details, but I think she would have assumed I already knew everything and I was embarrassed to admit the extent of my ignorance. I was the big sister, she should be the one asking me. And anyway, it wasn't the details I lacked. An encyclopedia we had when I was a child had informed me of those. It was the emotional side of the thing I couldn't comprehend.

If I had only thought to write to Daisy or Enid in advance…
Unfortunately, it hadn't occurred to me soon enough. When I had
tentatively broached the subject with Aunt Cecily, she had replied,
"Edmund believes in the teachings of the Church. I don't think you've
got a lot to worry about, Vivienne."

I tried not to remember Sam. It was important not to remember
Sam's eyes and especially his soft lips, and how I felt that time when
he kissed me goodbye with such tenderness and longing that I had
forgotten where I was.

I thought Edmund might want to undress me, but he could be
so fastidious sometimes. It was so easy to get it wrong with him and
I was afraid of making an error, but for once he too looked nervous
and uncertain. He switched on the plump table lamp with its stained
shade and then switched off the overhead light. The lampshade had
little tassels and for some stupid reason, my mind went straight to
the Windmill, where they said women danced with tassels on their
breasts for money. Edmund undressed himself down to his long
johns and vest and almost leapt into bed. I suppose it was fear that
set me to thinking, *Hop, little rabbit, hop, hop, hop!*

I chided myself. This was not the moment for silliness.

I wished I could speak to Olive. There were times I needed her.
She'd know what to do.

So, I did the same as Edmund, slowly stowing away my wedding
dress in the wardrobe. I was careful, so it wouldn't crease. I was
going to pass this on to our children. *Children*: that was what I had
to focus on.

Then I lay there, still as a breakfast bowl on a newly ironed
tablecloth, and he said, "Goodnight then." And the sense of wrongness
that has been a recurrent hum of my life, like the rumblings of the
Underground trains on the city streets, suddenly became a searing
pain and I almost wanted to cry out with it. But I didn't. I gathered
myself, and told myself, *We both want children. That will unite us
and keep us together. The daughter who will wear your wedding dress,*

the son who will have connections and a good job in a bank or maybe
even in the Indian Civil Service, you never know—the babies I will
push in a navy perambulator with big metal wheels through the park.
Those dreams were about to come true, I just had to hold my nose
and get on with it.

I said lightly. "Shouldn't we...do something, Edmund?"

He said he didn't mind.

"Have you...been with a woman before?"

Edmund went a dark shade of crimson. "I don't want to say."

I thought of the card I had found deep in the pocket of his gray
overcoat. The woman showing off her triangle of hair.

It sounded like he had. I didn't know if I was relieved or not. A
little relieved maybe. He readjusted his pajamas.

"Does that mean yes?" I persisted.

My eyes were level with his throat. I could see the awkwardness
of his swallow, the journey of his Adam's apple. "It means, not with
anyone important."

I lifted up his hand and placed it on my hip where the hem of
my nightie lay.

"Then we will learn together, Mr. Lowe."

I expected him to say something about my now being Mrs. Lowe
but he didn't. Maybe it was best he didn't. Maybe this wasn't the
time to think about Mrs. Lowe.

CHAPTER FORTY-ONE

1942—Now

Mrs. Burton asks me to babysit. Not the girls; they're "old enough and ugly enough" (they are not at all ugly!) to look after themselves. No, she wants me to look after the dogs, Laurel and Hardy.

She and Mr. Burton are going off for a celebratory night away. It's their anniversary. She's a September bride. *Twenty-five bloody years.*

How lovely.

"I thought he was a gonner in Coventry," she says often, and I always add, "We all did."

I agree to go over with Pearl. Pearl can cat-nap on the sofa. We will listen to the wireless and read.

Ethel is away, coping very well with the farm work. She is hardier than anyone expected.

Younger daughter, Sally, the bookish one, is all dressed up. Hair rolled, pretty cardigan, twirly skirt that has a life of its own. I've never seen her look so lovely—she's going to a Lindy Hop.

Mrs. Burton can't leave the house without having baked a cake, so Pearl and I share a sliver of a slice. The clock ticks slowly. I remember the first time I sat in this kitchen with my slippers on. How awkward I had been. Now, it's like a second home—a favorite home, really.

Tongue out, Pearl practices her spellings. I think the words are too difficult for a child her age.

Telescope. Telegram. Circumference. Circumstance.

Then I make her write them without looking at the words. Pearl's spelling is abysmal but she's good with the meaning of words, so I think we needn't worry too much.

At eleven o'clock, I hear footsteps—a rustling, a giggling beyond the front door. The bookish daughter is back. She is with someone. A man? Yes. He is wearing a heavy coat—he is a foot taller than her, maybe—and he wraps her in it.

I shouldn't be looking, but it is quite charming.

They smooch for a long time under the porch light.

It's not until he has turned to wave, a final yearning wave, that I can see who it is.

I avoid Mrs. Burton the next day. I queue for food, then play the piano and dominoes at the old people's home and do a big wash and iron. But on Thursday, there is no evading her. We're taking the tea van out to the train station, to meet the people off the trains. As I start the engine, I think, *Would Mrs. Burton tell me?* Yes, she probably would.

In my most casual voice, I squeak, "I didn't know Sally had a boyfriend?"

"She doesn't," replies Mrs. Burton.

Sally had come in that evening all friendly and oblivious. Her lipstick was smeared, her previously orderly hair was all over the place and she was all giggles and teeth.

"Oh, I see."

Mrs. Burton and I park up. We rinse the teapot with hot water to warm it, no skimping. The state-of-the-art urn is making all the right noises. We put the cups out and put a touch of milk in the bottom of each one. Saves time later. We brew the tea for five minutes, although if it's busy, we might end up cutting corners with just four.

"I think she *might* have a boyfriend," I say eventually.

"She's too young."

Just be factual, I tell myself. *It's the only way.*

Here comes the train. The first batch of tea-drinkers will soon be out. I wipe the counter again.

"I may have…I did, I think…I saw her kissing someone last night."

"Who?"

"Nathan."

"Who's Nathan?"

"Farmer Jones's evacuee boy?"

Mrs. Burton drops her cup and saucer and they shatter on the floor.

CHAPTER FORTY-TWO

1920—Then

Olive kept looking backward; I wanted to look forward. Plus, I didn't think looking backward all the time was good for her. You end up tripping over things.

"Why won't you talk about the war?" she would ask. Sometimes angrily, sometimes with an indecipherable expression on her face.

"Because it's over now." Or, "What else is there to say?"

A veil had been drawn across 1914 to 1918. Those were our amputated years. You don't go up to a man without a leg and ask how his leg is, do you? But an Armistice Day party was being held at the club Edmund's parents went to and they, and our father and Aunt Cecily and Uncle Toby, were looking forward to it. It seemed only *some* looking backward was frowned upon, some was danced at.

There were frills and flounces and the November air smelled of perfume, cologne, smoke and whisky. We were all dressed to the nines, even Olive, who'd reluctantly accepted my offer of a red dress and a black fur cape. She looked like a poppy. A shivering poppy.

"It's good for you to let your hair down," said Aunt Cecily, who was worried that Olive was both too thin and too serious about her work at the recuperation center. Olive made a face but said nothing.

"I regret getting her involved there," Aunt Cecily confided in me. "Mulling over it all the time can't be good for her."

*

If there was one thing Edmund could do quite brilliantly, both before *and* after the war, it was dance. He was unexpectedly light on his feet, while being exceptionally mobile in his hips. Although he would avoid meeting my eyes like an errant schoolboy, his legs and arms worked so gaily and brightly together it was impossible not to enjoy dancing with him. I laughed through the first few dances, knowing that our families—and not just our families—were watching us approvingly. Here we were, the bright generation, the survivors, the newly-weds. Things couldn't be too bad. Glorious to be so close to Edmund, to be the gay, bright couple everyone imagined we were. I didn't want it to stop.

Maybe tonight will be the night that Edmund and I will make love and something extraordinary will happen, I thought. We had been married nearly six months and my menses had disappointingly come every month without fail. I could barely bring myself to check my underwear any more.

I stole a look at him. He was one of the most handsome men there. King to my queen (Olive playing the jester).

After a few dances, Edmund said he needed a drink, and I had to admit I did too. Still, it was with reluctance that I went back to our table. I loved being on the dancefloor with Edmund. Seeing Olive slumped in her chair, sulking, made me feel uncomfortable. I thought she had been drinking too much, but I wasn't sure if I should point it out. I turned my attention to Aunt Cecily and Edmund's mother.

"We were just talking about you," Aunt Cecily said brightly, although Edmund's mother scowled, twisting her fingers agitatedly.

All eyes were on Edmund and me. I could feel their neediness as clearly as the fox stole on my shoulders.

"Oh yes?"

"When you have a son, you will call him Christopher Richard—Christopher Richard Lowe—won't you?" Aunt Cecily said. *Was it me being paranoid or was Edmund's mother grimacing? Was she annoyed with Olive? Probably.*

I nodded, non-committal. "We'll see."

Olive inhaled. "But what if you have a daughter?"

"I don't know," I said. "Maybe I'll name her after our mother?"

"How about the name Lena?" Olive asked. I shrugged. She persisted. "What's wrong with it?"

"Nothing!" I said, surprised. Were we really talking about this? I wasn't even pregnant.

"Is Lena an English name?" asked Edmund's mother, while Aunt Cecily said, rather more charitably, "Oh, I remember your poor friend Mrs. Ford, Olive. Lena was her name, isn't that so? What a terrible shame."

Olive leaned in to my ear. "What about Sam? I always liked that name. Or is that too Jewishy for you?"

I bristled and moved away from her. *What had got into her tonight?*

After a few more dances, I returned to find Olive still sitting in the same place, in the same unladylike position.

She looked up at me, bleary-eyed.

"Do you remember that time you were attacked in the ambulance, when that soldier leapt on you, shouting—"

"Why are you mentioning this now?"

"No one else will. Why shouldn't I?"

"Because we're at a *dance*, darling. We're supposed to be having a good time."

She dug into her handbag and took out her pipe.

"Not here, O," I warned her. "It's not...right."

"Just winding you up," she said. "God, Vivi, when did you become so conservative?" She produced a neat silver hip-flask. I'd seen men drink from them before, but never a woman and never my sister. She twisted off the cap and drank lustily.

"What's in it?" I asked.

She sniffed the bottle: "Ahh...It's a very fine liquor called Ways to Forget."

Edmund wanted to dance again. I looked back at Olive but it seemed she was determined to indulge her melancholy. I took Edmund's hand and we circled the room. My skirt flipped around my legs, and I knew my ankles looked shapely. We made an attractive couple. It was rare that I got to feel like this, like we were the married couple that everyone thought we were, the one they envied.

When I came back, I felt my patience with Olive running thin. "Dance with someone or you'll look like a gooseberry."

I meant it as a joke, but soon as I saw the hurt shock on Olive's face, I regretted it. I tried to pat her shoulder, but she wouldn't let me. Her cheeks were aflame.

Olive rose unsteadily from her chair. She pulled another face at me, like *Is this really what you want?* Then she circled the room, glaring at each table. It was quite unfriendly. People stared back at her—they didn't like her attitude. I saw one woman remonstrate with her husband, telling him to let her be. She tapped her head: "*Cuckoo.*"

My sister.

Olive had circled nearly the entire room when at last she found what she was looking for. A man in uniform with stumps for legs, in a wheelchair. Red, alcohol-flushed face, trembling hands. He looked up at her and, unlike the other guests, he seemed glad of the attention.

I watched them talk. He crushed his cigarette in the plate next to him and she took the handles of his chair. She whirled around with him. He must have felt dizzy, poor soul, but he didn't look like he minded. I shook my head at her, but at that, she actually climbed on his lap and sat there. He was half-cut too. I shook my head again. *For goodness' sake, what would people think?* To add to the indecency, directly above them was a picture of the King and the British flag. Edmund gripped my arm.

"Get your sister under control!" he said sharply. I went over to her. I didn't want to be noticed but I was. People were staring. I tugged at the back of her dress.

"You can't behave like this, Olive," I hissed.

She giggled, slid off the man's lap.

"Where are you going?" he called, disgruntled.

"I'll get us some more drinks." She smiled brightly at him and he relented.

"You had better come back!" he called. His words had an undercurrent of aggression that I didn't like.

"I'm taking you home," I said. Olive let me guide her out the hall and I thought she had acquiesced, but at the ornate doors, she grinned impishly at me and said, "See you, Vivi," and skipped off into the misty night.

CHAPTER FORTY-THREE

1942—Now

So, it's official. Mrs. Burton's youngest daughter, Sally, is walking out with Farmer Jones's Nathan.

"And why not?" says Mrs. Burton, once she's over the shock. "She's seventeen now." She grimaces. "God knows, I was only sixteen when I met her father."

And about the other thing? The fact that he is...you know?

No, Mrs. Burton doesn't care that Sally's boyfriend is Jewish. Well, she does *care*, she just doesn't object.

"Relationships are hard," she announces. "You know that."

I nod imperceptibly. *Yes, I know that.*

"And probably, maybe, it helps if you've got a lot in common—faith, background, type, I don't know—but..." she continues ferociously, "there's no guarantee of anything. If he can love my daughter, and be loved by my daughter, then that's good enough for me. I don't care if he's from Timbuktu wearing a sombrero on his head."

"I feel that's unlikely..."

"A fez then."

I sit in her kitchen, sipping my tea thoughtfully.

Twenty-five years has made a difference, I thought. "Times change"—isn't that what people say? No, "times" *don't* change...well, they do, but they don't change by themselves. People have to change, it's people who change the times.

I hadn't had the strength in 1916 to put all my own prejudice and stupidity behind me. And now it was too late. But maybe for the next generation, for Sally and for Pearl, things could be better.

CHAPTER FORTY-FOUR

1921—Then

Edmund and I moved to the house in Hinckley in August 1921. We had been married for one year and three months. In a rare moment of synchronicity, we both wanted out of London. I had my reasons. I'm not entirely sure what his were but he was offered a job in the Leicester branch of the bank. Apparently, he could go far.

I remember waving off the removal truck, fizzing with excitement. We took the train, promising to meet the truck at the new house. We were still trying to have children at that stage. At least, I was trying. And that day, it finally felt like Edmund and I were a team, or at least on the same side, going into our new life together. I was very excited.

The house was a new-build in a cul-de-sac. I had explained several times to different family members that the French word simply meant "bottom of the bag." Edmund's mother was quite disapproving of the "French influence."

"Is it because of the war?" she asked, nonsensically.

Edmund called our street a "dead end" and we had an ongoing joke about it between us. He did make me smile sometimes.

"A new start!" Edmund kept repeating. He actually patted my hand affectionately in the carriage. "It'll be good to get away from the temptations of the city."

I stared out at the uniform trees as they flashed by. There was something familiar about the landscape, even though it was new to me.

"Temptations?"

"You know what I mean," he said shortly, withdrawing his touch. He always punished me if I didn't stay in line.

"Leicester is better for raising a family," he said. And I smiled. *A family.* It was the one thing that we were on the same page about.

"Especially in a cul-de-sac." I smiled.

"Dead end." He smirked.

"I wonder what our neighbors are like?"

"Don't get too involved," he warned me. "I know what you're like."

"What am I like?" I asked coquettishly. *This has been a nice trip.*

"Easily swayed," he said, looking out of the window. He got up and pushed the glass down. "So hot in here, isn't it?"

We were both quite absorbed in our future plans. *Children!* The hope was that children would be the glue that held us together.

Olive was living in Newlyn in Cornwall. A pretty fisherman's cottage with stained-glass windows of dolphins. I'm not sure how she came to be there. I remembered Daisy's tales of the sea, the light and the clotted cream and how we all chorused that we'd love to go there some day. Olive must have been being serious when she said it.

I visited her once. It wasn't a successful trip and at the time I wasn't sure why. Things should have been on the up for both of us. The terrible war years were well and truly over. I had the husband I wanted. She was doing the art she loved.

The rain poured down every day, and I was affronted because the rest of the country was reportedly sunny and dry. "Cornwall has a mind of its own," Olive said. She liked that about it.

She was courting someone, she said. *You'll be pleased.* She didn't seem to be.

We went to meet him. He was a picture framer, Laurie, a bearded fellow with a black cat called Lucy. I'd been quite taken with the cat. Olive pretended he didn't stay over, but I think he might have. Small clues: cologne in the bathroom. Men's muddy boots by the back door. I thought there was something a little strange about him, but I didn't think much of it. A lot of people were strange. A gunner at Neuve Chapelle, he'd been captured and kept prisoner of war for over a year. When Olive told me, I thought, *Ah, maybe that explains it.*

I remember there was a moment when the rain stopped, and we tore off to play badminton on the beach. Playing badminton always reminded me of Sam although I tried not to let it. I was a married woman now with a home in a cul-de-sac.

We were eating buttered rolls when Olive said, quite out of the blue, "Did I tell you, Laurie? Vivi once saved a man from a burning plane."

Laurie stared at me. His eyes were very blue. I could not think of a single reason Olive should have mentioned it now.

"I wouldn't have expected her to have done anything else," he said. He was good with words.

When Olive walked ahead of us back to the cottage, he put his arm round my shoulders and squeezed for just a little too long. I didn't know whether to tell her about it, but when he did it again later, when she was in the kitchen, and again, when she was looking in a shop for new pencils, I knew I had to.

She said, "I thought so," and, "It's not just you, darling, don't worry."

"You aren't that keen on him anyway, are you?"

She laughed, a tight sound. "I'm not keen on him at all." She paused. "He is an awfully good framer though."

Olive was invited to hold an exhibition in South Africa. I could understand why she was tempted: I imagine it was well-timed. It made the split from the picture framer more decisive, more real. I still felt wrong-footed when she actually left though. I hoped she had put the travel bug behind her, but she said she had nothing to keep her here. I felt quite hurt, but tried not to let her know.

And it was in a big place, a big museum, and she would be the key artist; they called her a "war artist"—they didn't even call her a "female artist," just "artist." She would be the big name, the main attraction. Fancy that.

She said she couldn't believe her luck.

Even cynical Edmund was galvanized by this news. *International fame! A successful sister-in-law!* This, he liked. He had connections in South Africa, he told us; it was a place he'd always hoped to go. He told Olive about places she should visit and things she might want to read. He gave her addresses for the people she must call on, and even though I realized they were probably as far from the gallery as we were, it still struck me as generous. *See,* I told myself, *Edmund can be so thoughtful when he chooses to be.*

The trip was a great success. Olive made friends on the way out: on the ship, there were accordion players and comedians, singers and actors, the kind of people she liked best, and once she arrived, she was taken care of, courted and even feted. *The South Africans are fascinated by the war. And what's more, they are fascinated by me!*

She was having such a brilliant time that I began to wonder if she would stay out there forever, but when I suggested it, she wrote back.

No, I wouldn't want that. I would miss you all too much. What about Father? she asked (for the first time).

So, when the exhibition finished—and it lasted two months—she got on the first boat home.

I went to meet her in London. I think her letters must have given me a false sense of her well-being, for when we met, I found her distracted and agitated again. I couldn't help thinking it was as though she was back to square one, like those first few months after the war. At the risk of sounding like Aunt Cecily, I told her she looked too thin. I didn't tell her that her clothes were awful too.

We had afternoon tea near Father's office. She wanted to surprise him with me. "But he is expecting me," I explained, and she said, "Yes, but the two of us together, that will be a surprise."

If Father was surprised, he hid it very well. He was delighted though.

Olive had only been in the country for three days, but she had already been to Warrington Crescent. She wanted to find out more about what had happened the night of the bombing in March 1918.

"What is there to find out?" I asked nervously.

Olive scowled at me. "Well, Mrs. Ford was working on some new songs—"

"Was she?"

"Yes, and some of them were saved!" she boasted proudly. "'We Are Coming, Mother England,' 'When God Gave You to Me' and 'God Guard You.'"

"Are they any good?" I asked.

She frowned. "Yes, of course they're good. Mrs. Ford was a wonderful lyricist, one of our greatest."

"All right, O." I found these conversations surprisingly wearing. She would get so intense. We were talking about things that happened over four years ago now.

I wanted to hear about her trip to South Africa, not about the Fords, and I decided to tell her so. Olive grunted at me but, later, began recounting the wonder of it all: it was clear to me she was proud at how much traveling she had managed to fit in. She had been privileged to see elephants, giraffes and a strange creature called a wildebeest and did I know how fast a cheetah could run? And the shocking thing was, just one week before she had arrived, someone had been torn limb from limb by a lion.

"You would love it!" she declared. I was still reeling from her stories when she leaned forward over the scones and whispered that she was still unable to paint anything original at all and she was feeling quite, quite desperate about that.

I paused. I felt very much that I didn't want to say the wrong thing and I couldn't help feeling anything I did say would be wrong.

I asked if it was like the writer's block I had heard about, and she hummed and hawed before saying, "Yes, maybe, it is something like that."

She asked about the time we had been under fire and we had stayed put. "Frank Bellingham," she said. "That was his name. I wonder if he made it? Then we sang 'Keep the Home Fires Burning,'" she said breathlessly. "Didn't we?"

"Yes, Olive," I said. Her eyes were full of tears.

"And...And, Vi? Do you remember the first night, the last mission?" I knew which one she was talking about before she said it. "Vivi, am I imagining this? But the soldier—his face came off in my hands?"

I didn't know whether to lie or not. Eventually, I nodded and said, "You shouldn't go over it so much in your mind though, you know that."

"I can't stop seeing it." She rubbed her eyes. "It's always there."

CHAPTER FORTY-FIVE

1942—Now

This year, the school play is Charles Dickens's *Oliver Twist*. *Really?* I think to myself. This sounds too grown-up for Pearl, who still recites "Goodnight Children, Everywhere" with me and Vera Lynn at bedtime. But then I think everything sounds too grown-up for Pearl—maybe it's just me.

Trotting home, she chats excitedly about it. It will be performed in the village hall; the children are going to have to look really mucky.

I think that won't present a problem for Pearl. She's got scabs on her knees, scabs on her elbows and mud streaks on her chin.

"Do you want a part?"

I think of the brave little girl scrunched over her suitcase in the village hall three years ago. Who'd have thought it?

She beams at me. "YES! I want to be Oliver Twist."

Of course she does.

I start to caution her. "They might—"

"—Want a boy, I know. In that case, I'll be Nancy."

Nancy? If I remember rightly, things didn't go too well for her. "Which teacher is in charge of it?"

"Mrs. Bankhead," replies Pearl.

"Right."

I have a bad feeling about this.

We have parsnip soup—it's two days old but then, compensation for such a poor supper, we share a bar of chocolate that Mrs. Dean was sent from America. She has cousins who live there, generous cousins, and when their parcels make it across the Atlantic, the whole street is rewarded. Pearl practices for her audition while I slip next door to help Mrs. Burton see to two dogs: Toby, which makes me think of Uncle Toby, of course, and Rex. We get a satisfying amount of fur out of them. I ask Mrs. Burton if she knows *Oliver Twist*. She doesn't, so I explain it to her: "Poor Oliver is sent to live at an orphanage but flung out when he asks for more food. Found by the street gang, led by—" I suddenly realize where I might be going with this, "...an old Jewish fellow, Fagin. He's not very nice." I pause. "In fact, he's the worst villain imaginable."

"Who do you think they'll get Pearl to play?"

"Goodness knows," I lie. I *bet* I know what Mrs. Bankhead has got in mind.

Edmund says why would he want to go and see a school play in the village hall? It gets so drafty in there. He won't accompany me, so I get a ticket for Mrs. Burton instead.

A few days later, it's decided. Pearl swings while I hold her bags. She leans backward. Bliss! She loves the freedom of Friday afternoons. The clouds move above us slowly.

They chose an older boy for Oliver. A petite, softly spoken boy, nephew of the milkman. *This might be a good fit*, I think.

"And Nancy?"

"Mrs. Bankhead's daughter."

I didn't know she had a daughter.

But Pearl is smiling anyway. "I've got a good role, Aunty Vi, a big speaking part. I'm going to be Fagin!"

"I... Really?"

"Yes!"

"And you don't mind?"

"NO!"

"Then that's excellent, Pearl! I can't wait."

What would Olive do? I think of how she stormed out of the Lowes' at injustices and slights. She loathed any kind of intolerance or bigotry—but *was* this intolerance, *was* this bigotry? I'm not sure. And isn't it a small thing anyway, a buttercup of a thing? Wouldn't I be an awful fusspot to take it to the school? And anyway, Pearl is so, so excited. It would surely be strange to intervene…

I leave it.

But a few days later, I go past the village hall when the lower school are rehearsing, and I see what Pearl is performing and it is so riddled with ugly stereotypes, with racist propaganda, I almost feel dirty just watching it.

"Mrs. Bankhead!" I call—*it's now or never*—and she turns, unenthusiastically.

"Mrs. Lowe."

I can see it in her face: *over-involved host mother.*

"You have a class full of children and you chose Pearl Posner to be the…the Fagin. Is that a coincidence?"

"I don't know what you mean."

Thinking of Sam—*Things are very difficult for the Jewish people. When times are hard, those who are different are often blamed or scapegoated. We seem always to be at hand for that*—I plant my feet.

The debate does me no good. Mrs. Bankhead is, of course, unfazed by anything I say and I can't find the right words anyway. I feel Pearl being singled out to play Fagin is wrong, but I can't quite formulate why. For the next few days, I have a squirmy, shameful feeling in my stomach. Confrontation is not my strong point. However, the next Friday, Pearl comes bounding out of school, satchel swinging: "I'm the Artful Dodger now, and I like him best!"

"What happened to Fagin?"

"Mrs. Bankhead decided Keith and Bill will take it in turns."

I hug her, tell her I can't wait for the show. *What an amazing turn of events!*

She begs to go to Mrs. Dean's to call her mum with the good news. I agree, and rummage for the sixpence.

That night on the wireless, we learn that Singapore has fallen. Another country down. The dark tide seems relentless. The whole world must be wondering: *will the war never end? It can't go on for much longer, can it?*

But at least I have Pearl Posner, the Artful Dodger. They can't take her away from me.

CHAPTER FORTY-SIX

1923—Then

Olive and I sat on the back steps of Father's house. She smoked her pipe and I smoked my stress-relieving cigarettes. It was March and already I was visiting for my third time that year. I visited Portchester Terrace a lot. Edmund said I visited *too* much, but he never seemed bothered about me when I was at home in Hinckley so I figured it made little difference. By this time, he had already moved himself into the other bedroom. He said it was because I snored in my sleep. I was hurt by this and had resolved to ask Olive if it was true, but I could never quite bring myself to do it: whatever she said would have been hurtful.

I was pulled between here and there. My father's business was undergoing a post-war renaissance. The Middle Eastern routes had reopened. In the living room were two Turkish men with fine fabric strips and logbooks. Father said the quality was better and better all the time. He was sending rugs all over the country. I was glad he was doing well, yet it seemed part-rebuke that I was not there to help more.

"They've asked me to go back, Vivi."

"Go back? Go back where?"

A squirrel darted across the lawn.

"To the Front."

I turned to face Olive. She was staring into her hands.

"The Front? Why? Who's asked you to do this?"

"They want some artists to go and do some drawings. It's not just me." She laughed at the thought. "They're inviting a few of us, some who were there, some who weren't."

"And...and..." I didn't know what to ask. I couldn't think of her going back. I thought she had put all that aside, finally. "Do you *want* to go?"

"I don't know. I think maybe if I can go, I might be able to..." Her voice dropped so I could hardly hear her. "Draw a line under it all."

CHAPTER FORTY-SEVEN

1943—Now

It's spring and I've got dogs between my knees, I've got dogs coming out of my ears: Rex and Mossy, Joey and Bella.

Mrs. Burton is in her kitchen, combing out Baxter; while his owner *says* he is not vicious and won't hurt the other dogs, after much chaos we've decided to keep them all separate. Just in case. Baxter is what we euphemistically call "frisky." So, I've got all the others, and we had arranged to have lots in this morning. Edmund will go mad if he sees all the dogs running loopy in our garden, but something ugly has grown in me recently that almost wants to see Edmund lose his temper.

A car horn sets off the dogs and they howl like wolves at the moon; when one stops, another starts, louder. I shriek for Pearl to go out and see what's happening. Five minutes later, she hasn't returned. Irritated, I walk round to the front, to see her leaping into someone's arms.

It's Sam. Sam Isaac is here.

How on earth must I look?

Pearl is placed down carefully, like she's a precious jewel. Sam comes forward, hand outstretched for me like we are old colleagues, business associates. He's in a brown suit, a soft hat—*not a fez or sombrero*—and that same warm, old smile.

"Vivi," he says, "good to see you."

My throat is too dry to speak. This man. My pilot is here.

"And you," I manage. "Sam."

Pearl tugs my arm. "Can I go out? Can I go out with Uncle Sam? Can I, please?" Her face is alight with excitement.

"Wha— I...do you want some tea first?" I ask, both petrified and desperately hoping that he will say yes.

They do not.

Sam Isaac—Uncle Sam—must be nearly fifty-four now. (I remember the days when fifty-four seemed as ancient as Ozymandias.) His hair has changed color—but it's as though this is the color it should have been all along. Silver leaves, snowy plains...yes, I am being ridiculous. His eyes, those gentle eyes; I can't meet them.

Pearl runs inside the house to get her coat. I fuss over the dogs, trying to at least keep them from sniffing him. They are barking up a symphony.

"Are these all yours, Vivi?"

"No, no, no," I say. I'm flushed and so hot I'm afraid sweat might be visibly dripping off me. One of the dogs is rolling around in the cabbage patch, another has peed up the side of the shed. "None of them are. They are...just...for the war effort."

Sam smiles kindly at me. "I don't know what to say. You didn't get my letter?"

"No," I say flatly. If I had imagined our reunion a thousand times, it would never have been like this: me in an apron, my hair in a net, and with Laurel, the great lunk, hiding behind my legs.

"I'm sorry. I'll bring Pearl back tonight, if that's all right, about six?"

Pearl bounds from the house. She really can't wait. I hold the garden gate shut behind me so the dogs can't escape.

We look at each other, and at the exact same time both say, "Pearl loves cars." We laugh.

"Thank you," he says. He shakes my hand again.

Was this the longest day of my life? Sort out the dogs. Brush the dogs. Deal with frisky Baxter. Wait for them to be taken away. Baxter's owner, naturally, comes last. Queue for two hours at the butchers. Get a pig's head. Get turnips and cauliflower. Get beetroot. Pearl likes beetroot. Half-heartedly, jam some plums. Think about drying some apples—fail to dry apples not only because I lent Mrs. Dean my sulfur candles but because I am not feeling in a drying-apples mood.

I ask Mrs. Burton if she wouldn't mind putting curlers in my hair (she has offered before, it is not entirely out of the blue). She doesn't mind at all, and she doesn't ask why and when Mr. Burton comes home, and says, "Oh, Mr. Lowe not on duty tonight then?" she tells him, "Can't a woman do her hair without the French inquisition?"

I wear a favorite dress, which suddenly seems decidedly drab but never mind. Austerity means trying to look at old things with new eyes. I spritz on the last perfume in the bottle.

Sam and I could sit by the swings. We could walk to the village hall. We could...talk. There is so much to say.

And then at five past six, Pearl skips in on her own. She plonks her straw basket on one kitchen chair, sits on the other. Tells me she doesn't want tea. No, not even a beetroot sandwich, thank you. They haven't stopped eating all day, she says.

"You look nice," she says suddenly.

"What...wait, where is your uncle then?"

"Oh..." We both look out of the window. The car isn't there. "He didn't want to bother you," she says, casually.

"Oh." Disappointment floods through me. And here I am, sat with my gravy legs and nails like some...like some sad lady in a Tennyson poem.

I want to ask Pearl all the questions: *What did you do? Is he married? Is he happy?* He's bought her a book: *West with the Night* by Beryl Markham. *So,* I think, *he is good at books as well.* She wants to sit in bed and get started on it.

"Come with us next time?"

Has she been primed to say this? I look at her innocent face.

"I don't think so, Pearl."

She makes to go upstairs.

"Don't you need your bag, love?"

"Oh, wait," she says, "I got something for you." She carefully takes out a cardboard tube. "Uncle said he wanted you to have it."

And here inside it is Olive's picture. *In an Ambulance. A VAD lighting a cigarette...*

Olive didn't send it to the Fords, she gave it to Sam. Of course she did. Of course.

CHAPTER FORTY-EIGHT

1924—Then

Olive was away for well over a year that time and although she was only across the Channel in Belgium, she didn't come back to visit us, not once, even though presumably she could have. She wrote a lot though—to Father, to me, to Aunt Cecily; they read theirs aloud to me, and I read very selected bits from my letters aloud to them. The letters were very different: you would think they were written by a different person.

In her letters to them, Olive talked earnestly about her painting, her diet and how she was thrilled to be doing some good.

In her letters to me, she described the tin hut she lived in near the hundreds of Chinese laborers who had been part of the war effort and were now part of the cleaning-up effort. Chinese?! Edmund's mother would have had a fit at that.

She wrote about the artists she was with, not just painters, but photographers and writers and poets. Some of them even created films, she said. She had always been drawn to the cinema. She talked about the toxic water—the water supply had been contaminated early in the war. *Everything is toxic here, toxic, toxic*, she wrote. *The number of dead bodies they unearthed. Poor young men. People are flooding back to the area to rebuild, but it's not safe for civilians... other than us.*

She wrote that she was involved in a few incidents, had a spell of pneumonia and went to "a fabulous bar in Poperinghe—you would love it, don't tell the others, I don't want to worry Father," she warned. "But I am happy, Vivi, absolutely, happier than I've been in years. I really think I've recovered now..."

There was a poignancy to her tales, but her tone was not sad by any means. She was clearly in her element.

Perhaps I was in my element too. Small-town life suited me. I stayed in most of the day and cleaned and dusted. I liked shaking a feather duster at my bookshelf, gliding a cloth across the kitchen table. Aunt Cecily had given me a brand-new cookery book and I worked my way through the meat recipes. I was happy in my own company.

Friday nights were "honeymoon nights" and throughout the day, I worked at being as pretty and as desirable as any newly married woman. Unfortunately, Edmund often had to work very late at the bank on a Friday night and wouldn't get back 'til the early hours, which was disappointing. He would make us wait until the next week on those occasions.

Mrs. Lowe visited, sometimes with Mr. Lowe, mostly without. The first time she came, she looked around and I could feel her disappointment.

"I thought it was the countryside."

"Well, it is, kind of."

But she soon got used to it, and to us, and brought up salmon rissoles and pork chops made by her housekeeper, which were both a help and an insult at the same time.

I was a worshipper at the altar of routine. Predictability made me feel safe.

And then, it happened, my period didn't come on the day I expected it, nor the next day nor the one after that. I started to ache; my breasts felt heavy. My mouth felt metallic. I was nauseous but at the same time hungry. I was hungry but off my food. Unmistakable symptoms. The next stage of our marriage. It would involve change, yes, but it was the change I had long been waiting for.

I told Edmund's mother even before I saw the doctor. I thought she might have already guessed, but she hadn't. She was far more surprised than I'd expected, shocked even, but she said she was pleased: Lord and Lady Astor would be *charmed*—I'd made quite the impression at my wedding, apparently.

When I told Edmund, the smile on his handsome face made everything about our awkward, clumsy, post-war marriage worthwhile. This was how it was meant to be. We were back to the life we would have been leading if it hadn't been for that horrible, cumbersome war. Our rightful lives had been restored.

When Olive eventually came back from Belgium, although I couldn't put my finger on what exactly it was, she was different again. Her tone had grown knowing and wise. She talked in short sentences, then looked at me with a cynical raised eyebrow. She was staying with our father in London, and I spent a pleasant afternoon with them and Aunt Cecily. Olive always preferred to get me alone—*without dull Edmund*. I replied defensively, "I am often without Edmund, it's not like we are joined at the hip, but he *is* my husband."

"More's the pity," she said. "Only joking, Vi!"

She taught me some of the Chinese words she had picked up out there, for "Hello," "Thank you" and "You're welcome."

I said, "What is the likelihood of my needing Chinese in Hinckley?" and she said, "You never know, Vivi, do you?"

But there was something else about her that was different, not just her increased vocabulary, nor her mannerisms; there was something like a fizz, an electricity about her. It seemed to me that she was sizzling with something. At first, I wondered if she were ill. I asked her to visit, but she said she was spending the month on the Isle of Wight. "With great friends," she said. I let her get on with it, of course, and pretended I wasn't hurt, but then about six weeks later, she wrote saying she was back in London and she was *bored, bored, bored*, everybody who mattered had either died or had left, and could she *please, pretty please, come and stay*? I could have reminded her about dull Edmund, but I was always delighted to see her, and I was also intrigued about the source of her new euphoria, so of course I said an emphatic yes.

Edmund was disgruntled, but now that I was with child he had softened. Besides, it meant he could stay out longer without my bothering him.

I was full of excitement when I met Olive at Hinckley station. I couldn't wait to tell her my pregnancy news. It affected her too: my darling little sister would be the baby's aunty and I couldn't think of a better person for the role. She was carrying one large suitcase and her Gladstone bag. As we walked up to the house, she was shaking her head. "Could you have chosen anywhere more remote?"

"It's not as remote as the Isle of Wight!" I responded defensively. "We're only down the road from the city."

"Yes, but it's nothing like London, is it?"

I had lots of questions, but she kept saying, "Later, I'll tell you everything later."

So, there was something to tell?

She was wearing a black hat, and a dark blue dress that clung to her narrow hips. She looked quite the sophisticated woman for once. She usually hated comments on her appearance, but I found, without all the questions, I didn't have much else to say.

"I do like your hat, O!"

"This ol' thing?" She smiled to herself. "A friend lent it to me."

"Must be a good friend."

She shrugged, still grinning.

"It suits you," I continued.

She didn't approve of the house, I could feel it. It was too mundane, too ordinary for Olive. "A cul-de-sac, eh?" she said mockingly. I could almost see her thinking, *And that's the only French thing about it.*

I began to feel irritated. I had been so looking forward to seeing her. I wished she could make herself more agreeable. I supposed she'd have preferred a tin hut in no-man's-land with only Chinese laborers and English film-makers for company?

I imagine she found it plain. I told her that the wall-to-wall carpets were Father's wedding gift to us, and she breathed, "How wonderful!"

"Are you being sarcastic?" I asked, and she responded, more to herself than to me, "No, carpets are wonderful, aren't they?" And then she said, "I hear congratulations are in order."

"You know?!"

Aunt Cecily had only gone and told her. I couldn't help but be annoyed with my aunt about that—although I would never say so. It was my news to announce, wasn't it? I had a sense that I was going to have even less control over my life now. I had already become the business of other people more than I had ever been before.

"It's what you always wanted, isn't it, Vivi, Edmund's children? The Lowe family offspring."

"Ye-es . . ." I didn't like the way she put it.

"Very well done then."

She was more effusive about the carpets.

I made her tea, taking care to make it weak and not too milky the way I remembered she liked it, and I told myself to buckle up, everything was still going to be jolly. We were going to a Benjamin Britten concert in town the next evening. I had planned a few gentle walks; the doctor had told me that light exercise was just the ticket.

Mostly, I was really looking forward to our getting to know each other again. To spend time together again. Olive would be a brilliant aunty. Maybe not when the baby was very little, but once they were up and running, I knew Olive would be my perfect ally. She was a rock, if I'd let her be.

I smiled at her and she smiled back at me and I took in her face—like mine, but not like mine.

"Actually, Vivi, I have some news as well."

"You do?"

So, there *was* something.

"You've probably guessed it."

"I haven't," I said, "tell me?"

"Well, it just so happens, I met someone in Belgium."

I knew it!

"I'm so pleased!" I gushed.

"Yes," she said. "So am I."

But we had not reached the end of the story. Olive was standing, polishing an apple with her sleeve, but there was something else in the kitchen, a tension emanating from her. There was more to this announcement than met the eye. There was a complication, I felt it. I put my hand over my stomach. I was just thinking, *He's not married, is he?* when she jutted out her chin and the words seemed to run away from her mouth:

"And I think you'll really like her."

She busied herself with the apple.

I heard myself laugh, a solitary sound in the quiet room. "Oh, *Olive*, I thought you meant you had met someone"—I cleared my throat—"romantically."

Finally, she slid her teeth into the skin. "That's *exactly* what I meant, Vivi."

Then Edmund walked in, demanding to know what was for dinner. When he saw Olive, his good manners switched on like he had flicked on a switch. "Oh, hello, Olive, how wonderful to see you! And how was Belgium?"

*

We couldn't talk about it, whatever *it* was, while Edmund was there. I waited for him to clear off to his shed. But of course, tonight was the one evening he wouldn't go out. He was playing the good host; manners were important to him when it came to anyone but me. I felt suddenly hot and bothered and pretended to bury myself in my Agatha Christie novel.

Olive sketched a glass. She said it was always good to go back to still life. She had asked if she could draw me, but I felt too feverish to keep still and refused. I think she thought I was annoyed with her. I was, kind of, but I also suddenly felt so strange, I could hardly hold my head up.

She asked me to play something on the piano, but I didn't feel in the mood. I was sweating so much, I could see the underarms of my dress darkening. I had never perspired that much, not even when loading dead bodies into the ambulance in the midday heat in France.

We needed background noise. I put on the wireless, but it was one of those silly shows where if you don't listen carefully, you haven't got a hope of knowing what's going on. I could hear Olive telling Edmund about Belgium—a very sanitized version of what she'd told me; no tin huts or movie-makers featured—and I could hear him feigning interest, but it all felt very far away, very distant. I didn't think they were just three feet away across the room. She offered to teach him some Chinese, and I heard him say, "Not much call for it in these parts, I'm happy to say!" and it felt like everything was in slow motion.

I saw the hurt look on her face, and her weak attempt to cover it up.

"It's a fascinating language, Edmund, it really is."

My cheeks were flaming, heat like an explosion. I was waiting for O and me to be alone again. It wasn't until half past ten that I realized that Edmund didn't intend to leave us alone—that this was quite deliberate—and I would have to take measures.

"Let's go up."

How could she turn our spare room into her mess so quickly? It looked like she had opened her suitcase, dropped everything onto the floor and then rummaged it around. Papers were scattered over the new carpet. *Had she sharpened pencils onto the floor?* I felt achy, hot and cold. And resentful. *She treated everything with contempt, didn't she?* That was obvious. She'd pulled the curtains, but even that was half-hearted; she'd left a big space in the middle for the street light to get in.

"Can we talk about what happened in Belgium?"

"If you like," she said smugly. Kneeling on the floor, she picked up her papers and put them in a pile. I sat on the bed. I didn't mean to, but I couldn't stand up for much longer.

"Olive, how do you mean, I would like 'her'? I don't understand."

She chuckled to herself. "No, I knew you wouldn't."

"Tell me then."

"*She* understands me."

My mouth was dry. I was torn between letting rip at Olive and trying to keep a lid on my emotions in order to find out more. *What—what was going on?*

"*I* understand you."

She laughed. A cruel laugh.

"*She* makes me feel happy. It's as simple as that. She makes me feel special. She lost someone she loves too, during the war."

"Everyone did," I said shortly.

"Not all of us by choice, Vivi." She stared at me brutally.

"How do you mean?" I couldn't stop shivering.

"Some of us had our loved ones ripped away from us, but some merely skipped away from them and didn't even look back."

Did she mean me? Did she mean me and Sam? My stomach hurt. I felt like she had been kicking me. But surely she understood that Sam and I wouldn't have, couldn't have, gone very far. We came from such different worlds. Everyone would have been shocked and devastated and I couldn't do that to them. And then Edmund had been ill... Olive was still talking, but I had stopped listening. I tried to tune in once again.

"And she's a great person, once you get to know her."

"I don't *want* to know her!"

"Fair enough."

Having picked up everything on the floor, Olive began to get changed. She stood in front of me and unzipped, pulled down and removed her clothes. Somehow, the fact that she didn't cover up, she didn't have any shame, felt like she was making another statement. Finally, she stood in front of me, defiant in her nightdress and bare feet. Her toenails were long and unkempt. The hairs on her legs were like a soft animal down in the lamplight.

"You'll be outside of everything, Olive. Don't you understand that?"

The moment I said it, I felt a terrible shooting pain in my stomach and at the same time an incredible surge of both heat and chill.

She didn't notice. How could she? She shook her head, took a comb to her hair and did a cursory tidy-up. "Don't you see? The very last thing I want is to be like you, Vivienne."

She gestured around her, the room that I had tried to make homely for her, the picture I had hung, which I had hoped said: *I admire you.*

"As far as I can see, your life is really not all that wonderful."

I was being swept away by beating wings. I wanted to lie down there and then, to disappear.

"And I don't want to be with a man...any man."

I didn't want to face it. *I want to find common ground. I want to make everything okay.*

"But...but you were in love with Walter once, weren't you? You mightn't—"

She shook her head fervently. "No, no, I wasn't."

"What?"

"Poor, dear Walter," she said. She put down her comb on the windowsill. Long dark hairs were left between its teeth. "I was never in love with him, Vivi. I was in love with Mrs. Ford," she said simply. "How could you not have known?"

I went to the lavatory and there was blood. So much blood. I ignored it, choosing bed and hoping for oblivion instead. Suddenly I was in so much pain, I wanted to cry out, but I didn't want Olive or Edmund to know.

But after about an hour, I think—difficult to tell—it got much worse; the pain and the blood were too much for me to cope with and I knocked on the door of Olive's room. She was already up and pulling on her dressing gown. She must have heard me moaning. As she grabbed my wrists, I could see the fear in her eyes.

"Vivi, what is it? What's happening? Is it the baby?"

I remember her leading me back to my bed.

Her pale face peering into mine, seeking instruction. I didn't want her then, but I needed her: I couldn't face this alone.

"I'll get Edmund," she said.

"No."

What good had Edmund ever been at anything?

"I'll call a doctor."

"NO."

There was a part of me that knew if a doctor came it would really be over and I wasn't ready for that and I didn't want that. And anyway, I trusted my sister to take care of me. I had seen her tenderly soothe the wounded, I knew she would see me through.

But in the morning, as the sun rose over the garden, and my thighs were stained with a netting of what looked like an absurd amount of blood, I felt weaker and weaker, and at the same time, I grew angry with her again, so when the doctor came and asked why he hadn't been called earlier, I let her stand there, palms raised in surrender, and I let her take the blame.

And when he had finally left, I rallied myself and I told Olive *to go away, please. I had had enough.*

She resisted. She only wanted to look after me. *Let me, Vi, please. That idiot*—she meant dull Edmund—*wasn't good enough, he only ever looked after himself.*

She had always hated him, and this gave me the pretext I needed to get rid of her.

I shouted at her. I said *she* had done it, this was all her fault. Olive and her awful, disgusting news. I told her she was a liar. An animal. An aberration. I swore at her. Oh, the language I used makes me want to shrivel up and die when I think about it now.

CHAPTER FORTY-NINE

1943—Now

One Saturday, as I'm looking out of the window wondering if Edmund is returning for lunch, I see Mr. Burton arrive in a taxi. Ethel emerges from beside him. I haven't seen her for a long time, and I want to find out how it's going with the Land Army—Mrs. Burton has little information to dispense about farm life, only that Ethel is having "a whale of a time." I am about to barrel outside when I realize from her body language, from both their body language, that something isn't right. Mr. Burton's head hangs low and his shoulders are slumped. Ethel Burton follows him in reluctantly, all big hair and scowling lipstick, folded arms in her thick wool coat.

I hope there's no bad news about Cyril Fellows. The North African Campaigns, horrendous fighting in the heat of the desert, have been long and painful for our boys.

I don't see any of the Burtons over the weekend. I cook and prepare the house for the week and do sewing and knitting with the other WAVs at the village hall. Edmund doesn't come home for lunch or dinner. I play the organ at the church services. Pearl doesn't need help with letter-writing any more. She has to write an essay about meeting a famous person for afternoon tea. Have I ever met a famous person? Laughing, I tell her I nearly met the King of Belgium.

"Really?"

"No. It was a ship."

Pearl decides to meet Hitler. She will poison him with arsenic or maybe cyanide. She will drive him off a cliff—no, this would be a waste of a car. She will set a shark on him.

"Where will you get a shark?"

"All right, I'll set Laurel and Hardy on him."

"Laurel and Hardy wouldn't say boo to a goose."

"Then I'll just stab him through the heart."

"Is that really the sort of thing Mrs. Bankhead is looking for?" I ask, although the name of Pearl's teacher tastes like cod liver oil in my throat.

Pearl's face says, "Stupid question."

On Monday, I queue at the butchers, the grocers and at the post office, then go to Mrs. Burton's to knit and sew with the others. Everything and everyone seems just as normal, but when we're having a tea break, Mrs. Burton wipes her hands on her apron and whispers, "Please come over tonight, Mrs. Lowe. Once everyone's gone."

That evening, I've just sat myself down in her homely kitchen when she says, "So you'll find out soon enough. Ethel's got herself in the family way."

"Oh!" I say. "Oh."

"Indeed," Mrs. Burton says, squeezing her lips shut.

"I didn't know Cyril had been home—"

"He hasn't," she says.

"Oh."

Mrs. Burton shakes her head from side to side violently. I feel like I am in the presence of an unexploded grenade. Her face, I realize, is puffy. She's clearly been crying for some time. I reach my hand out across the table to my friend but she pulls out a handkerchief the size of a tea-towel—it *is* a tea-towel—and does an elephantine blow.

"The engagement will be off."

"Yes, I can imagine."

"And here I've been saving coupons and skimping and slaving over the damn wedding cake."

"Well... well, maybe this new fella—" I begin. I can't believe Ethel Burton would do this to her mother. How thoughtless and selfish could you be!

She shakes her head emphatically.

"He's not... It won't. No, that's not going to happen."

I think of sweet Cyril Fellows. His florid skin must be burning in the heat of the Middle East. How's he going to cope with this news? But then I think of poor Mrs. Burton, for she is such good friends with Mrs. Fellows, who might not be a member of the WAVs but has been a great support with the dog grooming and everything. How awkward this is going to be! The ripples of it will be felt far and wide. I wouldn't be surprised if Mrs. Burton is devastated by what her daughter has done— and this is without the worry an illegitimate baby brings to a family.

Mrs. Burton goes to her larder cupboard and there her shoulders rock up and down, but when she turns round, she is attempting a watery smile and holding out a large tin.

"Shall we, Mrs. Lowe? Just a little?"

"You don't mean—"

"What else can we do?"

Later, after we've each eaten a slice of the wedding cake and then tidied it up—somehow making it look almost whole again—Ethel trots down the stairs. She too is subdued and puffy—funnily enough, it's the first time I've seen how much she resembles her mother. She rests her arm over her stomach in the way I remember doing once. There is nothing to see yet though. Her skirt and jumpers—always too tight—still look... too tight.

"Say hello to Mrs. Lowe then," Mrs. Burton reminds her brightly. From under her fringe, Ethel sheepishly mutters "Hello" and I "hello" back. For the first time, I think, *Poor girl*. She's only a youngster. If you can't make a mistake when you are eighteen, when can you?

"More tea, love?" asks Mrs. Burton presently.

"Please."

I wipe the crumbs from my mouth. The wireless is on in the background and there is more shocking—or rather really shocking— news. There's been an uprising against the Nazis in the Warsaw Ghetto. Why do they have to use the word "liquidate"? I think of how distressed Sam will be to hear this.

Mrs. Burton tells us that she gave her saucepans to the aluminum collectors and is now struggling without enough pots. Ethel finds this both incredible and funny. Mr. Burton comes in from work, puts his hand on his wife's shoulder, squeezes, then pulls off his dusty boots. Laurel lets rip and everyone laughs.

"Huh! Why has he got no fur?" asks Ethel as though she has just noticed.

"Long story," says Mrs. Burton.

I leave them sitting round the table, the smelly dogs at their feet. My emotions are all over the place. I can't unpick them any more than you can unbake a wedding cake, but I know grief, regret, jealousy and shame are all stirred into that mix.

CHAPTER FIFTY

1924—Then

I was awash with yearning for my baby—the unborn baby. I dreamt of holding him. In my mind's eye, he was a boy, a boy I would have named Richard. I dreamt of his little shape in his first clothes and of stroking his soft, sweet hair. Of pinning his early artwork on the walls or rolling a ball across the garden for him. The perfect project for Edmund and me, the bridge that would bring us together.

Everything seemed so unfair; there were times I just wanted to scream but there was no time nor place for screaming: my father needed looking after now.

Six months or so after the miscarriage, our father sold the carpet business to two young Jewish men fresh from Poland with small round caps on the backs of their heads (how did they stay on, Aunt Cecily wondered) and firm handshakes. And in the following months, Father deteriorated right before my eyes. It was like a terrible theater performance with no happy ending. Like seeing a puppet without its supportive strings. His business had been holding him together, and now it was gone, and he was going to follow it out.

Once I started noticing his decline, I couldn't stop seeing it. I read it into everything he did. Every little slip of the tongue, every little stumble. Mrs. Webster had gone to bring her rampant efficiency to her widowed brother's household in Northumbria. I went weekly to London, the dutiful daughter, and when he grew worse, I would stay over there. It was not like Edmund could give a damn.

The doctors came and couldn't work it out, but their non-committal shrugs expressed that we had to understand: so many had died that anyone the age of my father—he was fifty-nine—was both lucky and disposable. He had had the luxury of a long life compared to so many.

I had seen my father deteriorate and then rally so many times that I allowed myself the delusion that he would always deteriorate and then rally. It was a stupid delusion for someone who has seen dead bodies piled up outside a hospital, but I wasn't prepared for the end of my own father. Perhaps no one ever is?

For a few days, Father ate only crackers and water, and then he stopped eating altogether. His lips cracked and his tongue grew so dry that he stopped speaking. I lifted him up for the bedpan, cursing Olive, for I was alone now. I didn't know where she was; she hadn't written to me since our row in Leicester. Aunt Cecily said repeatedly, "She says she's on her way," but still she didn't come. Letters came from her to Father, and I read them out to him, my lips curling, revolting against the world. I made my voice sound jolly, jolly, jolly because, "Oh, Father, it's super news, Olive is painting again!"

"That's my girl," whispered Father affectionately. The effort of saying that seemed to cost him dearly.

"Don't make her come if she's busy," he added, always putting us first. I cursed her as I sent down for ice—it was the only thing he could tolerate—and I cursed her as I ran it along his lips, then wrapped it in a cloth to lie on his heated forehead.

Another thing I didn't know, a thing I *thought* I knew: a "natural" death can be as painful as an unnatural one. It can even be worse.

The reluctant doctor eventually came back and this time agreed to give him morphine. I had to beg for it, and if it hadn't been for my years in France, I doubt I'd have had the confidence and I doubt they would have agreed.

Father raised his hand off the bed. "Did Olive come?"

I said she was on her way, and he said, "She's very good, you know."

Then I gave him the morphine, as often as I judged it needed. After a few uneventful hours, his breathing changed, and I knew it was time. I told him how we loved him, both Olive and I; that he had been an admirable father. Gently, I told him to join our mother, that she was reaching out to him now. At some point as I was telling him this, I'm not sure exactly when, he slid away from his bonds to this earth.

I am an orphan, I told myself, then shook myself. *Don't be so ridiculous. I'm a married woman.*

My father had many friends in the world of rugs and soft furnishings and they came in black suits to his funeral and greeted me solemnly and deferentially. We were a generation well acquainted with grief, so I suppose we were more practiced than most at how to behave at a serious occasion. Aunt Cecily was standing next to me at the door. She still wore her massive frocks; they were so old-fashioned that I expected they might one day be fashionable again. Her hair was pinned back into its usual bow but she now wore a net over it, so no strays could break free. She looked suitably severe. I had recently bought a pea-green coat that I was very fond of, but I hadn't wanted to wear green to the funeral, so instead wore an old black one that pre-dated my time with the FANYs. I made sure I smartened it up with a pretty scarf and my boots were shiny with polish. It felt very important to me to look the part.

Edmund surprisingly took a whole day off work and traveled back to London. His parents were coming, of course, Oh, the Lowes *loved* a good funeral. Edmund's mother never failed to make an impression as she entered the church. She always set the standard with the right clothes, the right manners. I saw her scanning the pews. I thought maybe she was looking for Olive—as I was—but when she tapped me on the shoulder, I realized it wasn't her she was interested in.

"Who on earth are they?"

"Who?"

She pointed at the two men in black with the yarmulkes on their bowed heads.

"Oh, they're the ones who've taken over Father's business."

"You couldn't find an English buyer?" She pursed her lips disapprovingly.

"I don't think we looked," I said, regretting it as soon as I saw the expression harden on her face. My father would always be the self-made man and she would never forgive him for it, even in death.

"Where is your sister?" she asked.

"I don't think she can make it."

She shook her head and I couldn't tell if it was about Olive or me *and* Olive, and she said, "She never could be relied upon." And I thought, *Well, actually that's not true, she has many faults but not that one in particular*, but I didn't say anything because I had to be grateful, for Edmund's mother had helped with the organization and the flowers. And the lilies were so very beautiful. In wreaths and in vases, they brightened the church and they were appropriate too, not too gaudy or showy. I heard someone say, "Impeccable taste," and someone else whispered, "It's the Lowe family. What did you expect?"

And it was a shock to hear how we had been incorporated into them, even Father, but it shouldn't have been because it was Edmund's mother who I had called first, in spite of myself, those first hours after Father had gone, and it was Edmund's mother who raced round with a doctor to sign the death certificate and with smelling salts for me if I wanted them (I didn't) and generally took everything out of my hands.

She had done Father proud, it couldn't be denied. She had the same get-things-done constitution as Mrs. Webster. Anyway, it was in Edmund's mother's interests to keep me sweet. We both knew that. I was the lone chance to keep the Lowe family name going now. And Edmund's mother felt desperately strongly about family names. If Edmund was King Henry VIII, I was the Flanders Mare.

Aunt Cecily had an awfully loud whisper and when she whispered that she had "left Uncle Toby at home with a kind neighbor," I'm sure half the attendants could hear. *Never mind.* She went on that he'd had a couple of bad days recently. Since every day now was a bad day with Uncle Toby this must have been quite diabolical. Uncle Toby didn't know where he was or who he was anymore. He didn't even remember Richard. My poor dear uncle and my poor dear aunt. Aunt Cecily unbuttoned her coat, then stretched like a cat in the sunshine. She smiled with her sad eyes. "Glad to get out of the house, quite frankly, Vivi."

And then, she did arrive. The prodigal daughter. Five days too late. Had Olive made an effort for the funeral? I was expecting her not to have, but I do think she had. Her hair was combed and pulled back into the nape of her neck. The style did nothing for her, but it was, at least, tidy. Her coat was smart and fitted, which made a change from her usual shapeless creations, and its copper buttons shone. As soon as I saw them, I suspected the hand of someone else on them. This was not Olive's work. I also knew that the lovely coat and its matching checked shawl would probably cover a multitude of sins: under that, she could be in anything from a nightgown to a smock with holes in. Her face was paint- and crumb-free. Her hands were silky and somehow naked-looking. Olive never wore rings. I felt like I was seeing those hands for the first time—perhaps it was only the first time for a long time I had seen them without the habitual splatter of paint.

I craned my neck around, desperate to see who she was with, but she was sandwiched behind Mrs. Webster and her son, Harry, in front of my father's barber, Mr. Tomassi. Seeing all these people from Father's life was a reminder that it wasn't just us—he *had* been well-loved—and it made me want to cry.

I kept looking at the people near Olive to see who was most likely to be the woman in question: there were two there, but neither seemed to fit, and that woman on her own—oh no, she wasn't on her own, she was with a heavyset man on crutches. I decided Olive must have come without her. Even my sister must have realized that bringing someone like that to her own father's funeral would be unreasonable. Her words swam in my head. *She lost someone she loves too, during the war. Not everybody did. Some merely skipped away and didn't even look back.*

That was probably one of the worst things she had said. *Is that what Sam thought about me too? That I'd walked away carefree—or for no good reason at all?* I had reasons, plenty of them—only now, when I looked around at the polite Polish-Jewish businessmen, their hands behind their backs, conversing with the vicar, I wondered if perhaps my reasons didn't add up as well as I had thought they had.

My aunt was leaning in to me. Her false teeth clacked slightly out of time with the rest of her.

"Please, darling, talk to each other. I can't bear to see you two like this."

"We *are* talking to each other," I lied. I couldn't even look up, I was afraid to meet my own sister's eye—the reactions I'd had when I saw her were too strong and too uncomfortable.

And I was pregnant again. Oh, I was nothing if not persistent. I think I was on week four, which meant thirty-six anxious weeks to go. This time, I was determined to hang onto it, and this time, it would know to cling on. It *had* to. I hadn't known how hard you had to work at it before...

Now we know. Now we know...

Aunt Cecily got up and insisted Olive move next to me. "Sit together, girls," she pleaded, not even attempting to keep her voice down now. Everyone looked round at us so that an objection was out of the question. Olive made her ungainly way along the pew, slender and sweet-faced as ever—I grinned at her despite myself, then tried to cover it up by looking indifferent.

"You're on your own?"

"Looks like it."

"Your... friend didn't want to come?"

She turned in the pew and peered at me. Her eyes were never brighter. "My friend?"

"Your..." at least I could do a proper hushed voice—"Lady friend?"

Olive laughed. She picked up the New Testament resting in front of her, flicked through it, then put it down. I don't know what she could have been looking for there.

"It's over."

"Oh," I said, momentarily thrown. "I can't say I'm sad." *What was this viciousness in me?* Was it purely about the girlfriend—or was it perhaps resentment that I had been left with Father and the ice cubes? *But that,* I told myself, *was a choice I had made deliberately.*

"No, I didn't think you would be," she said. She pulled her shawl around her so that there was no chance of it infringing on mine. We both stared ahead. My aunt tsked from further along the pew but I didn't know if it was at us or if something else had happened.

And then Father's coffin came in, and I could only gasp at how small and light it seemed, like a child's. I had forgotten Edmund was in the pew behind and when he put his hand on my shoulder, I shuddered involuntarily. His touch startled me nowadays, but he always played the good husband in public. I took out my handkerchief and covered my face with it. I could feel Olive glancing sideways at me. I don't know what she saw.

As the vicar spoke to us about light and darkness, I remembered makeshift funerals in sleet and hail at the back of Lamarck Hospital. You'd always try to go if you weren't working; you'd go to give the deceased a bit of respect and dignity, belatedly. It would make that letter back home more palatable: *We buried him in full attendance. He was much mourned.* The lies that were told in those letters, I can't tell you—those shallow graves, the tiny lopsided crosses. The promises we made: *We'll come back to it. Fix it.*

I must have missed half the service thinking about those days in France. When I next looked up, Father's coffin was being carried up and then out, out to the grounds. I felt a strange relief. I had seen the deaths of too many people to be heartbroken now: I loved my father very, very much but there were worse things than a mostly peaceful passing.

In the churchyard, out of nowhere, I thought of Mrs. Ford and Walter, taken prematurely, and how Olive had broken down in my arms.

I still couldn't believe it wasn't Walter she had loved all those years.

It was just Olive, Edmund and me who went back to Father's house. Father's business friends slipped away after more sorrowful handshakes. The two men who had bought his company kindly told me all was going well—a credit to my father. Aunt Cecily had to hasten back to Uncle Toby and Edmund's parents decided to go home. *The weather, you see.*

"They're taking over the country," was Edmund's mother's parting shot.

This piqued Olive's interest. "What did she mean?"

I covered for Edmund's mother. I don't know why; maybe because she was my family now. Plus, she had been so awfully good with the lilies and the doctor.

"Gray squirrels?" I suggested.

Molly had prepared enough food for ten. It made a sorry sight: that beautifully displayed stand with its delicious-looking cake at the center, and our best napkins in their shiny silver rings. That morning, Aunt Cecily had bizarrely sent round dominoes and some playing cards to entertain us. Perhaps she had forgotten that two of "the children"—Richard and Christopher—were dead, and of those of us who remained—Edmund, Olive and me—none of us were keen on board games. They were stacked haphazardly on my father's display cabinet.

Even Edmund didn't want to stay. He slipped away, minutes after we got back. When I asked where he was going, he looked sheepish. He said, in a low voice, he had an appointment with the estate agents about putting Father's house on the market. "Don't look like that, Vivienne, there's absolutely no point waiting."

The tower of cake made me feel small. I was glad Olive had come, but I couldn't help but feel resentment gnawing at me.

"So, why is it over?" I pressed.

She shrugged, helping herself to the seedy cake. She was the only person I knew who would eat plain seedy cake voluntarily. Everyone else hated it.

"She decided to get married instead."

"Married?" I repeated. "Really?" This most mundane of reasons was beyond my wildest imaginings somehow. Out there, somewhere in the universe, was a married woman who had been in a *romantic relationship* with my sister. I couldn't make head nor tail of it.

"Is that something you'd consider as well then?" I asked throatily. "In the future?"

She stared at me, balancing her tiny silver cake fork in one hand, a large china plate in the other. Her face was pale, the shadows under her eyes darker than ever. I hadn't realized it before, but she really appeared quite out of sorts.

"Why would I?"

"Look, Olive, it's just... can't you be normal? Think about it. You could move nearby and our children could grow up together and they'd be cousins. Don't you think that would be wonderful? We could be a *proper* family."

She sneered at me. "When will you ever learn?" She took one bite of cake, chewed it furiously, then slammed the plate down and left the room.

I sat staring into nothing for a while, then I got up to empty my father's wardrobes by myself. It was true: there was no point in waiting.

CHAPTER FIFTY-ONE

1943—Now

Sam suggests coming to Leicester. Not Hinckley itself, obviously, but somewhere nearby. I say no. But London isn't safe to meet either, for very different reasons. We decide on Peterborough. As the train pulls in, I think, *this is a terrible mistake.* Not just Peterborough, not just Sam. Everything. But I lean on Pearl, who, oblivious to my burgeoning fears, is simply thrilled at seeing her favorite uncle again. She has drawings to show him, and a poem to recite.

There are soldiers everywhere, even here. Some of them are Americans. We can hear their accents and we can see their jaws move rhythmically, and Pearl asks, "What is that they're doing?"

I explain that they are chewing gum, and she says, "Can I have some?" and one man overhears and says, "Sure, kid."

He is a good-looking soul with shiny white teeth and a square jaw. Mesmerized, Pearl asks, "Are you a movie star?," which makes him laugh loudly, and say, "You've made my day, kid."

My day is not made. I am petrified, and my heart is racing. And then here he is, Sam Isaac, standing in front of us, a massive hug for Pearl and a formal shake of the hand for me.

We go to the railway café as arranged. I have brought books, pens and papers for Pearl, tools to keep her occupied. Sam goes to the counter to order and I can't keep my eyes off him. *Please don't think I look old,* I think. But I know I do. My once *extraordinary* skin is less than ordinary now. I've kept my figure, just, rationing hasn't harmed it, but my body looks very different under my clothes. *What am I thinking?* At least I look better than the last time he saw me, chasing dogs.

"Tea, is it, Vivi?"

"Please."

I remind myself not to stare at him. On the table opposite, I can read the front page of the paper: Rome is being bombed by the Allies. I think of Mrs. Fraser, the dress shop owner's daughter, telling everyone the "truth" about Italy. I try not to think of Olive saying "*bellissimo!*" to everything.

We don't speak for a while; I am just breathing in the peculiar strangeness of our being there. The relief that I felt that he had come to meet us was quickly replaced with anxiety again. Pearl is offering him her drawing: her latest thing is to draw houses being bombed, and airplanes. Little stick men lie injured on the ground. Apparently the "townies" or evacuees are always producing work like this. To divert her, I taught Pearl how to do Spitfires instead. They look a bit like flying whales but they are better than they were.

Sam says, "Here, hand it over, Pearlie." That's what he calls her: Pearlie, or Pearlie Girl. He draws a biplane in the sky.

"That's brilliant, Uncle Sam!"

"I used to fly them." Sam raises his eyes to me but I can't trust myself to speak. "And crash them, occasionally."

Pearl is still chewing her gum madly. When her squash arrives, she carefully takes out the gum and puts it in the ashtray "for later." I wrinkle up my nose at her. *Manners!* She starts another picture obliviously.

"So?"

Was this a stupid idea? What was it actually for*? Why am I here?* I could have just let him pick her up, take her on a day out like last time. There was no need to involve me. And yet…

Sam is very gentle with Pearl. They chat, chat and chat. He tells me about the rest of their family and Pearl's brothers who are growing up so fast. He says he flew reconnaissance planes until the war ended and then he came back to live in London. Over the years, he built up a clothing factory. Now—at this he grimaces slightly—the only dresses they make are battledress. He says as soon as war broke out, he volunteered for the Air Force, the Navy, even the Army, but not one of them would take him on.

I can see how much this hurts him.

All they will let him be is an ARP warden.

"That's tough work though, isn't it?" I say, thinking of Mr. Burton covered in the ashes of Coventry and how Mrs. Burton, making me promise never to tell a soul, said he cries about it every night.

"Yes," he says grimly. "But I'd do anything to do active service again."

"And . . . and do you have any children of your own?" I ask, aware of how strangled my voice sounds.

He shakes his head. Licks his lips, then sips his tea. I've got to stop watching him like this. I'm like a scavenger haunting a carcass.

"And . . . and . . . are you married, Sam?" Heart beating. Banging. Waiting. *Oh God. Why would it matter if he's married or not? How dare I ask!*

He is weighing out his words in that steady way he has. Pearl is now writing postcards. Thoughtfully, she chews the pen. "How do you spell Peterborough?"

"No," says Sam. "No, I'm not."

"P-E-T-E-R-B-O-R-O-U-G-H," I spell out in a new, high-pitched tone. "Ooh, it's a difficult one!" I am full of lightness. I could spell anything now!

"What about your poem, Pearl? Are you going to recite it for Sa—your uncle?"

Pearl has been practicing her old favorite, "The Owl and the Pussy-Cat," for days.

"I've got another one now."

Okay . . .

She begins. "How do I love thee—" It is one of my favorites. She must have taken it from my bookshelf.

"No," I blurt out. "Not that one!"

She looks up, disappointment and confusion in her eyes. She takes Sam's tea and slurps it noisily. Sam looks between us.

"What's wrong with the other one, Pearl, the one you practiced with Aunty Vivi?"

"It's too babyish."

Sam gets up, crouches down by her seat. "Babyish? Never! That owl and that pussy-cat are my old friends. I've been waiting to hear it all year."

"Really?"

"For a very long time."

> And there in a wood a Piggy-wig stood,
>   With a ring at the end of his nose,
>   His nose,
>   His nose,
>   With a ring at the end of his nose.

We laugh, Sam and I, and he looks at me.

"She's brilliant," I say.

"I think she's got a brilliant host mother, haven't you, Pearlie Girl?" Sam blushes and so do I.

Sam takes out a Lucky Strike. He has a lighter—a Zippo, the ones the Americans love. We must remember at the same time.

"Thank you for returning the picture," I say.

He nods. "Olive was very talented."

"Yes."

Sam puts out his hand across the café table. It is there for the taking. I take it.

*

It's time for our walk through the woods. This is what we said we came for. Pearl swings off our arms between us. These trees have been here since the beginning of time. We're inconsequential nothings compared to them. Every time we see a squirrel, Pearl squeals with delight. We watch them run up trees and along the fallen leaves. We see them clinging to their winter stores.

"Have you been happy?" he asks me.

Such a big question. Far too big a question for one answer, and far too big for one conversation, in one day. There have been moments of happiness, I suppose. There have been glimpses of it, there have been times when most things felt right, yes. Not most of the time, no.

How can I tell him this?

That I have made wrong choices at every fork in the road, that I have made choices to please other people, choices through the eyes of other people, never my own; and, even worse than that, that all those other people I had made choices for... it didn't make a difference to their lives—only mine.

He is talking more about his life after the war, the places he went.

I am not listening to him as much as I should. I am staring at his face. Staring into his eyes. I can't stop myself. I am falling in love with him all over again.

CHAPTER FIFTY-TWO

1924—Then

A few weeks after my father's funeral, I had my second miscarriage. This time, it was more sadness than shock, mixed with the grief; there was more fear too. Perhaps this wasn't ever going to work for me. Perhaps I couldn't do this, perhaps there was something wrong with me. I rested and hated my body and hated Edmund and his body and I put the little things I had been collecting: a rattle, a bib, *oh, silly things for a tiny one*, out of sight.

Aunt Cecily visited. Tears came to her eyes as she advised me. "Don't put yourself through it again. There's only so much a person can endure," she said, but I felt she was talking about herself more than me.

Because we would try again, of course we would. Something had revealed itself to me over the last year. My marriage to Edmund was increasingly a joke but I *would* get something from it, *I would, I would.*

Edmund and I only made love for the purposes of making a baby. I felt about intercourse, I imagine, like soldiers in the trenches thought about going into battle. I was all right until those moments just before: *Eh up, time to go over the top.*

And I don't think Edmund relished it any more than I did.

"Do you have another woman?" I once asked him afterward, as he scrubbed himself down, in case there was a part of me left on him. "Or man?"

He gave me a look of such disgust that I felt like shrinking under the covers.

"It would explain a few things," I persisted. "It's not unheard of."

"Maybe in *the Mudie-Cooke* family it isn't," he hissed. The expression on his face! I think if I'd been a stranger in the street, he might have spat at me. "But not for the Lowes."

He left for his own room.

Once again, the person I leaned on most at that difficult time was Edmund's mother: she had become surprisingly tender toward me. Whenever we went to London, she would insist I sit in the window seat with a crocheted blanket over me. She would ask Edmund questions about my health, my piano playing. He would shrug and prevaricate, but she would be interested. She lent me her Agatha Christie books and enjoyed talking about them. Oddly, given her position on foreigners, she had no qualms about Inspector Poirot.

It felt so good to have someone on my side. Poor Aunt Cecily was increasingly entrenched in looking after Uncle Toby, and although I felt uncomfortable with some of Edmund's mother's opinions, to her surprise as well as mine she proved as good a mother-in-law as I had ever hoped for.

The next time it happened, the third time, I was six months gone. Further than I'd ever managed to get before. It made it better, it made it so much worse. I lay in the bath in a red so violent it reminded me of the worst nights in France, and I wondered if I mightn't just die there right now. I couldn't go on. I couldn't see a way forward. I was drenched in despair.

And then I got up, briskly toweled myself down, put on my dressing gown and shuffled to my bed.

This time, they admitted me to hospital because the bleeding was so heavy. Later, Edmund stood at my bedside like a schoolboy summoned to the headmaster's office who thinks he *might* get the cane but definitely doesn't think he deserved it.

He asked after my health and then in a low voice said, "It wasn't meant to be, perhaps?" and I nodded, hating him. What did he know how it was to carry a child, to love that child, to live, hope and dream for months, to then have it dashed upon the rocks?

He knew nothing, that's what.

"I've got something to cheer you up, Vivienne."

He thinks anything is going to cheer me up now?

"An automobile," he said proudly.

"What? How?"

"Father helped. We picked it up yesterday."

I wondered if he had waited for this to tell me, to ambush me with this when I was unable to get angry. I was too tired, too broken-hearted and too vulnerable to react.

But no, surely he simply thought a car for the baby? That's all. *Don't always look on the bad side, Vivienne*, as Aunt Cecily might say. *Edmund believes in the teachings of the Church. I don't think you've got a lot to worry about, Vivienne.*

"I thought you'd be pleased," he said irritably. I heard: *Your reactions are never correct, you can't do anything right.*

And I found I couldn't say, "I've just lost our baby, for goodness' sake!" It was impossible for me: I wasn't built like that, I wasn't in the habit. Years of not speaking up made it impossible to speak now. Instead, I pulled myself up on my hospital pillow, so I could be upright, more wifely and less unattractive. I hoped to say it with my eyes, my best feature, as wide as anything, and I leaned in to pat him on the wrist: "I *am* pleased, darling, I'm just surprised too."

I was on a ward with new mothers. Not as bad as it might sound—the babies were all in another room elsewhere, so I didn't have to see the other women's pink bundles of success. Small mercies. Occasionally, the new mothers were allowed to pad into the nursery, but sometimes they were kept away. The nurses were strict about visiting time.

"We need appointments to see our own babies!" one woman said to me. "I feel like a cow."

My breasts were engorged, great beached turtles lying on me. It felt like something stone hard was in one of them too and I didn't know whether to mention it or not. The mothers—I was not a mother, not yet, not yet—were neither kind nor unkind. They were indifferent to me, they were weary and absorbed in their own journeys. I'd been on that same journey, but my destination had been so very different.

Everything felt hopeless. My past and my future full of darkness. I realized I was in danger of sinking very low, but I couldn't pull myself out.

There will be a next time. I will not lose faith, I told myself.

But I did.

Every afternoon, the matron brought me a jug of cold water and a glass.

"You will get thirsty," she advised. "Drink."

I sipped obediently. I remembered holding water bottles toward shocked faces in the back of the ambulance. I thought about Olive and her painting of me and Sam, and suddenly I couldn't stand to think of her. It seemed to me that there was nothing I could think about her that wasn't painful, nothing that wouldn't make my heart ache. And perhaps I had brought this agony on myself by my general inability to get anything right. This explanation seemed to fit. My being so bold as to go to France, living and working among all that disease, plus my inability to love Edmund the way a good wife should, explained why this was happening to me, why I couldn't have a baby. It was punishment.

"What lookers they'll be!" Matron said suddenly.

"Who?"

"Your children."

I inhaled sharply.

"He's handsome, your husband. And you, well, you're as beautiful as a movie star, Mrs. Lowe. It'll be all right. I've seen this before. They come back, holding twins sometimes."

"I hope so," I said. My voice was tremulous. I realized I must have been crying again.

After Matron's kind words, I resolved something. I realized I couldn't go back in time, and I could do nothing about my war years, but I *could* make sure I never mentioned them again. It was the least I could do. I probably shamed Edmund by telling people what I had done in France. No one wanted to hear. And the other thing I could do was simple. I could *love* Edmund more. I could be a better, more devoted wife and keep a tidier house and make sure my pies had a piped crust and not plain.

I felt better already. I had steps to take. Action. Goals. I had something tangible to focus on.

When I next woke, three men with white coats were haunting the end of my bed like ghosts of pregnancies past, present and future. I thought Olive would be the only one who'd laugh at that and once more I missed her so much. *But maybe I never knew the real her at all.*

I had to trust what Edmund and I had. We were the family, the little family I had always dreamed of. I didn't choose Sam, I didn't choose Olive, I chose what was right and good. I chose what was normal. I hadn't done anything to be ashamed of.

It was strange: whenever I was with a doctor, I wanted to say, "I used to be on your team, cleaning and cutting, holding and hoping," but they would be looking at me indifferently, and it was with a sinking realization that I would understand: *I'm on the other side now, I'm a body on the bed. I'm just a collection of parts from a science textbook.*

No, they weren't looking at me *that* indifferently.

Something had piqued their interest: something in my notes. They pointed and gazed between me and the clipboard. I had their attention, that was for sure. So, I reached up, and stroked back my hair, hoping I was not looking too disheveled. The matron had referred to me as a beautiful woman only that morning, so surely it couldn't be that in just a couple of hours, I had become too ugly to have a baby.

Three doctors. *See no evil, hear no evil, speak no evil.*

Why won't they say anything?

Hauling myself upright, I said, "I have an aunt who had a miscarriage before she had her son, Richard." My voice, the story, trailed off. "He died in the Great War," I added, even though this information was redundant, my whole sorry tale was redundant. But perhaps if they had only known Richard, and what a glorious boy he was, they would treat me differently? If only everyone were a bit more like Richard—cricket matches, cream teas, big smiles.

"And," I continued uncertainly, "my mother died in childbirth. But this was a long time ago." I smiled nervously. "So, things have changed presumably?"

They stared at me.

"Is it..." I paused. "Is it a hereditary condition?"

The men looked at each other.

"Or could it be..." I forgot my resolution for a moment. "I served in the war. It was pretty filthy there and maybe the water was contaminated?" I added, thinking of Olive's letters from Belgium. "And I transported men who had been gassed. And all sorts."

One of the doctors laughed slightly, but I recognized that it was not an amused laugh—it was a fear-laugh. Olive used to do the same. She knew it was offensive, but she couldn't stop. The worse the situation was, the more she would cackle. The others nudged the fear-laugh doctor and he strode to my side resolutely; he even took my hand. I knew then.

It must be very bad news.

"Mrs. . . . ?"

He had forgotten my name; perhaps that accounted for the hand-holding. Perhaps he had good news. Perhaps my baby was not dead after all? Or perhaps they could just give me another one. Perhaps a woman had died and her baby needed a mother. *No one need know.*

"Lowe." I debated telling him "with an E," then decided not to. *Let him think I am low. I am* low.

"Mrs. Lowe," he repeated. He had a slight northern accent. Gentle hands, a whiff of cologne. I wondered if he made his wife happy.

"Do you want the good news or the bad news first?"

The fury came in fast, unrelenting crashing waves. The fury took me over; I was riddled with it, broken with it. It was not what they first thought. It was not syphilis—great news, Mrs. Lowe! No, it was a quite unusual mix of gonorrhea and chlamydia—a very interesting case—and unfortunately, while this was not life-threatening, Mrs. Lowe, it did have dire consequences, especially for a woman trying to conceive a child.

Those missing six months when I was in France and he was "in hospital." Intelligence work? An issue of the mind?

For goodness' sake. How could I have been so blind? Where was my intelligence—had I lost my mind?

But I was a woman who had never raged, not properly, never let her temper get away with her. My self-control was what people liked about me. My willingness to get on, to forgive, to be kind, was my distinguishing feature. I did not know how to react.

In my heart, Sam lived on. More vivid, more alive than ever before. In my heart, I could picture the carcass of the plane, the hunger of the flames—I could bring it all back, and I could make different choices. I could go back to the fork in the road and choose a different path…

But it was too late.

Edmund didn't come back to the hospital for two days. He was preoccupied with his new toy. "Breaking in the motor," he said contentedly. I said nothing. "How she purrs." He continued, reporting on the car and the state of the roads. *As if I cared!*

He picked up his newspaper and started to read. After some time, he must have noticed I wasn't my usual Edmund-pleasing self for he turned slightly pink around the collar and blustered. "How are you anyway? I thought they'd let you out sooner. They did last time."

"They've told me why they think it happened," I said quietly.

He slowly set down his paper and folded it. He wasn't looking at me when he said: "Oh?"

"Do you want to know what it is?"

"Do you want to tell me?" he said. Typical of Edmund: brush it off, hit it back.

"I'll tell you. You gave me gonorrhea and chlamydia, so that's fantastic," I said. I was practically hissing at him. "Fantastic. I can't have children. Ever. Because you managed to get yourself some filthy, rotten disease. You've ruined me."

He sat rigid in his chair.

"Aren't you going to say anything? Anything at all? How could you have married me, *knowing* that it would end this way?"

"I didn't think it would matter, Vivienne. I didn't think you'd be affected—"

"Did the doctors tell you that?"

"No," he grunted.

"You just decided it yourself?"

"Yes." He looked so sorry for himself, it made me want to howl.

I didn't ask how he contracted it; that's the word, "contracted"— an oddly formal phrase. I always thought it suggested a business arrangement. *You are contracted to purchase twenty rugs from Istanbul, five foot by five.*

Deep down, I *knew* how he contracted it. How couldn't I know? I had met enough girls in Calais so hungry that their ribs showed through their thin blouses, who would steal moldy bread off the ducks. Girls forced to do anything for money.

Riddled, infested, diseased, full of it. Filthy, dirty, poisoned, green, loathing, don't touch me, don't touch me. DON'T TOUCH ME.

Damn you, Edmund Lowe!

"Did your mother know why you were in hospital during the war?"

Edmund didn't say anything.

I grabbed his hands, I pulled at his arms.

"Did your mother *know*, Edmund?"

He nodded. He couldn't bring himself to say it out loud but the north–south nod was telling enough. *Yes, she knew.*

So damn you, Edmund's mother, too.

And all those loving letters to me at Lamarck Hospital made sense to me now: the belated welcome to the family. The delight at having a daughter. The hurry-up with the wedding.

She *knew* he was spoiled goods, she knew he was rotten: *that's* why I had become good enough for him.

At my request, one of the doctors brought me a medical encyclopedia. In my rage, I initially found it incomprehensible but kindly, the doctor sat with me to answer my questions. Apparently, it was not rare in soldiers of the Great War—or any time, he said wryly. "But it's not much talked about."

"I bet it bloody isn't."

This made him smile. He showed me a page of pictures of genitals black, swollen or shrunken, but explained that I was a carrier and not all carriers "show."

"You have no outward signs of infection or distress," he explained. I thought, *How typical: my version of this disease is private, turned inwards. Isn't that me all over? Tiptoeing through my own bloody life?*

A few days later, Edmund's mother had the audacity to come to the hospital. Presumably, Edmund had been as tight-lipped about this latest turn of events as he had been about everything else. She carried a big bouquet of lilies, the same ones that had been such a success at Father's funeral, and very pleased with herself she looked too.

"Exquisite," said Matron admiringly, whisking them away to find a vase.

"How are you feeling, Vivienne, dear?"

"You knew."

She didn't know what I was talking about at first. And then she did. I could see the horror rise in her eyes. They had been found out.

"You knew. You knew! You knew when he married me that he was diseased. That he would pass it to me."

"I didn't..." she started. "He didn't... We... we all hoped for the best—"

"Get out!"

She hesitated for a moment at the foot of my bed, but then just as Matron made her way back with the vase overflowing, she turned to go. I closed my eyes and she tap-tapped away down the ward. Some mornings, I can still hear that sound.

CHAPTER FIFTY-THREE

1943—Now

Pearl is curled up on the sofa. She's been tired a lot lately; could be the change in the weather, or maybe she might be homesick. Her mother and grandmother have moved to South Wales. Pearl's mother works on the land by day and sings at night. She comes to take Pearl out every two months or so. She is always impeccably turned out and always very gracious with me. The last time she came she brought a cabbage as a thank-you gift and the time before that, a punnet of blackberries.

Pearl loves to listen to Glenn Miller. "Chattanooga Choo Choo" and "A String of Pearls" are favorites, but she also adores "In the Mood" and "Moonlight Serenade." So do I. Everything is rationed but not music, as the old joke goes, nor singing along to your favorite tunes.

I am preparing rabbit. It's a fiddly, horrible job, and I like to be alone in the kitchen when I do it, no distractions. Pulling the foot out, getting the meat. It's like undressing something. Rabbit is not on the ration; you have to know someone who knows someone. Mrs. Burton does. I'll put it in a pie. There is no egg, but I've made a crust with potato and starch. The oil is six weeks old but I'm not changing it for rabbit.

Pearl's school books are all over the table. Fortunately, Edmund hardly comes in this room any more. He's barely in the house nowadays.

"I need to write about another country. It's a project for school."

Tapping her legs to get her to make room, I sit myself next to her. "If you're thinking about France, or Belgium or Italy, I might be able to help."

She screws up her nose. "I was thinking more of China?"

"China? I know a few words of Chinese."

She pulls her knees up to her chin. "Really?"

"Let's see, what can I remember? *Nihao. Xie xie.*"

She seems interested.

"My sister worked—"

"In China?"

"No, in Belgium, but there were many Chinese people there, during and after the war, helping us."

Pearl works on the project all weekend, her tongue out in concentration. I hear her repeating the words.

"*Nihao. Xie xie.*"

A few days later, we take the train to London. We're braving the city. This will be our sixth meeting with Sam—I'm counting—and this time we are going to stay over in a bed and breakfast so we will have all day tomorrow together too. Pearl and I will share one room, Sam will stay in another. Edmund is away again. It's October and you can smell the approaching autumn.

We have been to Yarmouth (my favorite), a car auction (Pearl's favorite), a stately home and twice to the woods. We haven't seen him for three whole months; I have been looking forward to this trip for what seems like an indecently long amount of time.

Sam still feels something for me. I know it. It's there every time we share a joke about the past, a hope or an observation. It's there when he stands up to let me pass, when he holds open a door or takes my coat for me.

Sam meets us on the platform at St. Pancras station under that glass and iron arched roof. It always feels like a special occasion here.

But why must I blush every time I see him? He asks if we would like to start with a movie, since there is such a damp chill in the air.

Yes, we do, of course we do.

"I haven't told you which one it is yet."

Pearl and I laugh. "Any!" she says.

"We love all the movies," I say.

Off we go, to the bright lights of Regent Street Cinema, where *Casablanca* is showing. I used to be a London girl but how unfamiliar everything in the city seems to me now. It's not just the war, it's my perspective, I think. Whereas once I strolled through London without a second thought, now I hardly feel entitled to tread on its pavements.

Sam knows the projectionist, of course he does. "Let's go and say hello," he suggests. Pearl and I make surprised eyes at each other. "Okay," Pearl says doubtfully. "If you say so." He leads us up the stairs to a box-like room, a cubbyhole. Pearl looks around in awe, at the bright lights and view through the glass. A wrinkled old man is operating the machinery like a wizard behind a curtain. When he sees Sam, he thumps him on the back.

"Is this her then? The one?"

"I don't know what you mean," Sam responds. He is a perfect salmon pink.

As we take our seats, I lean over and whisper, "What *on earth* did you tell him about me?"

"Nothing," he says unconvincingly. "He just watches too many love stories."

I try not to smile.

As we sit in our row, I remember watching the show *Chu Chin Chow* in the hospital with Sam. I am about to say something about it to him when, with one eyebrow raised quizzically, he leans over Pearl, who is happily nestled between us, and murmurs: "Remember *Chu Chin Chow?*"

"Who could forget?"

"That's the day I thought I'd died and gone to heaven."

"Was it the exotic dancers?"

He laughs so loudly that the people in front—who haven't been so quiet themselves—turn round and "Ssshhh!" at us.

Pearl swivels her head from him to me, then shrugs.

On screen, Ilsa Lund is just asking her ex-lover, Rick Blaine, to protect her husband, the Czech resistance fighter Victor Laszlo, when Pearl stands, hissing, "I need the loo."

She is gone ten, maybe fifteen minutes. I keep thinking of how Sam's hand had felt in mine that evening watching the show in Lanarck—over twenty-five years ago!—and I try not to think of our last goodbye kiss. What is the matter with me? It's some consolation to find Rick Blaine, the manager of Rick's Café Américain, is also struggling with the past catching up with him.

Pearl returns noisily.

"Couldn't you find it?"

"I found it," she mutters.

"Where are we going now?" Pearl asks after the film. She expects Uncle Sam to have a big plan. To be fair, he usually does.

"I thought I'd take you to the restaurant with the worst service in London."

Pearl squeals with excitement while I laugh.

"Ooh, you take us to the best places."

I try to take Pearl's hand but she won't let me, which is unusual but I don't want to make a thing of it. Not in front of Sam.

It's called Bloom's and it's in Whitechapel. Our bed and breakfast is just along the road from here. There are queues of people waiting to get in, but Sam . . . Sam has ways. I get our ration books ready.

"What do you want in your bagel?" the waitress shouts at me. I don't know what a bagel is. Sam is smirking at me. His eyes say, *I told you the service was bad.*

"Bacon?" I suggest. The woman gives me a glare that could turn me to stone. Sam makes a noise like a hiccup.

"This is a *kosher* establishment," she says. "If you don't like it, the door is over there."

"Then I'll have an er... kosher bagel, please," I say. I look at Sam— he can't stop laughing.

Pearl goes to the loo and once again she is in there for ages. After about ten minutes have passed, I go and tap on the cubicle door. It opens slowly. Pearl looks exhausted. Those old dark rings are back, under her eyes.

"I've got blood in my knickers," she says. "I soaked through my handkerchief."

"Oh, Pearl!" She is twelve now; there shouldn't be anything mystifying about this, but I am still completely wrong-footed. I did not suspect. She is so small.

"Are you sure it's not tomato soup?"

Pearl makes her what-is-wrong-with-you? expression at me. I am an idiot. "Sorry, darling, I mean it's your period. I'll... I'll find us a chemist, is that all right?"

"I want to go home," she whispers. She looks tearful. Of course she is. She wants her mum. Poor darling.

"Oh, Pearl, Mum's a long way away."

"I meant with *you*, back in Hinckley."

"Oh, oh, of course."

Uncle Sam understands. He walks us back to St. Pancras. I feel dreary that our long-anticipated trip has been cut short—will we two ever be lucky?—but I try to be jolly for Pearl. Next to the ticket office, she disappears to the loo and we smoke a cigarette each and

Sam tells me to keep his Zippo lighter, "until the next time," and I smile because it feels like this is his way of telling me we must meet again soon and also because it reminds me of the first time we met.

I'm ashamed at how devastated I feel about going home now. I know it's not right. I dread the return to Edmund, wishing instead that it was Sam, Pearl and me forever. But wishing won't get me anywhere. I have to act.

For this evening though, Mrs. Burton sorts us out: hot water bottle. Sanitary equipment. Praise for Pearl. What a big girl she is.

I tuck her up in bed. I think she has fallen asleep when she suddenly sits up and says, "You really like him, don't you?" I know who she means. Silly to pretend otherwise.

"Of course I do," I say. "He's your uncle."

She nods slowly in that way she has.

Pearl knows it.

A few days later, I read that Bloom's Restaurant is another one that's gone. Direct hit in the dead of night. And the row of streets and the bed and breakfast we would have been staying in were all destroyed too. Turns out we were quite lucky after all.

CHAPTER FIFTY-FOUR

I didn't know what to do with myself. Back at home in the cul-de-sac, after they let me out of the hospital, Edmund was surprisingly attentive. He did his own chores, and before he left for work in the morning, he opened the door to my room and called out hesitantly.

"I'm off!"

Yes, you bloody are.

I was resting and thinking.

I could go to London and live with Aunt Cecily, help her with Uncle Toby maybe? I could go to the city, or I could stay put. Everything seemed such a huge, gargantuan effort.

Edmund didn't require much feeding. He ate a hot meal at work and he was out most of the time. I could tolerate that.

Edmund's mother sent me flowers and cards. She offered to visit, but I told Edmund she could visit over my dead body (*that's not an invitation, Edmund*).

I considered getting a pet rabbit. I would put a hutch next to the shed, and it could be moved into the shed in winter. I thought this plan would make Olive smile, and I still loved to see my sister's smile but even finishing a letter to her seemed too difficult a task. I started several but abandoned them all. I knew it would be better to go and make amends with her face to face, but I didn't have the energy to wash my own pillowcases, never mind take a train and a ship to France.

*

It was the end of summer and I was whiling away the hours in the kitchen, gazing out of the back window. There were small mounds of dead leaves that Edmund must have raked. If I had had my baby, we might have been lying out on a rug on the lawn by now. It would be just about warm enough with knitted hats and cardigans with pretty buttons on. Maybe I would have been singing lullabies. I would have walked with my baby in his Silver Cross pram. Maybe, I would have pointed out the toddlers playing on the swings to him. People in the shops would have admired my baby's chubby cheeks.

The doorbell rang: two policemen were there. They were talking as I opened the door, and I felt like I was interrupting them, not the other way round. When they saw me, one went red and the other stammered.

"Mrs. Vivienne Lowe?"

"Yes."

Something ran through me. Not quite a thrill, but a feeling of doom, of fear, of excitement. *What had Edmund done now?* I knew it had been something abominably disgusting and finally, he had been caught. How fast my mind worked in those few moments. *Edmund—a bad man. Edmund in jail? This would be a solution to all my problems.* I would visit him once a week. No physical contact. But what would everyone think? No one need know. I would tell them his job had taken him to . . . somewhere obscure and unvisitable. The Scottish Borders maybe.

A black sedan car was parked outside. Out of the corner of my eye I saw the curtains of the house opposite twitch. I stared fixedly ahead. *Edmund could take his chlamydia and ride off in that. Be gone-orrhea.* My own joke. It was the first time I'd smiled in a while.

My good man! Edmund would say to the policeman, while thinking exactly the opposite. *My good man, can't we talk about this?* I might get to see him with handcuffs cutting into his wrists, being pulled along, staggering, hopefully, along the pavement...

For a moment, I thought the stars had given me all the solutions I needed. A solution I could never even have dreamed up. But they hadn't, of course they hadn't. Things didn't work that way, not for me. Nothing comes easily to me—I should have realized that by then.

"Are you the sister of Miss Olive Mudie-Cooke?"

I paused. *This was not about Edmund, then.*

"Yes?"

"Can we come inside?" The speaker looked at his colleague, then added uncertainly, "'Fraid we've got some bad news."

My love. My younger sister, my only sister, Olive, had taken her own life.

"She walked out into the sea. Deliberately," the younger man added. For some reason, he thought it was important that I didn't misunderstand this.

"As you will know, it's illegal. But—"

"Illegal?" I muttered.

"But under the circumstances, we won't be pursuing—"

The older man looked at his colleague. "There's no case," he told me gently. "Do you have anyone to look after you, Ma'am?"

I lied and told him I did.

*

Oh God, Olive, let her hear me once more, let us go back in time. Let me fix everything.

A rush, a crush of memories, press on my heart: her laughing, her drawing, her teasing me—and then it's there too. The other side of the coin: my shouting at her, blaming her, accusing her, resenting her.

I paced the rooms of my stupid house. I had chosen this family— Edmund, the Lowes—and abandoned my own. I had picked wrongly, I had made the most heinous mistakes, and look where it had led me. *I will look after you, O*, I'd said. And I hadn't. *I hadn't.*

Stupid things had swayed me, stupid, trivial things like family heirloom bracelets and leaping lords at my wedding, and having a husband who was *respectable*, who went to church and was friendly with vicars.

I had forgotten what was important.

If only I could have told her all of this. Face to face. Her pretty face. Her sheepskin coat and too-flat shoes. Her wide eyes and pointed chin. Her beloved pipe.

"Did she leave anything? Anything at all?" I had begged the kinder, older policeman.

A note. A note. Let her have left me a note. Or, no, a painting would have been more Olive's style. Or a pencil sketch that could have told me what terrible things had taken over her mind or shown me why ending the pain was more important than going on, than living.

"Nothing," he said apologetically. "There was nothing. I'm so sorry."

Olive's story was in some of the newspapers, usually on page nine or ten. Small columns, but columns nevertheless. The piece in the *Sunday Times* began, "Death of talented female artist." *That would have annoyed her. Why couldn't they just say "artist"?* It went on to say Olive had served in France and Spain (*Spain?*) during the war and her work was eviscerating and brilliant (*now that* was *true*).

Another article, this time for the *Herald*, said that Olive, like many women, had stepped up during the war and didn't know quite how to step down again. This phrasing made me pause a while. It continued: she had lost people she loved and, unbeknown to the many fans of her art, she had always struggled to come to terms with that. Another thing I hadn't known about my own sister.

The papers didn't report how she had died, of course. That absence, that hole in her story, would have told the careful reader everything they needed to know. I saw it, though. My darling, darling girl was as much a casualty of the war as the bodies piling up outside the hospital at Lamarck.

So, I was alone. No babies, no sister, no father, no cousin. No Sam. Just Edmund.

Edmund, our disease and all my mistakes.

CHAPTER FIFTY-FIVE

Edmund and I argue whenever we see each other. This is a new habit. I used to repress it, but now I seem to have found my voice. We have gone from silent film to full-blown talkie in technicolor.

Edmund is growing more spiteful. I'll be boiling some potatoes and he'll come in like we've been having a conversation—we haven't—and start up.

"You weren't the only one who served in the Great War, you know. I do wish you wouldn't harp on it all the time."

"Oh, remind me, what were you doing in France then? Paying poor young girls to sleep with you...Do they give out medals for that?"

He ignores me. *That* must not be mentioned.

"I haven't had it easy—"

"No one has," I persist. I want to say something profound: I want to tell him how he has hurt me, how he has wasted our marriage, our relationship and my child-bearing years. How I had been willing once, to work at this, us, but he had not, and I am losing my patience. But I can't find the words.

I don't suppose he would listen anyway.

Some weeks later, I have been queueing, waiting, stewing and visiting his parents—sitting there while they make their vile comments about the colored Americans in Birmingham—and it suddenly occurs to me: *I can't do this any more.*

I don't have *to do this any more.*

That night, I creep out to Edmund's beloved shed with a torch. I remember nights in France wandering around in deepest blackness and this spurs me on. I wrap my hand in my coat sleeve and smash the window. From there, it shouldn't be too hard to reach the internal door lock. It shouldn't be too hard, but it *is* hard. It takes me eight or nine attempts and the jagged edges of glass succeed in cutting my arm.

I'm in. It is full of—I don't know how I can describe it—postcards, yes, of women. All women. All shapes and sizes. Every variety. This is pornography. I'm not an innocent—I know how some men behave when they are unchecked, unregulated. Even in France I knew many soldiers kept pretty girls in their pockets. But these were different, these were my husband's pockets and these girls weren't just pretty.

This is what he does.

It appears to be, not a hobby, but a profession.

I look at the drawers. Each one is carefully cataloged with a name scrawled on brown paper. *Belle, Bertha, Bessie, Bettina, Betty.* All the way to Z. I look at V and it is full of *Victorian woman disrobes, Victorian woman naked.* U, T, S. *Saffron, Selina, Simona.*

It is the detail, the loving, obsessional detail, that kills me.

He never wanted me. Why would he have wanted me? When he had all this—this horrible fantasy world versus the reality of me. *Twenty-five years,* I think. Twenty-five loveless years down the drain.

Another spur-of-the-moment thing—I seem to be full of them these days. I race into the house and bring out the Zippo that Sam gave me at St. Pancras. First, I run around the garden like a madwoman, looking for and finally retrieving Charles from behind a camellia. He is chewing a berry, perfectly oblivious that he has lived through two world wars, through no fault of his own. *Better to be a tortoise,* I think.

Tucking Charles under my arm, I place him next to the house in safety, then I set light to the shed. I add some rushes and some twigs for an easier catch. Smoke and dust billows. Black clouds and then magnificent, hungry, licking orange flames.

I can hear Edmund running, footsteps in a flap, his heavy breathing suddenly next to me. I want to laugh.

"What the hell? How—"

"Bombs," I reply. I can't stop watching the devastation of his temple, it is hypnotizing.

"What? I didn't hear anything."

"Didn't you?"

I am revolted at him, revolted at myself.

"Oh well, there's nothing important in there, is there?"

The look on Edmund's face.

"Edmund, a room has come up at Mrs. Harrison's. I suggest you go there. Tonight."

"What?"

"It's over, Edmund. It should have been over a long time ago."

I don't know who is more astonished, him or me. He stares at me mutinously for a few seconds and there are dust and sparks and shouting from Mr. Dean next door, and then Edmund walks into the house. I see the lights come on, then when I look up just a few moments later, the lights have been extinguished. I hear the car start up and he is gone.

Later, Pearl and I sit round our bonfire, warming our hands.

"I have an idea," I say. I run into the kitchen to get our last bits of bread and we treat ourselves to a midnight snack.

CHAPTER FIFTY-SIX

1944—Now

Sam writes and this letter is addressed to me alone—and this time he says what I have been longing for him to say: "Can I see you?"

And I know what he means this time. He doesn't have to spell it out. He means, *alone*. Just him and me. No Mr. Churchill, no Mr. Hitler, no Finland, no Japan, no Coventry, no London, no war.

But I can't leave Pearl alone and Mrs. Burton has her own troubles—I can't allow her to look after mine, I can't just get up and go. I stopped doing spontaneity twenty-five years ago; even then I was a novice.

But then Mrs. Burton says, "Did you hear? They are taking the townies—I mean, some of the evacuees—to the seaside!"

"No!"

"Yes, they are."

"What? All of them?"

"Yes, all of them. First time for most of them too."

It feels like serendipity. It feels too much. The hand of fate is propelling Sam and me together.

I find myself inventing a cousin on the Mudie side. Thrice removed. Usually Mrs. Burton would be all over a new cousin like a rash, but she is distracted by Ethel, the impending baby and Sally and Nathan. And the way Sally has started drawing a line up her legs and painting them brown and the way she borrows curlers. Imagine, Sally, the bookworm who was never keen to spend time with bathwater! Now, she is always trying to break the water regulations. *And the hassle over the clothes coupons now you would not believe!* What a turnaround!

I nod and listen and knit faster and harder, for our troops are still needing us.

Pearl Posner will be building sandcastles in Lyme Regis. Edmund will be at Mrs. Harrison's, doing whatever Edmund does.

And I will be with Sam.

Sam doesn't yet know that I'm a filthy woman riddled with the grossest disease of all. That I take medicines for it, and most of them do work. I don't have symptoms, I am what they call asymptomatic— that's a kind of compliment, I think—except in that one crucial area, obviously. That place where it had counted so desperately.

How am I going to tell him?

Will he reject me when he knows?

I half-expect he will. I have been groomed to expect rejection, but the other part of me says, *not Sam, not Sam.* Although I hardly know him, I trust him more than I trust myself.

We can live somewhere quietly in the country, him, me and Pearl. We don't need much money. I can do without things. I've been doing without things for a long time.

A few weeks later, and we are at a dance hall. Sam has always wanted to take me dancing. Big band, big music. How many of us were in the Great War together? The musicians are the right age, or rather the wrong age. That smiling man on the clarinet, the serious one at the piano, were they out there too?

Sam thanks me again for coming, and I pull out his lighter and say flirtatiously, "I had to return this!"

He laughs, putting his arm round me. He says he's got some important things to tell me, some decisions he's made. His eyes seem to cloud over at this, so I press closer to him and murmur, "Later, Sam, let's have some fun first," and he bites his lip and agrees. I can hardly believe myself!

Sam is a different kind of dancer to Edmund. He is heavier. His hips are less swivelly. He doesn't get all eyes on him in the way Edmund did. But he throws himself into it; he is dancing with me, communicating with me, with fun and *joie de vivre*. And he keeps his eyes on me all the time, which makes me forget myself, then have to shake myself out of the dream. *I have to tell him first. Don't take anything for granted. He might not—he might not...*

We sit at a table the other end of the room from the band and he drinks the watered-down beer that is double the price that beer used to be—*war prices, Sir*—and I drink the landlord's homemade (illegal?) gin.

"Sam, you know I married Edmund?" I launch in without preamble. I have to tell him. I can't have him making decisions about us without knowing exactly what I am.

Lightly, Sam says, "Yes, Vivi." But he also knows there is more to this sorry tale, and so he waits. His eyes on me are full of sympathy.

"We have separated."

"Ahh," he says. He wipes the beer mustache with his sleeve, admits, "Pearl did mention he'd moved out."

"But the thing is...it's very difficult." I stare into my glass. *God give me strength*. I have never said these words aloud. Never. When I went to sign up with the local doctor the first time, I wrote it on a rectangle of paper, pushed it across Mrs. Carmichael's desk.

"I can imagine."

"No, it's worse than that. You see, he gave me a...kind of... disease."

Not disgust, not hate, not revulsion. I see something else come over his face, like the sun rising in the morning: *understanding, pity, respect.*

"Vi—" he begins.

"It's under control," I explain quickly. That's the word they use, "control," like they've chained up a rabid dog. *Under control*—not *my* control, unfortunately, but under *the* control of the medication. "The doctors say I'm not contagious. If...you know...you're careful. If *one* is careful, I mean. Not you."

"I understand," he says. "My darling Vivi, it changes nothing."

We have a small bed and breakfast and a landlady who doesn't ask questions. Walls that don't have ears. Flocked wallpaper curling up at the bottom. He apologizes for it. He thought it would be nicer than it is. I say he has no need to apologize and I mean it. This tiny shabby room feels like the center of the world. *The whole of my world.*

He sits on one side of the bed. My fingers shake so much I can't undo the buckles of my shoes, buckles I have undone countless times before.

"It's okay," he says. "Let's sleep."

I can't stop crying now.

He holds me, and I cry with his arms round me, not lean or spindly but strong arms and strong hands. This is the man I have loved for over two dozen years, this is the man I've always wanted. I've been a fool and a coward.

We could have had children. We might have had a little girl like Pearl. A family.

The next morning, waking next to sleepy-faced Sam, I have never felt happier. I know that this is how my life could have been if I had been braver but this realization is not as painful as it once was because this is how my life will be. From now on. There will be no more time-wasting. No more people-pleasing. We are together now.

We sit in the cramped breakfast room, giggling at the menu, for virtually all the items have been crossed out except for tea, crackers and eggs.

"And they'll be powdered," I warn him.

"Eggs, please," says Sam brightly to the landlady.

"Sorry," she says. They don't even have powdered!

Sam sits back in his chair, crunching on a dry cracker. There's more bad news on the wireless but that morning, it doesn't affect me like it usually does. I am here, smiling into Sam's eyes. Everything feels right. I don't feel guilt or shame or remorse. I think suddenly of Olive and how happy she would have been for us: she always wanted us to get together.

Sam, however, is listening hard. Suddenly he puts down his crackers.

"Such terrible things are happening. In Germany. In Poland. Even in France now. I have family still there."

I put my hand on his arm. *My* man's arm. I almost chuckle at the details of last night. It was everything I had dreamed of, and more. And the thoughts of next time make me smile too. *We mustn't wait another twenty years!*

"It's awful."

"I need to do something."

I can't stop smiling at him. I love him for his courage and his passion and his sense of duty and... everything about him.

"They won't take you, my love." I pat his arm confidently. Sam is still athletic. He is still strong. There's fire in his belly, oh yes, *I* know this, but he is—thank God—far too old for active service.

"It's true, the British military won't take me."

I nod, rearranging the pepper pot and salt on the table.

"But I have to do something..."

I'm not smiling any more. Sam is being serious. Suddenly he talks feverishly, "You won't believe it, Vivi." He lowers his voice to a whisper as though the landlady might object. "The people...my people, the Jewish people are being exterminated. They pretend there are showers, but it's actually poison gas. They are my cousins, Vi. If it weren't for my parents leaving all those years ago, it would be *me*."

It is hard to believe.

He reaches into his pocket, then pushes a photo across the table. I don't know where he got it and I don't know if it is real. It's people behind barbed wire. They aren't wearing tops, and they are skeletal: their ribs protrude, and their faces are just wafer-thin skin stretched over skulls. Dull eyes that have seen terrible things. They are more animal than human. Impossible to imagine they were once normal people. People like Sam.

"They bring them in trains, they sort them: the youngest and the oldest are sent to be killed immediately."

I think of Pearl and feel sick. Not Pearl, they couldn't do that to Pearl. With rising shame, I remember the conversations we had about Jews in the drawing room at the Lowes' or Aunt Cecily's. I have often thought Sam could read my mind. I hope he can't read it now.

They've got no loyalty to anyone. My words, all those years ago.

How Sam would hate me if he knew.

"There are mountains of shoes, false teeth, glasses. Baby shoes," he says. He is almost incoherent with fury. I think of Pearl's shoes. The old flannel she still holds against her cheek at night.

"The others, they tattoo numbers on them. They are just a number, and then they are allocated a job."

"Do...does our government know about this? Mr. Churchill— what does he say?"

He shrugs.

"But, Sam," I say wearily. My honeymoon bubble has well and truly burst. Everything feels dark again. "What on earth can *you* do about it?"

He leans across the yellow Formica table.

"I am going to join the resistance in Europe, Vi."

*

After we leave the bed and breakfast, we walk to Hackney Fields, past the bombed-out areas, the schools in ruins, destroyed houses, knocked-down garages. I have tears in my eyes. We sit on a bench near the ruins and he wraps his firm arms round me, but I sit stony-faced and unresponsive. I can't believe this is happening.

"You conned me!" I eventually say. "You got me to London for one sordid night, and now…and now you're off again!"

He's a fly-by-night—one of the type who got Mrs. Burton's Ethel in her predicament, a Johnny-come-lately. This is what they call a "one-night stand." And in the women's magazines, we are warned: "You would be amazed at the lengths men will go to get one."

I had given myself to him last night—and this morning—with such certainty. I could hardly believe I had done it. I had felt safe. Now, I hated myself for being such a cliché. A naive, stupid cliché. Good Lord, it might be excusable in a woman half my age, but I am nearly fifty. I'm too embarrassed to speak. I had thought this was the start of something beautiful, not the end of my dreams. I can't bring myself to look at him, although when finally, I do, I see his expression is incredulous.

"What? *Sordid?* What are you saying? How could you *possibly* think that of me? I love you, Vivi. I'd never walk away from you, *never.*"

"But…" My hands are trembling. "You may love me, but you don't love me enough to stay with me, to be with me here. Am I right?"

He sighs. "Vi, there is a war on."

"How dare you suggest I don't know it!"

"I'm not. I just…I have to do something to help."

"You can help from here," I exclaim, "and you bloody well know that."

"Ooh, I've never heard Vivienne Mudie-Cooke swear before." Sam smiles, stops as he realizes how serious I am.

"You're doing good, important work here, right now," I insist. *He can't go. He just can't. He wants to put himself in the firing line. What bravado is this?*

"I know." He looks at his hands. "But it's not enough any more. I used to be a *pilot*, Vi. I have experience, training and skills. I have the desire to do something." He grabs my hand. "Wait for me, darling. This time give me a chance. Let me prove myself."

I shake my head. "Don't go! You're fifty, not twenty-five. You'll be a joke anywhere you go. You can do more from here. HERE! What about the factory? And the ARP?"

Sam sinks his head into his hands. Suddenly I remember how my father broke down when we were leaving and how I had just stared at him. He had lost my mother and was petrified of losing us. And I had thought him pitiful.

"I don't want to go, Vi, but I have to. It won't be for long, I promise you. We'll finish Hitler off. And then my heart will be yours. Evermore."

"I don't want your bloody heart." This time he doesn't laugh. I continue furiously. "And what about Pearl? *She* needs you."

"Pearl has you," he says quietly.

"But... I want you here. Now."

He shakes his head. "You will write to me though, won't you, Vivi?"

I shake my head. "No, I won't. Not if you go."

I won't. I can't. I'm not going through this again. I feel betrayed and abandoned. I had made myself vulnerable to him, I had been awake all night, loving him, letting him love me, and now he is leaving me. I am a fool. I am no better than those young women who hang around the fences of the American airfield, hoping to be noticed. I am not going to be treated like that. No one is going to treat me like that. Not even Sam.

He puts his fingers on my lips, shakes his head. "I'm not losing you. Not again."

"You are." Tears fill his eyes. "If you go, you are! That's exactly what you are choosing," I say more forcefully. The man is a fool. He's not some youngster. What does he think he can possibly achieve?

"I'm going," he says. "I have to."

Through the tears, I whisper, "Then we can never see each other again."

"That's really what you want?" He can't hide the shock in his voice. He must be able to understand what he's doing, how much it took for me to come here, to be here and to open myself up to him. I need him now, not a vague hint at a possible future. I know what "after the war" means. I've done that before. I'm not doing it again.

"This is really what you want, Vivi?"

"I don't want you to go!" I repeat. *One more time and I can change his mind.*

If he loved me, he'd stay.

We walk back to the station. We don't hold hands and our shoulders are low. The platform is so crowded: he pulls me into the dingy waiting area with grimy windows. There is no one there but us. He says it again, he makes me repeat it, "Don't write. Don't call. Don't."

I can't bear it. I don't think he can either, but I'm adamant I'm not doing this. I will not be vulnerable again. I will not be abandoned again. I can't do it.

I can't see for the tears. I expect him to kiss me like he did when we parted the last time, all those years ago, in another country, in another war, but this time he is too furious with me. And I am too furious with him as well. *I would not have responded. I would have taken pleasure in pushing him away.* When the train pulls in he stomps out of the waiting room, leaving me there, the door swinging shut after him, not quite fitting its own frame.

CHAPTER FIFTY-SEVEN

1944—Now

Thank goodness for the WVS. I do believe they save my life. They keep me occupied. They keep me company. The dogs come and go, chew the furniture, give up their fur and nuzzle my neck. The knitting, the sewing, the tea van—the van is always in demand.

I change the house around now that it's just me and Pearl to please. I buy myself a telephone and for the first few days, Mrs. Dean and I call each other every morning just to joyfully say, "Testing, testing."

I put the picture Olive drew of me downstairs. It's one of the first things you see when you come into the house. I also frame the paper program from Pearl's school performance of *Oliver Twist*, starring Pearl Posner as the Artful Dodger! When she sees it, Mrs. Burton teases me about being a stage mother. I agree—I have no shame. Pearl has also made some changes to her room. She's stuck up some pictures of heart-throbs. The usual suspects: Rick from *Casablanca* and Rhett from *Gone with the Wind*. She's surprisingly pedestrian in her taste in heroes.

Pearl keeps me busy too. Twelve going on twenty, she babysits for Ethel's charming little boy, Peter, and borrows inappropriate books from Sally. I try to make her well-balanced meals on the diminishing rations. I have to feed up Pearl, my growing girl. We don't peel potatoes or carrots any more. Every little bit that can be eaten must be preserved. Those forgotten throwaway parts? Vegetable water, apple peel? That's where the nutrition lies.

We still listen to the wireless together, and I play with her hair and she plays with mine, but occasionally she says I smell of wet dog and refuses to sit near me. It's true, I do sometimes.

Pearl gets letters from her Uncle Sam. I don't. We don't talk about it, but each time those brown envelopes dive onto the mat, I think to myself, *Thank God, he's still alive.*

After we are weary of nearly five years of war, there is wonderful news: Leicester Council want to give Mrs. Burton a medal for her war service. I think of the mild-mannered neighbor who offered me tea and toys, the kind woman desperate to do her bit. She tells me in her kitchen, in her plain matter-of-fact way, Laurel flapping around her legs, Hardy dozing in the corner by the bin. "A grafter," my father might have called her. "Salt of the earth," the newspapers say about the unshowy army of women like her.

We hold a big party to celebrate. We dress up way too much for the church hall but the church hall is dressed up too, in reams of Union Jack bunting. We've even strung flags up in the trees out the front. Pearl wears an old dress of Sally's that was formerly Ethel's—she loves their clothes. We WAVs stand and giggle and clap like a troop of teenagers. Mrs. Burton says, "It's overwhelming, I've never been recognized for anything before."

Mr. Shaw nudges her: "I'd recognize you anywhere."

Even the mayor comes. The mayor, this time, not the deputy mayor! It shows what a big deal this is. He is—what a surprise!—landed gentry. As privileged as Uncle Toby, and as snotty as Edmund's father. We line up to meet him.

"And you were an ambulance driver in the Great War!" the mayor says to me, reading from his notes. I nod. "Good training." I nod again. "I bet you wish you could be overseas, in the middle of the action again!"

I was in the middle of the action once, yet I am in it still. Not only the devastating bombing of Coventry, or the deaths at Warrington Crescent, London, but the work we WAVs do every day—the washing, the ironing, the making, the mending, the dog-brushing. It is all worthwhile. Driving an ambulance in France was valuable. But so is this.

"Well, I have been quite busy here too," I say, "on the home front."

He moves on to Mrs. Dean, who, in her fluster, curtseys to him—a move I will tease her about *forever*.

There are journalists who want to talk with Mrs. Burton. The newspaper photographer's flash goes off with a boosh and everyone in uniform looks rather rattled. Some people get up and dance to the big band music—the vicar's gramophone is tireless—and then the mayor calls the numbers for the raffle. The prize is a big bunch of bananas. It feels appropriate that Mr. Burton wins, because everyone knows, it's the Burtons' night really, but he insists on giving out one each to the children there. Pearl takes hers and thanks him effusively—"Good manners, Pearl!"—then she nudges me: "What on earth is this thing?"

"It's fruit—a banana," I explain. "No, NO, Pearl, you have to peel it first."

Pearl runs ahead on our way home. She is my family. Her dress whips up around her thighs. One sock is up and one squidged down round her ankle. She has pulled her hair loose, out of her plaits, and now it flies free in the wind. I suddenly see with a painful jolt that she is one hundred shades of Olive. I know I don't deserve such joy in my life after all I have done, and I'm so sorry.

She calls to me, "Hurry up, we've got banana to eat," and I do.

CHAPTER FIFTY-EIGHT

1944—Now

Mairi Chisholm—the younger sister of Uilleam Chisholm—calls the day before she appears on my doorstep. She asks if I will be home and the word "yes" makes its way out of my mouth before I can stop it.

"May I ask what it's in aid of?"

"I have things for you," she explains, her voice deep and authoritative across the wires. I can't think what on earth she plans to bring—I have never met the woman before. In fact, I only ever met Uilleam himself a few times at Mrs. Ford's gatherings. Mairi apologizes again, and I say, as politeness prescribes, "Not at all."

She arrives in a black Austin Healey, a beautiful machine with shiny fenders and massive lights. She parks it and steps out, a vision of modernity in her dotty headscarf and sunglasses. I remember suddenly how Uilleam had described her: "Daredevil..."

"I would have come on the bike," she says, "but for this." She goes round to the back of the car, and there, alongside the spare tire, is a great big trunk fixed to the boot. She unfixes it as I stare, open-mouthed.

"Take an end for me, would you? I'm not as strong as I once was."

Between us, we manage to lug the trunk into the house. In the living room, she unlocks it, then, carefully, raises out the contents. It's Olive's artwork. There is so much of it. Olive hated being called *prolific*, as though this signified quantity over quality, but when I used the phrase I meant no such thing. She *was* prolific. She had done so much with her short time on earth.

Some of the papers were rough to the touch: Olive's hands had been here. Olive's fingers had rested, stroked, touched here. Olive's eyes had looked over these sheets, Olive had been present here.

I had seen some of the pictures. The ones she drew almost as soon as we had arrived at Lamarck Hospital. Just as we'd started driving on rain-tipped roads. She'd captured behind the lines: the monotony, the excitement, the teamwork and the loneliness, all with a few well-chosen strokes. My talented sister.

I flick through her sketchbooks: Sanctuary Wood. Stripped trees, naked fields. Nudes. There are written notes too, in that familiar curly scrawl. She always preferred a blue pen. She used to rail against writing in black ink. She was as bold on the page as she was in life, never afraid of taking up room. Her notes sound just like her speaking. It's all jumbled up; I think it's chronological at first, but it's not.

In the Belgium notes, she describes mothers and fathers quietly making pilgrimage to the battlefields after the war.

Moving like a very different kind of ghost army. Would they find the answers they sought? The last resting place. The Somme for clear-up. Women traveling out. Old men. Soldiers who didn't come back. Imagine what you had seen, you have been cooped up for months, and then out you look, and see this… nothingness, waste. Abandoned fears. Abandoned. What a place.

Mairi pulls out a picture. It is a painting of two tanks, rearing up, both shells of themselves. Skeletal, skull-like, flesh burned away from what had been the inhabitants.

Dop Dopter and D24. Two tanks, Polcapelle.

After the War: a VAD ambulance bringing in French peasants wounded by shells left on the Somme Battlefield. Beaulencourt Convoy.

This one, where the sky is grayer than Earl Grey.

Etaples: British Military Cemetery.

Mairi whispers, "I put this one in a frame, hope you don't mind."

I am so engrossed that for a moment, I had forgotten she was even there.

How could I mind?

I don't know much about art and what is good and what is not, and I know that was another thing Olive railed against. *Art is subjective, Vi, it's what is good to* you—but I also know Olive had done something exceptional here. She had captured the awfulness of war and the anguish of those involved behind the scenes. The ambulance drivers. The gravediggers. The civilians-turned-warriors. If only I could have told her how incredible she was. I hold the pictures tight, and it seems to me she is here, she is beaming, bounding around the room. She is more alive than any of us. I imagine she is calling out, *Do you love them, Vivi? Do you? Really? Do you?*

Yes, my darling, I do.

"She left them with me after her Belgium trip," Mairi explains. "Some of her work had been destroyed so she impressed on me how very important it was to keep these safe. She wanted them out of London."

I nod.

I realize, belatedly, that Mairi has traveled an awfully long way on this mission, and although we've had cake, the right thing to do would be to offer her some lunch.

Mairi wolfs down the fried egg and bread. I say, "I have plenty," but in fact that is my egg ration gone.

"I eat too much," she says with a sigh, dabbing her lips. "I think it comes from not knowing where my next meal would come from during the Great War...I find rationing a bugger."

"I seem to have lost all interest in food," I admit.

She smiles kindly at me. "Funny how it affects everyone so very differently. You were a FANY, like Olive?"

"Three years." I nod. "Only, I stayed in France. She went all over—Belgium, Italy. And you?"

"Three and a half. Belgium, near Ypres. I was invalidated out near the end of 1917."

"I'm sorry."

"It is what it is. Gas. Awful stuff. That's why I . . ." She inhaled, catching her breath. "Do struggle. Lungs. I'd have loved to do my bit this time round."

Mairi is the only woman I know who's been gassed. I pour more water and she drinks it.

"How well did you know Olive?"

"She visited me on the Isle of Wight a few times."

I try to imagine Olive traveling in her flat shoes, her big coat, buying the tickets, dreaming out of the train windows. *What did she and Mairi do there? How did they spend the days?* I suddenly remember the time . . . the time . . . Richard had died, and the way Olive had answered the door at the Fords' in little more than her underwear.

"She always talked about you," Mairi continues breezily.

I take in her short red hair, her freckles. Mairi isn't pretty, and I doubt she ever has been, but she isn't plain either. Her looks suggest someone totally indifferent to their appearance. Strangely enough, this is quite attractive.

"Can I ask you something?"

Mairi looks up like she has expected me to say that. She places her cup down onto its saucer carefully.

"Were you in a relationship with my sister?"

Mairi doesn't look horrified but she doesn't look startled either. She shakes her head. "No, Olive and I were always friends."

"But she told me there was someone after . . . after her trip to Belgium."

Mairi asks if she might have some more tea. I nod. She has three sugars. She takes her time before she speaks.

"She was in a relationship, yes, with a Miss Dobinson—Harriet. They stayed with me once. A lovely summer holiday it was. They weren't so compatible but I suppose they had something very powerful in common: they had both loved and lost. Olive was grieving."

"You knew about Mrs. Ford?"

"Olive loved her very deeply."

I find myself coughing. "You know she wrote that famous song?"

"Yes, Olive told me"—Mairi smiles mischievously—"several times."

Mairi puts on her driving gloves and we walk to her car. She ties on her headscarf and puts on her glasses.

"Oh, don't you want the trunk back?"

"It's all yours," she says.

Suddenly I don't want her to go. She is a connection with my sister. Maybe one of the last connections. It feels like she is an invisible thread running through us from here to then.

"I can't forgive myself for the way I treated her!" I burst out. "How could I have been so stupid?"

She looks at me gently. There is something so honest about her homely face.

"Everyone makes mistakes."

"Not like this, not like what I did."

"Yes, like this. *Exactly* like this."

She places her gloved hand over mine. "You're not alone, Vivienne."

"I can't forgive myself... I was so bad to her. Cruel."

"She loved you. She would have forgiven you."

"I should have taken better care of her."

"You need to forgive yourself."

*

That evening, Pearl and I cuddle up in my bed, and we go through my sister's pictures together. Pearl likes the one with the tanks best too.

She says, "It looks like a wild animal rising up on its hind legs."

There is such quiet around us in our house in this little cul-de-sac that it is strange to think we are still at war. At the end of my bed, there is a strong reminder: boxes and boxes of jumpers we have knitted, toys we have made, our WVS work.

"I wish I could have met your sister."

"So do I," I say. I lean over and switch off the lamp.

The next morning, I find something deep in the bottom of the trunk. At first, I think it is part of the lining itself, until I pull and feel it loosen. It is a page of sheet music. I can guess what it is before I examine it.

It's one of the first drafts of "Keep the Home Fires Burning," a version so early that the title is still "'Til the Boys Come Home"—the one everyone else wanted. The one I didn't.

How beautiful it looks, this page of music with its graceful black clefs, its parallel lines and its comforting white spaces.

Someone has circled some of the words: *and a noble heart must answer to the sacred call of friends.*

On the back of the page is written:

How proud I am of you to have gone away, to follow your heart, to serve and protect your people. Surely, that is the most honorable thing?

I will keep the home fires burning, my dear bravest girl. Never doubt my affection for you.

All my love
Lena Guilbert Ford

I put it back in the trunk. My heart aches at the tender words. My darling sister was loved. She was admired. She had someone waiting for her. I am so very glad of that.

The next day, I take out my best writing paper and I write a long letter to Sam.

EPILOGUE

After the war, Pearl asked if she could come and live with me. At first, I laughed it off, but then, when it became clear it wasn't a joke, I said, "We'll have to speak to your mum."

Eleanor, naturally, wasn't keen. I regret there were some choice words in her reply.

I said, "How would it be, then, if I came to live in London?"

"Would you?" squealed Pearl.

"Maybe," I said. I had Mrs. Burton and many friends here in Leicester, but I had been living with ghosts for a very long time, and suddenly, perhaps for the first time in my life, I felt in the mood for an adventure.

We sold the house and Edmund was surprisingly amenable about reaching a settlement. Mr. Burton said he'd always wanted a tortoise, so he and Mrs. Burton took Charles over the fence and, after a few days' excitement, even Laurel and Hardy left him alone.

I went to Edmund's father's funeral and held Edmund's hand throughout the service. His mother was still furious with me: Lowes do not separate, apparently. But she didn't have many people to speak to—no dukes, lords or ladies traveled to Leicester for the interment, surprisingly—so she stayed by my side for virtually the whole length of the occasion. As Edmund drove her back to Mrs. Harrison's, she thanked me for coming.

Edmund apologized to me more than once. He said, "I was a poor husband" and "You deserved so much better, Vivienne."

It meant a lot to me. I told him, "We should never have married," and he agreed. Finally, we had found *something* we agreed on.

I asked the Imperial War Museum if they would like some of Olive's pictures and they jumped at the chance. Her work would be safe there and it might get an audience some day. My sister deserved an audience, she deserved to be heard. She had a lot to say about the Great War and it's all there in oil and charcoal, both serious paintings and cartoons.

People have started calling the Great War the "First World War." It's a subtle shift, and I'm not sure I approve of it. But what can you do? Language evolves. Values evolve. We thought the Great War was "the war to end all wars" at one point.

Only a fool would try to hold back the tide.

I rent a flat along the Westway. It's not far from Portchester Terrace and sometimes when I'm walking to the high street or the park I walk by my old childhood home and try to catch a glimpse of who lives there now. My new place is small—just two bedrooms—but it does for me. The piano is in the hallway and there are pictures all over the walls.

They built over the houses that were bombed in Warrington Crescent long ago: they put up nice, Georgian-style homes, perfectly in keeping with the rest of the street. If you didn't know, you wouldn't know anything had ever happened. When I go past, I manage to smile at the memories: Mrs. Ford, Walter, David—or Ivor Novello, as everyone knows him now—Johnny, Uilleam, Olive and me.

I go to the theater and the cinema whenever I like. A couple of men—widowers, both—ask me to dinner, but I say no. Mrs. Burton comes to stay sometimes, when she needs to get away from Mr. Burton, Ethel and Peter, her darling grandson, who is "into everything." Sally, Nathan and their baby—yes—are living in north London, so she divides her time between us.

Pearl spends most weekends with me. She finds her little brothers irritating. They play with her things; she complains as is big sister's job to do. Her flannel has been washed, folded and put away in a drawer somewhere. She is still lousy at spelling and disagrees with country dancing. I pay for her to have Chinese lessons with an elderly woman in Soho and she diligently writes out little squiggly characters in a notebook.

If you ask Pearl what she wants to do when she's older, she'll say, "Hmm, something that pays well?" She wants to buy a car outright when she is eighteen.

Eleanor thinks Pearl will be an actress because she doesn't stop talking. I think Pearl might be an ambassador or a diplomat. Pearl, of course, says, "Why not both?"

It is a Friday, late afternoon, in March 1946. The rationing is even stricter than before and there is still conscription, but we have a new government and we have tentative hopes for a brighter future.

Pearl is late, *very* late, and I am tetchy because we are supposed to be going to see *Gilda* at the cinema and even though I've seen it once already, and Pearl's seen it twice, I hate to miss a start and she knows that. I am wearing new shoes—my first new pair for seven years—and they need wearing in. Perhaps that's why I'm so grumpy. All my dresses are old now too, but this is a favorite going-out dress that I know Pearl will approve of. She's become awfully picky about fashion all of a sudden.

It's a wonder to be without the blackout, to be able to look out to see gaslights in the street, or the beam of a car's headlights or the glow from the houses opposite. I stare out of the window, curtains pushed to the side, waiting for my girl to arrive.

Then I see her walking up the road. Here she comes with a black beret at an angle, the way Olive sometimes used to wear hers, and in a pretty mustard-colored coat that Eleanor managed to acquire from goodness knows where. Eleanor's resourcefulness is without parallel.

It takes a moment to register that Pearl is not alone. A man with a stick is making his way slowly alongside her.

It's Sam. Sam Isaac is here. Sam is at my doorstep, leaning against the front wall. I fly down the stairs, I fly.

"Look what I've brought you," Pearl says proudly.

He's not a ghost, *he's here, he's here, he's here.* I fall into his arms, full of questions, weeping at the sight of my lost love.

A LETTER FROM LIZZIE

Hello,

Firstly, and most importantly, huge, huge thanks for reading *When I Was Yours*. I do hope you enjoyed it. I have loved writing it.

If you want to keep up to date with my latest releases, just sign up at the following link. I can promise that your email address will never be shared and you can unsubscribe at any time.

www.bookouture.com/lizzie-page

This is the third novel I have written about women in the First World War, and as in *The War Nurses* and *Daughters of War*, it was inspired by the experiences of real-life women and is a celebration of them. For a long time women have been written out of history. This is an effort to restore them to their rightful place.

When I Was Yours differs from my previous two novels in that it has a dual timeline and focuses on the Second World War too. One reason I did this was because I was curious about exploring how it might have felt to go through one war and then have to go through another. I was particularly interested in exploring the lives of those who were approximately my age, late forties and early fifties, and how the Second World War might have been for them. I enjoyed having that longer time frame to play with and to explore more than just a snapshot of a life.

Another thing that pulled me to write about the Second World War was that I wanted to look at evacuation. My dad was evacuated—

from London to Hinckley—and I grew up hearing his tales, some of which I've borrowed here. Dad died two years ago, but he was always positive, and a loving support to me and my writing.

I was also interested in looking at anti-Semitism in *When I Was Yours*. As I was writing this, I would hear on the news that anti-Semitism is on the rise. I wanted to explore where it comes from, what it is and most importantly, what it requires to change. I believe, as Sam says, that it's often a question of scapegoating or blaming those who are different, but I'm also a firm believer that people, like Vivienne and her father, *can* change. It may require education, experience and open minds, but it can be done.

We should be so proud of those who serve and who served in the wars—and at the same time, we should never forget how truly awful a time the First and Second World Wars were. I sometimes worry that we idealize those days when in fact there is nothing beautiful about losing your loved ones—forty thousand civilians were killed in the Blitz alone—and there is nothing exciting about hunger or lack of medicines. It's very important that we recognize that people were immensely, astonishingly brave during those wars—but they shouldn't have to be that brave.

There is also, I think, a perception nowadays that previous generations were more "resilient" or "just got on with things." I think this is a mistake and it's something I wanted to address in *When I Was Yours*. Suicide, alcoholism, drug-taking and violence, particularly against women and children, was rife in the olden days—it just wasn't talked about. I'm very grateful that there is greater compassion and support toward those with mental illnesses than there ever was, yet more understanding and more help needs to be made available.

If you have a moment, and if you enjoyed it, a review would be much appreciated. I'd dearly love to hear what you thought and reviews always help us to get our stories out to more people.

It's always fabulous to hear from my readers—please feel free to get in touch directly on my Facebook page, or through Twitter, Goodreads or my website.

Thank you so much for your time,
Lizzie Page

        lizzie.page.75

        @LizziePagewrite

AUTHOR NOTE

When I Was Yours is fictional but there are characters here who were real and who were a great inspiration to me. If this novel inspires anyone to find out more about the lives of these remarkable people, then that would be brilliant.

Lena Guilbert Ford (1870–1918) was the American songwriter who cowrote the sensational "Keep the Home Fires Burning" with David/Ivor Novello.

Olive Mudie-Cooke (1890–1925) was a war artist who served as an ambulance driver in France and as a VAD in Italy and Switzerland. She had one older sister, Phyllis, who also served.

In an Ambulance: A VAD lighting a cigarette for a patient is one of many exceptional paintings Olive Mudie-Cooke created and it is currently kept by the Imperial War Museum.

ACKNOWLEDGMENTS

There's always a long list of people I want to thank and I always get very nervous that I'll miss out someone. But here goes. Many appreciations to:

ALL the fantastic book bloggers—where would we be without you? The internet would be a much less colorful place and us writers would feel far more isolated and bewildered. You really do take our books by the hand and deliver us into the world safely. Special thanks to: Emthebookworm at Shazsbookblog, Stacy at Stacyisreading, Emma at BookingGoodRead, Louise at WaggyTalesDogBlog, Frankie at Chicks, Roguesandscandals and Nicola at Shortbookandscribes. Annemarie at Bookaholic, Amanda at Gingerbookgeek, Kaisha at TheWritingGarnet and everyone who has read and reviewed my work. Your support and encouragement has given me so much confidence.

Stow Maries Airfield—a genuine First World War airfield with a small but perfectly formed women's museum and a lovely old-fashioned canteen—an atmospheric place to write! Special thanks to volunteers Dave H-G and Bookshop Tel.

Create 98 is a fabulous creative environment set up by Christine Wyatt and it's where I've been running some writing workshops. Thank you to my workshop cohosts, Richard Kurti and Jen Feroze, and to my students. I always learn so much from you.

Trauma Fiction is a Facebook group that have set me right on so many injuries and illnesses. Infinite gratitude also to spell-check for helping me out repeatedly and patiently with Gonorrhea. What a word that is!

My local libraries, especially Rayleigh and Southend Libraries, for their support. Libraries were very important to me: as a young girl with an Enid Blyton habit, as a student, as a mother of young children and now as a writer. Sadly, Essex Libraries are under threat from extreme cuts proposed by Essex County Council. I am grateful to those in the Save Our Libraries Essex groups fighting the proposals and I would like to continue to offer my support.

The Romantic Novelists Association is a fantastic organization and it's a privilege to be a member. Special love to the wonderful and welcoming Essex chapter, and indeed, the Bootmaker Restaurant in Chelmsford for hosting us.

Savvy Authors is a great Facebook group full of brilliant authors, where I learn all the things I need to know about this incredible industry (and some of the things I don't!). Other Facebook groups I love and appreciate include: Saga Girls, Book Lovers and Book Connectors, all wonderful groups of readers and writers, all places of great information and kindness.

My friends, old and new. You've been, and are, fabulous. I'm very lucky to know you all. (And a special mention to the brilliant Mariya Peneva, who really has kept these home fires burning.)

The Second World War Club on FB has been invaluable for research and ideas. I also want to shout out to an incredible reference book, *Wartime: Britain 1939–1945* by Juliet Gardiner. I have loved Crow's Eye Productions' beautifully atmospheric short films on getting dressed as a World War One nurse and a World War One soldier and a YouTube series called *Wartime Kitchen and Garden*.

Huge thanks of course to Bookouture, including the fabulous copyeditors, proofreaders, designers, marketeers, strategists, assistants, and never forgetting the multitasking caped crusaders and publicity gurus themselves: Kim Nash and Noelle Holton.

My fabulous editor—Kathryn "safe hands" Taussig. I was super lucky the day my first manuscript ended up on your desk!

My fabulous agent—Thérèse Coen at Hardman and Swainson—who, despite all the terrible ideas I throw at her, never makes me feel stupid.

Mum and Dad, who I know would have been thrilled by this book.

My sister, Debs, my gorgeous nieces, to my tolerant, if increasingly feral children, Reuben, Ernie and Miranda, to Lenny-the-dog, and last—but never least—to Steve.

WHEN I WAS YOURS

READING GROUP GUIDE

DISCUSSION QUESTIONS

1. The evacuation of children from the cities/seaside towns to the countryside was a huge organizational task. Do you think that could happen in a similar way today? Why or why not?

2. Vivienne didn't have any choice about being a host mother to an evacuated child. Do you feel she was a good caregiver? What would you have done if you were in Vivienne's situation? Or in Eleanor's situation as Pearl's mother? Would you be able to send your child away to live with strangers for his or her own safety? What would be your main concerns?

3. Which sister did you prefer—Olive or Vivienne? Who did you have more sympathy for? Olive pushed to volunteer overseas, and Vivienne went along with her. Yet Olive, the brilliant daredevil, found the demands of ambulance driving harder than the more reticent and cautious Vivienne did. Who are you more similar to? Who did you think was braver?

4. Were you surprised to find it was Olive and Lena, not Olive and Walter, who were in love? How do you feel Vivienne handled the truth? If Lena hadn't been killed by the bombings, what might have happened?

5. On anti-Semitism, Sam says, "When times are hard, those who are different are often blamed or scapegoated. We seem always to be at hand for that." Do you think this a fair summary? Were you surprised to hear of anti-Semitic attitudes during WWI in England?

6. Edmund's mother is a snob, yet she is also surprisingly helpful to her daughter-in-law and often provides her with practical assistance. Why do you think this is? How important is it to challenge people's prejudices?

7. Vivienne thinks, "I have made wrong choices at every fork in the road, that I have made choices to please other people, choices through the eyes of other people, never my own; and even worse than that, that all those other people I had made choices for...it didn't make a difference to their lives—only mine." Is this a reasonable summary of Vivienne's life? What should she have done? Why didn't she?

8. What impressed you or disappointed you about the way people handled terrible events of the war? What kinds of things do you imagine you might have done if you had been around in WWI or WWII?

9. What do you think happens next for Sam and Vivienne and Pearl after the book ends?

10. Some of the women in this book are based on real people, including Olive Mudie-Cooke, Lena Guilbert Ford, and Mairi Chisholm (who returns the trunk to Vivi). Had you heard of any of these women before reading the book? What other books have you read, or movies have you watched, that feature forgotten women from history, and what did you enjoy most about them?

THE CHARACTERS BEHIND
WHEN I WAS YOURS
By Lizzie Page

Around my forty-fifth birthday it occurred to me that anyone who was my (oh, relatively young!) age during the Second World War would have already gone through the First World War. The thought made a great impression on me, and I decided I wanted to write about a woman who had lived through both world wars—in the first as an active participant and in the second as a participant in a different way.

At about the same time I was mulling this over, I fell in love with a painting: *In an Ambulance, a VAD [nurse] Lighting a Cigarette for a Patient*. It's a beautiful study of tenderness. We see the vulnerability of the soldier, the gentleness of the nurse, and it seemed to me to portray the start of something special. I knew that it was what I wanted at the heart of my story.

The Artist

I found out more about the artist behind *In an Ambulance, a VAD Lighting a Cigarette for a Patient*, Olive Mudie-Cooke. There was a small number of women war artists, but Olive was not part of an official cohort. Instead, she had gone out to the western front as a volunteer ambulance driver and did some wonderful drawings and paintings once there. I learned that she served in France and then Italy. Olive was especially skilled at showing the mundanity of war through her art: volunteers laying a plank road, a driver's hut or a pill box. After the war, Olive went back to mainland Europe, to Belgium and France, with another volunteer group. There, she produced some more exciting, visceral work of the battlefields, cemeteries, and a tank on its side like some felled monster.

Tragically, this wonderfully talented young woman, brimming full of ideas and life, killed herself in 1925. She had an older sister who had also volunteered as an ambulance driver in France throughout the war.

I tend to write about the one who is the sidelined, the quieter one, and so it was natural to me to take on the voice of the less ostensibly remarkable sister—and so the older sister evolved into my narrator and main character, Vivienne Mudie-Cooke.

The Songwriter

Another character I borrowed from real life was Lena Guilbert Ford. I found her story fascinating. Lena was American, a single mother who had divorced and had come to London with her mother and son to pursue her dreams of making music. She cowrote "Keep the Home Fires Burning" with Ivor Novello—such a classic, enduring song with a sweet and wistful message—and yet no one seems to remember Lena's name. Neither do many people know that Britain was bombed during the First World War—and, unfortunately, Lena was the first American to die on British soil in that war. She was survived by her mother.

When I found out about Lena Guilbert Ford, I knew I wanted to write about her. I wanted the whole world to know about her. And it seemed perfectly logical to put this brilliant, rebellious character with Olive. Two enormously talented female artists, lost in time...

The Child

If the story of Lena Guilbert Ford came from the head, Pearl's story, the evacuation section, was one very close to my heart. When I was growing up, my dad always told me about being evacuated from Stepney in London to Hinckley in Leicester when war broke out in 1939. Dad and his older sister, my aunt Nita, went to separate homes, while his mum and baby brother, Moss, remained in London for a while.

My dad had quite a rough time. Like Pearl, he was chosen last in the church hall. He struggled with unfamiliar food (he hated pork chops), he was locked in the closet when he was homesick, and there was fighting between the "local" and the "townie" children.

Nita, by contrast, had the most amazing time. She was adored by her host parents and even requested to be adopted instead of returning to her own family!

So I was always aware that these things could go either way. For some, evacuation was the worst thing that happened; for others, it was the best. From a young age I always wondered what it must have been like to be an evacuated child. Hence the development of Pearl. I confess that she does share several characteristics with my daughter, Miranda, who is about the same age. (Sorry, Miranda!) Pearl Posner is also the name of my great-grandmother.

The Mother

As I got older and had children of my own, I also wondered what it must be like to look after someone else's child. I wanted to explore the pleasures and the pitfalls of that in *When I Was Yours*. I wanted to delve into the transformative power of caring and the way society often underestimates that role. All this informed the character of Vivienne, who starts the story depressed by loss, her sour marriage, and infertility and then undergoes change as she becomes a strong and loving advocate for Pearl.

The Neighbor

I love Mrs. Burton, her dogs, and the community she creates. She seems to me to represent something good, something simple and down-to-earth, something that affects Vivienne profoundly. If Vivienne's marriage is cold, Mrs. Burton's is warm and caring. Mrs. Burton manages to parent her daughters with unconditional love and humor even when she doesn't approve. I suppose Mrs. Burton is an idealized mother—but she is someone who Vivienne needs to observe and be with in order to change.

The Friend

Mairi Chisholm is a character from an earlier novel I wrote called *The War Nurses*, and she, too, is based on an incredibly brave woman who served along the western front in WWI. She connects Vivienne to her beloved sister and brings her the message that she is loved and forgiven. This allows Vivienne to move on.

The Husband

If there's a villain of the book, I expect it is Edmund Lowe. Yes, Edmund is a...bad guy. Nevertheless, I didn't want to make him *too* villainous. Vivienne's feelings toward Edmund were complex. She was bound to him by a sense of duty, yearning for a conventional family and a triumph of optimism over reality. Ultimately, like many couples, they were just wrong for each other.

The Boyfriend

Sam is the hero, but, again, I didn't want to make him too heroic. I liked the fact that he and Vivienne meet by Vivienne saving him—in a reversal of the old romantic tropes. He is a loving uncle and a kind and emotional family man. These are qualities I like. Plus, I don't know if you picked up on it or not, but Sam is also very handsome!

*

I hope you enjoyed *When I Was Yours* even half so much as I enjoyed writing it. I love all the characters even if I had to put them through a lot of painful stuff sometimes. I feel that sometimes World War I is the forgotten war when it comes to historical fiction, so I was really pleased to be able to incorporate both world wars in this story and to show how through those terrible times ordinary people ended up doing quite extraordinary things.

Thank you so very much for reading. I'd dearly love to hear your thoughts on *When I Was Yours*, so do get in touch via Twitter (@LizziePagewrite) or Facebook (facebook.com/lizzie.page.75).

ABOUT THE AUTHOR

USA Today bestselling author Lizzie Page lives in a seaside town in Essex, England, where she grew up. After studying politics at university, she worked as an English teacher, first in Paris and then in Tokyo, for five years. Back in England, she tried and failed at various jobs before enjoying studying a master's in creative writing at Goldsmiths College. Lizzie loves reading historical and modern fiction, watching films, and traveling. Her husband, Steve, three lovely children, and Lenny the cockapoo all conspire to stop her writing!

You can learn more at:

Twitter @LizziePageWrite